# DAMNATION

# DAMNATION

## PETER BECK

*Translated from the German*
*by Jamie Bulloch*

A Point Blank Book

First published in North America, Great Britain & Australia by Point Blank,
an imprint of Oneworld Publications, 2018

Originally published in German as *Söldner des Geldes* by Emons Verlag, 2013

ISBN 978-1-78607-327-3 (Hardback)
ISBN 978-1-78607-326-6 (eBook)

This edition has been published with the support of the Swiss Arts Council Pro Helvetia

swiss arts council

# prohelvetia

Printed and bound in Great Britain by Clays Ltd, St Ives plc

This is a work of fiction. While, as in all fiction, the literary perceptions
and insights are based on experience, all names, characters,
places, and incidents either are products of the author's imagination
or are used fictitiously.

Oneworld Publications
10 Bloomsbury Street
London WC1B 3SR
England

MIX
Paper from
responsible sources
FSC® C018072

*For the QoH, the queen of my heart.*
*In memory of my father.*
*And for my mother.*

# PURGATORY

*The Arab's burning better than the woman. Must be down to the kaftan, Strittmatter thought. The flames were licking at his legs. He was desperately looking for somewhere to land in these inhospitable mountains. Anywhere. The main engine cut out for a second. The helicopter dropped.*

*The fire hadn't yet reached the family photo beside the logbook.*

*This hadn't been an unusual job. His small but classy 'VIP Helicopter Transportation Corporation' often flew rich clients to spectacular sites in the Alps. In such magnificent surroundings, they were easier to schmooze. Ice and snow were particularly special for Arabs from the desert.*

*Shortly after a summer shower, the Arab and the woman in her elegant trouser suit had climbed into the back of Strittmatter's Bell 206. The young woman had smiled professionally as she handed over confirmation for the flight from Zürich to the Gemsstock mountain. There was a twinkle in her eye. She had brought the customary welcome gift, decorated with a fat bow in the colours of the private bank – a gigantic box of chocolates.*

*Twenty minutes after take off the woman was on her mobile.*

*'Fire!' the sheikh screamed.*

*'Where's the extinguisher?' the woman asked with urgency, but calmly.*

*'Under the middle seat,' Strittmatter answered with much less composure.*

*She pulled out the bright-red extinguisher, broke the safety seal and tried to spray foam onto the fire.*

*Strittmatter cast a brief glance over his shoulder. The helicopter was made of lightweight aluminium and the seats out of flame-retardant material. But the kaftan wasn't fireproof. The Arab was ablaze, a wreath of fire in his hair.*

*Screaming, the Arab squeezed himself into the corner. Apart from 'Allah!' Strittmatter couldn't understand a word. Earlier the Arab had spoken English. But mortal fear was suffered in the mother tongue. He hammered his fist in vain against the shatterproof window. All that broke was the glass of his expensive, mechanical wristwatch.*

*The fire extinguisher was empty and the woman's frantic efforts were to no avail. Terrified, she shouted, 'Land! Now! We've got to get out of here!' From the corner of his eye Strittmatter saw her trying to put out the raging flames on her white blouse with her bare hands.*

*They were spinning ever further downwards. In the steep mountains there were only bare rock faces, scree and ravines.*

*Steady the chopper. Slowly. Where the hell could they land?*

*The helicopter dropped once again and juddered, hurling its passengers across the cabin. He wouldn't be able to keep control for much longer, Strittmatter knew. His brow was slick with sweat and he let out a hacking cough. Black phlegm came up as the synthetic material of his shirt burned into his skin. The family photo went up in flames: first the edges, then his children, finally his wife.*

*They were still a hundred metres above ground when the engine cut out altogether.*

*A peaceful alp stretched out before the pilot. A squat hut, its two small, dimly lit windows staring back at him. Strittmatter saw black blobs on the pasture. Cows! They were lying languidly in the grass.*

*When the helicopter exploded at 20:44, the docile creatures leaped up awkwardly and bellowed in shock.*

Winter lay motionless in the filthy water. A thin film of grease covered the surface, trapping a mosquito which twitched as it struggled to avoid drowning. It was a hopeless fight against death.

The water had entered Winter's ears and made its way along the auditory canals to his eardrums. His eyes were closed, head and neck submerged. His Adam's apple and injured hand rose from the surface of the lukewarm water.

His hand was scratched, dirt engrained beneath the fingernails. A mixture of earth, clay and organic residue. One of the fingernails was split.

His pulse was weak.

And very slow.

The mosquito had stopped moving.

After a day of hard, physical labour he was relaxing in his bath, easing an aching back. He wanted to be on top form for Anne this evening.

He wallowed in the memories of their first date. How the scent of her Issey Miyake perfume had tickled his nostrils as they greeted each other with the traditional three kisses. How she had stood on the old, wooden balcony with her radiant smile and a glass of sparkling white wine.

He'd ventured an apologetic gesture as he showed her the half-finished terrace in his rampant garden, where the only edible things growing were wild courgettes, cucumbers and some berries. He could recall precisely the energy that had flowed through his body when, with a gentle laugh, she placed her hand on his forearm. She'd found his jungle 'romantic' and said how much she was looking forward to fresh raspberries and blackberries.

After that they'd taken it in turns to blow on the stone barbecue to get the fire going. She'd teased him and he'd almost passed out for lack of oxygen. When they'd finally put the steaks on the embers Anne was covered in soot. A black line from the edge of the grill ran across her T-shirt beneath her chest. His dishcloth had only made the mark worse. Since that moment Winter had been unable to forget Anne's belly button.

A warm feeling washed over him as he replayed that wonderful evening in his mind. Thoughts like that drifting through his head were a positive sign. His physical exertions on the terrace and the relaxing bath were doing him good.

After dinner he and Anne had sat there for a long while, finishing the bottle of Rioja. It gradually got dark and Winter lit the candles in the lanterns. The crickets were chirping. Later he made coffee and served the cheesecake he'd bought from his favourite bakery.

Anne had told Winter about her dream of watching lizards on the Galapagos Islands. Winter had raved about the nature reserves in Canada with their huge, unspoiled forests. They'd continued laughing late into the night, touching on every topic imaginable.

Apart from the bank. At some point he and his deputy had reached a tacit agreement that they wouldn't discuss work at his house. The superior and his subordinate. It was a fine line. A business lunch at the pizzeria was acceptable. As was a formal dinner with clients. But an intimate tête-a-tête was borderline. After much hesitation, finally feelings had trumped reason.

Winter slowly raised his head and surfaced from the water. With his right hand he carefully reached for the beer beside the bath. The cold bottle relieved the burning of his pierced blisters. He wondered how his battered hands would affect his shooting accuracy. Fortunately, there were few armed bank raids these days. Robberies now took place in back rooms. Instead of masks, the criminals wore pinstripes. Instead of dynamiting safes they hacked computers.

Winter downed his beer in one, climbed out of the bath and prepared to shave. Before applying the razor to his stubble, he examined his face in the mirror. He wasn't bothered by the lines that had started to appear. This evening, perhaps, Anne wouldn't just give him a long goodbye kiss, she would stay the night.

He'd met her at a judo competition. Winter was knocked out in the quarter-finals; Anne had won in her category. Sweating, he'd congratulated her on the victory and invited her out to dinner. She had declined, but when she saw from his business card that he worked at a private bank, she'd asked, 'Does your company recruit lawyers too?'

'Of course. Nobody else understands the contracts, though I'm not sure which came first: lawyers or contracts.'

She'd laughed, cocked her head slightly to one side and said nothing, which told him that she was not only a top judo fighter but also a sound negotiator.

'Send me your details and I'll ask our head of legal.'

Two weeks later there was no legal job for Anne, but there was lunch in a brasserie. That was the first time he saw her in one of her elegant trouser suits. Like him, Anne had studied law. After university she'd worked in a law firm whose name was so long that Winter was unable to remember it. But from her CV Winter learned that Anne had been with the police before university, working for two years as an officer on the beat while doing her matriculation certificate. And that's how she came to be his right-hand. Even though they'd only known each other for six months, they trusted each other implicitly.

Now he stepped out onto the balcony in bare feet, a towel wrapped around his waist: it was still pleasantly warm. The sun was hovering over the horizon. The weathered wood had retained the heat of the day. In the distance the mountains were clearly visible. A good sign for tomorrow's weather.

Winter went down the creaking, outdoor steps and fetched a bottle of Rioja from the cool, stone cellar.

On the way back he stopped beside his temporary granite store. Beneath the stairs were three towers of heavy slabs. His intention had been to impress Anne this evening with a finished terrace. He'd taken the day off and heaped up the earth behind the new drystone wall. But he'd underestimated the work it would involve.

He calculated what he had left to do. Laying the remaining granite slabs would take another day, after which he'd be able to lie in the sun on his deck chair and enjoy the view of the Alps. If his luck held out, it would soon be the two of them sitting here together. After all, Anne had certainly taken a shine to his little farmhouse.

The old wooden house in Eichenhubel, a secluded hamlet near Bern, had been a good buy. At first it was a shambolic building site. Now the water, heating and electricity were all functioning.

Winter was going to do the rest of the renovations gradually, when he had time. Working with his hands made for a good balance. You could immediately see the results of your labours. Maybe Anne would help him paint the shutters. At least the initial chaos had been tamed, Winter felt.

Being able to get your bearings straight away and act decisively amidst chaos was crucial in the security business too. Anybody who couldn't imagine the worst possible scenario wasn't paranoid enough to work in this field.

Lost in thought, he stroked the rough edges of the granite. They cut into his fingers. For a moment, those dead eyes from his past appeared again.

'Not today!' Winter thought.

Shaking his head, he climbed back up the outdoor stairs.

In the meantime Tiger had stretched out on the old wooden bench. The tomcat purred his contentment when Winter ruffled his neck. What could be better than a cat's life? To sleep as much as your heart desired, to be answerable to no one and to be presented with a full bowl of food every day. You only had to hunt the occasional mouse.

Winter went into the kitchen and put the bottle of wine on the shelf. He glanced at his mobile. A missed call. He probably hadn't heard it when he was in the bath.

From Anne.

*The telephone conversation was received by one of the American Navstar satellites, which sent the recording, together with millions of other electronic data, to the secret computers of the National Security Agency in the Nevada Desert. There it was automatically scanned by computer software. In the endless stream of bits and bytes the digital eavesdroppers detected a word that was on the list of defined key terms, marked the spot, took out the ninety seconds before and afterwards and sent the recording to NSA analysts. The net tightened a little.*

Anne's message on Winter's voicemail was from 20:41. Most likely a status report. Or to say that Al-Bader's private Gulfstream was late again.

'Hi, Tom. It's me. Everything's fine. We're on our way with a twenty-minute delay, but the sunset is fantastic, unbelievable.'

The noise of rotor blades in the background.

'I'll call again when I'm back at the airport...'

'Fire!' The sheik's voice. Screaming.

'Al-Bader's on fire!'

Winter froze. A shiver ran down his spine. It was as if a lightning bolt had struck the back of his neck and discharged itself down his vertebrae into the stone floor.

Muhammed Al-Bader was one of the bank's best clients, a relation of the Saudi king. A global investor with holdings around the world. A liberal businessman. A target for fundamentalist groups. Al-Bader would occasionally meet his business partners in the Swiss Alps. This was the first time Anne had accompanied him.

Winter pressed the phone to his ear and strained to make out the message.

First it sounded as if Anne were putting her phone down somewhere. *Clunk.*

Then he heard her voice, tinged with a hint of fear that only someone who knew her well could discern: 'Where's the fire extinguisher?'

Something that sounded like 'middle seat'. Probably the pilot.

After a 'Ffffsssssshhhh' sound that seemed to go on forever, Anne was suddenly cut off. Nothing but silence. Even the chirping crickets in his garden had stopped.

Winter sat down and stared at the large kitchen table without noticing the bottle stains and bleached patches on the massive piece of oak.

In his mind he pictured Anne fighting the flames inside the cramped helicopter. The sunset as backdrop. Helicopters are vulnerable, fragile, especially in the mountains and at night. But Strittmatter had always been reliable. Had he been flying himself or had he sent another of his pilots?

Winter listened to the digital recording again. And again. 20:41, twenty-minute delay, everything fine, sunset, Al-Bader on fire, fire extinguisher, hissing, end.

Winter rang Anne's number: no reply.

Next he tried Strittmatter's personal mobile. After three rings it went to voicemail.

There was no answer on the VIP Helicopter Transportation Corporation business number either. Another answerphone. This time a friendly female voice told him that calls were taken during the office hours of 8:00a.m. to noon, and 1:00p.m. to 5:00p.m. The same message in English. Winter hung up. As if planes and helicopters only crashed during office hours.

The kitchen clock, with its extra-large numbers for sleepy eyes, showed 21:02. 'No news is good news,' Winter thought. It was a maxim he'd always lived by: communication was only necessary when the situation changed.

Three dead ends later, the last resort was Ben, a friend from his days at police college and now head of security at Zürich airport. Fortunately he was on duty. Ben was paranoid too, a professional illness, which was why he was always on duty. He promised to call back in ten minutes, which gave Winter time to get dressed and make coffee.

After eight minutes the phone rang. Ben, with good and bad news. The good news was that they'd managed to locate the helicopter. It was stationary. Winter made a note of the coordinates. The bad news was that Skyguide air traffic control hadn't been able to establish communication.

'The pilot may have just gone for a piss,' Ben added. 'If there's still no sign of life after a while they'll send a rescue chopper. But at the moment there doesn't seem to be one in the vicinity, I'm afraid.'

'Christ. I get an emergency call and no one's doing a thing.'

'I know,' Ben said. 'They're all sitting here in the control room on their ergonomically tested chairs, thinking: maybe it'll all sort itself out, and if there's no sign of life then it's too late anyway and there's no need to hurry. I'm sorry.'

Winter thanked him and hung up. He looked for a detailed map of the region. The coordinates were in a rocky area. Here the map was grey, with black, curly lines close together marking cliffs and steep terrain. The place was known as the Höllentobel, 'Hell's Ravine'. Purgatory.

But how accurate were the coordinates?

Luckily there was directory enquiries. He had himself connected to the priest in Kargmatt, the nearest settlement. Presbyteries were usually well-positioned with a good view.

The call was taken by a woman with a strong local dialect.

Winter didn't understand her name, but he got the impression that it wasn't anything out of the ordinary for the elderly woman to take calls at this late hour. As the area was in the country's Catholic heartland, he assumed he was speaking to the housekeeper.

'Good evening, my name is Winter. I'm awfully sorry to disturb you, but I really need your help.'

'The house of God is always open, Herr Winter.'

'Thank you. A colleague of mine is on her way to the Gemsstock mountain, near your village.' Anne was more than a colleague, but he had never admitted that to anyone. 'She's in a helicopter and called me earlier to say that it was on fire.'

'Good heavens!'

'Have you seen anything?' Kargmatt was a kilometre or two from the Höllentobel. As an optimist, he didn't want to use the words 'helicopter crash'. Not yet.

'My dear man, the ways of the Lord are inscrutable, but I'll happily help you if I can.' Winter began to doubt that the kindly housekeeper would be able to help him.

'Can you see the helicopter?'

'The helicopter?'

'Yes,' Winter replied, trying to keep a lid on his simmering anger.

'Wait a second. I need to take a peek out of the window.'

*Clunk.* The telephone was put down on a hard surface. The same sound that Anne's phone had made.

An age later: 'Are you still there? I can't see any helicopter.'

'Are you sure?'

'It is rather dark, sir.'

'Have you seen a light?'

'The light of the Lord shines...'

'Or a fire?'

'Yes, down in the Höllentobel. Jakob sometimes burns cleared branches down there.'

Winter stared into the distance. A pause. Then the house-keeper finally twigged.

'Oh my God! You mean the helicopter crashed down there?'

Ignoring her question, Winter delved further: 'What's Jakob's full name?'

'Jakob Zbinden.'

'Does he have a telephone?'

'I believe he does have a mobile phone.'

'Do you have the number?'

'In the card index we have the numbers and addresses of our entire flock.' After what seemed like an eternal search, the housekeeper found Jakob Zbinden's mobile number in the presbytery's card index. The time was 21:17. The cowherd, who had to milk early in the morning, was probably in bed already. But Winter needed to be certain. Jakob answered after the second ring. A bad sign.

'Jakob.' Cool, terse, and youthful sounding, he pronounced his name in an American way. Not exactly the country bumpkin under the protective wing of the Church that Winter had imagined.

'My name's Winter, I'm calling from Bern. I got your number from the presbytery. Please excuse me for phoning so late, but I've got an urgent question.'

'Are you a journalist?' Jakob asked aggressively. 'Hot on the heels of a story?'

'No, I'm not a journalist. One of my colleagues was on a helicopter in your area.'

'I'm sorry.' All of a sudden the cowherd's tone was restrained. 'What happened?'

'The helicopter crashed in the Höllentobel.'

Purgatory.

## JULY 24 – 21:22

On the drive to the Höllentobel Winter tried to comprehend the tornado twisting inside him. He sought to observe the storm of his emotions from a safe distance, as if from a weather plane flying above a whirlwind. He saw the anger churning him up and hurling images through his mind. Anger at the helicopter that for some reason had crashed. An indeterminate anger at the people who were guilty. The pilot? A careless maintenance mechanic? A religious fundamentalist?

And beneath all this, anger at himself. For, in truth, it ought to have been *him* in that helicopter.

The anger mingled with the pain this had stirred.

Anne was his deputy, his right hand, but she'd become more than that in his head. They got on so well together. Earlier, he'd been so looking forward to the evening, the night and the day afterwards. Now the Höllentobel had devoured the helicopter.

A lightning strike.

Winter shook his head.

He wanted to see Anne.

He wanted to take Anne in his arms. Protect her.

Then, all of a sudden, Winter was in the eye of the tornado. Silence. A dull *why?* Winter was in the purring quietness of his silver-grey Audi. It was dark and there was little traffic. He drove quickly, over the speed limit. He couldn't understand the stillness. Was it fear? Fear of making a mistake? Fear of failure? Just one false move and the tornado would seize hold of him, tear the ground away from beneath his feet, suck him high in the air and throw him off course once more. The whirlwind left a trail of devastation inside. The dead eyes stared at Winter. Glassy. He screwed up his own eyes. He didn't want to visit this place in his memory ever again.

When Winter opened his eyes he found himself racing towards the taillights of a car driving at the right speed in front of him. He slammed on the brakes. The tyres screeched and smoked and the seatbelt cut into his stomach. The electronic braking system had just managed to prevent a collision.

Winter ran his tongue across dry lips. He consciously pictured himself placing a heavy lid on the past. From this moment he would focus only on the task in hand. He put his foot down again and overtook.

A helicopter crash involving a filthy-rich sheikh and a beautiful woman on the way to a remote mountain hut didn't fit well with the discreet image of the bank.

What disturbed him was the thought of the people who'd get to the helicopter before he did. The fire brigade, police, locals, curious journalists. A tabloid was advertising with the slogan 'Earn money with a single call!' It was purely a question of time. He had to be quicker.

As usual his line manager, Känzig, failed to answer Winter's call, so he rang von Tobler, but the private bank's CEO was at a barbecue. His booming greeting suggested he'd already had a few glasses. Winter pictured the boss in shorts with pale calves rather than a bespoke suit. Within ten seconds he'd managed to ruin von Tobler's good mood.

None of the guests chomping on their steaks would have had an inkling of what was going through von Tobler's head. The boss was a master of the art of jovial conversation and of the impenetrable poker face.

The account managers loved taking their clients out to eat with the boss, potentially bumping up their fees by two or three tenths of a per cent. On fortunes running into a hundred million francs, such a cut easily matched Winter's annual salary. But business was getting ever more difficult. The Asian banking centres were on the march. Swiss banking secrecy was crumbling.

Over the past thirty years the chief had run the bank almost singlehandedly and with great success. Profits had multiplied. When he realized a few years back that the bank was too small to keep pace with global growth, he persuaded the other family members to sell a portion of their shares in a complicated transaction.

Today almost half of the bank was owned by an anonymous financial group that consisted of a large bank, an insurance firm and two other private banks. At the time, commentators and financial analysts had been in agreement. The financial group had paid a hefty price for the bank; the timing of the deal – just prior to the crisis – was perfect and von Tobler's personal wealth had increased substantially.

Von Tobler was a patriarch of the old school and knew what he had in Winter. Winter had met him while still commander of the Bern police 'Enzian' special unit. Von Tobler's daughter, Miriam, had been abducted. The banker was prepared to pay an enormous sum to get back the apple of his eye. And Winter had negotiated her release in return for the ransom.

Winter had handed over the ransom money personally and brought Miriam to safety from the kidnappers, before arresting them after a frenzied pursuit. As a result the overjoyed chief made him an enticing offer.

For a few years now he'd been in charge of security at the exclusive bank, which boasted clients from all across the world. Clients who expected that nothing would happen to them and their money in Switzerland.

At the bank Winter enjoyed greater freedom and less bureaucracy than with the police. He was his own boss and could manage his own time, just so long as nothing happened and nobody was inconvenienced by the security measures in place. Normally security could be taken for granted. After all, this wasn't the Wild West. And here was the irony: as head of security he was doing his job best when nobody noticed anything. Nobody said, 'Thank you.'

Apart, that is, from von Tobler, who would give Winter the occasional clap on the shoulder in appreciation. But now the CEO didn't say much. He merely authorized Winter to do all he could to limit the damage to the bank and get to the bottom of why the helicopter crashed. Von Tobler wanted to be kept updated around the clock. He said he'd inform the board and, before hanging up, asked Winter to put the HC – head of communications – in the picture.

The telephone call with the HC, who'd declared public relations to be a top-level issue when he started his job a few months ago, lasted longer. Relations with the outside world were crucial. The perception of security was as important for maintaining trust as the actual level of security itself. Winter was pleased that it was the PR department rather than he who had to grapple with the media and their poisonous half-truths.

Helfer, the pretty boy, wanted to play for time, express the bank's sympathy and avoid commenting on the private activities of its clients. He'd stick to a strategy of passive communication – informal, off-the-record conversations with journalists investigating the story – and insist that the sheikh's trip had been a purely private one. The term 'private' was a mantra to be repeated over and over again, he added. The head of PR also told Winter that scientific studies had shown how messages with repetition turned out to be more believable.

Fortunately a tunnel cut off the call after almost a quarter of an hour.

The 'private' was where Winter's problems began, however. He didn't know much about Al-Bader. A lot of things in the bank functioned on the basis of personal relationships. Winter knew the salient features of the client relationship with Al-Bader: very high net worth individual, politically exposed person, successful businessman and investor, increased vigilance with regard to money-laundering, no known personal preferences or weaknesses. Just over a week ago all that Stefan Schütz, Al-Bader's account manager, said of the sheikh's foray into Switzerland was, 'Actually he's not here, he's at a conference in Norway.'

'Interesting. An Arab sheikh at a conference in Norway?'

'I don't know for sure what sort of conference it is. Something to do with global infrastructure investments. Given the current fluctuations on stock markets, buying a road can be a highly lucrative move.'

Noticing Winter's raised his eyebrows, Schütz explained further: 'You start with an investment. Let's say you build a motorway, for example. Later you raise the charges, claiming it's inflation, then you've got a nice little cashflow. Of course you need the loose change to begin with. But that's not a problem for Al-Bader. In fact, he's von Tobler's client.'

It was Schütz who'd asked Winter to organize the helicopter trip. 'He's planning to meet someone in Switzerland early in the morning of July the twenty-fifth. He'll be arriving the evening before in Zürich on his private jet and I'd be grateful if you could arrange for a helicopter to pick him up and take him to the mountain hut on the Gemsstock.'

Routine. The bank took care of practically every aspect of Al-Bader's visits to Switzerland. He loved the mountains and had already made a number of high Alpine tours at the bank's invitation.

'Who's he meeting?'

'No idea. Some investors.' Then, rather tersely, Schütz had added, 'Not our business.'

Now, in the cocoon of his car, Winter wondered what Al-Bader had been doing in Norway and who it was he'd arranged to meet here. Friend or foe? And why in Switzerland?

Did it have anything to do with the range of his jet? What was the range of Al-Bader's Gulfstream? Winter made a mental note to consult the manufacturer's web site. At the end of the day truth boiled down to physics. Metres, minutes and kilograms.

And chance.

Or destiny.

His original intention had been to pick up Al-Bader from the airport personally. But instead he'd sent Anne. He'd sent Anne on this flight because he wanted to give her the opportunity of meeting one of the bank's best clients. And it had suited him to take the time off and work on his terrace. And now, in all probability, Anne was dead.

Winter set aside his feelings of guilt and the nagging doubts, and concentrated on the immediate future. This was what he could influence, but only if he remained focused. Why had the helicopter crashed? Experience told him that the answer to this question would either be revealed soon or not at all.

He turned off the motorway. The road became narrower and the bends tighter. The headlights tunnelled into the night. Summer storms had descended on central Switzerland that evening. Winter opened the window and breathed in the cool air that smelled of wet grass. He drove through the narrow streets of Kargmatt and caught sight of the church with its presbytery.

Afterwards the road ran steeply downhill and across an old bridge. An unmarked turn-off. The dirt track road snaked its way through the forest and up the other side of the valley. The fir forest was dark and fresh after the rain. Winter could see the sickle of the moon through the trees.

It was midnight when the forest thinned out and the ever-chirpy voice of his sat nav informed him: 'You have reached your destination.'

At that moment the phone rang and Anne's name flashed up on the display.

Winter stopped, took a deep breath and brought his pulse under control. He looked around. A slope with cows chewing the cud. Stars in the sky. His mobile was still ringing and showing Anne's number. He cleared his throat and took the call. 'Hello?'

'Hello. My name's Oberholzer. I'm from the police. I do apologize, but we found the phone I'm using at the scene of an accident and your number was the last one called. Who am I speaking to, please?'

'My name is Winter, I know the owner of the phone and I'll be with you in a minute.' He broke off the conversation and clutched the steering wheel so hard his knuckles turned white. Winter stared up at the sky without seeing the crescent moon. He pulled himself together and shortly afterwards parked his car in the passing place by the single-track bridge above the Höllentobel. Before him lay the crash site.

Over the past few thousand years the torrential mountain stream had channelled a deep V-shaped incision into the ground. The deeper the water burrowed, the steeper the sides became and the more earth, plants and rocks were washed away. A vicious circle.

The Alpine herders had fought an unsuccessful battle against the water, which continued to devour fertile pasture. They had tried to tame nature with wooden structures and newer steel and concrete ones. The steel shafts of one such grill, which was supposed to hold back sliding scree, earth and avalanches, had bored through the glass cockpit of the helicopter.

The slim rear of the aircraft lay further down the slope. The small tail rotor jutted up from the road. Behind it was a red Toyota Land Cruiser and an old jeep with its headlights dimmed. The local fire brigade and police force. No ambulance; no survivors. The experts from the Federal Aviation Safety Investigation Board hadn't arrived yet. Two torches were flitting about by the outline of the cockpit up above.

Winter got out and approached the crash site. The surface of the untarred road was muddy and slippery. He saw debris from the helicopter everywhere. Part of the casing. Winter picked up the sheet of metal. Full of soot. The main rotor, bent out of shape, was further down in the ravine. The pilot had probably tried to make an emergency landing on the mountain but failed to get that far and instead ended up plummeting into the Höllentobel.

As Winter began to climb the slope the policeman came to meet him. 'This is the scene of an accident. Please stay on the road.' The voice from a few minutes ago.

Intent on seeing Anne, Winter kept clambering. The undergrowth was wet and prickly, the ground beneath it muddy. With each step he sank several centimetres into the sludge and slipped back. Sliding towards him in the mud, the policeman ended up right in front of Winter, far closer than would be ordinarily deemed polite. As he was on higher ground he stood a head taller.

'Please stay on the road,' the officer repeated.

Winter placed his hand on the policeman's forearm, a gesture that allowed him to grip onto the man and reassure him at the same time. Physical contact often had a far greater effect than a flood of words. He smiled, and with his other hand dismissed the officer's request. Certain things were best not discussed.

'Good morning, Herr Oberholzer.' It was past midnight. 'We just spoke. I'm Winter and I'd like to see the woman whose mobile you found. I know her. Her name is Anne. Where is she?'

Oberholzer nodded in the darkness. 'Up there next to the cockpit. She was thrown out on impact.'

'May I see her?' Winter leaned against Oberholzer, who abandoned his resistance. Without saying anything, the policeman turned around and they climbed the last few metres together to what remained of the helicopter. The bent skids pointed upwards. One door was hanging half off. Upside down and still belted in, Strittmatter stared at Winter with lifeless eyes. His blackened arms dangled from his body. There was the stench of burned flesh. The helmet microphone was stuck deep in his mouth. Strittmatter had piloted the flight himself. Once more Winter was gripped by feelings of guilt. He stared back and closed his eyes.

He turned his head and, opening his eyes again, saw a totally charred, twisted figure in the beam of the police torch. Al-Bader. It's probably going to be some time before he can be identified with complete certainty, Winter thought. After all, he wasn't here.

Beside the helicopter stood a fireman sporting a helmet, but otherwise in civilian clothes, and a lad with long, blond hair. The herdsman. Winter offered them his hand without saying anything and the two of them nodded a greeting.

'The woman's over there,' Oberholzer said. 'But don't touch her. She's evidence.' He pointed to a shady patch by a bush, about five metres away from the wreckage. At first glance it could have been mistaken for a dark rock. Suppressing the urge to break the policeman's neck over his clumsy choice of words, Winter merely said, 'Thank you.'

Anne had been flung sideways out of the helicopter.

As he cautiously made his way over to her, Winter stumbled against the fire extinguisher. She'd tried to put out the blaze and save Al-Bader. Winter stopped and drew the musty air of the Höllentobel deep into his lungs. He'd seen a few corpses in his time. But Anne was different.

She was lying face down, her trouser suit badly burned. The trousers worse than the jacket. Her clothes were ripped. Winter could see Anne's white blouse beneath her jacket, while in places her soft skin shone. Her legs were unnaturally contorted and her backbone bent. The impact of the collision must have shattered her spine. At least she hadn't suffered.

Winter ran his splayed fingers through his hair, screwed up his eyes and lifted his head towards the dark night sky. *Why? Why Anne? For Christ's sake!* The tornado inside him escalated into a hurricane. Defenceless, Winter was at the mercy of the tempest of anger, pain, grief and desperate guilt. A hard lump swelled in his chest. His organs went into spasm, forcing him to lower his head. His eyes were damp.

Crouching down, Winter finally plucked up courage to look at her face.

Anne's head was pointing towards the mountain stream. Her soot-covered face was resting on a rock, as though it were a feather pillow. Her hair flowed. Her eyes were closed and she looked wonderfully peaceful.

Here it was again – the calm in the eye of the storm. Just Anne and him. He was struck by a great sense of clarity. He would always love her, even though she was dead. Tom Winter stretched out his hand and stroked her hair softly; he swept a strand from her cheek.

Then he closed his eyes and, in some deep recess of his mind, saw Anne laughing. Standing in early summer on the unfinished terrace and jokingly making suggestions about the planting. Tuscany or the south of France. The most important thing was that it should smell of summertime in the country. He would never forget that levity of hers, that laughter. Her eyes sparkling with *joie de vivre*.

Opening his eyes again, he saw his hand caressing Anne's cheek. He stopped, withdrew his fingers and clenched his fist. Winter raised his chin and shook his head very slightly.

Noticing the decorative bow from the box of chocolates by Anne's left hand, he put it in his pocket. As a souvenir.

Winter got up and stood there with his head bowed.

The policeman came over with his radio, tearing Winter from his gloomy meditations. 'Who is the woman?'

Winter swallowed hard. 'Anne Arnold. She lives in Bern and used to be a policewoman.' He hoped that the authorities would make a special effort for one of their own.

'Do you know the other passengers?'

'Difficult to tell given the state they're in.' Winter was playing for time. Oberholzer's attention was diverted again by his crackling radio and Winter decided he'd seen enough here. He climbed back down to the road. The young Alpine cowherd, leaning on the bridge railings, was just lighting a roll-up.

'Did you see the helicopter crash?'

'Yes, I was having a smoke outside my hut.' He raised his cigarette. 'All of a sudden I heard a helicopter. That's nothing unusual here. They're always flying about the area, transporting something or other. But I thought it was a little late. The sun had just gone down. When the helicopter came over the ridge there I saw that it was on fire and spiralling.' The cowherd made a circular movement. 'It span round and round and then vanished into the Höllentobel. Then there was a bang. It all happened very quickly.'

'Did it explode?'

'I don't know; there was a bang. Why do you think it crashed?'

'I don't know either. The FASI board won't produce a report for at least six months.'

The cowherd took a drag on his roll-up.

Winter was on the way back to his car when he heard a helicopter. The air-rescue service had taken its time. Saving lives was more urgent than recovering corpses. The inclines of the Höllentobel restricted his vision. Straining his neck, he followed the noise of the aircraft, which was flying in a low arc above the mountain. The noise was coming from a small helicopter.

Winter didn't see the chopper until it appeared over the ridge. It was white. The Swiss air-rescue service helicopters were red.

The drone was deafening and the plants were blown in all directions. Winter squinted and saw two masked figures.

The chopper hovered about fifteen metres above the crash site and then tilted forwards slightly to get a good view of the wreckage. There was a flash, then the helicopter turned around and flew from the ravine towards the valley. Winter made a mental note of the registration number. He heard the chopper ascend in the distance and head northwards.

The apparition had lasted no longer than thirty seconds.

A grief-stricken Winter drove back over the alp, down through the forest and across the bridge to the other side of the valley. In Kargmatt he turned off and headed for the Gemsstock mountain. An hour or so later he parked at the end of a long, treeless valley, at the foot of a huge basin. Many of the angular boulders had been prised away from the rock face by ice in the cracks.

He took out his rucksack and climbed the path marked in red and white up to the Gatterli mountain hut. Winter knew this path at least. The lonely ascent in the cool, clear night blew away the grey clouds in his head.

Two hours later he was at the narrow strip outside the hut, set with flagstones. This terrace had been finished years ago. Against the sky the stone hut cut a triangular silhouette and snuggled up, crouched against the wind-protected recess high in the rocky slope. Up here, surrounded by the massifs, you felt small.

He approached the hut silently. The door and windows, barred by thick wooden shutters, looked untouched. No sign of any unwanted visitors. He opened the door, ducked his head and entered.

Winter paused and took in the atmosphere inside. It smelled of cold fire. Although his eyes had become accustomed to the pale, night light over the last few hours, he couldn't see in the dark corners of the hut – but his inner radar didn't register any unusual vibes.

Nothing suspicious.

Reassured, he opened the shutters, turned on the gas in the kitchenette and lit the ceiling lamp with a match. The room filled with warm light. He put on some water for coffee and found some condensed milk and sugar.

When the sun announced its arrival, Winter sat with his coffee outside the hut to observe the change in the light. As he waited for Al-Bader's unknown business partner he reflected on things. He was good at waiting. Security often meant waiting. Impatience could be fatal.

A good couple of hours later he saw a helicopter, small and white. It circled above the hut a few times before carefully tottering onto the improvised landing pad. This wasn't a pilot familiar with the local conditions. Winter could make out four dark shapes: a pilot and three passengers.

The rotors came to a stop and the three passengers got out, each wearing the same thick, red puffer jacket. Bought specially for a detour to the mountains. Thin legs in dark suits and black shoes stuck out beneath.

The men walked along the narrow path to the hut. Black hair, gaunt faces, tanned skin.

Winter stood on the terrace, his hands in his windcheater, and smiled as the three men arrived. An older one in the middle was carrying a briefcase, flanked by two younger men. A guest and two bodyguards. They scrutinized each other.

'Good morning, gentlemen,' Winter said in English. 'Welcome to the Swiss Alps. My name is Winter. I am your host. And who do I have the pleasure of..?'

'Good morning. Ali Husseini. It's a privilege to be here.' Oxford English with an Arabic accent. The man with the briefcase shook Winter's hand. Slender fingers, soft grip.

'How was your journey?'

'Fine, thank you. Very smooth.'

'Please do come in,' Winter said, gesturing towards the mountain hut. He turned around and stooped. Husseini and one of the bodyguards followed. They didn't have to duck as they entered the hut. Inside they looked around quizzically and then at each other.

'When's Al-Bader coming?'

Deliberately ignoring the question, Winter went to the hob, and asked over his shoulder, 'Can I offer you some coffee?'

'Yes, please. We were up early this morning.'

'Wouldn't you like to take a seat?'

Husseini put his case onto the table and sat with his back to the wall.

The bodyguard leaned against the doorframe.

Winter lit the gas again under the cast-iron kettle. He placed three metal cups and some sugar on the table then returned to the hob. Behind his back he could hear the two men speaking. The guttural sounds and rasping of the throat sounded Arabic.

Winter took the coffee powder, a plate and a packet of biscuits from a rack in the kitchenette. He opened the packet and shook the biscuits out onto the plate.

Husseini took off his puffer jacket.

The water boiled and the kettle whistled.

The briefcase was opened. The soot-blackened kettle was steaming hot, so Winter put on a thick, padded oven glove, which made him remember his grandmother when she'd baked cakes. He picked up the kettle and turned around.

Husseini was holding a pistol.

As was the man at the door.

Winter stood there between them, wearing the oven glove, remembering the calluses on his hands and making a cool analysis of the situation. It was not optimal. Both men were calmly holding their pistols.

Husseini had casually leaned his right forearm on the table and was aiming at Winter's chest. The bodyguard was standing with his feet apart, gripping the gun with both hands and aiming at the head. If they were intent on killing Winter they could have already done so.

Winter remained in the middle of the room.

'Where is Al-Bader?' Husseini asked for a second time, his voice now harsh and strident.

*Talking is good. So long as we're talking I'll stay alive.* 'In the Höllentobel – Hell's Ravine.'

When his guests raised their eyebrows, Winter jutted out his chin towards the window on the right. The Höllentobel was in that direction, more or less.

'What are you saying?' Husseini asked impatiently.

'In the Höllentobel,' Winter repeated. To emphasise the orientation, he lifted the kettle and pointed it northwards. 'Al-Bader is dead.'

Husseini stared at him in disbelief. Winter brought the kettle with the boiling water crashing down onto the table, where it toppled over. The hot water soaked Husseini's grey suit, scalding his stomach and nether regions. He dropped his weapon in shock. He tried to brush off the boiling water, but without success.

Overpowering the bodyguard was simple. Spinning around, Winter used his left hand to knock the arm with the gun upwards, then he grabbed the sleeve. Good, he was out of the firing line. Putting his right hand on the man's stomach, he rammed his right foot into his genitals. Winter fell onto his back and with his left leg gave a powerful kick from the floor. A Sumi Gaeshi judo throw.

The attacker went flying over Winter towards Husseini. When the bodyguard's head cracked against the wall it sounded as if a shot had been fired.

The door opened and the third man in a puffer jacket stormed in, pistol first. Winter knocked the gun out of his hand with a chair, grabbed the second bodyguard and gave him a karate chop to his larynx, causing him to stagger into the table. As he'd been outside in the sun he was practically blind. Now the pain and the change in light combined to dilate the bodyguard's pupils.

These men hadn't been playing fair, and Winter didn't like having guns aimed at him. He threw off the oven glove, picked up one of the pistols and gave it a good look. The weapon was loaded. Winter aimed it at the groaning men by the table.

'Is this how you repay hospitality in your country?' Winter sat astride a chair, waiting for his guests to pull themselves together. 'Yes, I admit the hut and the catering are a little on the modest side. But it's a damn fine view.'

He threw Husseini a cloth from the kitchen recess, so he could dry himself. One of the bodyguards was bleeding from the head; the other was rubbing his neck.

'From now on, no false moves,' Winter ordered. 'Hands on the table.' The men obeyed. 'Right then, Mr Husseini. I have a few questions for you.'

'What do you want?'

'Answers. Otherwise you'll all end up in one of the crevasses outside,'

'We're just ordinary businessmen.'

'Waving pistols around?'

'They're...security. We had an appointment to meet Al-Bader. He called us to arrange a meeting in Switzerland.' Husseini made an awkward movement in the confined space of the mountain hut. 'When we didn't find him here, I assumed you'd harmed him.'

Winter was filthy and sweaty from the Höllentobel and the climb. In this get-up he wouldn't inspire much confidence. More gently he asked, 'What sort of business do you have with Al-Bader?'

'A variety of things. Orafin is one of the largest firms in Egypt.'

Winter had never heard of Orafin. He raised the pistol. 'Be more precise. Please!'

'Various technologies.'

Winter slammed the butt of the pistol against the table.

The three men recoiled.

'We wanted to persuade Al-Bader,' Husseini sputtered, 'to help us build a nuclear power station for Cairo. He's got the money and we've got the contacts. The Egyptian government is in the process of changing the law. This will allow private investors to get involved in the energy sector too. Nuclear power stations are good business in our country.'

'Let me have a look.' Winter pointed the gun at the briefcase, which Husseini nervously pushed across the table. Winter examined its contents with his left hand while keeping an eye on his guests. In the lid he found Husseini's business cards with the Orafin logo. One side in Arabic, the other in English.

Winter put a card in his pocket.

Three plane tickets. Cairo – Milan Malpensa – Cairo. A leather-bound diary, stuffed with notes. With his thumb Winter turned to July 25th. Meeting with Al-Bader. LOI. Letter of intent. As well as a variety of contracts in English. Nuclear power station. Financing. Guarantees.

'Those are draft contracts for the letter of intent,' Husseini explained. We were going to discuss them here with Al-Bader.'

Winter saw some handwritten notes in some of the contracts. Others had gaps which presumably were to be filled in during the negotiations. He tossed the contracts back into the case.

'Who else is planning to invest?'

'Britain, France, Russia, India. Lots of people want a piece of the cake. Egypt is interested in new technologies. We still need energy after the Arab Spring. It doesn't matter whether it's Mubarak, Mursi or Sisi. The president needs energy if he's going to keep his promises.'

Winter gave a thin smile. He had no desire to enter into a political discussion with a diluted dose of the truth. Although the cards had been shuffled after the spring awakening, the networks between the Egyptian generals and the business world hadn't suddenly disappeared. Money looks for and always finds its way. And he'd long given up being shocked by the business practices of the bank's clients.

Husseini had now composed himself. 'You said Al-Bader was dead?'

'Yes, his helicopter came down last night.'

'Was it an accident?'

'I don't know yet. Why do you ask?'

'Al-Bader is from the modernising wing of the Saudi royal family and he has many enemies. The fundamentalist wing frowns upon his business activities.'

'How much was Al-Bader going to invest?'

'Two hundred and fifty million US dollars.'

After a few further questions Winter sent the Egyptians back to the waiting helicopter. The three men in puffer jackets stumbled away, climbed aboard and flew back to warmer climes.

Winter cleared up, closed the shutters and made his descent. He drove to Kloten Airport in Zürich, which had been renamed 'Unique'. As Winter approached the gloomy airport car park he wondered what was so unique about it.

He ignored his tiredness. He had a meeting with Ben: not only a friend, but also a specialist in counter-terrorism.

You couldn't miss Ben. Winter guessed that 'Grizzly' weighed more than 150 kilos. He had personally felt the full force of Ben's mass in close-combat training with police special forces. As a result of the many days sat in front of a computer with unhealthy food, lots of coffee and sugary drinks, the head of security had only got bulkier over the past few years.

The nickname 'Grizzly' didn't just come from Ben's laid-back nature, size and strength. Ben could also go at speed when hunting, like a real grizzly. He hunted terrorists and was always on the search for the needle in a haystack, for the one extremist amongst the millions of air passengers.

Winter also knew another reason for Ben's nickname, a more obscure one. Bears hibernate in winter. They dig themselves a burrow or creep into a cave, for months remaining invisible to the outside world. Other animals wander nearby without noticing them. Together with his IT team, Ben had developed a method based precisely on these principles. He would lie down to sleep virtually in critical places and look for conspicuous patterns in the electronic stream of flowing data.

When Winter stepped through the frosted glass door that led to Ben's section, Grizzly welcomed him with open arms. As ever he was wearing a suit with a matching black shirt.

'Winter, it's been a long time! You look as if you've just come back off holiday. Perfectly rested,' Ben said.

'Hi Ben. Yes, I've been in the mountains. Hiking.'

They shook hands.

'The helicopter's destination was the Gatterli mountain

hut?' This was more a statement than a question from Ben. Strittmatter's coordinates were in the system. Winter nodded. Ben had had a few hours to prepare for this visit. Although time was scarce in his job and he skipped any small talk, he radiated the serenity of someone who had all the time in the world.

'I've ordered us a late lunch.' Room service at the airport.

He walked along a short corridor and placed his palm against a small screen. The door to Ben's sanctuary opened. On a wall of flat screens two colleagues were monitoring the comings and goings at the airport. Ben headed for a recess housing more screens, keyboards and technological equipment.

'I've localized the transfer. The Gulfstream touched down yesterday evening at 20:14. It's a nice piece of kit: range of more than twelve thousand kilometres and a top speed of nine hundred kilometres per hour. Catalogue price: fifty million dollars. They arrived from Norway and got in contact ninety minutes before landing. They taxied straight to the apron, where the VIP Transportation Corporation chopper was waiting.' Ben had done his homework.

'Strittmatter was a reliable guy.'

'The helicopter landed at 19:47, received the passenger from the Gulfstream at 20:19 and took off again at 20:23. Al-Bader was our guest for four minutes.' Ben said.

Winter was not surprised that the airport's head of security had identified his fleeting guest by name, and asked, 'Has the FASI Board said anything about the crash yet? Informally, I mean?'

'I called them earlier and they're saying we're going to have to wait for the report that they won't be able to write until they've carried out a more detailed analysis. Examining the flight recorder alone takes a few weeks. They don't want to make any mistakes and end up in court with the insurance companies.'

'And informally?'

'The report will probably say that there was a fire in the cockpit, making the helicopter unstable and causing it to plummet into a ravine. The bodies of the passengers exhibit third and fourth-degree burns.'

Winter pictured the Höllentobel in his mind. Anne's twisted body.

Ben paused, before adding breathily, 'I'm sorry.' And after a longer pause, 'The other passenger was your deputy, Anne, wasn't it?'

'Yes. This was her first time accompanying Al-Bader.' An outsider would have found Winter's voice normal. Ben, however, could hear a latent quiver of sadness and anger. They both stared into space. 'It should have been me on board. I took the day off yesterday.' He raised his chin and looked across Ben's shoulder.

'It's not your fault, Winter. There's really nothing you could have done about it.' Pause. An invisible bridge. The silent offer to listen if Winter wanted to spill out his heart. Ben put his hand on Winter's shoulder.

Grateful, Winter tried a tentative smile. But he didn't want to talk about Anne, not now. 'What have they said about the cause of the fire?'

'Nothing. It's tricky. It could have been a burned-out cable, a spark in the wrong place. It wasn't lightning. The weather was fine.'

'Explosives?'

'No obvious traces. I'm assuming that parts of the helicopter are already in the laboratory in Spiez.' Spiez was home to the Swiss laboratory for analysing explosives, which worked closely with Ben, for obvious reasons. Every explosive substance has its own chemical composition and thus can be identified, even after an explosion. The more specific the characteristics, the easier it is to identify the manufacturer.

The late lunch only came as far as the security doors, where it was taken by one of Ben's colleagues and brought to the recess. Coke, four ham sandwiches and two chocolate bars. No wonder that Ben looked so comfortable. All part of the disguise. Ben typed something then bit into the first sandwich and pointed it at one of the screens.

The airport's security cameras had saved grainy images of the apron. The wet ground reflected the surrounding lights. It was raining slightly. Strittmatter landed at 19:47. He flicked a few switches, studied a checklist, then swapped his helmet for a baseball cap. He got out, walked around the helicopter and checked the passenger seats. He opened a hatch in the tailpiece of the helicopter, peered in, then closed it again before climbing back into the cockpit. He made a phone call and then started reading a paperback.

Ben pressed the fast-forward button until Al-Bader's taxiing Gulfstream came into view. On his last visit the sheikh had explained to Winter that his Gulfstream had only twelve seats instead of the usual nineteen. The extra comfort was of help when it came to discussions with business partners.

A young steward opened the door and converted it into some steps. Inside the plane Winter could make out the back of a figure in traditional white robes, handy for the desert. Al-Bader said goodbye to people on board. Business friends? Bodyguards? He came down the steps with a leather travel bag. Alone. Al-Bader was leaving behind his bodyguards and placing his safety in the bank's hands, in Winter's hands. Winter rubbed his burning eyes.

Right at the bottom of the screen a white car stopped, bearing the airport logo. Anne got out on the right. She was wearing one of her tight-fitting trouser suits and holding a cylinder-shaped carton in her left hand. The large box of chocolates with the fat bow was clamped under the same arm. Al-Bader loved Lindt & Sprüngli confectionery. Her right hand – her shooting hand – was free. Good.

Anne stood up straight, surveyed the situation and glanced up at the grey sky. A light drizzle.

The driver had got out too. He was wearing a customs officer's uniform and put on his cap. 'That's Heinz,' Ben said with his mouth full. Heinz went up to Al-Bader, who took a case containing his passport from a side pocket of his elegant leather bag. Heinz took a cursory look at the document, stamped it with a sort of punch, saluted and returned to his car.

Anne stepped forward and greeted Al-Bader with a formal handshake and a nod. Winter and Ben could only see her from behind. She said something and raised her left arm with the welcome gift. From Al-Bader's smile Winter inferred that Anne had found the right words. She pointed to the helicopter and they walked side by side across the wet tarmac.

At one point Al-Bader briefly turned around, but there was nobody at the door of the Gulfstream.

From inside Strittmatter opened the rear door of the cockpit and the two passengers climbed in. The rotor blades started spinning immediately. A few seconds later the helicopter flew out of the picture.

Ben pressed fast forward. The car disappeared from view, leaving tyre marks in the shining ground. Soon afterwards the Gulfstream vanished too.

'The Saudis are waiting for Al-Bader's body,' Ben said.

'I know. Can you tell me who else was on that plane?'

'No, we don't have a passenger list and as long as they don't pass through customs we don't have any authority to check who was on board.'

The screen showed an empty apron. For a while the two friends remained sitting in silence in front of the screen. Winter was lost in his thoughts and felt grief seizing hold of him again. He was thankful for this small oasis of tranquillity. Then he snapped out of it. 'Ben, could you get me a copy of that?' he asked, pointing at the screen.

Ben handed Winter a DVD sleeve from the table. 'Here you go, already done.'

'Thanks.' Another pause.

'Did anything strike you as unusual?'

'No, it was a perfectly normal transfer.' No sound apart from the quiet hum of the control room. Then: 'Did he always arrive without bodyguards?'

'Depends. He felt safe in Switzerland. Especially in the mountains. I think he wanted to talk to his business partners as discreetly as possible. In town, when he went shopping with his clan in Geneva or Zürich, he usually had his men with him. He's directly related to the Saudi royal family.'

'That's the problem.' Ben switched off the screen.

'What do you mean?'

'I need an espresso.'

Winter nodded. They passed through the security doors, then along a windy corridor until they came to a coffee machine. Ben put two plastic cups under the machine, swiped his smart card, pressed a button and waited patiently as the coffee was ground and the two cups were half filled.

Having given Winter one espresso, he emptied two packets of sugar into his cup and mixed it in with a flat wooden stirrer. Clasping the brew with his paw, Ben swilled the cup around thoughtfully, as if it were a tumbler of whisky. 'What I'm going to tell you now, you didn't hear from me, alright? Here at the airport I'm the one who makes the rules, but otherwise it's the intelligence service in Bern. And the Americans.'

'I'm quick to forget things, even my own birthday.'

'Al-Bader is pretty high up on the CIA list of individuals who supposedly finance terrorists. The Americans assume that his image as a successful businessman is just a disguise. It's alleged that he secretly bankrolls fundamentalist groups through his companies.'

'Where's the proof?' If it got out that his bank was aiding terrorism it would be dreadful for business. Just for a change, communications would have a real challenge on their hands.

'As far as I know,' Ben said, 'there isn't any, either for or against. I'm just telling you what I'm hearing on the grapevine. And for some people in today's world that's enough to launch a cruise missile or a drone.'

Even for Winter, a rocket in the Swiss Alps was something new. 'No, I can't imagine that.'

'Who knew Al-Bader was coming?'

'I don't know who he told. His business partners in Egypt, definitely. Have you ever heard of Orafin?'

'Don't they develop telephone networks? These countries aren't building fixed landlines anymore; they're investing directly in mobile networks. Leapfrogging a stage of development. That's lucky for us as it means the conversations on these networks are more or less public.'

Winter drank his already lukewarm espresso in one gulp. Horrid, but after such a night he could do with the caffeine. 'Ben, I need to ask you another favour: have you got an explosives detector? Dog or machine, I don't mind which.'

Ben grinned and, with a nod, gestured to Winter to follow him. After another march through the warren of the corridors they came to a hall where hand luggage and passengers were screened. Slightly to one side was the chemical detector, which was able to pick up the minutest volumes of explosives residue. Ben unclipped one of the belt barriers for managing queues and gestured to Winter to follow him.

'We use this thing as a hairdryer,' Ben said, grinning and nodding to his colleague responsible for the machine.

When Winter entered the cabin he felt the blast that blew the tiny, invisible particles from him. Taking the chocolate-box bow from his pocket, he held it in the wind for a bit, put it back, left the cabin and went to the screen behind.

A red light was flashing.

Explosives.

Winter drove into Zürich city centre, but got caught up in a traffic jam caused by a Lady Gaga concert, and so was late for the crisis meeting that Känzig had called for 16:30. He parked in the underground garage.

Housed in the historic building above him was the bank's most important branch as far as turnover was concerned. The head office was still in Bern, where the private bank had been founded. It also had branches in Geneva, Lugano and the tax oasis of Zug, as well as in the financial centres of New York, London, Singapore and Hong Kong. Most recently in Abu Dhabi too.

This branch might be soon be merged with one of the financial group's, which owned almost half the shares. Rumours were gathering apace that the financial group was intending to integrate the small private bank altogether. Was it a coincidence that the crisis meeting had been scheduled here in Zürich? Had there been negotiations today at their headquarters in the functional, glass building in the Zürich suburb of Glattbrugg?

Dismissing this thought, Winter locked the car and entered the lift. Using his black security card he went up to the fourth floor. The building was on Bahnhofstrasse, the city's most expensive street. It was more than a century old, but the inside had been completely modernized with glass and steel. The shell of the building, which was protected by a preservation order, radiated tradition, while the interior represented the modern element. The architect responsible for the conversion had explained that this solution allowed the bank to speak equally to young people with money as well as old.

The meeting had been called at lunchtime by his manager, Känzig. When Winter listened to his voicemails following his encounter with the Egyptians, he heard the rather terse message: 'Winter, where the hell are you? A helicopter crashes with one of our best foreign clients and you're not contactable. We're meeting at 16:30 in "Eiger" to analyse the situation and coordinate where we go from here.'

In the mirrored lift Winter was once more assailed by grief and anger. He put the grief aside for the time being and tried to channel his anger. The lift door opened. Nodding to the middle-aged woman at reception, smartly dressed in a suit, Winter made for the small conference room at the end of the corridor. He paused at the frosted-glass door. Behind it he could see the vague outlines of people. The room was soundproofed and beside the door it said in big letters, 'EIGER' so that their many older clients could read them without difficulty. All the meeting rooms in Zürich were named after mountains: *Mönch*, *Jungfrau* and of course *Matterhorn*. Was there a *'Gemsstock'* room too?

Winter entered, closing the door behind him, and saw Känzig in front of a flip chart at the other end of the room.

As usual, he was doing the talking.

The flip chart was full of keywords, some underlined. Känzig was wearing one of his virtually black suits, with a white shirt underneath. Today his uniform was completed by a tie, which like his suit was almost black, but sprinkled with tiny red dots. He's already gearing up for the funeral, Winter thought, before nodding to the assembled company and looking for a seat.

Känzig interrupted his flow. 'Ah, Herr Winter is honouring us with his presence. Better late than never.'

Winter smiled at his superior's sarcasm and ignored him. Känzig suffered from John Wayne syndrome: always intent on having everything completely under control, he was destined to fail from the outset. Swamped by too much work and emotionally drained by too little confidence.

With both hands Winter pulled the Egyptians' pistols from his waistband and placed them on the conference table. The barrels were aimed at Helfer, the head of communications, who slumped in his chair. Then Winter sat calmly in the one remaining free chair. 'Al-Bader, Anne and Strittmatter were killed,' he said. Now he definitely had the undivided attention of his colleagues.

'Who says so?' asked Känzig.

'I do. There was a fire on board the helicopter. I'm working on the assumption the fire was caused by an explosive. It was supposed to look like an accident.'

Känzig wrinkled his nose. 'Gentlemen, let's get back to the facts. We were just setting out our communications strategy.' Turning his back to Winter he gestured to the head of communications.

Helfer leaned back, made a triangle with his fingers and said, maliciously, 'As I said, we're lucky that the accident happened late yesterday evening. It wasn't an important enough story for the print media and it was too late to be researched. All we have is one brief report on a Lucerne local paper's website. Someone was probably listening to radio traffic and snapped up the story. But we weren't mentioned by name. There was too little information for the late-night news, and what there was wasn't interesting enough. It didn't add up to a story. On the internet more widely...'

Winter ran an eye over the individuals present. Opposite Känzig, at the other end of the small conference table, sat Schütz, the account manager, whose official title was the rather pompous 'Vice President, Client Relations'. He looked tired, absent and, in spite of his substantial weight, a little shrunken. One of his clients had crashed in the bank's helicopter, which obviously was going to put a substantial strain on client relations.

Although Schütz looked lethargic, he was known for his killer instinct in the closing phase. He could adapt perfectly to any client. In front of him lay an overflowing presentation folder.

Helfer had stood up and was clutching the flip chart. As he spoke, he wrote:

1. CONTAINMENT
2. PASSIVE COMM.
   KEY MESSAGE:
   – PRIVATE VISIT
   – MOUNTAINS = DANGER!
   – ACCIDENT!!!

To Winter's left sat Hodel, the lean chief legal advisor and the bank's chief risk officer. He came from Bern's aristocracy. In such circles it was the norm to speak with a French accent. He was elderly, highly methodical, a man of integrity and an old friend of the CEO. He was also responsible for the bank's salary and bonus policy. According to the organisational chart he was at the same hierarchical level as Känzig, but in practice he was the most powerful man in the room. He was listening with his eyes half closed.

Beside Känzig sat a man in a black suit whom Winter didn't know. He was around Winter's age and with his slicked-back hair looked like the ambitious sort. In front of him was a writing pad from the financial group. Out of the corner of his eye Winter watched his manicured fingers fiddle, bored, with an expensive fountain pen and make the occasional note.

Probably one of the financial group's watchdogs, tasked with the job of collecting dirt that could be used against the bank.

Helfer had finished.

'Am I correct in assuming,' Känzig asked, 'that Herr Schütz will be present at Al-Bader's funeral?' Känzig looked directly at Schütz, who was aware that this was an order rather than a question. Although Känzig wasn't his superior, he had the lead in this matter.

Schütz clearly had no desire to fly to Riyadh and idle away his days in a luxury hotel. 'Wouldn't it ultimately be better for the bank if we proceeded with discretion and didn't send a representative this time? I think it would be more appropriate.'

'It would be best if you went in a private capacity,' Känzig said. As an account manager you are in a way a friend of the family.

Turning to Schütz, Hodel opened his mouth for the first time. 'The boss wants you to fly over there and make sure that the Al-Bader family continues banking with us.' End of discussion.

'So who's going to Anne's funeral?' Winter said.

'You were her line manager,' Hodel said, 'and I think it would be right for you to talk to the Arnold family in person. Naturally, any of Frau Arnold's colleagues are welcome to attend the funeral. I will be there at any rate.' Shaking his head sadly, he looked around the table and said, 'Anne was far too young to die.'

Winter was astonished to hear Hodel use her first name and he nodded as he acknowledged his task. 'I'll visit Anne's parents this evening and on behalf of the bank express our condolences.'

At that moment the telephone rang in the middle of the table. A futuristic device for conference calls, with three legs for the loudspeaker and no receiver, it reminded Winter of the model for a space station.

Känzig pressed the green button. 'Hello?'

'Good evening, gentlemen,' the CEO's baritone filled the room. 'I'm glad that you are attending to this unpleasant business. We must do everything we can to maintain confidence in the bank. Känzig, I'd like a briefing please.'

'Good evening, Dr von Tobler. I'm pleased you rang. In the room we have, besides me, Herr Hodel, Baumgartner, Schütz,

Helfer and Winter. We have analysed the situation. Schütz has emphasized just how important this client is and he's going to fly to Riyadh, Helfer has the media well in hand, and Winter is claiming it wasn't an accident.'

'Winter, didn't the helicopter crash in the mountains?'

'Yes it did, but someone lent a helping hand.'

'Can you prove that?'

'Not yet. It's going to take time to investigate the cause of the crash.'

'You've got to be careful, Winter. Switzerland isn't Iraq. Our banking industry doesn't need any rumours about terrorists.'

'Of course not.'

Winter was reluctant to expound on his clues; he wanted to clear up one or two things first.

Unable to hold back any longer, Helfer interjected, 'Dr von Tobler, all my press contacts have been speaking of an accident and when the police called they also said it was probably an accident. There was talk of a lightning strike in a localized summer storm. It's going to take months before we get clarification. The dust will have settled by then. We've established our communications strategy: private visit, tragic accident in the dangerous mountains, our profound commiserations.' The last of these was missing on the flip chart.

Känzig interrupted Helfer with a wave of his hand and explained their plans for the funerals. He would send a card for Strittmatter.

'Agreed,' came the voice from the loudspeaker. 'And I've heard that Winter was already in discussion with Orafin this morning.' Evidently the boss was well informed. Winter wondered which strings had been pulled here. 'Orafin is a good client. As you know, I look after this account personally.' Winter had no idea, but he inferred from this that Orafin had a substantial fortune with the bank. 'And I want everything to be done to ensure that our bank can continue to grow with Orafin. I suggest, therefore, that Winter flies to Cairo and tells the gentlemen there at Orafin how secure and hospitable we are here in Switzerland. Okay?'

The boss had spent a long time in America and was known for his 'Okay'. In plain language it meant: Discussion over. Obey. March!

'Yes. I'll get the contacts from Schütz.'

Winter saw Schütz subtly shake his head.

'Excellent work, gentlemen. Känzig has the lead. I expect you to rectify the situation quickly.' Känzig suppressed a proud smile when von Tobler added, 'And Baumgartner. Give my best regards to the chairman. I will explain my position to him over lunch next week.' Winter had guessed correctly. The suit was the liaison for the financial group. And von Tobler didn't trust him either.

Baumgartner nodded, realized that von Tobler couldn't see him, and said in an astonishingly deep voice, but with a pinch of arrogance, 'Agreed, Herr von Tobler. The chairman has authorized me to let you know that head office is of course prepared to use all means to resolve the situation discreetly.' Was that an offer of help or a threat?

'I'm very grateful for that and I wish you all a pleasant evening.' The boss departed with a click. When everyone started gathering their papers and standing up, Känzig had no choice but to declare the meeting over.

On the way out of the room Winter had to pass Hodel, who motioned to him to stop and said, 'A quick word in private if I may.' Winter and Hodel went into a small room nearby, reserved for discreet client discussions. Hodel closed the door but remained standing.

'What facts have you got to support your idea that this wasn't an accident?'

'Fires don't just start in helicopters. Strittmatter was a good pilot – reliable and careful. His helicopters were always well serviced. It's likely that there were explosives on board. We'll have definitive proof when we get the laboratory analysis back. And the men from Orafin were slightly nervous this morning. My gut feeling tells me something's not quite right. Too many things don't fit. The left hand doesn't know what the right hand is up to. Since when has the boss been looking after Egyptian clients personally?'

Hodel said, 'Till now I've only been involved on the margins of our relationship with Orafin. Given the sums involved it's probably oil money from the Middle East. But the boss is being rather secretive about it. My assumption is that these shareholders want to diversify their portfolios too.'

'What sort of sums are we talking about?'

'I don't know exactly, but it must be in the region of a few billion. Which means it's definitely the boss's business.'

Winter made a mental note to undertake more detailed research into Orafin. 'How certain are you that Al-Bader and Orafin aren't financing terrorists?' he asked. 'Maybe we're just one stop on the money's path from oil to a dirty bomb. In your role as chief legal advisor and chief risk officer can you put your hand on your heart and swear that we don't have an unpleasant surprise awaiting us here?'

'The short answer is "No!" The long answer is more complicated. As far as the Swiss justice department is concerned, both Al-Bader and Orafin are officially clean. Somewhere between spotlessly white and light grey. But you can always hide a considerable amount of money amongst sums like that. And a few hundred thousand dollars of "expenses" will get you a long way in poor countries. What's crucial is our reputation.'

'And the truth.'

'We need to be pragmatic about this. Keep an eye on the Egyptians, but be discreet. If this really was a planned attack then I want to be the first to know who was behind it.' The distinguished aristocrat with the gaunt face bared his teeth.

When Winter stepped out of the lift in the underground car park, Schütz was standing beside his Audi. He'd put his slim briefcase on the roof.

'Can you give me a lift?'

'Hop in.'

They drove out of the city and took the Bern motorway. Schütz started complaining about the flow of information at the bank. The boss was withholding important material. 'How can I ensure professional client care if I'm not fully informed?'

'What exactly did Al-Bader want with Orafin?'

'He wanted more global investments. Diversify. He was most keen on infrastructure projects. For a long time he'd been building up large positions in utilities. And evidently Orafin has the same interests.'

Winter nodded. His business was security rather than risky investments. And yet the stake was often his own life.

'Did you bring me the Al-Bader dossier?'

Schütz clicked open his briefcase and gave Winter a folder.

'Anything of interest in there?'

'No, just the usual. I did a lot of investments, but it's unlikely we could have held onto Al-Bader in the medium-term. The Norwegians have been trying to poach him off us for some months now. Oil to oil.'

Winter dropped Schütz outside his family home and drove to Anne's parents in Fraubrunnen, a suburb of Bern. He didn't know if the police had already notified them that their daughter had died in a helicopter crash. Yesterday, he'd still been dreaming of a future together. He thought of the two sun loungers on his unfinished terrace.

He was her superior and he'd persuaded her to move to the bank. He'd sent her on that fatal flight. If it hadn't been for him Anne would still be alive.

Winter turned into Anne's parents' housing development. Her father was a specialist in a firm that serviced oil tanks. Her mother was a housewife and part-time carer in an old people's home.

He stopped the car in front of the semi-detached house with its small, but well-tended front garden. Shared costs for the oil tank. Sensible. In the drive was a green Renault and beneath the canopy a number of bicycles.

Further down the street children were playing hockey with a tennis ball. They'd marked out a pitch with chalk, including the shooting circles, and set up two wooden goals. Both goalkeepers were wearing impressive, full protective gear. Winter pictured Anne playing on this street as a girl – now she was dead. With an effort, he pulled himself together and got out of the car.

He rang and waited. Nobody opened the door. He pressed the bell again and tried peering into the house through the pane of glass in the door. Nothing. Winter walked around to the back of the house. Perhaps they were in the garden. Passing a small tool shed, he saw Anne's parents at the other end of the garden. They were sitting on a colourful Hollywood swing seat. When they noticed Winter, Anne's father stood up and came towards him.

This was the first time Winter had met Anne's parents. 'Good evening,' he said. 'I'm Tom Winter.' For good measure he added, 'Anne's boss.' He wanted to take his time and offered his hand in greeting. Anne's father took his hand and shook it, but didn't say anything. Their expression and demeanour made it clear that they'd already learned of their daughter's death.

'I'm very sorry about your daughter. I'd like to express my condolences, on behalf of myself and of the bank.'

'Thank you. Anne always said you were a good boss and she learned a lot from you. Thanks for coming.'

Letting go of Winter's hand, he returned to the aging swing seat. Although he was only around fifty, he moved listlessly, like a pensioner. The mother had tear-stained cheeks and was sitting perfectly still.

Behind them were shrubs and trees that demarcated the property from the neighbouring one, providing shade during the summer and framing the swing seat. There were five cast-iron chairs, a table and a kettle barbecue. The ground was paved with square flagstones.

'This was Anne's favourite place. She could spend hours here swinging, reading or just daydreaming.'

Winter didn't say anything.

He took a chair and sat beside the couple.

All three of them looked silently down the garden at the house. Now Winter understood why Anne had liked this garden. It tore his heart, and he was pleased that he could keep quiet for the time being. Anne's mother leaped up. 'I'm sorry, I completely forgot to offer you something to drink.'

'Thanks, but please don't go to any trouble.'

'I was going to make some tea anyway.'

She headed back to the house without waiting for Winter's answer and went inside. Lost in thought, the two men said nothing.

It was a pleasantly warm evening and in the distance they could hear the clamour of the children still playing hockey. Winter got the impression that Anne's father understood him without the need for words. He didn't know how much, if anything, Anne had told her parents about him. After a while the mother came back with a tray carrying a pot and three cups. She checked the strength of the brew and then filled the cups.

'Thanks very much.'

'You're welcome.'

'How are Angela and Andrea?' Anne had told him about the three As. AAA. Triple A, as it were.

'I called them straight away. Angela is studying in the US and will get here as soon as she can. Andrea was here this afternoon, but had to go back home because of the children.'

Winter stirred his tea even though he'd taken neither milk nor sugar. He stared as if mesmerized at the whirl in his cup and waited.

'May I ask you what happened exactly? All the policeman could say this afternoon was that it was a helicopter crash.'

Winter figured it would be best to answer these questions as quickly as possible. 'Anne met a client at the airport and was going to accompany him to a meeting with business partners. As you know, this is routine with rich clients. The client in question loved the Swiss Alps and wanted to fly to a mountain hut. We've been using this helicopter service for years and I knew the pilot personally. All I know at present was that a fire broke out on board and then the helicopter crashed. I'm sure that the Federal Aviation Safety Investigation Board will determine the precise cause of the crash. And I will personally ensure that no stone goes unturned.'

Anne's mother was still looking at him expectantly. Aware that he hadn't answered her real question, Winter was groping for words. 'I believe that Anne did everything to prevent the crash,' he said, thinking back to the voicemail message, 'and it all happened very quickly in the end. I'm certain she didn't suffer.'

Anne's mother dabbed at her eyes with a scrunched-up tissue and tried desperately to smile. A mixture of emotions twitched at the corners of her mouth.

'She loved her work. She always said it was a dream job: exciting people, a huge level of responsibility and trust, legal and police work under the same roof. She was wedded to her job.'

Winter nodded, letting her talk.

'Anne called in to see us yesterday, on her way to Zürich. We had a nice chat here in the garden. She was in a good mood and looking forward to the weekend. She was planning her holidays and asked me about Portugal. We went there on holiday when the girls were small, you see. But then she got a work call and urgently had to go back to Bern…'

Winter's ears pricked up. He hadn't telephoned Anne yesterday afternoon, and she worked for him and nobody else.

'She was here yesterday afternoon?' A rhetorical question to start with.

'Yes, but she wasn't going to stay for dinner.'

'What time did she get this urgent call?'

'Just before five. After Anne left we listened to the radio news.'

'Did she tell you who it was from?'

'No, all she said was that she had to dash back to Bern.'

Fraubrunnen was between Bern and Zürich, which meant that Anne would have had to drive back to Bern again. Twenty minutes there, twenty minutes back. The phone call put her on a tight schedule. It must have been something urgent, but minor – Anne would have surely called him otherwise. Who had gone over his head and made Anne turn back?

Now her mother had started talking about Anne's schooldays and the trouble she'd had as a small child in differentiating between the letters 'D' and 'P'.

All of a sudden Winter was in a hurry. He stood up, promising to get in touch if he had any news, and said goodbye to Anne's parents. The father, who'd sat the whole time in silence beside his wife on the swing, accompanied Winter back to his car. As a parting gesture he said, somewhat formally, 'Many thanks for having looked after Anne. It was nice to meet you and you're very welcome to drop in anytime.'

The sun was already low on the horizon and so Winter had to flip down the visor on the drive to Bern. He took the country road across the summer fields and opened the window. Winter barely noticed the countryside. He was wondering what Anne's father had meant by his open invitation. How much had she told her parents about their fledgling relationship? At what point does something become a relationship?

When he reached the city and parked near the bank, he contemplated his mission: to find out who had caused the helicopter to crash, thus murdering Anne, Al-Bader and Strittmatter.

# JULY 25 – 20:38

The bank's headquarters in Bern was in a five-storey, seventeenth-century sandstone building. The founding family's trust, which owned a variety of country estates and other properties, leased it to the bank. Originally this had allowed the family to cover its share capital. Today the ground floor was leased to a pizzeria, which was known for its crispy pizzas and loud Italian waiters. Winter had already spent a small fortune in this restaurant. With Anne too.

From the outside you had to look closely to see it was a bank. Beside the pizzeria was a discreet entrance with a tarnished sign bearing the bank's name. As Winter approached the entrance he saw a man waiting there. Nothing unusual in that – people often arranged to meet outside the pizzeria and would stand there waiting for friends. But Winter was certain it was no coincidence that this ordinary-looking man was here today. If he'd asked passers-by whether they'd seen anyone, most would have answered, 'No'.

The man was of medium build, around fifty years of age, with a short-sleeved shirt and thinning brown hair. A well-thumbed newspaper was clamped beneath his left arm. He wore imitation-leather shoes with tiny holes. Meister looked like a lonely official who didn't know what to do with himself of a Saturday evening and was now waiting for the bus.

Such an impression only told half the truth – intentionally so – for Meister was section head at Fedpol, the Federal Office of Police in the Swiss Department of Justice and Police. From his desk he ran the division that dealt with organized crime.

Winter had met him years ago when still with the Enzian unit. Meister worked in the background combating the same crimes that Winter's special unit was deployed against: international organized crime, abduction, the drug trade, counterfeit money and corruption.

Meister, a lawyer by training, had also helped set up the money-laundering reporting office a few years back. An authority that no bank could dare ignore. This is why, after his switch to the private bank, Winter had kept up their relationship. The geographical proximity helped: Fedpol was within walking distance. Winter nodded to Meister and took out the key that would open the heavy wooden door. 'Are you coming in?'

After all these years the two men still addressed each other formally as '*Sie*'. There simply hadn't been any reason up till now to switch to the informal '*Du*'. Winter was comfortable with that.

'No thanks, I ought to have been home long ago.'

Winter had no idea where Meister lived and found it difficult to imagine him as a husband, in spite of the wedding ring.

'How did you know I'd be coming to the bank this evening?'

Smiling sheepishly, Meister tapped the breast pocket of his shirt with his newspaper. In it was a slim mobile phone. Meister had followed the movements of Winter's own mobile. Good to know. Technology was both a blessing and a curse.

'Doesn't that infringe my constitutionally guaranteed rights?' Winter said with an ironic grin.

'I've heard that a helicopter crashed with a client and employee of the bank.'

'You heard correctly.' Winter wondered where Meister was going with this.

'The helicopter crashed for reasons as yet unknown. The Federal Aviation Safety Investigation Board is working in conjunction with the forensic officers of the Central Swiss cantons to identify the causes. The Valais lot are there because of Strittmatter. The Saudi embassy was informed by the Federal Department of Foreign Affairs. The laboratory in Spiez is investigating whether explosives were involved. I've said that we'll take care of the bank. The name Al-Bader set a number of alarm bells ringing in our office. Money laundering and terrorist financing cannot be excluded.'

'Al-Bader was one of our best clients and we're very sorry about his death. As far as I know he never did anything wrong. And personally I liked the guy.'

'I'm sorry. But that's irrelevant. By our criteria he was on the radar. Do you have any idea why he disappeared?'

He hadn't 'disappeared', he'd been burnt alive. But Winter was too tired to argue the point. 'No idea. He was one of many clients.'

'Did you spot anything unusual at the crime scene?' Meister could be a real pain, but that was his job. He'd clearly tracked all of Winter's movements electronically.

'A wrecked helicopter, a policeman out of his depth and a local fireman. Three charred bodies. That was no accident. Someone deliberately planted a bomb on board.' Sooner or later Meister would come to the same conclusion.

'Do you have any proof?'

'No, but I do have a hunch.'

'Me too.'

Winter looked first at the key in his hand, then at Meister, who said, 'Call me if you find something.'

'Likewise.'

A few seconds later Meister had vanished. It was a pleasant Saturday summer's evening. The offices were deserted. Winter went up to Anne's office on the first floor and unlocked the door with his skeleton key.

To begin with Winter just stood by the door, then he sat in Anne's swivel chair. The windowless room was neat and tidy. No papers on the desk. No personal items. Nothing. Anne was scrupulous about the security procedures. Just a single, family photo on the desk: Anne's parents and the three girls laughing in a pizzeria. The photo had doubtless been taken by the waiter, the family huddled tightly to fit into the picture.

Deep in thought, Winter opened the desk drawers. In the top one he found Anne's large address book. He leafed through it. Under 'W' Anne had jotted down his birthday. Underlined twice. With a sigh, Winter tore himself away, locked the door and went into his own office next-door.

Winter's office had a window onto a dark inner courtyard. It was above the pizzeria kitchen, at the back of which the extractor pipe hummed. The rooms for receiving clients were higher up in the building; the more important the client, the more natural light they were granted.

But he rarely sat at his desk. Nor was he dependent on impressing the people he met with a prestigious office. Desk, telephone, computer, printer, cupboard and wall safe were enough. His only luxury was the crumpled leather sofa, where he went to think. Piled on the limited shelf space was an assortment of magazines, old newspaper cuttings, miscellaneous books, travel souvenirs, boxes and all manner of odds and ends.

Winter got a coffee from the machine in the corridor and made a to-do list. The most important and urgent tasks first, everything else later.

Then he booked his flight to Cairo and browsed the internet and the bank's databases. Orafin was a not particularly transparent conglomerate that invested in everything imaginable. There wasn't much in the client database, but he did find some contact addresses. Most of these were in Egypt, but there were some in Kuwait, Washington, Delhi and Beijing too. The database had been carefully updated by the CEO's office. Winter printed out the list. He was unable to find any detailed client documentation, and after half an hour he gave up. He emailed an urgent request to the head of the analysis and research department, asking for a comprehensive report on Orafin.

Realising how tired he was, Winter decided to study Al-Bader's dossier at home. He was just about to close down his computer when someone crept in silently.

'Hello, Winter.'

Winter gave a start and saw Dirk in the doorway. Dirk was the head of IT and one of Winter's favourite colleagues. Both of them had the COO Känzig as their superior, both worked cross-departmentally and from time to time both liked to stray from the strictly conventional way of doing things. For a bank employee Dirk had remarkably messy hair and tested the dress code to its limits.

'Hello, Dirk. What are you still doing here?'

'The trading platform is playing up again.' The usual. Then, with an expression of concern, he said, 'I heard about the helicopter crash. How are you?'

'Not so bad. I've got to go to Cairo tomorrow. On a mission for the big boss.'

'Why the hell did it have to be Anne?'

'I don't know. Not yet.' A pause. 'It ought to have been me in that helicopter.'

'Don't beat yourself up about it. The ways of the Lord are unfathomable,' Dirk said, raising his eyes and hands to the heavens.

'Like at Microsoft?'

'No. I'm being serious here. There's really nothing you could have done.'

'Yes, I know. Thanks.'

'That's what friends are for.' Dirk grinned.

'Dirk, could you find out who Anne spoke to on the telephone over the last few days, yesterday in particular?'

'No problem for the landline. We have all the VOIP records saved on hard disc. Secured and mirrored twice. Here and in the bunker. For her mobile I'd need a bit of time as I'm reliant on the provider. I hope my contact isn't on holiday.'

'And while you're at it, could you check Al-Bader's numbers too? Who did he call at the bank?' Winter opened Schütz's dossier, jotted Al-Bader's numbers onto a Post-it and gave this to Dirk.

'You don't believe it was an accident, then?'

'I don't know. Just in case. Very few people on our side knew that Al-Bader was coming, let alone when and how. I just want to be sure we don't have a mole.'

Dirk nodded, waved the Post-it note by way of a goodbye and left the office. Winter stretched. It had been a long day. Wrapped in his thoughts, he walked to the car park and drove home.

The whole affair was a puzzle. Who benefited from the crash? Al-Bader was a businessmen and must have enemies as well as friends. But why here and now?

As he turned off the main road and drove cross-country, the hamlet with his house came into view on the horizon. Once again Winter couldn't help thinking of Anne. Yesterday evening he'd fantasized about how wonderful it would be if they were together. Today his plans for the future lay in ruins in the Höllentobel. He was overcome with grief again.

He stopped, switched off the engine and remained bent over the steering wheel for a moment. He was tired, hungry and needed a shower.

Tomorrow was another day. Picking up Schütz's documents and his small rucksack, he got out and walked across the muddy area in front of his farmhouse. When it rained, this was boggy; when the weather was dry, it was dusty. Ever since he'd moved in he'd had the same thought each time he crossed this space: I really ought to gravel it over. But now this recurring thought was joined by another: *unfamiliar footprints.*

The footprints were fresh and Winter couldn't place them. He knew those of the farmer who cultivated the land around his house and always wore Wellington boots. He knew the prints of the postman who drove his motorbike as close as he could to the front door. But these were from someone wearing large trainers.

Although his neighbours ensured that the comings and goings were closely observed, Winter had installed a rudimentary security mechanism: he'd drilled a small hole into the edge of the door and the jamb. Beside the door hung a bunch of dried flowers. Whenever he left the house for a considerable time he would place a dry stem in the hole. Now he saw that the stem was broken. Someone had opened the door.

Setting down his rucksack, Winter took out one of the Orafin pistols, silently released the safety catch and crept around the house. If the burglar was still here they would surely have heard his car being parked. Winter ducked and peered into the sitting room.

In the dim light he saw the silhouette of a figure scuttling to the balcony door.

Winter slid along the exterior of the house, moving his way down the slope, and crouched beneath the wooden steps by the entrance to his wine cellar. Above him somebody was hurrying across the balcony. Whoever it was, wasn't making any effort to stifle the noise of the ancient wooden planks. The intruder dashed down the steps and found himself staring into the barrel of the pistol.

'Good evening,' Winter greeted his uninvited guest.

The man was about Winter's size, between fifty and sixty years old, wearing jeans and a roll-neck sweater. He had a small sports bag, but no weapon as far as Winter could make out. His face showed no fear, only apparent irritation that he'd been caught.

A professional, Winter thought. 'Drop the bag and slowly put your hands on your head so I can see them,' he instructed. 'It's been a long day and I've no desire to dispose of a corpse.'

The man obeyed without hesitation, but Winter could see his eyes scanning the area for an escape route.

'What are you looking for here?'

'Nothing, I was just on a walk and hoping to find something to eat around the house.'

'Poor joke. Right, now you're going to take a few steps back – slowly!' The intruder carefully moved backwards in the direction of the stable. 'That's it. Now stay where you are.'

Winter crouched down and opened the bag with his left hand: technical eavesdropping equipment. Not the latest model. Winter stood back up. 'Move!' he barked. 'We're going for a walk.'

On their way up to the stable some distance away, they passed the dung heap with the slurry pit. With his right hand Winter gave the intruder a karate chop to the neck. As the man struggled to keep his balance, Winter kicked him in the knee.

There was a crack.

Screaming, the intruder tried to keep himself on his feet, but tumbled into the slurry pit. The exchange of pleasantries was over.

The slurry pit had been built after the Second World War with cheap concrete mixed with sand. The round tank was seven metres deep and two metres in diameter. The farmer regularly pumped the stinking, but nutrient-rich, liquid from the pit to fertilize the surrounding fields.

Today the tank was half full and Winter had to take a few

swift steps back to avoid being spattered. He heard the man's cries of pain being choked. The slurry in his windpipe muffled the screams.

The visitor spat, cursed and tried in vain to push himself up.

Winter returned to the house, taking his guest's bag with him. He turned on the lights and made a quick search of all the rooms. Nobody. He fetched the rucksack with Al-Bader's documents, put some coffee on and embarked on a more thorough inspection of his sitting room, which also served as a study.

He checked the low-hanging lamp, unscrewed the receiver and base station of the telephone and followed the cables leading from his computer. Behind the router he found a small nondescript box that he hadn't put there. He left it where it was.

Time for a little chat. He took his coffee and went back to his guest. 'As I said, I don't have any time. Either you can tell me the truth in the next sixty seconds or I'll let you perish down there. If I cover the pit, in a few minutes you'll be knocked unconscious by the methane and then you'll drown. But at least you'll serve a useful purpose as fertilizer.'

'Get me out of here. Please!' came the grunted plea from the pit.

'What were you doing inside my house?'

'I'm a private detective. This evening some guy rang me, gave me your address and asked me to monitor your computer. Internet's my speciality. He said you weren't at home.'

'Name?'

'The guy called himself Müller and he rang from a pre-paid mobile. I checked. He paid immediately. The first ten thousand were transferred to my account within five minutes.'

'What were you supposed to give him?'

'Everything I could get, especially your emails.'

'For how long?'

'Until he called again. He promised me two thousand a day plus my set-up expenses.'

'How were you going to deliver the information?'

'He gave me an email address.' The detective spelled out an anonymous-sounding address. 'He ordered me to send him all the files straightaway.'

'Did you notice anything unusual? Did your client have an accent?'

'No, he spoke Swiss German. No particular dialect. From Zürich perhaps. I somehow got the impression that this wasn't the first time he'd commissioned a job like this.'

Winter drank his coffee and mulled over the situation. As he couldn't think of anything else to ask the detective he fetched a tow rope, attached it to a hook and threw it in. The private detective clambered out. He looked pitiful and he stank to high heaven.

After Winter had taken a few prudent steps back he said, 'I'm going to let you go now. I found your address in your bag. You'll go home and carry out the assignment as requested. Give him what you agreed. If I find that you haven't done that, I'm going to pay you a visit. Is that clear?'

The filthy man just nodded and hobbled off into the darkness.

Winter sat in one of the two loungers and stared into the night sky. Shooting stars. But he wasn't in a position to wish for anything. After an hour he got up, sent a few emails, lay down to sleep for five hours, packed his foldable toothbrush in his rucksack and flew to Cairo.

The full aeroplane landed late. Winter had been forced to make do with a middle seat. The sandwiches wrapped in perforated plastic film had been unpleasant. He hated flying. And when he ducked his head to step out of the plane and into the tube connecting them to the airport, he was assaulted by the heat. Cairo in July. Not a good idea. He went through customs with his express visa and when asked, 'Tourist or business,' he replied, 'Business.'

He was one of the first passengers from the flight to enter the air-conditioned terminal with its slightly curved, steel roof and real palm trees. Winter wondered whether Orafin had been responsible for the building.

The fifty metres in the dry, dusty heat to the taxi rank were enough to make him break out into a sweat. On the way to the city centre he switched on his phone, which gave him the choice of three Egyptian mobile networks. He decided against the Orafin one, called Dirk and told him about the bugging installation at his house. 'Double-check the bank's firewall. Our friends appear to have deep pockets.'

'Absolutely. There hasn't been any suspicious activity recently. The hackers are on their summer holidays too.'

Winter asked the taxi driver to drop him at the Shepheard on the Corniche. It was the only hotel he knew in Cairo. Centrally located: it was a few hundred metres from Tahrir Square, near the Egyptian Museum and with a view of the Nile. The name wasn't from a breed of dogs, nor a shepherd, but an Englishman who'd established the hotel. The Shepheard had cold mineral water in the minibar, air-conditioning that worked and an empty computer room in the business centre.

Winter went for a walk. He changed money, bought a city map from a peddler with his Egyptian pounds and dived into the chaos of Cairo. Millions of Egyptians lived in this city by the Nile. A good number of them were honking their horns in cars manufactured in the factories of the former colonial powers. Young people on Japanese motorbikes with cool sunglasses and Western clothes snaked their way perilously through the traffic. Groups of elegant women with colourful headscarves walked the pavements, along with fully-veiled women – and corpulent businessmen trying not to sweat in their suits.

The streets around Tahrir Square were freshly cleaned. It was patrolled by new policemen, or soldiers who were barely old enough, wearing their excessively large uniforms – or at least armbands – with pride. And amongst them a farmer in traditional white robes smoked on a donkey-cart piled high.

Winter went with the flow. He passed a Coptic church, a presidential palace with a park and water sprinklers and allowed himself to get sucked up into Port Said, the wide thoroughfare. Port Said divided Cairo into the traditional and modern part. On the opposite side of the road it was all a bit mediaeval and *One Thousand and One Nights*.

Because of the way the Nile flooded, the original Cairo didn't evolve on the river itself, but was built on a slight elevation. It was only in the last 150 years, after the river was tamed, that the city extended westwards, first nestling up to the Nile, then crossing it.

According to the client file, Orafin's headquarters were on Port Said. The house numbers weren't easy to read. Winter wandered more than a kilometre to the north until he found the building with the Orafin logo: a five-storey glass construction with a 1970s façade, stained with soot and fumes. The air-conditioning units jutted out at regular intervals. There was old scaffolding on the roof. It was tax efficient never to finish the building, at least not officially.

Egypt in summer. Around lunchtime. Really poor timing. He went into the lobby and stopped for a moment. Beautifully cool. Almost cold. And astonishingly quiet. Four security guards equipped with radios. Two in uniform flanked the entrance, two sat looking bored on seats by the lift. Their age and tubbiness suggested they were on the verge of retirement. For a moment Winter envied Orafin's head of security, who clearly didn't have to scrimp on staff. There was also a lot of white marble, golden ornamentation and a reception with three very pretty women, also in uniform.

Smiling, Winter stepped up to the counter and said in English, 'Hello, my name is Winter and I'd like to speak to Mr Kaddour.' This was von Tobler's contact and probably a big cheese at Orafin. In the client database the 'Title' field had been empty.

'Good afternoon, sir,' the woman in the middle answered in almost accent-free English. 'Do you have an appointment with Mr Kaddour?' She didn't consult the bulky, ancient-looking computer and gazed with her perfectly made-up eyes at Winter, who was already a touch sweaty.

'No, I'm sorry,' he said. 'I didn't have the chance to arrange a meeting with Mr Kaddour. But it's an urgent matter and I'd really be very grateful if you could hand him my business card.'

Winter had learned from experience that you made quicker progress in these situations by remaining as polite and unassuming as possible. He gave the women a business card that bore, besides 'T. Winter', only the name and logo of his bank and a telephone number. It was a high-quality card, slightly larger than the standard ones. It left many things unanswered.

She gestured to a group of red-leather sofas hidden behind columns. Winter nodded and watched the woman go through a door behind the reception. After seven minutes, the door opened again and the woman smiled at him. 'Mr Kaddour is terribly busy at the moment, but he would be delighted if you would accept his dinner invitation for this evening. He will pick you up from the Shepheard at 8:30P.M.'

'Thank you very much.' Winter smiled, said goodbye and wondered who'd announced his arrival. He hadn't told anyone which hotel he was staying in. Clearly he was being followed.

With several hours till dinner, Winter took the afternoon off. On the way back he walked through the Khan El-Khalili souk and marvelled at the ornate displays of the traders. He didn't know most of the fruits and spices, but he was beguiled by the intense aromas and colours. He took his time and had no inclination to worry about anyone tailing him.

At the Al-Azhar mosque he removed his shoes and took a gentle stroll around the vast courtyard. In a shadowy corner he saw a group of young men on the ground, listening to an older man. The mosque was also a university.

Winter climbed the narrow stairs of one of the minarets and was rewarded with an excellent all-round view of Cairo and the mosque's courtyard with several exits. Winter looked calmly at the people in the house of worship. He bet himself that his tails were the two not-so-young men in grey, Western suits. Amongst the majority of people in traditional robes they stood a little lost at the edge of the covered walkway on one side of the courtyard. This gave them a good view of the minaret and they were acting as if deep in discussion. Winter couldn't make out which direction they were looking in, but from the position of their heads he concluded that they were taking discreet but regular glances up at him.

Winter went back down to ground level. To avoid the worst of the heat and turn his mind to the puzzle of the helicopter crash in peace, he sat in a quiet corner of the courtyard. From outside it looked as if he were having a nap. Suddenly he felt hungry. What harm would it do if he cashed in his bet?

At a stall outside the mosque he bought a flatbread filled with meat and vegetables. And, for good measure, a Coke. The sell-by date had been smudged. But it was cold. He ate standing beside the stall and glimpsed the men in grey suits loitering nearby.

Winter took a taxi back to the hotel, but asked to be dropped off on the Nile side. As he paid the driver he watched in the rear-view mirror the two grey suits get out of a taxi too, around a hundred metres behind him.

Between the road along the Nile and the hotel was the hotel's private park. Palms and head-height red and white oleander bushes provided shelter from the traffic noise.

He nodded to the gardener-cum-security guard, who was dozing in a green hut by the entrance, hurried halfway to the hotel, then dived sideways into the oleander bushes, where he crouched. After a minute he saw through the leaves the two men coming down the path. Once they'd passed he straightened up, stepped out of the bushes and asked, 'Can I help you, gentlemen?'

Visibly startled, the two men spun round. Winter had to suppress a grin. They stammered something about 'visiting a friend' and pointed at the hotel.

Amused, Winter asked, 'Could I invite you for a drink?'

The men looked at each other blankly.

'Surely it would be nice for us to get to know each other?' Winter continued.

'My name is Winter and I arrived from Switzerland this morning.'

A key function of communication was to say, 'Hey, I'm here!' As language evolved in the jungle it was important to keep talking to each other. It was how people could be sure that everyone was still alive, rather than having been gobbled up by a wild animal.

So Winter continued, 'It's pleasantly warm here. A little hot for me, but nice and dry.'

But communication often creates confusion too. People often talk at cross-purposes, understanding only a fraction of what the other person has actually said. Sometimes this was a bit tedious, but in certain situations it was quite practical.

'As I said, my name is Winter.'

He held out his hand.

Baffled, the man on the left also held out his hand. 'My name is Faruuk. Pleased to meet you.'

Taking Faruuk's outstretched fingers, Winter gave him a limp handshake and looked him straight in the eye. As he withdrew his hand, he grabbed Faruuk's little finger, thrust his arm up in a flash and swivelled through the arch formed by their limbs. Jiu-Jitsu for beginners.

As he turned around he could feel the joints in Faruuk's little finger being dislocated. Twice there was a crack and a jolt. Winter got goose pimples. Faruuk suppressed a scream. He snarled and screwed up his eyes in pain. Winter calmly held on to the little finger and asked, 'Why are you following me?'

'We're visiting a friend in the hotel.'

Winter shook Faruuk's twisted finger. A tried and tested method. No weapon. Minimal damage. Maximum pain. Few parts of the body were more sensitive. The earlobe, perhaps. As a rule, the gums were a bit unappetizing.

The second man stood there as if thunderstruck.

'Well?'

'Mr Kaddour is keen that nothing happens to you in Cairo. He said we should make sure you didn't get lost.'

That was better, and was probably half the of the true story. Winter let go of the little finger and the man stood up straight.

'That's very kind, but you don't have to go to so much trouble.'

Winter left the two of them standing there, went up to his room, took a shower and had a rest. Then he sat on the terrace and ordered a large bottle of mineral water and an Egyptian beer. He waited and watched the sunset on the other side of the Nile. He'd been rather popular recently. Yesterday a private detective, today two men in suits. When the sun vanished fully below the horizon, images of the crash site, Anne, Al-Bader and Strittmatter resurfaced.

Two hours later a steward pointed at Winter and behind him a man appeared on the terrace. Kaddour, around fifty with a slight paunch, wore a dark suit. Too many business dinners. From the way he treated the steward, he must be used to issuing orders. His upright gait and short hair suggested a military career.

But Winter's thoughts were distracted. Behind Kaddour, a woman of about thirty stepped onto the terrace. She was wearing a light, sand-coloured trouser suit, a white blouse with a pointed collar and she was almost as tall as Kaddour. The woman had long, black hair and moved gracefully, about half a pace behind Kaddour and to the side.

Winter stood and the two men greeted each other. Close-up, Winter could see that Kaddour's suit was dark brown and tailored from fine wool. Beneath this he wore an ivory-coloured shirt with a short stand-up collar. As they shook hands Winter noticed a seemingly genuine, gold, mechanical watch. Kaddour's handshake was firm and bore out Winter's initial impressions. His facial expression was neutral and difficult to read.

'Good evening, Mr Winter.' English, as expected, with a faint accent.

'Mr Kaddour? Delighted to meet you.'

'The pleasure is all mine. May I introduce you to my right-hand woman, Ms Hakim – Fatima Hakim?'

Fatima Hakim gave a reserved smile as she offered Winter her hand and nodded. Winter briefly looked into her dark eyes with their broadly arched brows. Mascara. He noticed large gold earrings and a fine necklace, also gold, its pendant hiding in the décolleté of her silk blouse. When he bowed his head slightly, he detected the hint of a subtle perfume.

Winter gestured to them to take a seat. 'Shall we have a drink?' He had chosen a round table and now he pulled out one of the thickly-padded garden chairs for Fatima.

'Good idea. We'll have our aperitif here and then go on to Giza. I've reserved a table in a restaurant I'm sure you'll like. No tourists.'

A waiter came. As Winter had a beer glass in front of him, Kaddour opted to join him. Fatima ordered something in Arabic. Kaddour made himself comfortable in his chair, his hands together in front of his belly.

'I'm terribly sorry we're late, but we are in Egypt, and the clocks work differently from in Switzerland. One Egyptian minute corresponds to about five in Europe.'

'No problem. I'm just pleased we can chat in peace. The climate was a little chillier last time.'

'Oh, you mean Husseini, my dear controller? He came back raving about the mountains and your hospitality. He said the view was magnificent.'

Kaddour grinned, his beer arrived and they clinked glasses. Winter offered a toast to Egypt, Kaddour to the evening and Fatima to the future. They talked about Cairo, its traffic jams, the new bypass and the impact of the Arab Spring on tourism. Small talk. Kaddour used to be CFO of Orafin, but for a number of years now he'd been managing the operative side of the business.

When Winter asked where Fatima had learned her accent-free English, she beamed at him. Then she explained that her father was a British diplomat with Indian roots. She'd spent her childhood in a variety of metropolises. London became her second home and she'd studied finance at the London School of Economics.

Kaddour was proud of his right-hand woman. He also made no secret of the fact that he knew von Tobler personally. Kaddour appeared to be well informed about him and Winter. On one of his visits to Switzerland, he'd learned from von Tobler that you eat 'rösti' there. He wished Egypt was as green as Switzerland and had as many lakes.

After the small talk they got into the black Mercedes with its tinted rear windows. Kaddour drove and Fatima insisted that Winter sit in the front. They crossed the Nile and sped towards Fayum. Not everyone on the roads had lights, but Kaddour's adventurous driving and his large saloon car gave the clear message: out of the way! Winter wondered whether Kaddour simply liked driving or whether he wanted to ensure that nobody was following him.

They left the bustle of the city and half an hour later Kaddour turned right off the wide Malyk Faisal Road. The restaurant turned out to be a single-storey mud house on the edge of the desert, its red façade illuminated by blazing torches. In the sandy car park were a dozen fancy vehicles, in the company of which the Mercedes no longer stood out. The entrance was covered by a canopy and on the floor was a woven carpet.

Recognising Kaddour, an elderly waiter greeted the party and led them through the building into a spacious palm garden with a few tables covered in white cloths and lit by candles. The host showed them to a round table in a corner.

Muffled scraps of conversation mingled with soft background music. It was a mild evening. Sweet scents hung in the air.

The garden was surrounded by a knee-high wall, beyond which the desert began. In the moonlight Winter could see tracks in the sand. An emaciated cat, whose eyes reflected the candles, slunk past, keeping a respectable distance. On the horizon, the small triangles of the illuminated pyramids were visible. Son et lumière for the tourists.

The food was outstanding. Fatima explained to Winter what the individual dishes were and how each was prepared. Kaddour recounted Egyptian anecdotes which, if they weren't true, were at least well crafted.

Winter drifted with the flow, unaware if this was the result of the beer or his sated stomach.

Kaddour and Fatima were in perfect harmony. They were used to entertaining guests together and Winter wondered whether their relationship went beyond the purely professional.

When the dessert arrived Fatima explained that it was called Esh el Seraya: 'Palace Bread'. These flatbreads, soaked in honey, were substantial and sweet.

Kaddour put a tiny piece in his mouth. 'In the old days only the pharaohs could afford honey. Today everyone can buy it. The same is true of paper. Papyrus used to be reserved for rich people and priests, but now everyone can use paper. And we are on the verge of the same development with our communications network. Soon all Egyptians will be able to call everywhere with mobiles. Orafin is making this possible. To achieve it, the land by the Nile needs the right infrastructure: roads, concrete, antennae, fibre-optic cables and electricity.'

Winter's hosts kept gleaming with pride at the long and distinguished history of Egypt. It was only a small step from the pyramids to Orafin. And it was irrelevant whether Mubarak, the Muslim Brothers or Sisi were at the helm. It was all the same to Orafin whether Younes, Balbaa or El-Markabi was in charge at the energy ministry. Egypt needed electricity, and no government can afford blackouts.

Leaning back, all Winter said was, 'And that's why Orafin wanted to cooperate with Al-Bader?'

'Yes, we have to think beyond our national boundaries. America consists of the United States of America; the European Union has integrated the national states of the Continent. We want the same here in the Middle East. Sooner or later the

progressive countries will form an economic union. The Gulf
states have the oil money, while we have key contacts and,
more importantly, a large number of consumers. Compared to
Europe our growth is phenomenal. It's a huge opportunity for
our country. The next step is the nuclear power station north
of Cairo. It will provide electricity for everybody.'

'I can well understand that,' Winter nodded. 'We'd be happy to
help organize the necessary transactions. Switzerland is neutral
ground, it's discreet and very secure for such development.'

Now Kaddour leaned back too. 'So you don't believe it was
an accident? The latest statements from the Swiss police are
still saying that there could have been a number of reasons for
the crash.' Kaddour had been doing his homework.

'The investigation is being carried out by the public authorities and they work to a different rhythm. Even in Switzerland,
official minutes last a little bit longer. But I'm afraid I can't rule
out an attack. I'm sure it was an isolated incident. But I keep
asking myself: who might have something against Al-Bader?'

'I'm sorry I cannot be of assistance here, for there are a
lot of people who might benefit from a delay. Progress is not
embraced by everybody. Religious fanatics have no interest in
it. Second, the old generals are vying for power, which puts a
block on many decisions.'

Kaddour was sticking out a finger for each possibility.
'Third, the competition is fierce. Our rivals would like to get
involved with the nuclear power station too. Fourth, you have
the Americans, who are unhappy when countries like Egypt
expand their knowledge of nuclear technology. As far as the
CIA are concerned, it's only a small step from the peaceful,
environmentally friendly use of nuclear technology to the
bomb. Just look at Iran. And fifth, perhaps it was just a former
business partner Al-Bader ripped off. He is... he *was* a damn
fine businessman, and hard as nails.'

Now Kaddour stuck out the little finger of his other hand.

'And sixth, the Saudi royal family are not exactly famous for all getting on with each other.'

In truth they knew nothing. Fatima had kept quiet, but Winter was certain that she'd been listening very carefully. He wasn't surprised, therefore, when she said, 'Perhaps we're thinking along the wrong lines. If it was an attack, how do we know for sure that Al-Bader was the target? To my knowledge there was a second passenger on board, besides the pilot. Who was that?'

'A colleague of mine. Normally I would have accompanied Al-Bader, but I took last Friday off. I'm in the process of renovating my house.' Everybody's building in Egypt, Winter thought; they can understand that. Then he added, 'But I'd swear by Anne.'

'I see. So it was pure chance that you weren't in the helicopter yourself?'

'Yes. This time I was lucky.' And Anne unlucky. His feelings of guilt roiled again.

'How do you know that you weren't the intended victim?' Kaddour said.

Gazing out into the night, Winter saw the pyramids in the distance and, close-by, a Bedouin walk past with a camel in the pallid light from the restaurant. He had to admit that this was not a completely absurd possibility. He'd made the odd enemy in the past. Occupational hazard. 'Maybe I was. Not many people knew that we'd swapped places. But there are simpler ways to get rid of me.'

There was a pause in their conversation. After a while, Winter said, 'I still think Al-Bader was the more likely target. He's rich, usually well protected and not loved by all. But we know far too little. For example, why now? Was it just opportunity, or did something trigger it? Are your dealings at a critical point?'

'Permanently.' Kaddour laughed out loud and added, seriously, 'No, we have to be fairly flexible with the timeline.

Because of the protests following the blackouts, the government is reforming energy legislation. We don't know how quickly that will go. But we were just *one* of Al-Bader's business partners. He told me he was at a conference in Norway on issues of infrastructure and that "we" should meet in the middle. I estimate that Al-Bader's family is worth six to seven billion – US dollars, of course. And I'm assuming that his investments are spread around the world. It might be worth taking a closer look at his business contacts. As a banker you must be perfectly placed for that.'

Kaddour raised his eyebrows.

'I'm just in charge of security. At any rate, Swiss banking confidentiality would prevent me from talking about other clients.'

'Oh, come on. Don't give me that old line. Your boss is much more talkative. He once told me about a well-known German who got rich with yoghurts and moved from Deutsche Bank to your outfit because of your boss's charm. Out of gratitude he now has free yoghurt till the end of his life. Next time he's going to seek out a brewing baron.' Kaddour laughed.

Winter thought this was a good opportunity to throw in an awkward question. 'Why did you send Husseini the day before yesterday? Wouldn't it have been more appropriate for *you* to come to Switzerland?'

Kaddour stopped laughing. He hesitated a moment too long to sound convincing and shot Fatima a sideways glance.

'Originally I was intending to come to Switzerland myself. I love your country. But I had to go to the ministry at short notice. The energy minister wanted my advice and that's why I sent Husseini.' Pause. 'Have you come across anything in Switzerland to suggest that I'm in danger too?' Either Kaddour hadn't taken Winter's direct question personally or he was good at diversionary tactics.

'Here we need to keep an eye on the fundamentalists, you see,' Fatima interjected. 'We keep receiving threats, but we're convinced that progress cannot be halted.' Winter wondered who Fatima meant by 'we'.

'No, no. You can rest assured that I've heard nothing of the sort back at home. But there are rumours that Al-Bader has financed Islamic terrorists.'

'That's absolute nonsense! Al-Bader is much closer to the Americans than to Al-Qaeda or ISIS. In the West, anyone with an Arabic background and money automatically ends up on a list of terrorists.'

'I thought the same,' Winter said. 'But in my business you can't take any chances.'

The discussion went back and forth, becoming ever more speculative. After midnight Kaddour excused himself and went inside the restaurant. The bill? Toilet? Phone call?

Winter was alone with Fatima. She was stunning and Winter was slightly unsettled. For a while they were silent, then she bent forwards and looked imploringly at Winter with her large eyes. 'I'm frightened. Kaddour was a bigwig in the military and now he has lots of enemies. If you know of anything that could be of a threat to him, you must tell me! Please. He is a good man. I've been working for him for three years and he only wants the best for Egypt.' Winter was taken aback by the intensity of her pleas and spontaneously he placed a hand on Fatima's for comfort.

'I really haven't seen any evidence, and nor has my boss said anything.'

'Thank you.' Although she didn't pull her hand away, she was clearly a touch embarrassed by the situation. Winter opened his mouth. For a moment they looked at each other and Winter felt an invisible connection. The pyramids were the only, silent witnesses.

Fatima broke the spell and said, rather formally, 'You ought to know that the president of Orafin doesn't dare step out of his house any more for fear of being the target of an attack.

He only leaves his house when it is unavoidable, and he has arranged round-the-clock protection for himself from armed guards.'

Kaddour came back out onto the terrace, with a mobile phone in his hand and a slightly fixed smile on his face. 'Right, my turtle doves. Shall we go?' Winter let go of Fatima's hand and they got up.

As they were saying goodbye to the owner beneath the canopy, Kaddour's telephone rang. He checked the display and excused himself.

A confidential conversation.

Meanwhile, Fatima was chatting to the owner.

Winter took advantage of the opportunity to relieve himself before the drive home. He went back into the restaurant and found the door to the toilet hidden behind a curtain. He stepped into the dimly lit room and held his breath. Winter relaxed and emptied his bladder. Bye-bye beer. He was peering through the filthy window into the night when a deafening explosion shook the building. For a split-second Winter saw the yellow fiery glow, then the glass shattered and a piece of metal from Kaddour's Mercedes hit his skull.

# JULY 27 – 17:03

When Winter woke up, he was lying in a bed on his back. Naked. Covered with a coarse sheet. There was a hellish pain in his head. The blood was throbbing against the inside of his skull.

Where was he?

Then his memory returned: *Cairo!* Kaddour and Fatima. The restaurant with the filthy bathroom window. The dazzling explosion.

Somewhere outside, a muezzin was calling to prayer; the incomprehensible monologue penetrated his aching skull. Street noise. Winter tentatively opened his eyes. A simple lamp hung from the brownish ceiling.

He carefully turned his head.

Light slanted in through closed shutters.

Winter cautiously checked his temple and found a large dressing, padded with cotton wool. There were smaller dressings on his nose, cheeks and chin.

The slivers of glass from the window.

Beside the bed was a chair with his things placed carefully on top: watch, wallet, keys, phone and a neatly folded handkerchief.

And a glass of water too! His throat was as dry as a bone. Winter was grateful for the drink. And for the fact that he was alive. He sat up. The glass was covered with a saucer. He sipped the lukewarm water hesitantly at first, then gulped the rest.

The clock showed six minutes past five. Morning or afternoon? Impossible to tell from the way the light was coming in. Beside the bed and between the two narrow

windows stood an antique chest of drawers with a marble top.
On it were some clothes. In the backlight Winter could make
out his trousers. At the foot of the bed was a door with a key
in the lock. Not prison, then.

Good.

From the way the room was furnished, it didn't look like
a hospital either. To the left, above the bed, hung a yellowed
photograph – at least a hundred years old – that showed
a half-finished Eiffel Tower. If I'd paid better attention in
history lessons, Winter thought, I'd be able to date this photo
accurately. Wasn't it a world exposition?

Winter was too exhausted to think. His head hurt. The best
thing would probably be to get more sleep. He closed his eyes.
After a while he heard someone carefully opening the door. He
didn't move and pretended he was asleep. Someone entered the
room, moving softly and circumspectly. Shuffling on the balls
of their feet.

He smelled Fatima's perfume and opened his eyes.

She gave a contented smile and said, 'Nice to have you back.
How do you feel?'

'Better.' Discovering how difficult it was to speak, Winter said
no more, opting instead to feel the plaster on his temple again.

'That's good. You slept the whole day.' It was evening, then.

'What happened? Where am I?'

'Kaddour is dead. Those bastards blew up the Mercedes.
They found you unconscious in the toilets. You were struck by
a piece of metal and probably have concussion.'

She was wearing a loose, beige, cotton blouse; ankle-length,
brown and very wide trousers, and her long hair was held up
with a comb slide. No jewellery.

When Fatima sat on the edge of the bed Winter could feel
her weight on the mattress and, through the sheet, that she was
close to him.

'The owner of the restaurant drove us back to Cairo in his

car and I put you up here. I told the police you were a friend
of the family. They were pleased that they didn't have to worry
about a foreigner too. But in cases of concussion the patient
has to be monitored.'

For a moment Winter wondered what 'family' she was
talking about, and said, 'Thanks. Thanks very much. I think
I'm much better already.'

He was happy not to have ended up in hospital. He gave
those places a wide berth wherever possible. After all many
people didn't actually become sick until they got to hospital,
even in the so-called First World.

'Bastards!' All of a sudden Fatima was seething with rage. Her
composure was gone and she was clenching her delicate hands.
'Those fucking extremists. I always thought Kaddour was pretty
safe, but clearly they will resort to anything. He was only the
operational head.' She paused, then added sadly, 'For me he was
more than a boss. He was my mentor, almost like a father to me.'

'I'm really very sorry.'

Fatima sighed, her anger subsided, and then she smiled
ruefully.

'Are you sure it was extremists?' Winter asked.

'Yes. Well, I can't be certain, but they must have followed us.
The police found a detonator. When Kaddour went to his car
the bomb exploded. It was a primitive device. Typical of fundamentalists.' She shook her head.

'What about you? Did nothing happen to you? You were
under the canopy at the entrance.'

'I was lucky. I was talking to Ali, the owner. We were
standing, thank goodness, behind his delivery van, which
protected us from the explosion.' She cocked her head and
added, thoughtfully, 'We were extremely lucky. Kaddour had
gone to fetch the car. If he weren't such a gentleman we'd have
probably been in the car too. If, if, if... It's simply fate. Allah is
great.' She stood up.

'If you feel up to it, we could have dinner together this evening. Just something simple.' Winter smiled and gave a weak nod. 'The bathroom is next door and I've put out my father's shirt for you.' She pointed to the door, then the chest of drawers.

'Thanks.'

Stroking the marble ledge with her hand, Fatima peered out of the window and then turned back to Winter. Once again he said, 'Thanks.'

'You're welcome.' She left the room, closing the door behind her.

Lying in bed Winter thought a bit. Then he got up, carefully. His brain was still a little sluggish, and with each movement it felt as if it knocked against his skull. Wrapped in the sheet, he spent a few minutes looking through the gaps in the shutters at the pulsating activity in the street. But in truth all he saw were colours. He'd lost all sense of time and felt as if he'd been in Cairo for months, even though he couldn't remember a thing.

After a while he padded his way into the bathroom, which was astonishingly large and cooler than the bedroom. The walls were decorated with oriental tiles. The basin was yellowed and supported on either side by a metal rod. The fittings were too short and impractical. The mirror had a wealth of grey spots at the edges.

Winter examined his head covered in dressings. People would think he'd been shaved by a blind barber. Gently lifting the large, padded dressing from his temple, he saw that the wound wasn't completely dry. The dressing would stay.

The bathtub was old and with feet in the form of a predator's paws. The shower had been built subsequently in a corner. Winter turned on the squeaky tap. The water spluttered along the pipes. He found a large bar of soap and carefully washed around his head wound. The cold water revived his spirits.

Back in the bedroom he listened to his voicemail messages.
Dirk, the head of IT, confirming that he'd checked the firewall
but not found anything. A friend wanting to go out for dinner.
Känzig demanding a 'progress report – immediately!' Nothing
from Ben. And Schütz this afternoon from Riyadh, asking him
to call back because he'd heard 'interesting' information at
Al-Bader's funeral. Winter phoned Schütz. As the connection
was made Winter wondered where Schütz was at this moment.
Egypt must be an hour or two behind Riyadh.

'Hello, Winter,' Schütz said. 'Thanks for calling back. Are
you still in Cairo?'

'Schütz. Yes, I'm still in Cairo.' Feeling his plaster, he decided
against mentioning the attack. 'How are things in Riyadh?'

'Hot. I'm in one of these luxury hotels. Everything made of
gold. A sheer waste. We really have to open a branch out here.'

'So you've got some interesting news?'

'Yes, we had a buffet reception in the family's villa. The
brother invited all the guests. An astonishing number of
Americans and Europeans were there, especially from the
Nordic countries. I spoke to a Norwegian from Bergen who
manages a fund specialising in infrastructure investments.
Starting sums of ten million. And after the fourth vodka the
Viking told me that Al-Bader was in the process of making
massive investments into global infrastructure projects. Hence
the conference in Norway.'

'And?'

'Well, when I got my sixty-second audience with the brother,
he told me that the investment process was in the interests of
the entire consortium and that it had to continue at the same
speed, in spite of Al-Bader's death.'

'Yes, and?'

'The most interesting thing was that the brother mistook
me for a Norwegian to begin with. Must have been my blond
hair and blue eyes. When I told him I was from Switzerland he

immediately dismissed me with a wave of the hand as if I were no more than a nuisance.'

Schütz laughed scornfully. 'And, being the idiot I am, I always thought we were Al-Bader's main bank. He probably just kept his petty cash with us. Imagine that! It seems that oil sticks to oil. If that thing about the consortium is true then the investment sums are enormous. You could put a murder on expenses. You can't make an omelette without breaking eggs.'

'Are you saying that Al-Bader used a Norwegian fund to invest in infrastructure like Egyptian nuclear power stations and that he was killed for these investment programmes?'

'No, I wouldn't put it as bluntly as that. All I'm saying is that Norway wasn't just about Al-Bader, but a whole group of investors from the Middle East. A consortium. And Al-Bader was merely one of them. If you make a rough estimate you easily arrive at several billion dollars. An amount that can move markets.'

'Do you know if the conference in Bergen is still running? If so we'd have all of them in the same place.'

'Yes, the conference goes on to the end of the week. I'll email you the Viking's business card. That should serve as an entry ticket.'

'Thanks.' Winter ended the call and thought: Norway's cooler than Egypt.

With much on his mind, Winter left the room, walked down the stone steps and through an open wooden door entered an inner courtyard. Shielded from the noise of the street by the house, the courtyard was a cool oasis full of flowering plants. In the middle was a rectangular, tiled pond with a water fountain. A covered arcade led around the courtyard. It was already quite dark but the last rays of the sun lit up the roof.

Fatima was sitting with a laptop at a round, cast-iron table in a corner.

'What a wonderful courtyard!' Winter said.

'Yes, I love it here. I can concentrate on work much better than in the office.' She bashfully made a sweeping gesture. 'This is my mother's family's house. But at the moment my parents spend most of their time in London. I live here with my grandmother. She looks after all the plants.' She closed her laptop. 'Are you hungry? Yes, you must be starving after such a deep sleep.'

Winter nodded gratefully.

Fatima got up, went inside, and within a few minutes came back out with a tray full of Egyptian snacks from the kitchen. They ate straight out of the richly decorated dishes. After a while they started talking about the parallels between the helicopter crash in the Höllentobel and the explosion of Kaddour's Mercedes. Was it coincidence? Was there a connection? Fatima was desperate to know who was behind Kaddour's death. 'Al-Bader is the only obvious connection.'

'I'm not sure. Maybe it doesn't have anything to do with Al-Bader or Kaddour as individuals, but with the planned nuclear power station.'

'Nobody was aware that Al-Bader was going to invest.'

'Nobody?'

'You never know. But there are several other interested investors besides Al-Bader. The fundamentalists can't murder every single one of them.'

'No, but they can send a clear message to other potential investors and poison the atmosphere.'

'In the worst-case scenario the Orafin project will be slightly delayed. At any rate we are going to continue our conversation with Al-Bader's family.'

Winter rubbed his throbbing temple. 'The money trail isn't easy to follow. But if we knew who might profit from the murders then at least we'd have a concrete motive. The difficulty is that in such cases those issuing the orders rarely get their hands dirty themselves.'

'I'll ask around at Orafin. Money leaves a trace too.'

Winter nodded and contemplated his next steps. He didn't speak any Arabic and had only superficial contacts in the Middle East. Fatima could be useful. There might be another parallel besides the victims and the money. 'I'd like to compare the explosives. If they're the same, that's a clue we're dealing with the same attackers. Where is the metal splinter from my head?'

'Are you saying it will have traces of explosive on it?'

'I think so. I can get it analysed in the laboratory back in Switzerland.'

Fatima got up and and fished the walnut-sized piece of metal from the bin. It was painted black, smeared with blood and had a sharp, jagged edge along the line where it had broken.

They sat there, well into the early hours, drinking strong Egyptian coffee, talking and then not talking. It was a comfort and time stood still.

They spent the following day apart. Fatima went to Port Said and sorted out Kaddour's affairs. Winter slept in to alleviate his concussion. A police inspector came by and Winter politely answered his questions. They still had no clue as to who had carried out the attack. Then Winter went to fetch his things from the Shepheard, sent a few emails, checked out, spoke to Känzig and tried to do some research into the Bergen conference, but was unable to find anything about it on the internet.

Winter called a colleague at Nordea Bank, one of the largest Scandinavian banks, and asked him about the conference. He didn't know anything about it either, but he called back an hour later. 'Hello, Winter? It's not a conference, but a forum. A former colleague of ours works for Galaxy and says that the discussions are all completely under the radar. Lots of sheikhs have brought their families and are on holiday at the

Hardangerfjord. They're staying in the "Sole Bad", at least seven stars with a private yacht marina. Not for people like us.'

'Thanks. Who or what is Galaxy?'

'Galaxy is the private equity fund that has organized this meeting. Not much is known about them. They operate practically outside any scrutiny and are not keen to become known by the wider public. They're not in the retail market. They specialize in quantitative, mathematic models. Galaxy makes a lot of money investing billionaires' money.'

*When Aleksi drove carefully into the dark tunnel late in the evening, the first thing he did was to turn on the windscreen wipers. The dried-up plastic wipers creaked across the filthy windscreen of his heavily-laden Russian tanker, only partially wiping away the water that dripped from the tunnel ceiling. His weak headlights groped along the rough walls.*

*He bent over his large steering wheel to give him a better chance of avoiding the potholes. The headlights of a Mercedes came towards him. A new SLK-Class on its way to Moscow sped past.*

*After five minutes, the road inside the almost four-kilometre-long Roki Tunnel became a gentle downward slope. Aleksi shifted up a gear and left the Russian Federation. The Roki Tunnel pierced the main ridge of the Caucasus Mountains, connecting the north to the south, North Ossetia to South Ossetia, Russia to Georgia. Theoretically. Because of the armed struggles for independence that kept flaring up there was no official border up here. In the worst-case scenario there might be checkpoints guarded by paramilitaries. His cousin Vladimir kept him updated. Tonight the coast was clear.*

*Aleksi looked in the rear-view mirror. At the market in Ergneti his client, the Russian-speaking boxer with the black leather jacket, had said little but paid well. With these euros Aleksi could finally afford a new incisor. Out of gold. He grinned at himself in the mirror with his exposed gums.*

*All there was left to do was to have breakfast in Gori and leave his*
*tanker full of petrol in the roadside car park for half an hour. It was*
*none of his business who would be transporting the heavy wooden*
*crates in the chassis cavity from there. The military crates would*
*probably keep heading towards the Black Sea along the highway*
*beside the Gazprom pipeline. Thinking about it, would he be better*
*off investing his euros in the buxom Lucie?*

That same evening Fatima and Winter ate in the courtyard
again. She'd heard many rumours on Port Said. Ali Husseini,
for example, had said that Al-Bader's younger brother was
likely to take over. Apparently the family wanted to spread
their risks more widely and were in conversation with other
wealthy families. At the conference in Norway the sheiks were
discussing how they could put their money into one large pot.
Following the example of the billion-dollar state funds they
were intent on making diversified investments.

'Galaxy.'

'Galaxy?' Fatima frowned at Winter and he told his hostess
what he had found out earlier. Independently of each other
they had heard about the Norwegian conference. It was no
coincidence.

The two of them agreed that the money trail was hot.

For that reason they went to the airport together the
following morning. They checked in for Bergen with transfers
in Zürich and Oslo. Fatima showed her burgundy British
passport, Winter his red Swiss one.

At Zürich airport, Winter asked for Ben, but he was indis-
posed. He slipped the walnut-sized piece of metal from the
mudguard of Kaddour's Mercedes into an envelope and sealed
it. The woman promised to pass it on to Ben Halter as soon as
possible. Winter left a message on Ben's voicemail, requesting
him to send the splinter to the laboratory in Spiez for analysis.
Then he bought two new shirts.

During the transfer he got some Norwegian kroner and bought a travel guide: *111 Places You Must See in Norway*.

On the flight to Bergen Winter wondered what exactly the arrival time on flight schedules referred to. Landing? Docking? Or leaving the aeroplane? At any rate the schedule of this flight gave SAS – Scandinavian Airlines – plenty of leeway to be punctual.

Bergen airport was small and functional. Within a few minutes they were at the car-hire desks. 'Unfortunately' – because it was holiday time – the Hertz representative didn't have anything left apart from a Jaguar Convertible XKR. A special promotion for newlyweds. Perfect for driving up, with a beautiful woman, to a luxury hotel full of rich sheiks. As they made themselves comfortable in the new Jaguar, Winter soaked up the tasteful privacy of this high-end vehicle. It smelled of precious wood and fine leather. He put on his sunglasses and they set off.

He had planned the route during the flight. They began by taking the motorway northwards through a few tunnels in the greater Bergen area. Then the traffic decreased, Winter opened the roof and they cruised eastwards on the country highway, the engine purring. On one side the Hardangerfjord, on the other steep mountain faces.

The coast of Norway was frayed. The fjords ate deeply into the land and the mountains rose into the Atlantic like gigantic fingers. On the map the coast looked much shorter than when you navigated it by car.

Unlike Cairo, where the sun dropped below the horizon within a few minutes, the Norwegian summer evenings were extremely long. As they were only a few hundred kilometres south of the Arctic Circle the evening sun set gently at their backs. The shadows gradually grew longer, the light warmer. After a day of physical inactivity they were full of vim and raring to go.

Fatima laughed. 'It's like being on holiday. Almost.'

Winter stared at her for a moment. He nodded and had to admit that he was enjoying the drive too.

'Do you think there could be a connection between the religious fundamentalists and the rich investors?' Fatima asked later. 'Somehow it doesn't seem right. Surely investors need stability?'

'I'm not sure. As far as I know Osama bin Laden was the son of a wealthy family. And investments in nuclear power stations are always controversial. The Egyptian state is behind the Orafin project isn't it?'

'Yes, the government is substantially involved.'

'Good. Now I'm excited to find out where the money trail is going to lead us here.'

'Me too. I want Kaddour's killer.'

After a pause, Winter could sense Fatima scrutinising him. 'How's your Arabic?' she asked.

Flattered that she imagined he might have any knowledge of the language at all, Winter said apologetically, 'Non-existent, I'm afraid.'

'I'll look after that side then.'

'That's what I'm counting on.'

Fatima was one step ahead of him. 'And we need a story to explain why we're here. We've got the Jaguar for newlyweds. Our best bet would be to keep on spinning this line. What do you think?'

Winter felt caught off guard. It seemed oddly forward, or was that wishful thinking on his part? He thought on it further. Fatima had been to university and she was a successful businesswoman, with London as her second home; she was hard to read.

A succession of tight bends with traffic coming the other way forced Winter to shift down a gear. 'Good idea. But because of our different passports it would probably be better to say we're only engaged.'

Fatima leaned her bare arm out the window, her fingers splayed against the wind, and nodded seriously.

There was a silence.

Eventually Winter said, 'I'm going to seek out the Viking from the private equity firm who Schütz met in Riyadh. Hopefully he can tell me what Al-Bader was planning.'

Fatima blinked slowly, and then she licked her lips.

As the sun was setting they got to the hotel. It stood on a spit of land by the Hardangerfjord. The hotel consisted of a main wooden house from the early twentieth century, painted yellow and white, a more modern annexe and an array of outbuildings scattered around a generous-sized park. In the broad lobby an open fire was roaring. Fatima opted for a bungalow right beside the sea.

A powerful Norwegian woman in her fifties carried Fatima's suitcase through the park with all its roses and sun loungers. They passed a modern conference building, partially set into the rocks. Its glass frontage that gave onto the Hardangerfjord was covered with dark curtains.

'Nice spot for a conference,' Winter said.

'Yes,' the sturdy Norwegian woman replied, 'but our guests aren't interested in the view.'

Winter gave a quizzical look

'Yes. We often have conferences. Last week and this week it's bankers. Next week it's plastic surgeons.' The Norwegian woman's tone did not disguise what she thought of these professions; she didn't seem to be interested in money or external beauty. They passed children's toys lying on the ground, and with a sneer she added, 'Some of our guests are here with their families. The children are treated like little princes and princesses.'

The bungalows were slightly isolated from the other buildings. Each house had a wooden terrace that projected out into the water and served both as sundeck and mooring. The Norwegian woman unlocked the door, slapped the suitcase down and disappeared before Winter could give her a tip. The large room was divided into a sleeping area with an extra-wide, double bed and a living area with a sofa. He'd probably take the sofa.

Fatima opened the curtains. The floor-to-ceiling windows gave them an evening view of the *Hardangerfjord*. In the distance a number of dark islands loomed out of the water. They saw the lights of passing ships. 'What a wonderful view!' she exclaimed.

Winter nodded and stepped outside the bungalow.

Fatima moved out onto the large deck over the water, connected to the bungalow by a small jetty. She took off her flat shoes and tested the water temperature. 'We're so far north and yet the water's really warm.'

'That's the Gulf Stream. It brings warm water from the Caribbean.' Breathing in the sea air, Winter noticed Fatima's slim silhouette against the dark-blue sky. He was overcome by a mixture of sadness and guilt. He felt disloyal. His heart jolted, and he took another deep breath.

'Winter, let's go for a swim,' Fatima interrupted.

'I don't know. It's already pretty dark.'

But then he looked at Fatima again, and suddenly he wanted to feel life, to feel alive. It was an overwhelmingly powerful sensation.

Minutes later they were swimming side by side out into the deep Hardangerfjord, their bodies slipping through the dark water with ease.

Winter was wet and standing naked outside their bungalow when it exploded and went up in flames. He ran to the car park, his wet feet slapping on the flagstones in the park. He stood by the Jaguar and wondered why it was suddenly black and had no mudguard. When he unlocked it with the remote control the car exploded too.

He spun around and was about to enter the bank in Bern when it was shaken by an earthquake and collapsed like a tower of wooden blocks. To save himself, Winter ran barefoot, panting and sweating across scree, to the helicopter pad, which was on the top of a mountain. As he opened the cockpit door the helicopter broke in two and exploded on either side of him. Anne plummeted to her death before him. He tried to grab onto her, but his dripping hands couldn't find purchase and she slipped inexorably into the Höllentobel.

Bathed in sweat and his eyes like saucers, Winter woke up. Half sitting up, he took a deep breath and tried to orient himself. Daybreak was shimmering through the cracks between the heavy curtains.

Once his heartbeat had calmed, Winter thought about the previous evening. Fatima and he had returned to the bungalow to find that while they were out swimming someone had placed in their room a bunch of roses, a bottle of champagne and a fancy card that said 'With the compliments of the management'.

After they had drunk the champagne, Fatima had said simply, 'Winter, I just want you to hold me in your arms tonight.'

He'd nodded; he thought Anne would understand. And so Fatima had fallen asleep in his arms.

It had felt good. Very good indeed. Anne had understood, Winter was sure, despite the dream.

After a while he carefully got out from under the covers, dressed quietly, took an apple from the fruit basket and went into the park. He wanted to enjoy the early-morning peace and quiet, and to explore.

The air was clean and fresh, the sky light blue. A few high, passing clouds were already being lit up by the sun that was still below the horizon. The *Hardangerfjord* was perfectly still. In the distance an illuminated cruise ship drifted past.

As Winter made his way up to the main building, he was invigorated by the fresh air. He passed the conference centre, where the curtains and the windows were now open. On one of the garden chairs in front of the building sat a man in black. Black jeans, black T-shirt and black baseball cap with a stylized lion and a large 'S' for security. Bored, the man was rocking on the back legs of the chair, staring into space. Winter knew this well: waiting, waiting and more waiting. The early hours of the morning were the most difficult on the human body.

'Morning.'

'Morning.'

'Fabulous day, isn't it? Do you think the weather's going to be good enough to go out in a canoe?' Winter swept his arm out in the direction of the fjord. The man in black stopped rocking, slowly stood up, stretched his shoulder blades, gazed up at the high clouds, swung his head from side to side. An I-don't-know-I'm-not-really-sure gesture.

'Maybe.'

The security guard fished a crumpled pack of cigarettes from his jeans, knocked it against the back of his left hand and offered one to Winter, who shook his head.

'No, thanks. My father died of lung cancer when I was a kid.'

The security guard shrugged and lit himself a cigarette, took a big drag. He had plenty of time. Winter began to eat his apple.

'At least you knew your father.' Good English. 'Mine buggered off to an oil rig before I was born. Never to be seen again. That arsehole wasn't even a bad role model.' Melancholy. Pause. Change of subject. 'What's it like to be just married?'

Winter wondered that too. He gave a nod of acknowledgement. 'How did you find that out, detective?' He looked down at himself and, as if to refute it, held his left hand up to his chest. No ring.

'Nothing to worry about – it was easy. Yesterday evening I saw the chambermaid – the one who looks like a bodybuilder – bring roses and champagne to bungalow number two.'

'That's observant. If I'm being perfectly honest it feels a little strange.' After the night just gone that was no lie. He tried not to think of Fatima falling asleep in his arms. He reminded himself that he was here to find out who had the deaths of Al-Bader and Kaddour on their conscience. He gave a friendly grin and asked, 'So what are you guarding? I always thought Norway was one of the safest countries on earth.'

'Yes, you're right. Normally it's not necessary. But they've got a conference here with filthy-rich businessmen. And one of them is no more. So they called us and I've been here ever since. Twelve-hour shifts. But that's better than the drunks on the ferries.'

'You mean someone was killed?'

'Yes, my boss said he was blown up.'

'Does anyone know who did it and why?'

'No, no idea. My boss says it's all about world domination again, which means you've got to expect deaths. But if those moneybags don't feel safe anymore, it's not good for business.' The security guard flicked his cigarette away and asked, 'Where are you from? Germany?'

'No, I come from Switzerland.'

'Nice. I went skiing in Laax once. They've got the biggest ice bar in the world with the sexiest snow bunnies.'

'Talking of bars, do you know where I could get a coffee at this time of the morning?'

The guard put a hand on Winter's shoulder. 'Come with me. They've got a decent coffee machine in here and there's not a soul about at this time of day.' He took Winter through one of the glass doors into a seminar room.

The tables were arranged in a horseshoe, with black swivel chairs. A projector was attached to the ceiling and a screen stood at the front. In one corner were two flip charts, in the other one a small table with a coffee machine and a fruit bowl. The guard walked across the room and asked, 'Coffee, espresso, double espresso, latte, macchiato? We've got almost everything here.'

'Regular coffee would be fine.' With Swiss pride, Winter noted that the machine was manufactured by Jura.

While the security guard was busy getting the coffee, Winter took a closer look around the conference room. On the tables were loose photocopied sheets, bound presentations, plastic sleeves and glossy brochures. Figures and graphs.

There was a sort of matrix on one of the flip charts. Probably the result of a brainstorming session with an evaluation using different parameters. Cost–benefit analysis. Down the vertical axis was a long list: Telcos, Ports and Shipping, Roads and Rail, Airports, Energy (Gas, Coal, $H_2O$, Nuc), Drinking water, Pipelines. Along the horizontal one it read: 'Return, Necessary investment, Risks.' Everything in billions of US dollars. Most were three-digit figures.

'Sugar? Milk?' the security guard asked.

In the realm of milk and honey, all the same. 'No, thanks.'

Winter took the coffee he was offered. 'Thanks. This will wake me up.'

He turned around and made for the glass door. But when his foot got caught in a cable he had to hold onto the nearest table to steady himself, and some coffee spilled on the table.

Winter looked around for a cloth, at the same time searching his trouser pockets in vain for a tissue. 'I'm so sorry.'

'Don't worry. We'll have that cleared up in no time.' The guard left the room. Winter grabbed a pile of loose documents that looked like summaries, an agenda and a list of participants, folded the pieces of paper and stuffed them in his trousers behind his back. His jumper hid the documents that in a few hours one of the people at the meeting would miss.

The security guard came back with a bundle of paper towels, wiped away the coffee stains and said, 'Let's go.' They left the conference room. Winter waited till his coffee was the right temperature, smiled as the guard wished him fun with the canoe, drank up his brew and left for the main building. The sun had risen.

Winter sat in the lobby and read his emails. He didn't open Känzig's message entitled 'Status report ASAP'. Schütz had sent the contact details of the Viking he'd met in Riyadh: Dr H. Hansen, President, Galaxy – IIS Individual Investment Solutions. An address in Bergen with telephone numbers and a personal email address. 'Best of luck, Schütz', followed by a PS: 'He looks like a Viking who's fought more than one battle...'

At that very moment a colossus of a man entered the lobby. He was followed by a tiny suitcase on wheels, like a dog. His black, tailor-made suit was crumpled and the man was clearly in a bad mood, because he just grunted when the woman at reception cheerfully greeted him by the name of Hansen. Winter got up, strolled to the lift and stood beside him, noticing he had big rings below his eyes and was unshaven. Where his unfastened collar had been rubbing against his fleshy neck it looked greasy. He smelled bad – of sweat, cigarette smoke and a long journey.

'Good morning, Dr Hansen. My name is Winter and we have a mutual friend who's now dead.'

They arranged to meet at breakfast. Winter went straight into the large, almost empty dining hall and sat at a table in the corner. He had a good view of the unoccupied tables, the growing breakfast buffet and the Hardangerfjord. The world was a peaceful place in the morning. A silent waiter poured him a cup of coffee. Winter nodded his gratitude and waited for Hansen: viking and money manager.

Hansen arrived twenty minutes later. His gait and stature suggested that he had once been a strong, powerful man. He was between thirty and forty. The rings under his eyes were not merely those of someone who'd hadn't had enough sleep; they were also indicative of too much food and too little exercise. The fat on his cheeks made the rings appear deeper. His blue eyes wandered calmly across the room and inspected Winter's face.

Hansen was not a man easily ruffled though, neither physically nor psychologically. Good nerves were necessary when you bet on the stock market with large sums of foreign money and high leverage.

A violet-coloured, silk handkerchief was perched in the breast pocket of his pinstripe jacket, beneath which he wore a fresh, light-pink shirt with broad, violet stripes and a fat, matching tie. Hansen smelled of his morning shower. Golden cufflinks flashed on his wrists. Winter couldn't help smiling. The Viking was terribly British. He'd probably worked in the City of London.

After their wordless greeting Hansen ordered coffee and a Full English breakfast. A waitress swiftly brought a large, silver pot of hot coffee. Winter helped himself modestly at the buffet, taking some fruit muesli, toast and orange juice. He ignored the lavish towers of salmon. Fish for breakfast wasn't his thing.

It was early in the morning and neither man had any desire to waste energy on exchanging pleasantries. After the coffee started to take effect Hansen said, 'We both have an interest in finding out who killed Al-Bader. He was your client, and mine too. What do you have so far?'

'Not a lot. The official investigation is still in progress. I'm working with the assumption that the helicopter crashed as the result of an explosion. The list of possible motives is long. Obviously I'm wondering what sort of business Al-Bader was pursuing here.'

Hansen stirred two cubes of sugar into his black coffee.

'Galaxy's vision is to become the world's largest and most profitable private equity fund for investment into essential infrastructure. I can also say that we'll soon need a more ambitious vision.' Winter nodded and thought of the security guard who had quoted his boss. 'World domination' took on quite a new meaning. Whoever controls water, energy and transport is in command; something the rulers of the Roman Empire realized a couple of millennia ago. Hansen was a well-paid mercenary. 'Galaxy offers its clients a unique service. We act as brokers between investors and promising infrastructure projects.'

'Uh-huh.' Let him talk.

'Western governments need to save and sell the family silver to private buyers. And the projects in the Third World and emerging nations really need investors with deep pockets and stamina.'

'Are you saying that Galaxy has both?'

'Galaxy is only open to clients who are prepared to invest an adequate sum over several years. For private investors, such as Al-Bader's family, we're opening doors that would never be opened otherwise.'

'As a head of security I'm only an educated amateur in such banking affairs. Can you explain what that means?'

'It's easiest if I give you an example. International trade is going to grow in the future too. Which means more ships. Which means more ports. These are mostly owned by regional or national governments who want to invest, for which they need capital. We provide that for them on favourable terms. The point is that the oil sheikhs have difficulty in getting close to these investments. Ports are strategic, geopolitically important infrastructures. Which Western nation is going to sell them to a Muslim?'

'And that's where Galaxy comes in?'

'Yes. I don't need to tell you, a Swiss citizen, about the value of neutrality. As a Norwegian private equity fund we are completely neutral politically. The only thing that counts is business. Norway isn't in the EU and because we're a Norwegian fund we aren't subject to the pressures of a particular financial centre either. It's one of our unique features that our fund is located here on Norway's beautiful western coast, far removed from the everyday frenzy of the stock markets. Here we can focus squarely on the long-term trends.'

'What about your clients? I'm assuming they're big players from the east?'

'Correct. Quality above quantity. I'd rather have a hundred professionals than ten thousand grannies wanting to invest their cash under the pillow in the railways. A few Russians, more and more Asians, but mainly Arabs value our services. Oil to oil.' It sounded like ashes to ashes. Winter wasn't the only one who thought so, as Hansen grinned and crossed himself. 'We have specific skills in this area. And they love Norway: cool and secure. In fact, I'm amazed that you Swiss didn't invent this business model.'

'In Switzerland private equity funds are strictly regulated, which scares off lots of investors. One man's joy is another man's sorrow.'

When Hansen's breakfast arrived his face visibly lit up at the sight of fried eggs, sausages and bacon. Winter spread some cloudberry jam on his toast. To prevent Hansen's flow from drying up, he said, 'I envy you this idea. First you take the money, then you fleece the sheiks with all manner of fees. Congratulations.'

'Don't underestimate them. Alright, I admit that some have more money than sense. Not all of them are Einsteins. But most are sharp, professional investors seeking to diversify their portfolios. There's little correlation between our performance and the stock markets. Some are semi-state investors who want to get the best global yield on their citizens' money based on their risk.' One sausage per bite. Winter made a bet with himself that Hansen would soon order seconds.

'So what are you doing here in the "Sole Bad"?'

'We work very closely with our clients. Twice a year we invite them to a presentation of our projects and vehicles. As we have a seventy per cent stake in this hotel we can kill two birds with one stone.' Hansen grinned once more. 'The discussions here give us the opportunity to listen to the clients' needs. Often they'll come with other interested investors who are eager to meet us in an informal setting.'

'How well do you really know your clients? Were there any signs that things between Al-Bader and other investors weren't totally smooth?'

'I didn't see or hear anything. We've been involved in the Middle East for years. The winner is the person who's always a few steps ahead of the competition. Your Schütz was impressed at any rate. Have you ever been there?' Hansen pointed his fork, grinning. 'And don't get dazzled by all that gold. The sheikhs are buying up half of America and nobody's noticing. They come, they buy and they profit.'

'In the wake of the financial crisis the Americans need the money to pay off their debts.'

'Yes, you're right. George Bush senior saw it years ago. He's got good pals in Saudi Arabia. Which is great news for world peace. Who's going to start bombing their own assets?' Hansen waved at a waiter, pointed to his plate and ordered more.

The bet was won.

Leaning his elbows on the table, Hansen folded his hands, rested his chin on them and said, 'Did you know that the Abu Dhabi Investment Council has bought the Chrysler Building in the heart of the Big Apple? Those with debts have to sell. It's as simple as that.'

Winter gave a feeble smile. His gut feeling told him that Hansen had warmed up and it was time for some concrete questions. 'What role did Al-Bader play in these investments?'

Hansen glanced towards the kitchen. A pause for thought or just a craving for more sausages? The stomach is half an hour ahead of the brain. It's only with a half-hour delay that the brain registers you've eaten enough and you're not actually hungry any more. But Hansen wasn't a Slow Food advocate. With him everything had to go quickly, although he hadn't said anything of substance yet.

'Dead clients are bad for business. That's why I want us to find Al-Bader's killer. He should rot in a hole for the rest of his life. If needs be I'll smash his skull in with my own hands.' But he still hadn't answered the question.

Winter probed further. 'Was Al-Bader a special client then?'

'Every client is special. Al-Bader represented his family, his clan. And I'm hardly letting you in on a secret if I say we're not talking about pocket money here.'

'What sort of sums *are* we talking about?'

'You're worse than the journalists.' More eggs, bacon and sausages arrived, putting Hansen in a generous mood, which is why before launching his assault on the plate he condescendingly added, 'They've entrusted Galaxy with a few billion.'

Winter looked out of the window, tried to imagine an amount with nine zeros and by the time he'd turned back to Hansen, the man's plate was already half empty.

'In your opinion, who might have a reason for killing Al-Bader?'

He shrugged. 'The Al-Bader family has been with us since the beginning. From time to time they've helped us win new clients on the Arabian Peninsula. But the answer is: I don't know.'

'Could you speculate?'

'I was at Al-Bader's funeral in Riyadh. And when I looked at this family I couldn't imagine that everything's harmonious all the time. Too much money at stake. Perhaps he trod on someone's toes. You know what I'm talking about. One enemy too many. I really don't know. You're the expert. Isn't it your job to find out?'

'Maybe.' Winter didn't want to talk about his job spec, and certainly not about his sense of duty.

Hansen was keen to know something too. Abruptly he asked, 'Was the helicopter shot down?'

'A fire broke out in the cockpit and currently the authorities are investigating what caused it. I'm inclined to believe it was an explosion.'

'Who had access to the helicopter?'

'Al-Bader, the pilot, the service engineers, the passengers on that or the preceding flight, the pilot's wife, airport staff.'

'If it was an explosion, have they found a detonator?'

At this point Winter could easily imagine how a firm's management would feel if it were being grilled by Hansen. 'No, as far as I know, no detonator has been found yet.'

'How was it triggered?' Hansen was more interested in the technical aspects than the human ones.

'A timer? On the internet you can find all sorts of instructions for building a bomb. Or a mobile phone. One call is enough.'

Hansen shook his head and rubbed his smoothly-shaven double chin thoughtfully. After a dismissive grunt he contemplated the problem from another angle.

'Who's got the strongest motive?'

'That's what I'm trying to find out.'

'There were no terrorists claiming responsibility? No call to a tabloid?'

'No, not as yet. I've been trying to reconstruct Al-Bader's last few days. Do you know why he left the conference here?'

'Al Bader's family is investing directly in the Middle East. All he told me was that one of his projects in Egypt needed his urgent attention. He wanted to be back the following evening for the presentation on the subject of water.'

'Who was he going to meet?'

'I don't know. A minister?' Hansen grinned. 'Was there no suitcase full of money found?'

'Al-Bader was scheduled to meet Kaddour, the number two at Orafin. On July the twenty-sixth, Kaddour was killed by a car bomb in Cairo.'

'Jesus Christ!' For a second or two Hansen forgot to eat.

Too many dead clients spoil your appetite, Winter thought. Then he said, 'I'll bet you that greed is behind it. Al-Bader and Kaddour are dead. So be careful.'

'Listen, Winter. There's often a bit of showmanship in our business. We're operating on a public stage. Why did someone choose to kill Al-Bader in this particular way? He could have been poisoned silently and without fuss. I'm sure it would have been simpler.' Hansen poked around his almost empty plate a little sheepishly. 'I think that the method of the killing – if that's what it was – is a message too. The explosion of a helicopter in safe Switzerland is a sensational act and thus a particular sign.'

'From whom to whom? A deterrent? I'm inclined to think they meant to disguise the attack as an accident.'

Hansen pulled his vibrating mobile from his pocket, glanced at the screen, declined the call and said, 'I don't know, but if I can help you, I will. I have contacts. I'll lend you my jet if you like. Tell the hotel you're my guest. But find the murderer.' His plate empty, Hansen looked at his watch and shook Winter's hand. 'Best of luck!' he said and then he was gone.

Winter remained sitting there, digesting both his breakfast and what he'd heard. He was still lost in the view and his thoughts when a waitress approached him and said in a tone that wouldn't allow for any buts, 'Please leave the dining room at once and go straight to the car park!'

When Winter raised his eyebrows at the waitress, she explained, 'We've had a bomb alert and we're evacuating the hotel. Please go quickly.'

He nodded and thought of Fatima. His heart tightened.

Winter knew the drill and got up. Statistically most bomb threats were false alarms. But he also knew the dilemma of the person in charge. In a very short time they had to decide whether to take the threat seriously or not. If you evacuated and nothing happened, there would be trouble with the guests. If you didn't evacuate and there was an explosion, you were responsible. This risk meant that in most cases the building would be evacuated, sealed off and searched.

After the events of the last few days Winter didn't want to rely on statistics. Probabilities were helpful, but sometimes deadly too.

He left the dining hall and jogged towards his bungalow, meeting hotel guests coming the other way, most of whom had been startled out of their sleep. Many of the guests were still in pyjamas or they'd quickly put something on. A few Arabs in white robes with wives, aunts, cousins and lots of children in tow came rushing past. The children were shrieking with excitement, but otherwise nobody seemed to be in a panic.

Winter saw three security guards dressed in black, directing the guests to the car park that was set some way back from the hotel. The hotel's evacuation plan earmarked the car park as the assembly point.

Hopefully not another car bomb, Winter thought. That would be a catastrophe. First lure all the guests to the car park and then detonate the bomb. In Iraq and Afghanistan insurgents had refined this tactic to perfection over the years.

As he passed the conference building he saw Hansen and a similar-looking, but younger man hectically collecting up all the documents that were lying around. Both men had red faces and looked stressed. What had Hansen said? Two birds with one stone. If the hotel were blown sky-high it would affect the guests and investors. Winter felt behind him for the documents that were still stuffed into his trousers. Nobody would notice that anything was missing.

Winter got to the bungalow.

The stocky chambermaid from the previous evening was outside the door, knocking on it with her fist. Winter wouldn't have been surprised if she'd tried to break down the door with her shoulder. 'Sir,' she said, 'we have a bomb alert. Please go straight to the car park with the other guests!'

'I know.'

The door opened a crack and Fatima's large eyes were even larger than usual. Her long, black hair was dishevelled. 'What's wrong?'

Somewhere in the main building a siren went off.

The chambermaid hurried to the next bungalow.

Fatima was holding a towel to cover herself.

Winter grabbed Fatima's head with both hands. 'Bomb alert. Get dressed, quick. We've got to get out of here.'

She slipped on her jeans and a jumper. Winter threw the rest of their things in the suitcase on wheels and grabbed his rucksack. Then they hurried to the car park. Fatima walked across the gravelly car park in bare feet. About a hundred guests were milling around, chatting and on the phone. Some were taking photos of the hotel, and for a moment Winter was seized by the macabre thought that they might be trying to capture the explosion.

Before. After.

Fatima sat on a rock and put on her shoes.

Winter went up to the Jaguar. He had the electronic key in his hand, but he hesitated, remembering his dream. The Jaguar was parked between a blue Polo with Norwegian plates and a claret-coloured Mercedes. It looked untouched. He walked around the convertible.

A cat had left its paw prints on the bonnet. Cats love warm cars. Winter was always a bit disconcerted when his cat treated his Audi the same as it did him. It seemed to make no difference to Tiger whether he was cosying up to Winter's legs or the Audi's tyres. He would purr on Winter's lap just as he did on the warm car roof. Could you be jealous of cars?

The windscreen was full of insects. He didn't notice anything suspicious on the lock of the boot. He kneeled on the ground and looked under the sports car.

Nothing.

He cautiously tried the door handle on the driver's side, which was still locked. About five centimetres beneath the window of the passenger door was a barely visible horizontal scratch! The Hertz rep hadn't said anything about that. Winter had given the car no more than a cursory glance when they'd handed over the keys. The scratch could be from anything, such as a branch brushing the chassis or a picklock that had slipped. Winter ran his thumb over the scratch and checked the passenger door as well.

He looked around.

Fatima was sitting on the rock and the other hotel guests weren't taking any notice of him. He heard sirens and two fire engines arrived. If something blows up now, Winter thought, then at least the fire brigade's here. He took a few steps back, stood behind the next row of cars and pressed the unlock button. The Jaguar responded with a flash of its lights. Winter breathed a sigh of relief.

'What's wrong?' Fatima appeared beside him.

'Nothing, I just had a bad dream.'

He packed the luggage into the boot and they sat inside the car. From their vantage point they had a good view. More fire engines and police cars arrived. In contrast to the holiday guests, most of whom were lightly dressed, the firemen were wearing full protective gear. The hotel had now been sealed off with yellow and black tape. The safety zone around the main building was about fifty metres. The fire brigade was putting hoses in place.

The initial frenzy started to die down. People waited tensely. A Saab came along the drive and Winter saw the large logo of a newspaper emblazoned on its side. The press. The bomb alert would make it into the regional paper at least. Two young men got out and started looking and asking around.

'What are we going to do now?' Fatima asked, flipping down the sun visor to check her appearance in the mirror. When Winter didn't reply she turned to him.

Winter felt as if they'd already known each other for ages. He attempted a reassuring smile and said, 'Wait,' unsure of what else to say. He continued watching the activity outside.

After a while he remembered Hansen and told Fatima about his breakfast with the money manager. He pulled out the documents from the conference room, leafed through them and passed some on to Fatima. The week's schedule and detailed daily programmes: presentations and discussions on selected topics of global infrastructure. A list of around thirty names – mostly Arabic and some Chinese – with telephone numbers, emails and contact addresses.

Recognising some of the names, Fatima commented, 'In the Middle East they're part of the Establishment.'

A three-page list entitled 'Partners' gave addresses and contact persons for banks, financial institutions, authorities, specialists,

experts, advisors, as well as public and private university institutes. There was a comprehensive list of books and studies,
arranged by topics such as energy, transport, mixed. Someone
had marked a few titles with a pink highlighter. This participant
was obviously interested in shipping and wanted to invest in
ports and container ships.

The bundle of paper also contained some PowerPoint
presentations and prospectuses of Hansen's private equity
fund. Wearing a pink tie, he smiled at Winter from page
three, extolling the achievements of his investments. The
graphics were impressive. Growth, profitability, performance.
Everything was going up at a giddying rate.

Another police car, a panel van, sped up the drive and
skidded to a halt outside the hotel. Winter could make out the
word 'Bergen'. Two uniformed officers got out and yanked
open the doors at the back. Two Alsatians leaped out and
were put on a lead. The specialists from Bergen with their
sniffer dogs. Winter checked his watch: 07:42. About half an
hour since the evacuation. The dogs were excited and looking
forward to their search. For them it was just a game.

Fatima pointed at a document. 'Look, here's a presentation
about nuclear power stations by Al-Bader. "The peaceful use
of a clean technology – the sustainable yields of nuclear power
stations." He was actually trying to persuade others to invest in
our nuclear power plant.'

Winter skimmed the presentation. It looked like all those
beautiful pieces of paper from his bank. He'd study it later.

The hotel had set up an improvised breakfast buffet and
were providing the waiting guests with tea, coffee, rolls and
fruit. The waitress from earlier wandered through the crowd
with a tray full of plastic cups.

The children had drawn lines in the gravel of the car park
and were playing hopscotch. They hopped around, laughing
and trying to make each other lose balance.

The security guard Winter had chatted to that morning was strolling along the lines of cars, inspecting them. He held a cup in his right hand, switched it to the left, stroked the Jaguar and said, 'Nice car. I wish the company gave us these to drive.'

'Just a rental, I'm afraid. But she drives beautifully. A bit large for the narrow roads in this part of the world. On the drive here I learned a few words of Norwegian: *Automatisk Trafikkontrol.*' Winter grinned.

'Oh yes, our lovely speed cameras.'

'Got everything under control?' Winter asked, pointing at the hotel.

'I think so. Probably a false alarm.'

'You only ever know that after the event. Where did the alert come from?'

'It seems as if a number of guests got an email this morning warning them that the hotel would be blown up at zero eight hundred hours. They woke up, dozily checked their mobiles and then couldn't get back to sleep.' The guard gave the time in military fashion. His fake golden Rolex showed ten to eight.

'Who sent it?'

'Some Islamic committee. The Arabs took it seriously at any rate. The committee is demanding that they' – he pointed to the Arab hotel guests – 'stop doing business with the infidel.'

'What was the exact name of the sender?' Fatima asked.

'I don't know.'

'What will happen if they don't find a bomb?'

'We'll wait a few hours. The police will give the all clear and that's the end of the scare.'

Through an open window on the first floor of the hotel they saw one of the handlers egging on his dog. Ten minutes for the entire building was tight, but not impossible. There were thousands of scents inside a hotel and the dogs had to focus on just a few. These trained animals were still far superior to any technology; they could sniff out explosives in an instant.

But the three-storey main building of the hotel had around sixty bedrooms plus attic, basement and kitchen. Then there were the large reception areas. A hundred rooms, two dogs, ten minutes. Five rooms per minute. And if any explosives were found there was no guarantee that these could be defused in time.

The security guard walked over to a Mercedes SLK-Class, giving the outward impression of calmness. Winter and Fatima waited. They couldn't concentrate on the documents any longer and the clock was ticking more slowly than normal. The police officers from Bergen asked the guests to move further away from the hotel. The firemen donned their helmets, flipped down their visors and shouldered their equipment. One of the reporters had set up a tripod on a rock at a safe distance and mounted a camera.

The handlers came out of the hotel, shaking their heads. They patted their dogs and gave them a treat, then the animals obediently jumped back into their cage. A brief bark. Otherwise silence all around. The hotel guests had stopped chatting. Winter checked the time: 07:59.

## JULY 30 – 08:00

A mobile phone rang and a portly Arab took the call. The people standing nearby turned to him. He nodded, made a brief gesture, muttered something, then energetically flipped his phone shut. The journalist placed his right hand on the camera and checked his watch. Ready to shoot. The firemen were pawing impatiently in the starting blocks.

The unnerved guests moved further back.

08:00 passed uneventfully.

Bent over the steering wheel, Winter stared at the hotel. After a few anxious minutes the guests came to life again.

Relieved, he leaned back in his seat and gave a long sigh. Winter looked at Fatima. She was relieved too. He was alive, well and with an intriguing woman. Then the image of Anne laughing came back to him and superimposed itself on the present. He fancied she gave him a look that was at once searching and inviting.

He shook his head. When would the future begin? Turning away, he said, 'Come on, let's go for a bit of a walk. Waiting any more is going to drive me mad. We'll get a good view from the cliffs over there.'

Behind the hotel they found a narrow path alongside the fjord. They passed small, weekend houses with white timbers, terraces and boathouses. The air was thick with the sweet scent of ripe cherries. To the left lay a cherry orchard, to the right a stony bay with patches of sand. In the distance he could see a ferry. Although the sun was already shining strongly, the air was still fresh from the night.

Fatima seemed to like the tranquillity here. It offered a contrast, at any rate, to the dust and noise of Cairo. They strolled along the bay, both buried in their own thoughts. It was peaceful; the explosions now seemed far away.

At the end of the bay, cliffs plunged into the fjord. After a short climb they reached a rugged, barren plateau, where they were met by a cool wind that ruffled Fatima's hair. The black cliffs fell forty metres vertically into the water. The waves of the fjord frothed against the crags that lined the cliffs in multiple rows, like shark teeth.

They sat on a bench bearing the logo of the local tourist board and gazed out at the fjord. Where the Hardangerfjord met the horizon, the blue of the water melded into the blue of the sky.

Winter wondered where the fresh water of the fjord finished and the salt water of the sea began. Did the salt content increase gradually or was there an invisible boundary? When did his feelings for Anne end and when did they begin for Fatima? Anne was dead. That was a clear boundary at least. But he did not want to forget her. Confusion. After a while, Winter said, 'I'm so relieved that the bomb threat wasn't carried out.'

'Me too.'

Nodding, he bent forwards, rested his elbows on his knees and said, more to the water than to Fatima, 'Somehow it all happened too quickly for me. On the day the helicopter crashed I was actually meant to meet up with Anne. We got on well outside work too.'

'I know. Did you love her?'

'No.' He hesitated before adding, 'Yes. I don't know. I mean, not in the way you're thinking.' She rocked her head from side to side, but said nothing. Winter was finding it hard to disentangle his feelings in his head, let alone articulate them. He felt Fatima lay a hand on his back, then said, 'Yes, I did love Anne. Maybe I'm still in love with her. But I was her boss and I never told her. I'd planned to a few times, but I never managed it. I just didn't want to embarrass her.'

'I can understand that.'

Winter remembered Kaddour and how he'd spoken about Fatima, how he'd looked at her. Then the explosion at the restaurant near the pyramids. Deciding it was going to take time, he turned to Fatima and said, 'Let's think of the future.'

'Yes, let's see what fate Allah has in store for us.' Fatima smiled, thoughtfully at first, then with a broader grin. Laughter lines at the corners of her eye. Somehow fate seemed to be the right word here, Winter decided.

'Yes, good.' He paused. 'What do you think is behind the bomb scare?'

'I don't know.'

'It was effective. The investors are going to think twice about transferring their money to Galaxy. Getting hold of those email addresses isn't exactly rocket science. They're publicly accessible. I expect an insider heard about all the people who were meeting here and told an acquaintance who knows someone who knows someone else. And sending an email anonymously from an internet café is risk-free. The timing was good in any case.'

Winter rubbed the scabby scar on his temple and continued thoughtfully, 'Sending a bomb scare by email is not the same as the two murders. My gut feeling tells me that somehow they don't go together. The sequence and style don't match.'

'Maybe a copycat. Maybe one of Galaxy's competitors sent the email to disrupt the conference.'

Winter nodded and scratched himself pensively. 'What I want to know is why Al-Bader and Kaddour were targeted. Why were they singled out to be killed? And why precisely now? Did the two of them have other joint projects?'

'Apart from the nuclear power station, no. Or not that I'm aware of. I knew Kaddour fairly well. He often asked me for advice. He always wanted to know my opinion. To begin with that was difficult, especially when my opinion was different. He didn't always take my advice to heart.'

A faint smile emerged on Fatima's lips before vanishing again.

'No! I'm certain that Kaddour didn't have any other business with Al-Bader. We enquired about him last summer. Someone Kaddour knew was dealing with Al-Bader's brother and that's how we came into contact.'

Hearing the sadness in Fatima's voice, Winter looked at her and said, 'We must find out more about the consortium's plans. We've only scratched the surface so far. What we do know is that there's a huge amount of money at stake and it's being invested in Western infrastructure. That's a politically contro-versial tightrope walk.'

'I know.'

'Being Swiss, I'm not going to get much out of them. But you could pretend to be a journalist and ask some questions. If you tell them you're a freelance journalist working for Al Jazeera and you bat your eyelids I'm sure you'll be able to coax something from one or two of them.'

But she shook her head resolutely. 'No, that isn't a good idea. I don't want to put on an act. Why would businessmen talk about their affairs with a stranger? Business in the Middle East only functions through connections.' After a pause she added, more gently, 'And those take time.'

'Oh well, it was just an idea. But how are we going to continue following the money trail?'

They gazed at the water.

'Let's go back. I'll try to get talking to the women. Maybe they can help us further. Although they only operate in the background, in general they're better with the money.'

Winter looked at Fatima, unsure if she was being serious. But it was a good idea.

'Alright then. Maybe they've given the hotel the all-clear by now.'

They stood up and walked back. In the distance they heard the siren of a car ferry approaching from behind the cliffs and heading for the hotel's landing stage. Fatima and Winter paused and watched the ferry advance with its belly full of cars and a bow wave in its tow. The crew was preparing to dock and a handful of passengers were waving from the deck.

A few minutes later they were back at the hotel. The main building was still sealed off. In the car park were uniformed officers, firemen, the security guards dressed in black and a few plain-clothed police, standing around their vehicles and discussing the situation. The car with the dogs was empty; no doubt the sniffers were doing another thorough search of the building. They walked in an arc around the hotel and entered the park.

Making a virtue out of necessity, the guests had settled down in the expansive park for a picnic. They sat or lay in the grass. Waiters and waitresses hurried back and forth, serving more food and drinks from the kitchen, which must have been reopened. It was quite a trek from there to the guests, who were used to being waited on. In the middle of the park was a rotunda, a sort of summer house with a metal roof that had turned green, a table and curved cast-iron benches around it. Five Arab women in traditional dress were sitting there, chatting animatedly.

Fatima headed for the rotunda.

Winter stayed where he was for a moment and watched her. He sighed and returned to the Jaguar, where he met the security guard. The man told Winter that they still hadn't found anything and that it had probably been a hoax. Winter didn't disagree. The hotel and bungalows were given a final methodical search. In all likelihood the guests wouldn't be able to return to their rooms until the afternoon. Winter accepted the offer of some water and drank from the bottle.

The guard kept chatting away, expressing his astonishment at how large the Arab families were, something particularly apparent now at this improvised picnic. He knew that they'd travelled with kith and kin, but in the wake of the bomb scare he could actually see them all together. He'd read that in Norway the average family was only 3.2 people. And if it went on like that the Western countries would sooner or later die out. Half listening to him, Winter drank his water and then he had an idea.

Al-Bader was the head of a large family. It was perfectly possible, therefore, that in spite of the funeral back home, a distant cousin was holding the fort here in Norway to represent the family's interests. Winter gave the security guard a grateful clap on the shoulder and took his leave.

The hotel had set up a temporary reception by the rose-covered entrance gate at the edge of the park. Beside the large granite that bore in metal letters the hotel's name and a welcome in three languages, stood a table, behind which two slightly lost-looking receptionists sat. Winter ran his hand through his hair and asked, 'Excuse me, have you seen Mr Al-Bader anywhere?'

The two uniformed women smiled their receptionist's smile, said in stereo, 'Just a moment, please,' and leafed through some pieces of paper. These were computer printouts of the bookings, marked with green and yellow highlighters. The provisional reception had to make do without computers.

'We've got two Al-Baders. The others left a few days ago. Which one would you like to leave a message for?'

Winter had no idea. He smiled sheepishly. 'I can never remember the Arab names. He's a bit older.' There was always an older one. And throughout the world it was usually the case that the older you were, the more influence you had.

The receptionists consulted in Norwegian and the elder of the two said, 'It's probably this one.' The younger woman said with a smile, 'He must be seventy at least.' Realising her indiscretion, she quickly added, 'Mr Al-Bader is a very spritely man.

What message can we pass on to him?' Winter glanced at the finger on the computer printout. Suite 31 was booked for the entire week.

'Nothing right at the moment. You don't happen to know where I might find Mr Al-Bader now, do you?' He looked around. Unfortunately the two women were unable to be of any further assistance. Winter thanked them and embarked on his search for the elder Al-Bader.

He walked back around the main building to the park. Fatima was sitting in the rotunda with the women. They were having a lively discussion, gesticulating fervently. Her back was turned to Winter. In the rose garden, a few Arab men were sitting in a circle of garden chairs, engaged in a vocal conversation.

He strolled through the park, looking out for a spritely looking old man. Hansen was panting his way up from the bay and Winter asked him where the elder Al-Bader was. The money manager, glad to be able to take a breather, pointed into the distance and gasped, 'Over there. The one with the stick.' At the far end of the park, where the cultivated area turned into woodland, was a herb garden with white stones and light gravel paths.

On a park bench at the edge of the herb garden sat an elderly man with white hair, looking out at the fjord. His stick was leaning on the bench. Winter walked through the herb garden, took in the different aromas and felt the sun reflected on the light stones. His shoes crunched on the gravel. Winter couldn't read the dark, weather-beaten features of the old man's face. Was he impassive, relaxed, tired?

'Please excuse me for disturbing you. Are you Mr Al-Bader?'

The old man looked at Winter with watery, but clear eyes. His face was deeply furrowed. The man had spent much of his life outside and looked more like a Bedouin than a businessman. When he rocked his head Winter couldn't be sure whether it signalled a Yes or a No. In very old-fashioned English and with a strong accent, the man said, 'Good day. With whom do I have the pleasure of speaking?'

'I'm a friend of Muhammed Al-Bader.' And after a pause, 'I work for a Swiss bank and we met a few times. We were in the mountains together.' The 'friend' bit was a slight exaggeration. Relations between him and Al-Bader had been purely professional. But Winter had always tried to get to know him as a person too.

'The last time we met a few months ago he told me about his falcons.' The normally reserved Al-Bader had once raved to Winter about his passion for falcons. The old man looked out at the fjord. High above them a bird of prey was circling.

After a while the old man said, 'Muhammed was a good man. He had no fear of the future. He was interested in new things and travelled all around the world. He was in China and America.'

'May I sit down?' Al-Bader nodded, gestured to the space beside him and Winter sat on the bench. They stared at the fjord together. To the left were the bay and the cliffs, to the right the fjord opened out to the sea. Small, colourful boats bobbed up and down on the water. The old man was quiet. At his age you had plenty of time. Or none at all. Or a different sense of time. Perhaps the old man simply had more patience than Winter.

'I'd like to find out exactly what happened.'

Winter adjusted to Al-Bader's rhythm and after a while was rewarded. 'I'm a cousin of his father who died three years ago. May Allah have mercy on his soul. After his death Muhammed became another of my sons.'

Winter said nothing.

'And now Muhammed is dead too. I really ought to have gone back to Riyadh for his funeral, but his younger brother asked me to stay here.' He sighed.

'I've spoken to Mr Hansen from Galaxy. He told me that

your family and other wealthy ones from the Middle East are investing money in the West with Galaxy's help.' Winter stated this as fact rather than putting it as a question. All the same he hoped to get confirmation from the uncle. Years ago his law professor had impressed on him the importance of cross-checking. Assumptions only became facts when they were checked from different angles.

'When I was a child,' Al-Bader said, 'I lived in the desert. My grandfather bred camels. He was a well-travelled man with friends in distant countries. Once he took me with him to Rabat. He told me that a good businessman always had to be a friend, too. Please do not misunderstand me. My grandfather was a tough character who wanted to earn money. Wealth means a large harem.'

A throaty laugh rose from the smoker's lungs of the elderly man. 'But even if he was able to buy a camel cheaply he always made sure that he showed respect to the seller. That took time. You need patience in the desert. We often talked all day and drank tea, then talked more. As long as it took for us to understand each other.'

A long pause. 'These days everything has to happen so quickly. Muhammed had his own aeroplane and would race off to Paris, London or Hong Kong to shop.' The old man shook his head.

After more silence Winter asked, 'Did Muhammed command the respect of the whole family?' He couldn't think of a politer way to enquire about possible private quarrels within the Al-Bader clan.

'Did we argue, do you mean?'

Winter nodded.

'Yes, there were always arguments. But that's all part of it. Muhammed was the head of the family. He and his younger brother believed it was our holy duty to help build up the Saudi kingdom. The oil will not flow forever. For this reason we need friends around the world. Other family members don't think it's right that we're building roads and ports in Europe and America.'

'What's your opinion?'

'I'm just an old man. I have always tried to mediate. During the Second World War my family lost almost everything. So I could understand Muhammed when he said it was better to invest money across the globe. But my home is the Arabian Peninsula and there is nothing I wish more dearly for my brothers than peace and prosperity.' After another pause he repeated, 'I'm an old man who only partly understands the world of today.'

If the murderer came from within the family it would be difficult. Winter didn't understand the language, had no clue about the culture and no contacts. But wouldn't a family member have had better opportunities to strike? Brutus had slain Caesar in the Roman Senate. Why in Switzerland? Was the place intended as a big red herring? Or perhaps it was another clan?

'May I ask you another question? I'm not familiar with the traditions of the Middle East. Could this be a vendetta? Did Muhammed have enemies in Riyadh or anywhere else on the Arabian Peninsula who might go so far as to kill him?'

'Young man,' Al-Bader began didactically, 'I advise you not to believe everything you see on television and read in the newspapers. We are not gangs of murderers. We are a civilised people. We were creating great things when Europe was still in nappies.' Another smoky laugh.

'Please excuse me, but I am a prisoner of my history.'

'That's alright. I forgive you your youthful presumption.'

Relieved, Winter moved away from the controversial topic. Resisting the desire to dig deeper he posed a simpler question. 'Was Muhammed Al-Bader happy with Galaxy?'

'The stargazer helped us in Europe. Because of the oil they

got on well. All this palaver here helped us invest the money in the right place. My grandfather's camels were famous for their big feet. Some people called them "flatfoot camels". Broad feet are important to stop sinking in the sand. The less a camel sinks, the less water it needs, and the less thirsty it is, the further it can walk. The stargazer is like a breeder; he brings the best camels together. But although he looks like an Englishman he doesn't have a clue about America.'

'America?'

'Yes, Muhammed always said that he wanted to go to the United States. He studied at Harvard.'

'I didn't know that.'

'It was Muhammed's conviction that so long as countries were doing business they wouldn't wage war against each other.'

'At least not with weapons.' The words slipped out of Winter's mouth.

'The Americans believe in the market. We believe in the market. We can build on this foundation. It's much better than people bashing each other's skulls in Palestine. That costs the lives of many innocent people.'

'Are there controversial projects in America then?'

'America isn't Riyadh. There's a lot of mistrust in this world. And you must learn to listen.' At this the elderly man stood up, grabbed his stick made of burr wood and took his leave with the words, 'Many thanks for your company and your time. It was a great pleasure to talk to you. I learned a lot from your questions.' With astonishingly lithe movements he left the herb garden and went back across the grass to the hotel.

Winter stayed sitting on the bench. What had he missed? He replayed the conversation in his head again. The old man had talked in metaphors. But what did his grandfather's camels have to do with the nuclear power station in Cairo? Talking of which, the scar from Cairo was itchy. Winter had to stop himself from scratching it till it bled. He heard soft footsteps in the gravel and turned around. Fatima.

'Hello. Did you have a nice tea party?' he asked her.

Sitting down in the camel-dealer's place, she gave him a reproachful look and said, 'We got all worked up about the fact that Afghanistan only lets its female athletes compete if they're covered from head to toe. Just imagine that. Sprinters with veils.

'Yes, I can't really picture beach volleyball in Afghanistan either.'

'That's different.'

There was a right time for every topic and this was not it, so Winter changed the subject. 'Did you talk about Al-Bader as well?'

'Yes. They're all very shocked by his death. They blame it on the American project.'

'The American project?' Winter echoed.

'Yes, Al-Bader started up a bank in Boston.'

'Starting up a bank is a bigger crime than robbing one.' Not recognising the quote, Fatima hesitated, so Winter added, 'Not my words, but Brecht's.'

On the drive back to Bergen airport, Winter put the Jaguar through its paces. He'd charge the fines from the *Automatisk Trafikkontrol* to expenses. Winter was determined to be at Anne's funeral the following day. Bergen had only one flight to Oslo late that afternoon, which they had to hurry to catch.

They couldn't talk on the plane, nor did they want to. Winter used the time in the air to think. He felt as if he were poking around in the dark. They flew through gigantic banks of cloud, their form constantly changing. The flows of air and money were invisible; only the effects were palpable.

Due to turbulence the captain asked the passengers to keep their seat belts on. Airline advertising would have you believe that flying was having your every need attended to as you glided smoothly above the clouds. In truth, like livestock on an industrial sheep farm, you were herded through airports, then wedged on board to save maximum space. Winter had caught himself envying Al-Bader's private jet. But Al-Bader was dead. Perhaps a scheduled flight was better after all.

What were the invisible currents that had led to the murders? Winter could only guess at Al-Bader's cash flow, his capital streams. Känzig, Schütz, Kaddour, Fatima, Hansen and this morning Al-Bader's uncle all had their own interests, their own perspectives. Al-Bader's investments were controversial. Were the currents political? Was there a clash of national interests, or was it a conflict between the traditional and the modern? Al-Bader had been a modern Arab with mercenaries around the world.

During their transfer in Oslo, Fatima had downloaded her emails onto her laptop and was now typing away industriously. Out of the corner of his eye Winter could only see her long, black hair, screening her face like a curtain. She hadn't eaten much and had offered Winter her dessert. He loved sweet things, but this felt to him like a parting token.

They landed punctually in Zürich and Fatima had no reason to miss her connecting flight. The two of them stood there, lost in the flow of the business travellers heading home. To the left was another endlessly long walkway to the gate for Cairo, to the right lay the exit. The lighting was harsh, and a buzzing, cleaning machine was heading in their direction. For the last two hundred metres Winter had studied the advertisements for watches and banks, still at a loss as to what to say.

Fatima had a better grip on the situation. 'Right, this is where I think we part company.'

'Indeed, many thanks for your help.' Winter stroked the encrusted scar on his temple. 'It's a shame that we met under such circumstances.'

'Under other circumstances we wouldn't have met at all,' Fatima retorted with clinical logic. When she smiled her teeth shone in the neon light. 'It's better for me to be in Egypt. I just got an invitation from the owner of Orafin. He's asked me to come to his house, his palace, to discuss Kaddour's successor.'

'Does this mean congratulations are in order?'

'No. And keep it under your hat. I haven't got a concrete offer and I don't know if I could accept it anyway. I mean, Kaddour was blown up.'

They didn't say anything for a while until Winter broke the silence. 'It would definitely be a great challenge and I'm sure you'd do it very well. In any case you would be a role model for the younger generation, especially Egyptian women.'

'We'll see.' She held out her hand formally. 'I'll be in touch if something turns up in Egypt.' As soon as Winter took her hand he moved to embrace. They made do with three awkward kisses on the cheeks. 'I'll keep you up to date my end. All the best and I wish you success.'

As he watched Fatima walk off, he felt a twinge in his heart and wondered whether he'd ever see her again. He was surrounded by a horde of Japanese travellers with a flag at the front. When he had room to breathe again, Fatima had disappeared. All of a sudden Winter was terribly tired. Perhaps this was the after-effect of the concussion, the fruitless search for a killer or killers, their parting or simply the flying.

Winter wondered how Tiger was. His cat probably hadn't even missed him. Tiger was self-sufficient and would schmooze anybody who came past, particularly warm car tyres. Passing through the green customs channel, Winter was apprehended.

Keen to see Winter, Ben had set a flag in the electronic data flows to let him know when he was there. Ben looked tired, but shook Winter's hand far more firmly than Fatima had just done. 'Winter? How were the holidays? You look old somehow.'

'Thanks. Same to you. The water was pleasantly warm.'

'Coffee?'

'Have you been spending time with mind-readers?'

'No, but habits make up half a personality, whether you're a terrorist or a banker.'

'Is there any difference between them?'

'Sometimes I'm not sure.'

When they arrived at the coffee machine Ben silently filled two cups. They went into a multifunctional office with no decoration or windows.

Ben kept it short. 'My plate's full with a strike at Heathrow. To prevent the baggage-handling from going completely tits-up they're using staff who've only been subject to minimal security checks. All they need to do is fill out a form and present a photocopy of their passport. It makes your hair stand on end. But that's not your worry. How was Bergen?'

Winter gave Ben an outline of his visit to Norway, concluding with the contradiction that although Al-Bader was on the CIA terrorist list he'd also been starting up a bank in America.

'Maybe he's got a split personality,' Ben said. 'Or the various American agencies aren't working in tandem. It wouldn't be the first time that the left hand was unaware what the right hand was doing. I don't know what you need exactly to start up a bank, but I can imagine that Al-Bader was doing it via a firm or front man, rather than directly.'

'I'll check with our analysts. Heard any more from the Americans?'

'No, not directly. But since Al-Bader's helicopter crash they've raised the alarm level for vital infrastructure.'

'What does that mean?'

'The US Committee on Homeland Security regards the probability of an attack on oil rigs, and gas, water and electricity supplies to be higher than last week. Protecting all electricity masts, water pipes and pipelines nationwide is no easy task. Put yourself in a terrorist's shoes. You want to create a climate of fear. With as little effort as possible you want to carry out attacks that have big impact and get lots of publicity. Imagine a ship full of TNT, piloted by determined suicide attackers, sinking a Western oil rig. Or Los Angeles's water supply being contaminated by a poison you can neither smell nor taste, but which infects millions of people.'

'And you think Al-Bader was financing this sort of stuff?'

'I don't know, but being the owner of a bank gives you lots of possibilities. All it takes is not to be so particular about issuing credit cards to the wrong people.'

'All of that is speculation,' Winter countered. After a while he added, 'Did you get in touch with the explosives laboratory in Spiez?'

'Yes, the molecular analysis of the traces from the helicopter and from your Egyptian mudguard show they don't come from the same explosive.' Ben paused.

'Thanks,' Winter said. He knew there was more to come.

'The explosive in Egypt is based on nitrates you can also buy as fertilizer. The authorities are tracing the sample back to the various manufacturers. But they're not optimistic because we're talking about a very common consumer product; there's no paper proof of sales and any idiot can get the instructions to build those sorts of bombs from the internet.'

'What about the explosive in the Höllentobel?'

'Most likely from Swiss military supplies...' Another, more dramatic pause. '... combined with a flammable liquid from the supermarket. The crash was supposed to look like it had been caused by a fire.'

Ben and Winter looked each other in the eye. Both of them knew that munitions or even explosives sometimes disappeared from exercises during compulsory military service. In a detonation it was impossible to verify whether all the explosive had been used or if a few hundred grams had been set to one side.

'Is the department in the picture?' Winter was referring to the Federal Department of Defence and Civil Protection.

'Yes, they've launched an internal investigation. I'm no specialist, but the various stocks are marked with trace elements, so perhaps they'll be able narrow it down.'

Winter couldn't resist a sarcastic remark, 'Down to the male population eligible for military service, you mean?'

Ben just shrugged his massive shoulders and dismissed the comment with a swish of his hand. 'But they found the detonator.'

'Military equipment too?'

'No, a specialist detonator that reacts to differences in air pressure. It went off as soon as the helicopter reached a certain height. The Federal Aviation Safety Investigation Board asked me for my expert opinion as this technology is of particular interest to the airport and we have a lovely collection.'

Certain that this collection was interesting, Winter ran through the options and said, 'No timer?'

'No, they didn't find any timer. But we can't rule out the possibility that a number of trigger mechanisms were linked. The detonator was badly damaged and they weren't able to reconstruct it fully.'

'Strittmatter was based in Valais. So he flew over the Alps. If there was no timer involved the bomb must have been brought on board in Zürich.'

'If, if, if... Perhaps Strittmatter had other passengers?' Winter had great respect for Ben's cool logic, and he had to admit that he'd been putting off the homework he needed to do in this area. He made a mental note to enquire at the VIP Helicopter Transportation Corporation.

'Do you have any idea where the detonator comes from?'

'Internet. Mail order. Direct import. No. No idea.'

'I've got one more request.'

'Just one?' Ben said with a grin, and Winter knew it would be his turn to pay for the steaks next.

'Yes, just for once I'm being modest today.' On some notepaper he jotted down the registration number of the helicopter he'd seen above the Höllentobel. 'Who does this helicopter belong to?'

'That's an easy one.'

It belonged to one of Strittmatter's competitors.

On the drive home Winter asked himself whether he might not have been following the wrong leads over the last few days. In the comfort of his Audi he was gripped once more by tiredness on the motorway. To prevent himself from nodding off he

made a few telephone calls, even though it was late. It was
summertime and people were either on holiday or enjoying
the balmy evening.

As usual, Känzig didn't take the call, so Winter left a brief
message that he designated as a status report. That's how
simple it was to cross one item off his to-do list. Box-ticking.

Schütz was in the garden and had time. For two whole
minutes Winter listened to Schütz recount his triumphs as a
barbecue maestro, then enquired about his children and asked
for details of the funeral. They wished each other goodnight.

Dirk had set up an improvised open air cinema screen in the
garden and was watching an action film with friends. A DVD
through his laptop.

'No,' there was nothing new on the IT front. The bank's
firewall hadn't been attacked and, no, he couldn't localise the
email address of the person who'd ordered Winter's house to
be bugged, let alone identify its owner. 'Yes,' he'd bring the list
of Anne's phone calls, both mobile and landline, in tomorrow.
Unfortunately he still had no information about Al-Bader's
calls. And 'Yes, the mood in the bank is a bit peculiar. But in fact
it's business as usual.'

They discussed what to do next and a minute later Dirk was
back with his friends and the film. He'd probably erased Anne
from his short-term memory already. Delete. A colleague from
the security department was just a simple cog in the whole
machinery. Security in the bank was a matter of course.

Finally he rang the VIP Helicopter Transport Corporation.
He heard the call being diverted a number of times. 'VIP
Helicopter Transportation Corporation, Strittmatter, how can
I help you?' A woman's voice. In the background the sound
of cars driving past. He explained who he was, expressed his
condolences and discovered he was talking to a cousin of Hans
Strittmatter. She sounded composed and told him that the
police had already been. As far as she knew Strittmatter had

flown directly from the base over the Alps to Zürich for the Arab sheik's transfer. But she would check for sure.

'Do you know if he refuelled in Zürich?' Winter didn't utter the name of the dead Hans Strittmatter.

'Yes, well no, we have our own fuel here. It's cheaper than at the airport. They're crooks.'

Winter ignored the comment and said goodnight.

If it were true that no timer had been involved to detonate the bomb, the explosive device must have been taken on board at Zürich airport by Al-Bader or Anne. On the security video Winter hadn't seen anybody else near the helicopter.

Winter left the motorway, drove cross-country in the dark and parked his car. In the light of the moon all he saw in front of his house were the prints of the farmer's wellies and the tyre marks of the postman's motorbike. The stem in the door was undamaged. As Winter entered his house he felt as if he had been away for weeks. He opened the windows, hoping that the sticky air would cool overnight. No important post. On the balcony he was greeted by Tiger, who proudly showed him a dead, tattered little bird.

When he sat down on the balcony and smelled the antique wood and the night, he was overcome by a great feeling of calm. The mountains and stars had been around long before humankind and would still be there long after. The broad horizon made his problems seem small. Nature soothed Winter. What a contrast to the airport, with its artificial atmosphere, stressed passengers and their perspiration. Here was the peaceful stillness of the night with chirping crickets and the pungent whiff of cowpats. Each to their own.

Gradually a plan took shape in his head, which was less the result of logical analysis and far more the sum of the impressions that had consolidated there. It was like the dot-to-dot pictures he'd loved as a child. To start with there were just the numbers scattered across the page, but once he'd joined the first few with lines he usually got an idea what the finished picture would be. Even then his aim had never been to draw the lines especially straight, but to identify the overall picture as quickly as possible.

Winter relaxed for half an hour and stopped thinking. Then he got up for an inspection of his unfinished terrace. Afterwards he poured himself a glass of twelve-year-old Talisker single malt, switched on the TV and DVD player, and watched the video from Zürich airport. Several times.

Until he finally saw the obvious. Or didn't see it.

Anne didn't have her pistol. She normally carried her weapon, a .22 SIG Mosquito, in a holster. Either at her hip or on her back, depending if she were wearing trousers or a skirt. And the desk drawer where Anne kept her gun had been empty. It's difficult to see what isn't there. Where was her gun?

# JULY 31 – 09:17

Winter slept fitfully, but couldn't remember any of his dreams. During the night the temperature had fallen below twenty degrees. Immediately after he woke up, this freshness momentarily deluded him into thinking that everything was alright. Then he remembered that today was Anne's funeral, and he became weighed down by a leaden sadness. He breakfasted merely for fuel. Stepping out onto the balcony, he stared at the blue morning sky and thought of Anne.

He drove along country roads with the window down. The bends and the wind stopped him from thinking too much. Normally he would have delighted in the green of the meadows and enjoyed the winding drive. But today he couldn't care less about the magnificent summer.

On the way he bought a deep-red rose. None of the fresh flowers in the florist's had cheered him. Anne loved flowers. She was an optimist, blessed with a talent for injecting joy into almost every situation. Once again Winter resolved never to forget her laughing face with those tiny wrinkles around her sparkling eyes. Deep in thought he drove up the hill past a parade of expensive cars to the small, white, country church. He grew even gloomier when he saw the people dressed in black with their funereal expressions.

Winter recognized the CEO's Mercedes. The driver was standing in the shade, smoking. Right in front of this was Schütz's Audi with his yellow-and-black football scarf on the parcel shelf.

Winter parked and walked slowly up the old, cobbled road to the church, which formed part of a mediaeval castle that had burned down and been rebuilt several times. The path became a right-hand curve that ran around the hill. As with most mediaeval castles, a right-hand bend was advantageous to those under siege. The majority of attackers would wield a sword in their right hand and a shield in their left, leaving them exposed to the defenders. Back then, battles were hand-to-hand combat. You could look your opponent in the eye. Somehow Winter found that fairer.

He made his way slowly up the hill, trying not to break out in a sweat in his suit. It would be cool in the church at least. Other funeral goers walked ahead of and behind him. Some whispered to each other; most were silent. An elderly, heavily-made-up woman in a wheelchair was being pushed by a young man, sweating as he struggled up the steep, uneven road.

Winter didn't know anybody. Loneliness.

It wasn't until he entered the inner courtyard, which served both church and castle, that he saw some bank colleagues.

Schütz waved at him. Winter headed for the bunch of people who had grouped around the tall, suntanned and white-haired CEO. Känzig was hanging on his every word. Winter could hear the sonorous voice of the alpha male, who was recounting an anecdote about his tailor. Winter shook his colleagues' hands and nodded to them without saying anything.

Känzig couldn't refrain from passing comment. 'Ah, Winter. Nice to see you in person again.' Ignoring these words, Winter silently offered him his hand and gestured to Schütz that he wished to speak to him in private.

They withdrew to a quiet corner, next to an arrow slit in the fortifications. Winter handed Schütz the documents from Bergen. 'I'd be grateful if you could run your eye over these. They're Galaxy's seminar documents. I'd be interested to know if anything strikes you as unusual. The documents got lost in Norway.'

Schütz nodded, leafed through the presentations and

whistled through his teeth when he saw the list of participants. 'In the Middle East these gentlemen are the *crème de la crème* of investors. Between them they could easily rustle up a few hundred billion US dollars. Without leverage.'

He pointed to a column full of names. 'To my knowledge some of these are also clients of our bank. Especially direct investments in Swiss blue chips. But they're looked after directly by the boss,' he said, nodding towards the group.

At that moment Anne's family came out of a side building, which had once been a stable. Her mother was in tears and flanked by Anne's sisters. Her father walked stony-faced ahead of the gangly priest.

The murmur in the courtyard died down and for a moment there was silence. The family entered the church, followed by the mourners. First the elderly uncles and aunts. The woman in the wheelchair. Then the distant relatives Anne had perhaps seen once a year, who would return to their normal lives this evening and forget her.

A handful of younger people came next. Some manifested their grief with just a black tie or a dark blouse. Clearly they'd had no reason till now to buy themselves a black suit. Probably this was their first funeral. Many of Anne's friends were tearful, unable to comprehend such an early death.

Who could? Perhaps they'd been to the gym together last week, or spoken on the phone or gone shopping. Certainly, many of them would remember the last time they'd seen Anne. Some would regret unresolved matters, loose ends.

As if from afar he heard Schütz say, 'Hey, Winter, are you alright?' Schütz had noted Winter's absent expression and sympathetically placed a hand on his shoulder.

'I think so.' Unwilling to enter a discussion about his grief, all he said was, 'I'm sure that Anne's found herself a comfy cloud in heaven.' Schütz looked as though he didn't know whether Winter was joking or actually did believe in angels on clouds.

Winter didn't know either. Moving away from the wall, he said, 'Let's go in.'

Anne's bank colleagues filled the last two rows in the church. The simple wooden coffin, decorated with a summer bouquet, stood before the altar. Sunflowers and white roses. White, the colour of mourning in the East.

Winter found himself between Schütz and Dirk again. He looked at the backs of people's heads and ignored the priest's soothing words. Bare beams were visible on the ceiling of the church. Suddenly everybody stood for a hymn. Winter was relieved. The elderly relatives sang at the tops of their voices while his colleagues just moved their lips.

Only the CEO's attractive assistant surprised him with her rich and really tuneful voice. Winter recalled the documentation from her security check, which stated that she came from the traditional Emmenthal and played the accordion. Nudging Winter with his elbow, Dirk pointed his chin at the assistant and grinned.

Angela, Anne's youngest sister, stood up, placed a hand on the coffin and told stories from Anne's life. In her other hand she held a crumpled piece of paper full of writing, which she ignored. With considerable composure she spoke of the holidays they'd enjoyed by the sea, sandcastles, the treehouse – and how Anne had protected her on the way to and from school. Winter was moved and struggled to prevent his colleagues from noticing. The sister talked about how the three of them had spent a summer holiday going from one European city to the next, without much money but plenty of time.

Winter could hear stifled sobs in the front rows. Angela went on to say that Anne had been a right tearaway but someone you could always rely upon. He was grateful to Angela for her honest words and resolved to tell her this.

To Winter's amazement now the CEO stood up next, walked to the coffin with his head raised and turned to the congregation. He was clearly used to speaking in public. His deep voice resonated in the five-hundred-year-old church. He spoke of her talent, her wonderful personality, the suddenness with which Anne had been plucked from the prime of life and the painful loss, especially for the family.

Winter found it a bit out of place that the CEO, who had barely known Anne, should give a speech. He had to admit, however, that von Tobler had found the right words, bringing some consolation to the people who had gathered. Von Tobler finished, bowed his head and sat back down in Winter's row.

Another hymn. The small organ played. The priest quoted from the Bible, blessed the mourners and asked everyone to say the Lord's Prayer together. Winter's thoughts were with Anne once more. Images of moments they'd spent together flashed past.

Now the service was over and everybody stood. There was slight confusion about who was going to carry the coffin. Four elderly men from the third row, probably brothers of the father or mother, carefully lifted the coffin and followed the priest out of the church.

The sunlight was harsh and Winter frowned in the glare.

Walking around the church and down into the sloping cemetery, they gathered around the open grave. The coffin was gently lowered into the earth with the help of a green metal cradle. The priest prayed again and, one after the other, the mourners threw handfuls of earth from a battered wooden box into the grave. Winter was one of the last. He dropped the rose into the grave, closed his eyes and bowed his head for a few seconds.

Then it was over.

On the way back to the courtyard he had to pass through a small archway and shake the priest's hand. It felt clammy and a shiver ran down Winter's spine. The mourners huddled in groups in the courtyard, waiting to express their condolences.

After a few minutes of awkwardly hanging around, Anne's colleagues followed their boss, shook the family member's hands in turn and muttered a few words of comfort. When it was Winter's turn to speak to Angela he told her his name and said he'd been Anne's direct superior in the bank.

'Oh, Herr Winter,' she said. 'Nice that you could come.'

'I had to be here. I owed it to Anne.' Winter offered Angela his hand. 'What you said about her in the church really touched me. I wish you all the best. My deepest condolences,' he said, making to move on to avoid holding up the queue.

But Angela held on tight to his hand. 'Thank you.' She looked at him with tears in her eyes. 'Anne really liked you.'

What had Anne told her sister?

She smiled feebly and added, after a pause, 'Why didn't you speak?'

'I don't know.' Then he stuttered out an excuse: 'I'm not good at speaking in public.' He composed himself. 'If there's anything I can do for you, please give me a call.'

'Thanks,' she said, nodding at him with smiling eyes.

Then she turned to Dirk, who was standing somewhat awkwardly behind Winter. The guests were trickling out of the castle courtyard. Mediaeval attackers were better able to defend themselves with their shields when in retreat. On behalf of the family, the priest warmly invited all the mourners for a small reception in the restaurant 'Bären'. Winter wasn't hungry and he had an appointment.

Dirk nudged him. 'Such a sad story.'

Winter said: 'I need to understand it.'

'What do you mean? You really don't believe it was an accident, do you? That's the reason for all the research.'

Winter shrugged his shoulders.

Dirk continued, 'I get it. You've been away the last few days. But the bank's internal news and the newspapers talked of an accident. Caused by a fire.'

Winter hadn't read a paper over the past few days, nor had he checked the bank's intranet. The police were often reluctant to release information and the intranet's news site was nicknamed 'Pravda', Russian for 'truth'. 'I'm not sure,' Winter said out loud. He shook his head. 'It's my job to be paranoid. Do you have the details of Anne's phone calls?'

'Yes, here you are,' Dirk said, pulling out some folded computer printouts from his inside jacket pocket. He leafed through the lists that were stapled together. 'Her calls to and from landlines in the bank over the last four weeks. Thanks to VOIP that was a doddle. Here.' Dirk continued looking through the printouts and pointed to the third page. 'The calls to and from her mobile phone, also for the last four weeks. That wasn't so easy, but because we're a good client the provider was prepared to give us the data individually. Some of the numbers are anonymous, which means the caller withheld their number or the call came from a computer.'

The lists showed the caller's number, the date and the start and finish times of the calls, down to the second. Where the numbers were withheld only the duration of the call was given. Dirk handed Winter the list.

'Thanks. I hope this helps. What about Al-Bader's number? Any success there?'

'No, I'm afraid not. Not a chance. Zero. Nada. His number isn't registered in Europe and we had to go via the official channels.'

Winter turned to the fourth page. The two last calls from Anne's mobile were to a number Winter knew well. 24/07, 20:41:22 – 24/07, 20:41:45. Anne's status update. 25/07, 00:08:06 – 25/07, 00:08:22. Anne's call had lasted twenty-three seconds, the one from the policeman in the Höllentobel sixteen seconds.

Winter heard Anne's voice. 'Hi, Tom. It's me. Everything's fine. We're on our way with a twenty-minute delay, but the sunset is fantastic, unbelievable.' Then he pictured again her filthy, twisted body in the Höllentobel. Now, at least, Anne had been cleaned and was lying straight in a simple, wooden coffin. For a moment at least, this idea gave Winter the curious impression that everything had been cleared up. Thank goodness he'd brought the rose. He shook his head to disperse the images inside his head.

Looking at Dirk, Winter asked, 'Have you found out anything about my intruder and his client? Surely the guy's email address must lead somewhere.'

Dirk shrugged and shook his head. 'No.'

'Is it really that hard for a whiz like you?'

'You underestimate it. And maybe it's got nothing to do with the helicopter crash. Maybe…'

'Bullshit!' Winter barked. He couldn't restrain his anger any more. The funeral had shredded his nerves. The grief was affecting him badly. It made him furious. He was furious that he didn't know who was behind the murders. He was furious at himself because he hadn't made any real progress yet. And now he was venting his anger at Dirk, who was only trying his best. After a while he calmed down. 'I'm sorry, Dirk. I didn't mean it like that.'

Dirk looked away. 'It's okay.'

'What's wrong?'

'I'm sorry, but Känzig made it quite plain that I mustn't do any more "private" stuff at work and that I've got to focus squarely on the IT.'

'Fucking bullshit. Since when have you listened to Känzig?'

Now Dirk was getting worked up. 'He gave me a bit of a roasting because of the trade platform and your private affairs really aren't my number one priority.'

'Calm down. It's fine. And thanks anyway for this.' Winter pocketed the lists. Having reached Dirk's Passat, they shook hands and Dirk got in. Winter's Audi was a hundred metres further down, slightly on its own by the side of the road.

Everyone's in a hurry, he thought, either to get to their next appointment or to the reception.

Sitting on a bench, from which he could gaze down at the village surrounded by fields, Winter concentrated on the lists. But the figures swam before him. Finally he was on his own and no longer had to maintain his composure. The corners of his mouth twitched. Putting the lists to one side he leaned back. The unending, dark emptiness that had been pursuing him all morning enveloped Winter and took possession of him.

Anne was dead and buried. He'd never hold her in his arms again. He'd never hear her laugh again. He'd never see her sparkling eyes again. It was his fault, but there was nothing he could do about it. Winter slapped the bench.

He'd never told her that he loved her. What an idiot! Winter pressed the heels of his hands against his temples. The physical pain was nothing in comparison to the grief he felt inside. He bit his lip and felt his eyes becoming damp.

He bent forwards and tore his hair. With his elbows digging into his knees and his hands clenched tight he stared at the picture postcard landscape before him.

Without seeing it.

People at the foot of the hill were merrily hanging up paper lanterns for Swiss National Day, August 1, and getting ready for their family celebrations. The sunny landscape infuriated Winter. Perhaps it would be easier if it were autumn and starting to rain. He shook his head. He couldn't change the past. His mistakes would pursue him forever. Only the future remained. He could influence that. Or at least he believed he could.

Winter took a deep breath. After several more he calmed down. He would focus on solving the murders. Where were the telephone lists? Grabbing the papers, he got up and rested his foot on the bench for support. As he stood there he studied the printouts.

The calls from the bank were easy to identify because the first three digits were always the same. Winter leaned back and gazed into the distance. A sea of green. Then he turned back to the lists and remembered an unanswered question. Who had called Anne when she stopped at her parents' in Fraubrunnen on the way to Zürich? Around the time in question – about five o'clock – there were two calls:

24/07, 16:55:12 – 24/07, 16:55:52. The first three digits 'belonged' to the bank.

24/07, 17:02:01 – 24/07, 17:02:42. Number withheld.

## JULY 31 – 12:10

Winter slammed the Audi door, chucked the lists onto the passenger seat and drove off. As he passed through the village he had to concentrate on not driving too fast. Children in swimwear frolicked in the spray of a sprinkler, its water running into the road.

Grief and anger mingled. He felt angry at his lack of progress and at his colleagues, who were taking liberties with the truth and thinking only of themselves. And he was livid at the diffuse, intangible powers behind the murders.

He'd sunk his teeth into finding the murderers like a dog. But emotions were a double-edged sword. On the one hand they helped you make quick decisions. Emotions could animate you. Anger in your belly could unleash unimagined powers.

On the other hand, emotions blurred the senses, sometimes inducing rash behaviour. Winter knew that he could only strike at precisely the right moment if he were composed and patient.

During the drive back he focused on his next task. He programmed his GPS with the address of the firm where the helicopter was registered, the one that he'd seen circling above the Höllentobel.

Strittmatter's competitor had his base in a rural hamlet whose name Winter hadn't heard of till yesterday, and which lay in the Zürich–Basel–Bern triangle. An enormous sign in the shape of a helicopter pointed the way from the main road through a wood to a large clearing. The wood screened off the noise.

The helicopter base was an old farm. Winter drove across the clearing, past a herd of cattle and two, white, Robinson helicopters. He parked on the forecourt, switched off the engine and got out.

There were half a dozen cars: two gleaming off-road vehicles with broad tyres and advertising stickers with helicopters, and dark saloons with Zürich number plates. Business cars. A military vehicle from the air force. The barn had been renovated into a hangar. An orange windsock hung limply above the corrugated iron container that served as an improvised tower.

Winter closed the car door and headed for the shack. An information board was affixed outside; Winter ignored it. He knocked at the door and entered without waiting for an answer. The inside of the container was dark and divided into two by a sort of counter. Behind this, a man in a cap sat at a double desk, eating a pasta ready-meal and drinking a can of Coke.

When the man stood up Winter could make out in the dim light a smooth-shaven, tanned face. Clear eyes, around thirty-five. A helicopter logo on the cap. The fan on the counter was struggling in vain to battle the heat inside the container.

'Good afternoon. How may I help you?'

The man wore a short-sleeved, khaki shirt with loops buttoned onto the shoulders for attaching badges.

Winter took out his old police badge from his breast pocket. Resembling the Swiss identity card, it was genuine, with a Swiss cross at the front, a photo from earlier days and his name. The expiry date was printed on the back in small digits; it was some years ago now. When he left the police they'd forgotten to seize his ID.

'Good afternoon, please excuse me for interrupting you,' Winter said, pointing at the pasta. 'My name's Winter and I'm investigating a helicopter crash for Bern.'

Bern could refer to a number of things; the Swiss capital

was the seat of many different authorities. The man's hand was rough with residues of dirt beneath his nails from working in the stable. As they shook hands vigorously, Winter smiled at the man and put his badge away. Peering outside, he motioned to the window with his chin and asked out of curiosity, 'Doesn't it disturb those cows when choppers take off and land?'

'No, on the contrary, I get the impression that they rather like the activity. My father's been logging their milk output for ages and it's increased over the last few years.'

'May I ask how you hit on the idea of providing a helicopter service? It's a rather unusual idea.'

'I've always wanted to fly. But it's not easy for a farmer. When I visited my friend who'd emigrated to Canada, I got hooked on helicopters.' With a proud smile, he continued, 'These days everyone wants to be up in the air. Our speciality is photo flights. You can't imagine how many people want a photo of their house from the sky.' Stuck to the walls of the container were long photographic panoramas mounted on cardboard.

'Exciting.' Winter returned the smile and felt that the man was sufficiently warmed up for him to be able to broach the reason for his visit. 'The truth is, all I wanted to know was which of your clients was in one of your helicopters from the night of the twenty-fourth to the twenty-fifth of July – that's last Friday to Saturday.'

'None.'

'I wrote down the registration number.' Winter took a small piece of notepaper from his wallet and showed it to the man.

'Yes, that's one of my Robis.'

'But none of your clients chartered a Robi that night?'

'No. We flew ourselves.' Raising his cap slightly, the man scratched his head. 'We were commissioned to do it. A strange job. But we priced it based on the night-time tariff.'

'What does that mean?'

'I couldn't say. I don't like to give out information about my clients.'

'Oh, come, come. We can sort this out here, or would you like me to have you summoned to Bern?'

'No, okay.'

'How was it a strange job?'

'It came at short notice and late in the evening. By email.' Winter just nodded. It sounded familiar. 'You can book us via our website, you know. It was a freelance journalist for a local paper, wanting pictures of a helicopter crash. It was something I was interested in personally and we specialize in photography, especially night photography. We're completely booked out tomorrow: sunsets with bonfires. He sent us the coordinates, made an offer we couldn't refuse and we were on our way.'

'We?'

'Me and my brother. I fly, he snaps away.'

'What happened to the pictures?'

'As soon as we got back we uploaded and emailed them. So that our client didn't miss his deadline.'

A lie. Much too late. They would have had to improvise. 'Can I see the email?' Winter asked.

The helicopter pilot turned around and woke the computer from its sleep mode. Clicking through his emails, he found the relevant one and waved. Winter went around the counter and bent over the pilot. The sender called himself Harald Schneider and said he was a freelancer for the *Schwyzer Landbote*. No telephone number. A Hotmail address. Another trace that would get lost in the infinity of the web. 'Did he pay?' Winter asked.

'Yes, he posted cash in an envelope. Rounded up to the nearest hundred.'

'What about the photos?'

'They were good. We used a Nikon with a fast lens and thermographic filter.'

He opened one of the attachments in the email reply and the accident site filled the screen. It was a ghostly setting and almost as light as in daytime, but with a green tinge. The helicopter wreck shone brightly because of the heat it emitted. Winter could make out the policeman, the fireman, the alpine cowherd and himself standing next to the car. Anne's twisted body was pale yellow.

Taking a closer look, the pilot said, 'Is that you?'

Winter just nodded. His face was easily recognisable. The email had been sent at 01:42. Someone had spotted him in the photo and issued the order, via another anonymous email address, to monitor his computer. Who knew him?

On the drive back to Bern Winter received a call from Strittmatter's cousin. On July 24 Strittmatter had indeed flown directly from his base in Valais to Zürich across the Lötschberg. Winter thanked her for having called back, then put his foot down. He left the motorway at the football stadium and drove into the third underground floor of a public car park in Bern city centre, where the bank had eight spaces permanently reserved for clients and staff, marked with the bank's logo and a sign that read 'Private: clients only'. There were internal rules detailing the procedure to follow if you wanted to book one of the expensive parking spaces.

He parked beside Anne's Mini Cooper S, an old original. She'd loved this car. Winter recalled her almost childlike excitement when she'd found it in a classified ad and bought it in good condition off an elderly teacher. She'd cruised around everywhere in that Mini.

On the day she died Anne had driven back to Bern from Fraubrunnen. A journey of about twenty minutes. Then she'd left the car in the underground garage. In all likelihood, Anne had removed her pistol before visiting her parents, then left it in the car.

The SIG Mosquito must be here.

What then? Was Anne picked up? By the anonymous caller? Did she opt to take the train because of the risk of getting caught in an evening rush-hour jam? After all you could comfortably get to Zürich in an hour by train and it stopped right at the airport.

Although Winter didn't have a key, he did have the relevant experience. One of his training instructors had been a reformed car burglar. In a nearby bin he found a strip of metal three metres long and a centimetre wide, the sort used to fasten boxes on palettes, and folded it in the middle.

Winter looked around. Nobody was watching.

Carefully he slipped the metal strip between the glass and frame of the driver's door, then jiggled about inside. Luckily these old cars didn't have electronic central locking. Winter was a bit out of practice, but within a few seconds he found the hidden mechanical lever and the door unlocked with a click. A Citroën drove past. Winter opened up, squeezed himself into the black seat behind the wheel and closed the door behind him.

A green, miniature Christmas tree dangled incongruously from the rear-view mirror. He looked around, wound down the window, switched on the radio and the volume made him jump. Music reverberated loudly around the walls of the underground car park and Winter quickly turned down the volume. In the glove compartment he found the car's papers, some tissues and a pair of gloves. He felt beneath the driver's seat. Nothing. He leaned over to the passenger side and put his hand under there too.

Winter felt the cold metal of the pistol and the leather grip. Anne had slid her gun beneath the seat so nobody could see it. Winter took out the pistol.

It was 3:00P.M. and time for the hourly news bulletin. Winter listened with one ear while he checked the weapon. The magazine was full and the gun clean. The newsreader said something about an opposition party calling on someone to resign. Winter wasn't listening properly and suddenly felt the urge to get out of the underground car park as quickly as possible.

Then he sat up and focused on the voice coming from the radio: '... the oil rig sank in a few minutes. There are no clues yet as to who might be behind the attack. The authorities estimate that up to thirty people have died. The Canadian prime minister has interrupted his holiday to visit the site of the atrocity. In a statement, Greenpeace has expressed its concerns about the leaking oil. Stock markets have reacted to the news with significant falls in share prices. Berlin: today the German chancellor welcomed the Russian president...'

Winter put the pistol in his pocket and switched off the radio.

He leaned back, exhausted, and laid his head on the low headrest. He took a deep breath. Was he seeing ghosts or was he just tired? His eyes were burning; he probably looked ghastly. The rings under his eyes must be dark black. He flipped down the sun visor for its mirror. An envelope fell into his lap.

It was white, rectangular, made of quality paper and folded once in the middle. He turned it around. It said 'Anne' in elegantly looped handwriting.

Winter was wide awake again. He carefully opened the unstuck envelope. Inside was a piece of paper, folded twice, written by hand. Smoothing the letter flat, Winter held it beneath the courtesy light. He thought he recognized the handwriting. Five paragraphs. A love letter to Anne, an unequivocal love letter, signed, 'All my love, J.'

Winter took the motorway to Lake Geneva. The engine purred at 3,000 rpm, complementing U2's *Rattle and Hum*. The evening sun shone into his face and he put on his sunglasses.

The letter had stirred his hunting instinct. He was determined to find out who had been bugging him and who had sent the helicopter with the photographer. Counter-espionage.

Winter had a busy afternoon behind him. He'd been writing too, but not a love letter. In an internet café he'd sent himself a message from an anonymous email address he'd set up. In bad German, shot through with French expressions. Sender: a nameless banker who was shocked when he'd heard about the crash and was desperate to talk to Winter. But only in private, because the information he had was sensitive. Highly sensitive!!! Three exclamation marks. They should meet at 'Le Baron Tavernier' above Montreux.

Tibère, a colleague from Geneva who'd become a friend over the years, had been earmarked for the role of the Geneva banker. When Winter called him, he agreed at once, but on two conditions. He insisted first on paying and second on choosing the restaurant himself. He knew one above Montreux with a good view and excellent food. Winter was sceptical. Normally the rule was: the better the view, the worse the food. And vice-versa. But he trusted his friend. Moreover, the restaurant and its setting were right for the purpose.

Later, back home, Winter agreed by email. The little box in his connection would do the trick. The bait had been laid. Winter was certain that his opponent would be waiting for him and, more importantly, for his pretend informant. He would turn the tables.

The motorway dropped steeply, 'When Love Comes to Town' was banging out and Lake Geneva stretched out before Winter. The water was turquoise, the French mountains beyond Évian dark blue and the sky, light blue. Playground of the beautiful and rich. Only platinum record sellers and Formula 1 world champions could afford the astronomical property prices here. Or Charlie Chaplin.

Leaving the motorway, Winter drove across the terraced hillside vineyards. Arriving at the restaurant car park five minutes later, he turned off the engine and the music. Tibère had been right about the view.

Before Winter got out he switched from relaxed driving mode to hunter mode. He studied the parked cars and made a note of the registration numbers. Most were parked forwards. Only two drivers had made the effort to reverse into their places.

Le Baron Tavernier had an open lounge outside for drinks and a glass-covered area for eating. The guests met outside for an aperitif or two, then sat in the weatherproof section for dinner. It was still early evening and both terrace and restaurant were only just half full.

Winter sat in a square, thickly cushioned wicker chair, ordered a glass of the local white wine and waited for his friend. It was a grand panorama, but Winter was working.

The restaurant was nestled on the hillside and only accessible via steps. Restaurant and terrace were shielded from nosy onlookers by walls and hedges.

Studying the guests, Winter wondered how he would try to shadow someone here. The people who had him under surveillance knew the time and place of his meeting. They would play it safe and have arrived earlier.

They were probably within a radius of twenty metres.

Someone was probably keeping a watch on the car park.

Probably near the entrance.

They had probably reserved a table.

The problem for his pursuers was that they didn't know the informant and couldn't be certain if the restaurant was just meant to be the meeting place or whether they'd stay there for the evening. To cover all options the tails would be positioned so that they could move quickly in any direction.

Winter reckoned it would be a man and woman posing as a couple. That would look most natural in the lounge. Or two men pretending to be out on a business dinner.

Winter focused on four people. A young man in a suit, with gelled hair, sitting in a wicker chair beside the entrance, a bunch of red roses on the table in front of him.

Sitting at the neighbouring table were two elderly men in suits and loosened ties, both with paunches and briefcases. Salesmen. Winter had picked up scraps of German when he stepped onto the terrace. One was drinking Coke, the other had a glass of whisky.

The fourth candidate was an elegantly dressed woman in the entrance area, around thirty years of age. She was pacing up and down on her mobile, gesticulating with a Latin temperament. Winter couldn't see the expression on her face. Was she liaising with a partner keeping watch over the car park? These days a woman on the phone was the man reading the newspaper of yesteryear. Conspicuously inconspicuous.

The wine arrived with a bowl full of exotic nuts. Winter insisted on paying immediately. A first test. Out of the corner of his eye he could see that the woman was still on the phone, the two old men hadn't interrupted their conversation, while the young man picked up his mobile. Was he calling his girlfriend or informing his partner?

Winter made a bet. Favourite was the young guy with gelled

hair, second place the woman on the phone, and third the two businessmen.

The young, white wine was refreshingly cool and effervescent. He took a second sip and put the glass on the table.

Time for test number two.

He got up, took off his jacket and hung it on the back of the chair to mark his territory. He wandered to the restaurant. When he opened the glass door he saw that the woman on the phone had taken a few steps in his direction and turned her upper body towards him. She was interested in him. Whether professionally or otherwise he couldn't yet tell. He went to the toilets. As he was washing his hands, one of the two businessmen with a paunch came in. The race was wide open again.

Back on the terrace he saw Tibère coming down the steps. He seemed in a good mood and was wearing a light, linen suit, an open-necked, white shirt and pointed leather shoes. Elegant as ever. Tibère was at home in the clubs and bars around Geneva. They shook hands, gave each other a clap on the shoulder and both said how happy they were to see each other again.

The young man with gelled hair and the woman at the entrance were both on the phone. The businessman was back on the terrace. In French, Winter said, 'Come, I'm sitting at the back.'

Placing a hand on the arm of a passing waitress, Tibère ordered a cocktail that Winter had never heard of. Tibère explained in detail to the pretty waitress what he wanted, then sat down with Winter.

'How lovely that it worked out this time!'

Winter could see that a young woman had joined the man with gel in his hair. He half rose from his deep armchair. They kissed. From a distance it all looked genuine. He handed her the flowers. Either they really were together or the woman had been responsible for monitoring the car park.

Tibère told the anecdote of a client who had put his
valuables and identity documents into a deposit box, lost the
key and forgot his code and then couldn't prove his identity
because his passport was in the safe. A dilemma. Listening with
one ear, Winter grinned and watched the woman talking to the
waiter by the glass door.

After a while they went into the restaurant. Tibère had
reserved a table to the rear with a view. Winter had a good
sight of the guests and divided his attention three ways: one
third for Tibère, one third for the view and one third for his
tails.

As he and Tibère ordered, the young couple entered the
restaurant and were allocated a table two rows away from
them. The woman on her mobile had vanished and the two
portly men were still on the terrace.

The red wine arrived after the salmon carpaccio. Tibère
tasted it, nodded and the waiter filled the balloon-shaped
glasses one third of the way up. They toasted and wished each
other the best of health. Winter sniffed the glass and took a sip.
'Excellent choice, Tibère.'

'Thanks. The owner of the vineyard is one of our clients. I
buy a few boxes off him each year. He managed to modify the
land-use plan of his commune so that part of his vineyard fell in
the construction zone. Now he's a gentleman of independent
means. But he's one of the unluckiest fellows I know, because
he's terribly bored.'

'Well, money on its own never makes you happy.'

'But it is a comfort.' They laughed, then Tibère asked
seriously, 'Have you found anything out yet?'

Winter outlined his research and they discussed their plan
for the evening. Winter described the behaviour of the people
he suspected. Tibère was sitting with his back to the tails,
but didn't need to turn around. Out of professional habit, he
too had made a mental note of the people in his vicinity. He

recalled having seen the young woman who'd been given the flowers in a car in the car park.

'A VW Passat with Zürich plates?' Winter asked.

'Yes, parked backwards. She looked like she was putting on make-up.'

The steaks arrived. Rumours were circulating that Tibère's bank was aiming at taking over a specialized part of the financial group behind Winter's bank. Rumours were rumours, fuelled by speculation. The conversation moved to Winter's house, his unfinished terrace. When the double espressos arrived the two friends were up to date with each other's news and looking forward to the special dessert.

The couple had decided against pudding and were now having coffee too. The businessmen had only moved into the restaurant half an hour ago and were waiting for their main course. Winter wondered about the woman with the mobile. Was she lurking in the car park?

After much discussion Winter was finally able to take the bill off Tibère. Today his arguments definitely carried greater weight. After all, Tibère was working for him in a sense. As they left the restaurant, joking, out of the corner of their eyes they could see one of the businessmen stand up. And the young man was waving his wallet.

Tibère and Winter slowly climbed the steps. Once at the top they had an unhurried look around. The sun had set around half an hour earlier. A lost cumulus cloud glowed pink in the sky.

The two of them took a post-dinner walk. They strolled along the narrow road that snaked through the vineyards high above the lake. The asphalt radiated the sun's warmth stored during the day. An emerald lizard darted past, disappearing between the limestones. On either side, amongst the sea of leaves, Winter could see wine grapes already well formed, but still small and solid. They smelled of summer.

The wine-growers had terraced every conceivable patch of

ground. The head-height vine stocks stood in rank and file, fastened to wires tensed between metal posts. The terraces covered the gently curved slopes like a patchwork quilt.

The two friends were enjoying a leisurely chat. With each footstep Tibère's elegant shoes made a clicking sound. They stopped at a viewing point, leaned against the railing and gazed down at Lake Geneva.

Behind them they saw the young couple, arm in arm. They were walking fairly slowly, not wanting to overtake Winter and Tibère.

Simple, Winter thought.

The couple stopped about thirty metres away and started kissing passionately. The bunch of roses rocked back and forth.

They waited.

A small, noisy motorbike came from the opposite direction and chugged past.

The two men looked at each other with raised eyebrows. Romeo and Juliet. Had they been mistaken? Was it a genuine couple kissing for real? Or were they just pretending? In the twilight they couldn't make out the faces. The man had put his arm around the woman and his summer jacket tightened. The outline of a holster was visible at the man's lower back. Romeo was armed.

The couple stopped kissing. They leaned on the railings and looked out at the lake. The man pointed with his right hand to the far side of the lake and whispered something to the woman. A right hander.

Otherwise not a soul to be seen on the road.

Winter wanted to keep the momentum. He motioned to the restaurant with his chin and they slowly got moving.

The couple made a point of ignoring the men.

When he reached Romeo's blind spot, Winter took a few silent and rapid steps towards him. 'Good evening!' he said, tapping him on the shoulder.

The couple spun around and Romeo aimed a matt silver pistol at Winter's head. For Winter, the next few moments passed in slow motion. He knew exactly what he was doing because he'd practised these movements ten thousand times.

With a smile, Winter turned his head towards the lake and the young man's eyes automatically followed his gaze. This split second was enough for Winter to grab the barrel of the pistol.

His left hand wrenched the barrel down and outwards. Any shot fired would miss. Then his thumb dug into the pressure point of the hand holding the pistol and, with a circular movement, Winter's right hand seized the gun. He waited for resistance, then with both hands locked the man's wrists, elbows and shoulders.

Romeo was disarmed, bent forwards and in a painful lock. If necessary, Winter could dislocate his shoulder with a little jerk. The shoulder capsule was full of sensitive nerves.

Juliet shrieked and launched an attack with the bunch of roses. Tibère had no wish to end up with a scratched face. He ducked beneath the roses and used the momentum to put the woman in an arm lock. The flowers were on the floor and Tibère announced, 'Sorted.'

Winter tossed the young man's pistol into the roadside ditch, manoeuvred him to the railings and forced his head through them. With his free hand Winter grabbed the gelled hair and yanked the head back. Romeo had a great view but couldn't enjoy it.

'If you lie I'll break your wrist, followed by your elbow, then shoulder and finally your neck. Is that clear?' To give emphasis to his threat, Winter slightly increased the pressure each time on the pertinent body part. The young man nodded as best he could. Winter heard a rasping 'Yes'.

'Right, then. First question: What's your name?' Always good to start with a simple one.

'Romero.'

His guess had almost been spot on.

'And?' A little tug on the hair.

'Sanchez.'

'Where do you live?'

'Zürich.'

'Address?' The man gave the address of a working-class district of the city.

'Who do you work for?'

'I'm a freelance PI – private investigator.'

'Who's your client?'

'I don't know.'

Without any warning Winter broke the man's wrist. When the tendon snapped it made a noise like a guitar string breaking. The cartilage between his forearm and the back of his hand crunched. The man let out a stifled scream.

'Second attempt,' Winter continued. 'Who is your client?'

'Please don't!' Romero panted and with his hand in the man's hair Winter could feel sweat streaming from his head. He waited. He had all the time in the world.

The man gasped and mumbled something.

'Louder, please.'

'This afternoon I got a call from the detective agency Schmitt, Berger & Partners.' Winter had heard of them; they specialized in financial crime, charged horrific fees and operated within the grey areas of the law. 'If they're short on people I sometimes work for them. They get the jobs I find hard to come by.' Under gentle pressure it suddenly all came spurting out of the young man. 'Schmitt said he had a simple but urgent job in a large case of financial espionage. He wanted to know *who* you were meeting. I agreed and Schmitt emailed me a photo of you and the address of the restaurant. That's all.'

Winter said nothing. He wanted to sense if the young man was deliberately withholding something from him. He shifted his weight and increased the pressure on Romero's shoulders.

'Please let me go. I've told you everything,' the whining detective said.

'Where's the photo of me?'

'In my inside pocket.'

Winter let go of his hair, wiped the sticky residue of the gel on the man's shoulder and felt in his inside jacket pocket. The photo he pulled out had been substantially enlarged. It was from the brochure for an international conference on fighting financial crime. Anybody could find this photo. Winter put it in his pocket.

From the man's back pocket he took out a wallet. A driving licence in the name of Romero Sanchez. Cheap business cards. A loving photo of Romero and his girlfriend in a bikini on some beach. Winter stuffed the wallet back into Romero's back pocket and said, 'So she's your girlfriend?'

'Yes, I thought we could spend a nice evening together.' That's why it had looked so genuine. Romero had wanted to mix business with pleasure.

Winter let go of the man's arm. Romero hit his head against the railings. He stood up and inspected his broken wrist. Tibère let go of Romero's girlfriend, who picked up the bunch of flowers.

Juliet exploded and savaged her boyfriend with the roses, now badly damaged. 'You told me we were just going for an evening out, you idiot! With a bit of observation on the side. But then these two,' she said, pointing scornfully at Winter and Tibère, 'almost killed us!' Romeo tried as best he could to defend himself against his girlfriend's attacks.

Winter and Tibère grinned at one another and returned to the restaurant car park. Meanwhile the couple continued to argue at the tops of their voices.

Tibère wiped his hands and said, 'Why would Schmitt, Berger & Partners be interested in you?' He looked at Winter and added, after a short pause, 'Or did you break one of their friends' wrists?'

'No idea. I've never had any direct dealings with them over the last few years. I expect I ought to pay them a friendly visit in the coming days.'

'Let's have another drink.'

By now the sky was almost black and the two men could see the moon and the stars. Via the steps they went back to the terrace, which was practically empty. Winter ordered a Talisker, Tibère a gin fizz. They let the evening come to a close exchanging tall tales. Around eleven o'clock they shook hands in the car park and Tibère sped away towards Geneva in his Alfa GT.

Before Winter got into his Audi, he took a final glance at the lake and the lights of the villages along its bank. Tibère had been right: the view, food and company were excellent. Winter started up the engine and switched on his headlights and car stereo. U2's 'Helter Skelter'. He released the handbrake and looked in the rear-view mirror. There was a movement behind him.

The wire noose of a garrotte strangled his neck. Immediately he tried to thrust his fingers beneath the wire yanking him against the headrest and cutting off his air passage and blood flow. Winter's fingernails dug into his neck's skin, drawing blood as they scratched in desperation.

Pressing his chin to his chest, Winter tensed every neck muscle. He tried to hoot his horn, but his fingers were trapped by the wire. He braced himself with his feet against his attacker. The engine screeched momentarily before dying. Winter jerked to one side. But the garrotte was looped around the headrest, preventing any sideways movement.

In the mirror he could see a dark figure with a stocking over the head with eyeholes. Unlike the amateur earlier, this was a cool professional. Were he and Romero working together?

Time was running against Winter. 'Helter Skelter' was finished. Did Tibère have a passenger too? Was his final hour striking? The food, view and company of their last supper had been excellent, was his last thought. Then Winter lost consciousness. How deathly quiet it was. Nobody had noticed the attack.

With his gloved right hand, the man took out a roll of industrial-strength tape, tore off a strip and stuck it over Winter's mouth. He fastened a longer piece over Winter's eyes. Just to be sure, he kept hold of the two wooden ends of the garrotte with his other hand.

You could never tell if someone was really unconscious or just pretending. Still using one hand only, he took out a cable tie, of the sort used by half the police forces in the world to tie hands and feet. These single-use ties could only be pulled in one direction. He wrapped it around Winter's wrists, which hung limply beneath his chin, and pulled the ribbed, plastic loop tight. Only then did he loosen the garrotte and free Winter's fingers. His bound hands fell into his lap.

The man on the back seat took out a second plastic tie, raised Winter's arms and fastened his hands to the passenger headrest. Then he removed the stocking from his own head, got out of the car, opened the passenger door and dragged Winter over. First his torso then his legs. Had someone happened to witness this scene from a distance they would thought it was a drunk person being hauled into the seat by a mate. The man walked around the car, made a quick call on his mobile, got in and drove off.

When Winter regained consciousness he was freezing. It was dark. He couldn't see anything or open his taped mouth. He was slumped outside on some hard, narrow bench. Someone was pouring water on his head. He shivered, shuddered and realized that his numb hands were bound.

His jacket had been pulled down over his shoulders, restricting his arms. The bench had no backrest. He tried to move his feet, but these were bound too. A voice behind him said, 'Morning. Sleep well?'

Winter shook his head. Although his eyes were blindfolded by thick tape he could make out a light-grey strip. His nose tautened the tape across his cheeks, allowing a small slit for his eyes.

He craned his neck and thrust out his chin, but all around him was night. He was definitely not inside, for a wind was blowing and he could smell water, mould and moss. The blood throbbed inside his head.

He felt dreadful and was afraid he might throw up. He didn't want to choke on his own vomit.

But if the man had intended to kill him, he could have done

it ages ago. The fact that he was alive meant that they still needed him. Winter carefully moved his head and attempted a recce of his surroundings through the slit between his nose and the tape. It took a while for his eyes to function again properly. The grey was water. It was about fifty metres below him. On either side he could make out black, wet cliffs that fell vertically.

He was not sitting on a bench, but on the broad handrail of a bridge, his feet pointing outwards. A mere nudge from the man behind him would send Winter plummeting. His pulse was racing. A sadist.

When the man clapped him on the shoulder, Winter's stomach contracted. 'I'm just the messenger,' he said.

He tore the tape from Winter's mouth and Winter greedily sucked air into his lungs. The oxygen calmed him, and after a few deep breaths he asked, 'Good work. Who are you?' Nobody was immune to a compliment and he had the feeling that he didn't have much time left to get to know his abductor.

'Thanks. You can call me Max.'

Winter tried to place the dialect, but without any success. He was sure that Max was a false name, but that was irrelevant. He needed to keep the dialogue going. As long as they were talking he was alive.

'Max. How nice. May I enquire why you abducted me? What have I done to you?'

'Nothing personal.' Max wasn't particularly talkative. Winter could hear the man fiddling with something behind him. He tried moving his head to glimpse through the slit what was happening. But he couldn't turn around too emphatically without slipping from the rail and plunging to his death. Max seemed to be alone – a sign of self-confidence.

Winter slid backwards. Noticing this tentative escape Max said, 'No way!' grabbed Winter by the belt and shoved him back into his original position. Max was both strong and observant. Winter's brain was working on overdrive. There must be some sort of opportunity. He tried moving his legs but they were tightly bound at the ankles.

'That's that done,' Max said to himself. And to Winter, he said, 'Pay attention. I want you to give a message to your boss.'

Why can't he just send an email? Winter thought. Then he said in disbelief, 'Känzig? What has that bastard got me messed up in?'

'No. The old man. You're to tell von Tobler to keep his nose out.'

Herr Dr von Tobler, CEO of the bank. Winter's mentor and guardian. Winter had no idea what von Tobler was to keep his nose out of.

'Out of what?'

Max hesitated briefly, Winter sensed he was having to improvise. He hadn't been banking on a counter question.

'He knows. You lot need to keep out of the business in the Middle East.'

'Max, that doesn't help me. We work across the globe. None of this is going to be of any use if you don't tell me what it's about.'

'Shut it! Enough chit-chat.' Winter could hear Max moving away, opening a car door and closing it again. Then he felt Max run a knife down his spine, the blade cutting open his wet shirt as it went. His back was wet. His arms were bound by his rolled-down jacket, his hands by the cable tie.

'Max, what do you want?'

'Shut it!' Max repeated. Winter felt Max writing something on his back in felt tip. His throat burned. Max was making sure that the message would be delivered if Winter died. 'Did you use a permanent marker?' Winter asked.

Max gave Winter a slap from behind. 'What did I tell you? Shut it!'

'Listen, mate, you've got to work on your vocabulary. Shut it, shut it, shut it. Not very imaginative.' Winter changed his tactics and mimicked Max. Chatting hadn't helped. Perhaps Max would make a mistake if he provoked him instead.

Time was running out.

Max wrote slowly and carefully and Winter got the impression that he was going over letters twice. Then he felt Max write an exclamation mark and underline the message – double underline.

Max took a few steps back, inspected his message and said calmly to himself, 'Right.' He put his mouth close to Winter's ear and said softly, but unmistakably, 'Keep out! Is that clear?'

Max vanished. Winter used the opportunity to try to free himself from his straitjacket. He twisted his shoulders and arms. The jacket slid further down; now he could move his elbows. Max came back and put a knife to Winter's throat.

'Stay nice and still, and nothing will happen. Do you get me?'

Winter nodded and contemplated trying a head butt. If Max was standing right behind him, he could catch him on the forehead. But there was the risk of slipping and falling. He could feel Max doing something at his feet. Then Max sliced through the cable tie fastening his hands.

Winter immediately grabbed onto the wall.

Ripping the sticky tape from Winter's eyes, Max said, 'Bye bye.'

The gorge yawned before Winter and seemed to drop into infinity, bordered by black, shining, wet cliffs.

Suddenly he could hear the rushing of the water. Or was that the blood in his head? Winter looked up. An orange stripe glowed above the fir forest. Sunrise. Executions always took place at sunrise. Luckily, however, he was not in a gloomy prison yard, but outside in nature. And he was still alive.

Winter tried moving his feet, but they were still bound. He slid from the wall and found his footing on a narrow ledge. Then he let go with his right hand and swivelled around in a flash. Winter grabbed the sleeves of Max's coat.

Max was wearing black. He was blond, pale and quiet. Even his eyebrows above deep-set eyes were blond. Max jerked himself free and took a step backwards. Shifting his weight to his left foot, which was in a laced-up combat boot, he shot a karate kick at Winter's ribs. Winter couldn't get out of the way and his spine made a cracking noise. For a moment he thought it was broken. The momentum of the kick spun Winter around, his feet slipped from the ledge, and now he was just holding onto the railings with his left hand.

Beneath him the water and rocks.

His fingers were slipping.

Above him were the railings and Max's silhouette. 'Happy August 1st,' Max said, giving Winter's fingers a firm kick. The boot broke the nail of his middle finger, digging into the sensitive skin. Winter screamed and let go of the railings in pain.

# AUGUST 1 – 03:53

Winter plummeted. His arms flailing about, he kept falling ever further. Slowly to begin with, then gathering speed. With his bound legs he tried to stop himself somewhere. Hopeless. Gravity was pulling him inexorably into the depths.

His head overtook his feet.

Winter saw the ravine beneath the bridge.

He saw the arch of the bridge from below.

Greenish blocks of stone.

Winter was spinning head over heels. The smooth black cliffs, the water and the orange stripe of sunlight flashed past his eyes. He'd expected that the final moments of his life would pass by in time-lapse. Winter sucked in the nature around him. The colours were brutally intense. The orange stripe on the horizon was dazzling, the wet cliffs, jet black. A verdant fir tree flew past. A Christmas tree? In summer? He closed his eyes.

From his throat came an uncontrolled, guttural scream.

It wasn't a scream of fear but liberation. It was over and Winter was on his way. The water beneath him was steel blue, reflecting the morning sky. Winter felt relief. He would plunge into the water rather than being splattered into pulp on a rock.

The only question was how deep the water was at this point. Generally you could wade through these little rivers. An image from his childhood popped into his mind. Once, on a school trip, they had to cross a knee-deep stream barefoot. The adolescent Winter had bravely supported the pretty girl who sat one row in front of him in class. The girl reminded Winter now of Anne. Anne laughing mischievously.

Impact. His head plunged into the water, followed by his neck, shoulders and his back, with the message written on it. The water was cold and shot into his mouth and nose. Then Winter was yanked back. As he sailed up through the air, his first thought was: This must be the way to heaven. Turning his head, he saw that he was hanging from an elastic bungee rope.

Winter laughed out loud in relief. He flew up about half the distance of his fall, before plummeting back down and diving into the water for a second time. He ended up hanging head first in the water. He could feel the flickering tension of the rope on his ankles. His lungs were empty from screaming. He didn't want to drown. A gentle current pulled him under water, tugging on the rope.

Tensing his stomach muscles, he held on tight to his trousers and pulled his head above water. Deep breath. His lungs filled with the morning air. The wet cliffs were still there. Far above him he saw the black strip of the bridge, but no sign of Max. The sky was bright.

Winter tore the tape from his feet and hauled himself up. He untied the rope and let himself fall back down into the water. He was free. Saved. Winter stretched out his arms, manoeuvred himself beneath the bridge and waded ashore onto a small gravel beach. There will be barbecues here tonight, Winter thought. To celebrate Switzerland's national day. Piss-up included.

He inspected his freezing body. Abrasions on his wrists, neck and ankles, but no permanent damage. Most painful was his broken fingernail. Then he made an inventory. His keys and wallet were still there. They were wet, but Max hadn't got his hands on them. Astonishingly his mobile phone was still in his coat too, but it wasn't working any more. The electronics didn't like the water.

A biting wind blew through the ravine. Shivering, he climbed the steep footpath to the road. He carefully crept the last few metres through the thick undergrowth, but the bridge was empty. Max had stolen his car. Winter walked to the middle of the bridge, looked down and shuddered once more. The rope was hanging limply from the railings.

His body frozen, Winter began jogging along the road. Perhaps a car would take him to the nearest station. But on August 1st nobody was driving to work. Apart from a dairy farmer on his way to the creamery. Cows didn't have holidays.

After about five minutes the terrain became flatter and soon afterwards the forest thinned out. The sun had just risen and was casting long shadows. The church spire of the nearest village was about two kilometres away. In the distance Winter could see a railway line and a road. He was back in civilisation. The rattle of a small motorbike sounded behind him, growing louder. A fat man in a long, black, leather coat chugged past with half a dozen shopping bags hanging from the handlebars.

He jogged towards the village through yellow cornfields. Now the sun was warming him too. A bilingual place-name sign told him that he was somewhere near the border between French- and German-speaking Switzerland. Winter passed a farm and reached the heart of the village. A few stone houses, the 'Hôtel du Cheval Blanc', a post office, a small general store and a white church. Not a soul about. He would surely find a phone booth at the station.

Winter was amazed to find his car beside the station shelter. How obliging of Max to park here. Either he'd been collected by an accomplice, or he'd simply jumped on a train. Winter circumspectly walked around his Audi. The bonnet was still warm. No visible traces on the tarmac outside the station. Winter peered under the car and carefully pulled the door handle. Locked. He put his hand between the right rear tyre and the mudguard and felt around. Luckily he had a spare key in a small metal box.

Before Winter drove off he called Tibère from the payphone of the unattended station. There was no reply on his landline. He left a message, asking him to call back. Tibère's mobile number wasn't listed in directory enquiries and his damp mobile, where Tibère's number was stored, wasn't working. He'd try again later.

Forty minutes later he was back home. The dry stem in his door frame was intact. Inside he took off his damp clothes, left his mobile and wallet out in the sun to dry, and went into the bathroom. Just as he was about to get into the shower he remembered his tattoo. Studying his shoulder blade in the mirror, he deciphered the smudged letters.

'Keep out!' underlined twice. Thinking back to Max and the bridge, Winter shuddered. He got out his digital camera and photographed his back. Then he had a long, warm shower. He was tired after the night he'd had. Although it was a public holiday Winter was unable to relax. He couldn't reach Tibère on any of his three numbers. Winter left a message on each while making himself some coffee.

He printed out the photos of his back, ate a substantial breakfast, filled sulky Tiger's bowl and sat on the wooden balcony. The terrace beneath him still looked the same. Although it was only a few days ago that he'd been working on it, now it seemed like an eternity. After Anne's death he was no longer in the mood to finish it. First he had to find out who had called her, and who had sent the love letter.

As he drank his third cup of coffee, Tiger came skulking up, leaped onto his lap, curled up and allowed Winter to fondle him. Tiger had probably had a strenuous night behind him, too. He was a hunter. Tiger purred blissfully.

The fact that someone had taken the effort to tail Winter and push him from the bridge meant that he must be close to something.

But what?

It also meant that this someone was sparing no expense. Romero, respectively Schmitt, Berger & Partners and Max weren't exactly cheap. Winter studied the printout of his back. Keep out!

Of what?

What had Max said? 'You lot need to keep out of the business in the Middle East.' Schütz had talked about opening a branch there.

Max was just the messenger.

Von Tobler owed him some answers. Pensively, he rubbed his sore neck. He had no choice but to ruin von Tobler's August 1$^{st}$.

Von Tobler lived in Oberhofen on Lake Thun. Winter had about half an hour in the car to prepare for his conversation with the bank's CEO. A shower, fresh clothes and coffee had worked wonders.

After the motorway exit at Thun he meandered along the narrow roads to Oberhofen. The commune was on the gold coast of Lake Thun, a paradise for rich pensioners with a view of the lake and the Alps. The fancy golf course at Interlaken was a short drive away and the place was full of restaurants with starched linen napkins.

Winter steered his Audi slowly through the narrow streets of the winding village centre and drove past Oberhofen Castle. This feudal residence, now open to the public, dated from the era when Bern still owned half of Switzerland and parts of France. Over time this poor fishing village had become one of the richest and most tax-efficient communes.

Because of the August 1st celebrations the village square was closed off. A few men were building a small stage with a lectern for local politicians, while women were unloading floral decorations from a van. Winter turned and took a narrow road up the hill. Von Tobler lived a little outside the village in a grand eighteenth-century villa, which he had 'slightly upgraded' to include a heated pool and private tennis court.

Winter drove along an avenue of poplars that led to a wrought-iron gate decorated with the crest of an old Bern family. He stopped, checked out of professional curiosity the fine electric wire on the wall overgrown with ivy, looked into one of the three cameras and pressed the intercom through his open car-window.

'Good morning.'

Winter recognised the voice.

'Hi, Stefan. It's me, Winter. I have to talk to Dr von Tobler.' Winter had appointed the security guard almost two years ago. As a policeman on a pursuit in his patrol car, Stefan had knocked into a suspect fleeing on foot and squashed him against the side of a house. The suspect turned out to be an innocent tourist who had learned to avoid the police in his native country. He broke his thigh. An underemployed lawyer sued Stefan for damages and threatened to go to the press. His superiors urged him to leave the force of his own volition. The door opened automatically.

'Von Tobler's on the tennis court.'

'Thanks.'

The gate closed again behind him, and Winter parked in front of the former stables that had been converted into garages. There was the gleaming black Mercedes S600. Winter thought of the black of the cliffs beneath the bridge.

Von Tobler's company car was custom built with bullet-proof glass and a reinforced floor. When he'd joined the bank Winter had regarded these security measures as excessive. Now he could understand von Tobler. If Kaddour had driven this car he'd probably still be alive. Winter got out. The bonnet of the S600 was warm.

Winter went down the steps to the entrance and rang. A real bell pealed. A maid in traditional costume opened the heavy door and wiped her hand on her apron. She raised her eyebrows and said, 'How may I help you?' A strong local dialect.

'Good morning. I'm very sorry to disturb you, but my name's Winter and I'd like to speak to Herr von Tobler, please.' When the maid hesitated, Winter added, 'It's urgent.'

'Are you from the bank?'

'Yes, I'm responsible for the bank's security.'

'Oh!'

It wasn't until the maid from the Bernese Oberland had slowly processed this information that she opened the door. She turned around and Winter followed her through the entrance hall. Large, gold-framed mirrors hung on the walls and for a moment Winter saw his image reflected a thousand times. It was nice and cool inside the house. They walked past the broad staircase, and delicate Louis XV furniture, to a door that led to the garden behind the house. The maid pointed to the tennis court.

'The Herr Doktor is playing tennis. I've got to get back to the kitchen. We've got a party today.' She smiled coyly. 'A masked ball.'

'I know. Thanks very much.'

She gave the hint of a curtsey.

Winter walked through the symmetrical beds with roses and ankle-high hedges, across the manicured lawn and past a large white marquee, beneath which stood bulky garden furniture. He went around the putting green with its three colourful flags and came to a tall hedge that screened the tennis court.

He heard the pock of tennis balls and saw the hulking figure of the CEO running back and forth. He was playing against his third wife, Mari, who had Swedish roots, moved gracefully and was about the same age as von Tobler's daughter, Miriam. Winter paused for a while beneath the trees and watched the mismatched couple. He waited until there was a break in the game and then stepped onto the court. The Swede noticed him first and waved with her racket.

Von Tobler turned around. 'Ah, good morning, Winter. Up so early? What's wrong with you?'

Every time Winter heard that deep voice he envied von Tobler for it. The white teeth grinned at him from a tanned face. Dripping with sweat, von Tobler grabbed a towel on the way over to Winter and wiped his face and neck. He offered his hand and stated the obvious: 'We're just practising.'

'Good morning, Herr von Tobler. I'm very sorry to disturb you, but I'm afraid it's important. May I have a word in private?'

'I'm just going to take a quick break, darling,' von Tobler told his wife. 'I'll be right back.' To Winter, he said, 'Let's go on the terrace.'

Von Tobler's terrace had been finished a hundred and fifty years ago. 'How's Miriam?' Winter asked.

'Fantastic. She's finished her studies. Finally! And now she's working freelance as a fashion designer. In Zürich and London.'

'That's good to hear.'

'You ought to pay her a visit some time. Her shop in Zürich is only a minute from Bahnhofstrasse.'

'I will.' Fashion wasn't Winter's thing.

As they passed the kitchen, von Tobler barked through the window, 'Could I have something to drink?' The maid in traditional costume hurried to the window and von Tobler asked Winter, 'Fancy a drink too?' Winter nodded. They walked around the house to the seating area on the terrace. Winter sat at right angles to his boss and looked out at Lake Thun. The mountains on the far side were closer and steeper than at Lake Geneva yesterday.

'Al-Bader's death is a tragedy for the bank,' von Tobler said.

Not a word about Anne. Winter nodded. The maid arrived with a jug containing a pale-orange liquid. An isotonic drink. Without saying anything she placed the jug and two glasses on the table and left. Von Tobler served Winter then himself.

'My secret recipe. Orange juice and tonic water. I have to watch my waistline.' He gave a hearty laugh, raised his glass to Winter then drank half of it in one gulp. Winter drank too and had to admit that it was a refreshing combination.

'Aah, the first sip is always the best. Like with women.' He grinned again. 'But you had something important to tell me. How was Egypt?'

'Interesting. As you know, Kaddour was murdered too. Orafin was looking for investors in a nuclear power station outside of Cairo. Al-Bader was interested. That's why they were going to meet in Switzerland.'

'And?' In a flash the jovial *bon vivant* had become the hard-hitting power-monger. Von Tobler's smile disappeared and his eyes narrowed.

'Early this morning I received a message for you,' Winter began. He gave von Tobler a concise account of his encounter with Max. To get answers he had to pose questions. 'What business are we doing in the Middle East?' By 'we' he meant the bank and specifically von Tobler.

'Why do you ask?'

A defensive counter-question, playing for time, Winter thought. 'Because Max said, "Keep out of the business in the Middle East!",' he told von Tobler. From his jacket pocket he brought out the photograph of his back with the double-underlined message: 'Keep out!'

Von Tobler took the photo and gave it a long, hard look before replying thoughtfully, 'The growth in the East is phenomenal: Abu Dhabi, Riyadh, Doha. The riches there are like the sand in the bloody desert. The Arabs want to put their money in a safe place. We make a bomb on it.' Either he hadn't realized his unfortunate choice of words or he wasn't letting it show. 'We can offer them that safe haven. Politically stable. Neutral towards the entire world. And we ask far fewer questions than the Americans.' Von Tobler had said nothing that Winter didn't know already.

'Do we have any problems there?'

'Don't think so,' von Tobler replied curtly.

'What business relations does the bank have with Orafin?'

'Orafin's on the lookout for financial investors and they

asked us what role we wanted to play in the financing of the nuclear power station.' Kaddour was history already.

'And?'

'Is this an interrogation?'

'No. I'm just trying to clear up the murders of one of our colleagues and two of our clients. I think it's important to understand the motive.'

Von Tobler bent forwards and put his glass down on the table.

'Okay. We're in the process of creating a private equity fund specialising in essential global infrastructure. We're only at the planning stage at the moment. Al-Bader was going to provide the money of his Arab friends, and us the links to the Western financial world. To ensure success we would need a certain sum of money at the launching stage. In preliminary talks with Al-Bader and some other rich clients I sounded out their willingness to participate. One of the projects involved is Orafin's nuclear power station near Cairo.

'What sort of sums of money are we talking about?'

'Blackstone in the States has about twenty to thirty billion of equity capital, the French firm Wendel and the Australian Macquarie have about five to ten billion each, depending on the climate of the market. They leverage this money, thereby controlling many firms that are worth twenty to thirty times that much. You can do the maths yourself.'

'Money is power,' Winter said to himself.

Ignoring him, von Tobler continued, 'And over the last few years the capital return has almost always been substantially more than fifteen per cent. I call that alpha. And the best is still to come. Investment in these infrastructure projects produces a regular cashflow that is pretty independent of the markets and thus comparatively crisis-proof.' Realising that he'd worked himself up into a sales pitch, von Tobler stopped abruptly and changed topic: 'What's with your neck, Winter?' He made a hand movement that a rapper would have been proud of.

'It's not so bad. One of the risks of the job.'

'Are you after a risk bonus?' Von Tobler was the jovial, but authoritarian boss again. But Winter wasn't ready to change the subject yet. 'At what financial level do we launch the private equity funds?'

'It should be at least three or four billion capital. But as I said, we were only in preliminary talks.'

'Had Al-Bader already agreed?'

'In principle, yes. But these things take time. Most of the money belongs to his family. He was confident of being able to persuade them. His brother has taken over now and we're going to have to do a bit more convincing.'

'Best of luck. At any rate there are some radical Islamists who won't be pleased if the money goes flowing to the West. They think it's better for the money to stay in their own countries.'

'Oh come on, Winter. People earn nothing in those countries. Bribes, procrastination and wars devour all returns. Look at Nigeria or Venezuela. Everything ends up being nationalized.' Opening out his arms, von Tobler added theatrically, 'We're investing in peace.'

'In oil rigs too?'

'Yes. If that Canadian oil rig had been financed with Arab money it would still be standing. The interlinking of capital prevents wars, Germany and France being the best example of this.'

'Do you really believe that the Americans will allow funds from an Islamic country to buy up their ports?'

'It's already happened. That's the market. It's always right. Till now capital has always been distributed most effectively via the free market. It's just a question of time. The Americans are bankrupt. The future lies in the East.'

'But there are those who won't shrink from blowing other people up. You should be particularly careful at the moment.'

Max is a professional, Winter thought. He could eliminate

von Tobler without much risk if he really wanted to. The bank's security system was designed for Switzerland, where even federal ministers wandered around in public without personal protection. The tennis court was an easy target for a sniper. But how could he forbid the bank's CEO from a bit of sport with his attractive wife? The evidence was too thin.

'I'm not afraid. But it would probably be better if we held back a bit over the coming weeks.'

'Have you noticed anything unusual recently?'

Von Tobler frowned pointedly and said, 'No.' He shook his head. 'Who would kill me?'

'The same people who killed Anne, Al-Bader, Strittmatter and Kaddour.'

Unconvinced, von Tobler shook his head again.

'Do you have any plans to leave Switzerland in the next few weeks?' Winter asked.

'I'm not going to change my travel plans just because of a few lunatics. But don't worry, Winter. I'm not going to Afghanistan. Next week I'll be in St Petersburg.' In Russia, even von Tobler wouldn't go anywhere without two security guards, and his partners there would probably wear bulletproof vests. 'And then, of course, we've got our annual conference. Don't forget.'

Now von Tobler was the head teacher wagging his finger and admonishing his pupil. Winter had received the invitation a while back. He hated these compulsory functions. He would be forced to wear a new suit, eat canapes and listen to meaningless chit-chat.

'Of course not.'

'The more I think about it the more I'm convinced that the whole affair has nothing to do with the bank. Al-Bader and Kaddour probably trod on someone's toes. These feuds have nothing to do with us. Maybe it was a vendetta. They still happen, apparently.'

'What about Max?'

'Don't worry. Neutrality is our strength, Winter.' He gave his head of security a patronising pat on the thigh. 'Stop your investigation and concentrate on the basics: the bank's security. There's bound to be another attack.'

Was von Tobler right? What was the point of poking about in the dark? What business of his were cockfights between enemy clans or internal family struggles in the Middle East? He rubbed his neck. He'd done his duty. He'd talk to Stefan and instruct him to inform Winter the moment he saw anything suspicious. He'd call the security firm in Moscow and get them to ratchet up the security level a couple of notches when they escorted von Tobler's visit. There wasn't much more he could do for the time being. Von Tobler had been warned. 'Okay,' he said. 'And sorry, again, for disturbing you.'

'Don't worry. At my age you're pleased to be able to take a break. My wife was thrashing me.' Von Tobler grinned, finished his drink and they stood up.

'I'll find my own way out. And enjoy your party this evening! Looks like you've got the weather for it.' Winter gazed up at the sky. 'You can never rule out a storm.'

Von Tobler shook Winter's hand, clapped him on the shoulder and said, 'Relax. Enjoy your day off.'

On the way back to his car he paid Stefan a visit. The security room was in the house where the gardener had once lived, which stood apart from the villa. They discussed additional security measures and Winter raised the security level here too. He ordered Stefan to keep a close eye on the land around the property.

On the way home Winter stopped at an open-air café. Here too the staff were hanging up garlands, lanterns and red-and-white flags. He sat in the large, gravel-strewn garden and ordered a double espresso with a glass of water. A few elderly men were playing cards. The sun shone through the plane trees, casting an irregular pattern on the red, metal tables.

When the drinks arrived he asked if they had a telephone. The waitress was from Eastern Europe and he had to repeat his question. Winter called Tibère using the cordless handset from the bar. Mobile number: voicemail. Bank landline: answerphone. Private number: answerphone. Maybe Tibère was travelling again or just didn't want to pick up the phone.

He rang his own voicemail and heard Fatima's voice. 'Hi, Winter. Hope you're well. Are you celebrating today? I've got some news. Please call me back.' There was a pause, then she said, 'Speak soon' with a hint of hope in her voice.

Winter listened to the message again, jotted down Fatima's number on a beermat and leaned back. It was nice hearing from her. He drank his double espresso in one gulp, washed it down with water and then dialled the long number in Egypt.

After two rings Fatima answered and said something in Arabic. It sounded very energetic.

'It's me, Winter,' he said. 'I'm calling from Switzerland. I just picked up your message.'

Fatima switched to English. 'Hi, Winter. Nice to hear from you.' She really did seem pleased. 'Are you celebrating the birth of your nation today?'

'Oh yes. Switzerland is an old lady, founded in 1291.'

'Many happy returns. But that's nothing compared to Egypt.'

Winter said, 'How are you? Did you take the job?'

'I'm fine and yes, the president has given me his confidence. I'm going to try to be a good example for Egyptian women.' She hadn't forgotten Winter's words. 'Anyway, I spoke to Al-Bader's younger brother and found out that they didn't set up any bank in America. The women in Bergen hadn't quite understood. Together with a professor from Harvard the Al-Baders established a private equity fund that invests globally in infrastructure.'

Winter swallowed. Von Tobler and Al-Bader had the same plans, but von Tobler hadn't said anything about America. Had Al-Bader been leading von Tobler on? Was that a motive? Von Tobler hated it when his business affairs weren't successful. 'A private equity fund for infrastructure projects,' Winter echoed.

Then he heard Fatima say, 'Yes. They pool their money and invest together. I'm flying to Boston in a few hours to meet Al-Bader's brother. He has taken over and I want to secure the investment in the nuclear power station for Orafin. We're meeting at the headquarters of Pyramid Investment Partners.'

'Did Al-Bader's brother say anything about the helicopter crash?'

'No, but you could ask him yourself if you like.'

Winter didn't know what to say.

After a pause Fatima added, 'If you came with me.'

He felt torn. He wanted to see Fatima again. Winter pictured her sitting at the table in the courtyard of her family's house and imagined that in the background he could hear the pattering of the little fountain in the tiled pool. Pensively, Winter rubbed the healing scar above his ear and said, with slight embarrassment, 'Boston?'

He looked around the café and ran things over in his mind. He could pay his friendly visit to Schmitt, Berger & Partners

later. And Boston was lovely at this time of year. On the other
hand, there were risks. If something happened to von Tobler
while he was in America, it wouldn't be good. And he could get
into trouble if he continued the investigation off his own bat.
But Winter was only bound to his conscience.

'Hello? Winter? Are you still there?' Fatima said.

'Yes, I'll come.'

It turned out that she'd booked a hotel already and Winter
promised to call as soon as he arrived. At the end she asked,
'Tell me, are you really alright?'

'Yes, apart from a few scratches I'm fine.' And – if he ignored
the exhaustion – this was the truth. His fall from the bridge had
pumped his body full of adrenalin. He'd sleep on the plane.
The Americans were six hours behind. 'I'll tell you all about it
this evening.'

Winter booked a seat on the afternoon flight to Boston.
Fourteen hours later he landed at Boston's Logan Airport. He'd
asked the stewardess not to disturb him on the flight and he'd
slept the whole way. He felt astonishingly fresh. In the long
corridors of the airport he switched on his dried-out phone. A
text from Tibère: All OK, party soon. A winking smiley.

The US immigration officer in her glass cabin was in a
good mood. She reminded him of one of those women who
sometimes presented the weather on CNN. He handed her his
passport, smiled at the camera, gave his digital fingerprint, said
'Business' and 'Parker Hotel' and was rewarded with a beaming
smile and wishes for a pleasant stay. He crossed the border into
the United States of America unhindered.

The weather forecast was right: outside the temperature
was an agreeably mild twenty-two degrees. In a few minutes a
taxi took Winter through the Sumner Tunnel under the port,
past some remaining Big Dig construction sites and into the
centre of Boston. During the drive he called Fatima, who'd

arrived at the hotel half an hour earlier. 'Suite 62,' she said brusquely.

*Six time zones to the east, midnight was long past. Piet watched a group of drunk Japanese businessman stagger out of a karaoke bar lit up pink in the Viennese district of Mariahilf, to the south of the Westbahnhof. A passing patrol car slowed down for a second before accelerating again. Glancing at the green digits of the clock on the BMW's dashboard, Piet cursed and rubbed his nose, which had been broken several times.*

*Over the course of his chemistry and civil engineering studies in Cape Town he'd learned to work with accuracy. Precision. The customers of his specialized import–export logistics firm valued his reliability. Quality had its price. He stretched his back. The drive to Vienna had been long, but uneventful. He'd arrived on time at the meeting point. Punctuality. Of all people it was his contact from Switzerland who was late.*

*When the massive 4x4 stopped behind him and flashed its headlights twice, Piet tossed the cigarette out of the window and muttered, 'Better late than never.' He got out and eyed Max.*

*Without saying anything the man with the pale face chucked Piet an envelope. A thick bundle of thousands. Swiss francs. At this price Piet was even happy to help lug the heavy military crates from his trailer into the boot of the off-roader. All part of the service.*

*This was why Max didn't dispose of his deliveryman until after the transfer. A silenced shot to the head. Max took back the brown envelope and stuffed Piet into the empty trailer.*

They stopped at a red light. As Winter absentmindedly watched a guided group of Asian tourists at Faneuil Hall, he wondered how things with Fatima would go from here. What did she want? He wasn't sure, and when the taxi got moving again he decided he'd let things take their natural course.

Winter paid the driver and went into the hotel lobby. The Parker was old, at least one hundred and fifty years old, but fresh looking and stylishly renovated. Lots of polished wood on the walls, huge lights and liveried pages with golden luggage trolleys. Avoiding an extended American family, Winter passed the reception and took the lift to the sixth floor. More red carpets, sucking up the sound. Stopping outside number 62, he knocked and said, 'It's me.'

Fatima was wearing a white blouse with large collar, a fine golden necklace and black trousers. The uniform of a successful businesswoman. But on second glance she looked worn out and fairly delicate. Winter could see dark rings beneath her eyes, which couldn't just be a result of the time difference.

They gave each other three air kisses.

Winter said with a smile, 'It's good to see you again.'

She scanned his face with her large, brown, but tired eyes. 'Does it still hurt?'

'No, it still itches a bit sometimes, but you did a good job patching me up.'

He looked around. The heavy curtains were drawn, the three-piece suite in the sitting area was furnished with abundant large cushions. An open laptop sat on the antique desk, beside it a bottle of mineral water and papers. The large room was an L-shaped suite and had an enormous double bed with a thick, decorative quilt and dark-red cushions. The smaller area with the sofa and armchairs could be sectioned off with a sliding door.

'Nice room.'

'Yes. I love old hotels. They have much more character than those modern blocks.'

'I'm hungry. Can I invite you to dinner?' Winter's stomach reminded him that he'd only had liquid sustenance since breakfast.

'It would be my pleasure.'

'Give me ten minutes to have a shower.' Winter opened his rucksack and took out the box of handmade chocolates. 'Here. I brought something for you.'

'Thank you very much. I love chocolate.'

Fatima kissed Winter on the cheek and he went off for his shower. When he came out of the steaming bathroom with wet hair five minutes later, half the chocolates had gone.

'I couldn't resist,' she laughed.

From his last visit Winter remembered a little Italian trattoria in the old part of the city, in a side street between Salem and Hanover. After a short taxi ride they found themselves being looked after personally by the manager at a table with a red-and-white checked tablecloth.

They ordered pizzas, Winter's extra hot with salami, Fatima's with four cheeses. And a bottle of Barolo. By the time the salad arrived, Winter had told Fatima the story of the bridge. As they ate their salad, Fatima spoke about her visit to the palace belonging to Orafin's president. And when the wine came she was telling Winter about how the investigation into Kaddour's murder was going. Winter tried the wine and gave a nod of approval. The waiter poured some into two large glasses, which rang out when they tapped them together in a silent toast.

They took a sip of wine, carefully placed the glasses on the small table and neither said a word for a moment.

The pizzas arrived.

'Well, the police informer knew that an attack was planned in Egypt,' Fatima said. 'He was also sure it would be a bomb. But he didn't know the target. The target is only ever revealed at the last moment.'

Leaning forward, Winter rested his elbows on the table and put his hands together. 'And?'

'The police have arrested a few suspects, including known members of fundamentalist groups. Three young men apparently confessed to placing the bomb of their own volition, but they don't belong to any of these groups. A little later they withdrew the confessions. Of course, the political leaders of the fundamentalists are vehemently denying that they knew anything.'

'Is there any indication that the bomb near the pyramids is in any way linked to the helicopter crash in Switzerland?'

'I know the deputy chief of police in Cairo a little. He plays at the same tennis club as my brother. We spoke.' She paused as the waiter put a candle on the table and lit it. When he'd gone, Fatima said. 'No, I'm sorry. Nothing so far. The bombers hadn't heard of Al-Bader and the house searches didn't turn anything up.'

'The explosive was not the same either,' Winter said. He told Fatima that the laboratory in Spiez was working on the assumption that two different types of explosive had been used. 'It's likely we're looking at two different sets of killers. As the two attacks occurred so close to one another I just assumed that there must be a connection.'

'Perhaps the connection is you.'

Winter shook his head. He couldn't believe that was the case. What the murders had in common was the business relationship between von Tobler, Al-Bader and Kaddour, the business connection between his bank, the Al-Bader family fortune and the Orafin project. They knew each other. He, Winter, only came into the equation as a result of the explosions.

'Has von Tobler contacted you?'

'Yes.' Fatima looked a little embarrassed. 'He called to congratulate me soon after it was made public that I had taken over Kaddour's role.'

'What would we have to do to make Orafin conduct more of its business via our bank?'

'Nothing, to my knowledge. At any rate the chief financial officer is happy. We conduct a substantial proportion of our European transactions through your bank. I look forward to meeting von Tobler personally. Kaddour always spoke of him with great respect.'

'Was my boss actually going to invest in the Cairo nuclear power station too?'

'He mooted an interest. But I explained that we work with investors from the region wherever possible. That's why I'm meeting Al-Bader tomorrow. He wants to invest via the private equity fund here. If Allah is merciful we will sign the letter of intent in the next few days.'

'Why here in Boston?'

'Apparently the Al-Baders have been collaborating with American universities for some time now. They've financed research projects here and they sponsor a chair for alternative investments at Harvard. That provides financial know-how and connections. The Al-Baders and acquainted families want to invest globally. And Boston is a good base for this. The Middle East, unfortunately, isn't exactly a haven of political stability.'

'The Al-Baders have plenty of irons in the fire.'

Winter understood why Al-Bader had been flying around in his private jet. He wasn't just looking to hand his family's oil money to a few banks to manage; his intention was to invest it himself. By investing throughout the whole world he was lowering the risk. Making the fortune secure was the precondition for increasing it.

Like the Sun King, Louis XIV, Al-Bader played cabinet politics. He siphoned off knowledge from a variety of professionals who knew nothing of one another and compared facts. That's why he met Hansen in Bergen, and that's why he had cultivated relations with von Tobler and probably dozens of other investment specialists. Divide and rule.

The aim was not to have his own bank, but a private equity fund. These were far less regulated and an ideal vehicle for a reasonable number of rich investors to pool their money discreetly. Winter regretted the fact that Al-Bader's mobile had been destroyed in the crash. His list of contacts would have been highly interesting.

The owner came and recommended his world-famous tiramisu for pudding. They allowed the topics to meander towards more personal issues. They laughed often and for a while completely lost sense of the time.

Later, Winter paid cash – he didn't want his credit card leaving a trail – adding a generous tip, and thanked the owner in Italian for his hospitality. The owner shook their hands vigorously, showered Fatima with compliments, and slyly winked at Winter as he accompanied them to the door.

As it was a pleasant evening they decided to take a stroll and they walked leisurely down Hanover Street towards the expressway. They allowed themselves to float in the stream of people as they peered into restaurants, cafes, confectioners and shop windows. At the end of Hanover Street they came to a pedestrian underpass that led beneath the main road into the more modern part of the city.

They passed a beggar showing his amputated leg and went down into the dimly lit underpass, which stank of urine. On either side, metal bars hung with plastic sheeting screening off a building site. Footsteps echoed. There were people walking behind and in front of them, but Winter could feel that Fatima was close beside him.

On the other side they were met by the modern glass buildings of the financial district in which only the occasional window was still lit. 'Let's take a taxi,' Fatima said.

'Good idea.' Looking around, Winter spotted a free taxi about fifty metres away, its engine running. He waved, the car started moving and they took a few steps towards it. When Winter opened the back door he eyed the driver, as was his habit. He was wearing a clean shirt and looked trustworthy. At that moment he heard Fatima's stifled scream.

Fatima recoiled. A man was sitting on the back seat. Winter just saw his legs, which were in suit trousers. The driver's left hand was on the wheel, his right somewhere in the depths of the car. Winter couldn't make out if he was holding a pistol.

The pedestrians exiting the underpass walked past them without noticing anything.

Winter switched his focus. Slow motion. Every last nerve in his body on red alert. His antennae taking in his surroundings with greater clarity and intensity, able to sense the slightest vibration around him. He'd spent years refining this skill of shifting his consciousness at a stroke.

In his profession the focus was on observation and analysis. He'd spent days tailing people. Waiting patiently. And then, all of a sudden, something would happen that would smash the passive lethargy and demand an instant decision, a specific response.

Only a tiny proportion of his time was taken up by rapid, precise action. It was like playing golf. During a round lasting several hours you only swung the clubs briefly. These few swings represented practically nothing in terms of time. And yet they decided everything.

In hand-to-hand combat training they thought he had magic eyes in the back of his head. But it was pure physics. Nobody could launch an attack without disturbing the airflow around them. And now the fine hairs on Winter's neck were telling him that someone was approaching from behind. He stood up straight.

Indeed, a couple of metres behind him stood two men in black-leather jackets and jeans. Hands in their jacket pockets. He remembered seeing them at the end of Hanover Street, thinking they were a gay couple. They were a little too close for it to be a coincidence. There was no obvious reason to stand where they were; passers-by had plenty of room here.

Winter wasn't armed and his opponents were numerically superior. If he'd been on his own this wouldn't have troubled him. The two men in the car were restricted in their movements. He'd be able to deal with the other two in leather jackets. But Winter couldn't be certain how Fatima would react. Would she break out in panic and scream or freeze? He didn't want to put her in danger.

Winter concluded that it would be best to avoid any escalation for the time being and find out what the men wanted. He put his hands on the roof of the car and bent down, which served two purposes. First, he signalled that he wasn't about to reach for a hidden weapon. Second, it allowed him to look inside the car.

The man on the back seat had short hair and was wearing a dark suit. Around fifty years of age, he had leathery skin and his legs were crossed in a relaxed pose. Winter's initial impression was that this was someone from the military top brass in civilian clothes. 'Good evening,' the man said. 'Please get in.'

A polite request, but his tone made it perfectly clear that this was an order; his voice was deep and composed. He gestured briefly with his hand for them to join him in the car. Fatima had taken a further step backwards and not moved a muscle since. Winter smiled and said in his most elegant English, 'Excuse me, sir, but are you looking to share the cost of this taxi with us? May I ask where you're heading?'

When the man bent forwards Winter saw grey at the temples and deep lines in his face. Deathly serious, the officer in civvies replied, 'Although the budget discussions in

Washington aren't easy for us, we'd be happy to cover your costs for the journey.'

'Who are you?' Fatima said.

'That doesn't matter. I'm not important. But if you get in we'll drive you to the Parker Hotel and I'll tell you.'

Fatima glanced at Winter and he nodded. They walked around the car. Winter opened the back door for Fatima and then got into the passenger seat. The security locks of the doors clicked, the window closed, the internal lights went out and the car set off silently.

Winter turned around and saw the two men watch the car drive away.

The man behind him said, 'Smith. Deputy Director of the National Security Agency and responsible for coordinating all operations in the Middle East.'

Smith leaned back and addressed Fatima in Arabic. Winter couldn't understand a word. All he heard were the names Orafin, Kaddour and Port Said. The discussion between Fatima and the NSA man went back and forth, like their question and answer game in the Italian restaurant. Fatima was feisty, shaking her head vigorously a few times. In the fast flow of the Arabic discussion the word 'Winter' suddenly cropped up and the NSA man asked in English, 'Are you Mr Winter?'

Winter nodded. 'Most of the time.'

'Would you mind showing me your passport?'

They glided through the evening traffic. The man had assumed that Winter understood Arabic. Winter wondered whether he should invoke his civil rights and refuse. The image of orange-clad prisoners in Guantánamo flashed through his mind. Winter didn't want a confrontation. He removed his passport from his inside pocket and Smith inspected it with practised eyes and hands.

'May I ask in what capacity you've come to the United States?'

'I'm here for the shopping.'

'Don't make jokes.'

'The dollar's at a good rate at the moment.'

Fatima looked at him sternly and then explained, 'Mr Winter is helping me with security issues.'

Winter hadn't been aware of that, but he didn't feel any need to be specific. He even felt flattered somehow. He'd learned that you don't get any answers without questions and so said, 'And what are *you* doing?'

'We're protecting the American people and making the United States more secure. We pay particular attention to the financial flows of terrorist networks. No money, no attacks. We have reason to believe that Orafin has moved large sums of money to the United States and my agency is keen to see that these are invested according to the law.'

'Do you have any proof that Orafin is working with terrorists?'

'No, at the moment we just have a few suspicions. But prevention is better than cure. And what we're doing here is prevention.'

'Okay. So you're abducting innocent tourists?' Winter said, turning around and looking Smith in the eye. The NSA man was unruffled; he wasn't going to succumb to provocation. He had the tunnel vision of the determined hunter on a mission. 'I'm sure you heard about the sinking of the oil rig in Nova Scotia,' he said patiently. 'The cutter the terrorists used is registered in Port Said and originally belonged to a trading company that Orafin has a share in.'

Fatima stated vehemently, 'Many of our exports go via Port Said. Orafin has over a hundred investments. That's a sign of long-term thinking. We want ours and the partners' goals aligned.'

Winter listened with interest. Smith had probably found out that Fatima had arrived in the US. As the CEO of Orafin she was on a watch list. Maybe the US immigration authorities had even used one of Ben's programmes. Fatima entered the country and Smith was taking the opportunity to have a discreet, informal chat with Orafin's new CEO. One of the lessons of 9/11 was that America's contacts in the Arab world were inadequate. 'The American people have a right to security,' he heard Smith say.

'Are you a nationalist or a capitalist?' Fatima asked.

When Smith didn't reply immediately she said, 'I hope the Americans have nothing against the free flow of capital and still believe in the power of the market.'

She's shrewd, Winter thought. But clearly Smith had no desire to get embroiled in a political discussion. The Lexus drove past the market, stopping at the same red light where Winter had waited a few hours earlier.

Striking a conciliatory tone Smith said, 'Please don't get me wrong. We're trying to get to the bottom of the attack on the oil platform and prevent the next terrorist atrocity. For that we need to employ all means at our disposal.'

Winter could understand him. He didn't care for political discussions either. He was a pragmatist. In every democracy, political show-fighting was a necessary evil to demonstrate power. And it was a hundred times better than war.

'One of these means is a good partnership with open-minded forces around the world,' Smith went on. He smiled at Fatima and gave both her and Winter a business card. 'If you want to talk to me you can get me on this number 24/7.' On the card with the NSA logo was the name 'Smith' and below it a telephone number. Nothing else.

The car pulled up outside the hotel, the security mechanisms of the door clicked and Winter said ironically, 'Thanks for the ride.'

'My pleasure.'

Reflecting on the responsibility weighing down on Smith's

shoulders, Winter added seriously, 'And best of luck with the hunt.' They shook hands and Winter fancied he saw the hint of a grateful smile.

They got out and the Lexus glided away, vanishing into the night-time traffic.

Fatima and Winter stood outside the hotel, looking at each other for a moment. Winter shook his head and took a deep breath.

'Nice man.' Fatima said sarcastically.

'What did he want?' Winter said. 'I didn't completely understand the conversation in Arabic.'

The liveried doorman, a gigantic, elderly, black man, opened the door and they entered the hotel lobby.

'Unofficial access to Orafin's books,' Fatima explained. 'Because of the attack in Nova Scotia. And I told him, "Over my dead body".'

She realized what she'd just said and Winter tried to defuse the situation. 'At least we saved ourselves the taxi fare.' But Smith had succeeded in thoroughly ruining the relaxed mood of the evening.

Fatima and Winter said nothing as they waited for the lift with other hotel guests. Winter suddenly felt how tired he was. His body was craving sleep.

They entered the room. The double bed had been turned down and on both pillows lay a small box with three Lindt & Sprüngli chocolates. The same ones Anne had given to Al-Bader. This supposedly sweet greeting had a bitter aftertaste.

Fatima darted into the bathroom. Winter got undressed, climbed under the covers, crossed his hands behind his head and stretched his back. He could feel the effects of the long flight and a lack of exercise. Maybe he'd go for a jog in the morning. He relaxed, let his thoughts meander and fell asleep immediately.

Rather than go to bed, Fatima stuck her USB stick into the

laptop and started working through her encrypted emails. She organized a meeting with Orafin's head of finance and sent him a list of detailed questions. She invited the owner of Port Said's shipyard to Cairo. Then she concentrated on the precise wording of the letter of intent for the nuclear power station. The devil was in the detail – what goals were realistic in Egypt? How could they distribute the risk optimally? How could the investors' needs be reconciled with the needs of the constructors of the nuclear power station? Fatima was confident of moving a stage further tomorrow.

Occasionally she peered at Winter through the crack in the sliding door but she didn't stop what she was doing.

# AUGUST 2 – 05:07

Winter woke from his deep sleep shortly after five in the morning, his internal clock still set to European time. The heavy curtains were almost totally drawn. Only in one narrow strip of light could he see dust particles dancing. Someone ought to give this room a deep clean sometime.

Turning his head, his nose was caught up in Fatima's hair. The hilly landscape of the heavy duvet beside him rose and sank slowly. She was sleeping soundly. Winter lay back and closed his eyes.

After a while he got up and put on some jogging shorts, a T-shirt and his running shoes. On a hotel notepad he wrote, 'Good morning, Fatima. I've gone for a jog and am looking forward to having breakfast together.' He closed the door to their suite quietly behind him, left the hotel via a side exit and set off.

Winter loved the early mornings. The air was fresh. The sun slanted between the red-brick houses and reflected in the puddles. He overtook a slow, street-cleaning vehicle and ran across Boston Common. The ground was springy and his joints and thoughts limbered up. A flock of ducks took flight; a young terrier chased fruitlessly after them. A group of Chinese people were practising Tai Chi.

He crossed the glittering Charles River via a narrow pedestrian bridge, passed the Massachusetts Institute of Technology and after half an hour reached Harvard University's boathouse. He turned away from the river and passed several libraries and research institutes before arriving at the campus. Soon, perhaps, one of these buildings would be named after Al-Bader. How many millions of dollars did you have to donate to have a building called after you?

Winter had committed to memory the address and location of the Pyramid Investment Partners HQ. Another two hundred metres. The symbiosis between university and private business functioned geographically too. Leaving the campus he came to a quiet side street containing two rows of old, three-storey town houses, each with a narrow strip of front yard.

The place was home to medical specialists, lawyers, financial advisers and PR agencies with meaningless made-up names. The entrance to a plastic surgeon's was decorated with a marble Aphrodite. A street for rich people. A man carrying a large bag was delivering copies of the Boston Globe.

The HQ of Pyramid Investment Partners did not stand out. An elegant sign with a pyramid logo. In front of it a few square metres of white gravel. Vertical slats screened off the windows. No one to be seen.

The street was lined with expensive cars on both sides. In the last parking place was a grey Lexus with a man inside on the phone. Winter jogged past slowly. The bonnet wasn't radiating any warmth. From the corner of his eye Winter could see a small map with an officious eagle logo on top of the dashboard, and a camera with telephoto lens in the driver's lap. No personal items. Company car. The driver could monitor the comings and goings in the street. Someone kept an eye on the area.

Winter turned around and ran back, his mind whirring. What were the authorities hoping for by keeping an eye on Pyramid Investment Partners? Ben had warned him that Al-Bader was on America's list of terrorists. But why hadn't Smith, the NSA man, said anything about Al-Bader yesterday evening? What did Smith know of the helicopter crash? As he jogged back to the hotel Winter tried to make sense of it all.

***

The alarm was shrill. It got louder for a few seconds, before subsiding and beginning all over again. It hurt his ears and Winter was pleased that he hadn't been startled from his sleep by such a siren. Whoever had come up with this noise must have been an experienced torturer who knew the precise frequency at which the human ear suffered most.

Winter saw Fatima, her eyes closed, grope for her mobile phone and blindly switch off the alarm. He opened the curtains energetically and sunlight flooded the suite.

Eyes half-shut still, Fatima sat up amongst the claret cushions. In the sun her silk lingerie shone the colour of sand. She opened her eyes properly. Physically she was all there, but not quite yet mentally. She put her phone back down.

'A wonderfully beautiful morning.'

'Winter?' Looking at him against the light, she grimaced. 'What's happened? I mean your T-shirt.'

Winter peered down at the sweaty fabric. 'I went for a little morning jog.' He pulled the T-shirt over his head and took a half-litre bottle of mineral water from the minibar. 'Did you sleep well?'

'Reasonably well, but somehow it's almost too quiet for me here.' She laughed.

Winter thirstily drank half of the bottle of Evian, refilled it with orange juice and shook his isotonic cocktail on the way to the bathroom. He returned with a towel and sat in one of the armchairs. 'It was quite peaceful along the Charles River this morning too.'

Leaning back against the headboard and cushions, Fatima watched Winter alternate between rehydrating and wiping the sweat from his neck.

Standing up, he said, 'I'm going to take a shower.'

The bathroom was as large as his bedroom back home. Too

lavish. Too much marble. And the old-fashioned, mock-gold fittings were impractical. Winter took a long shower. With cold water first, then hot. The shower itself was modern with a drencher head. As Winter let the water pelt down on his body, for a second he imagined Fatima in there with him.

After a while he turned off the water, stepped out of the wet room and felt for a large bath towel. The room was a steam bath, the mirror fogged up. Winter wiped the water from his eyes and dried himself. What would today bring? Should he shave or could he leave his stubble? With the palm of his hand he cleared part of the mirror and decided that it could wait. He opened out his arms, threw the towel over his head and massaged his back diagonally.

When he looked in the mirror again he saw Fatima behind him. She was standing at the other end of the bathroom, eyeing him in the mirror. He stopped. How long had she been standing there?

They gazed at each other in the mirror. And then Fatima went to stand behind Winter, her body almost touching his. He had never felt so naked. For a moment Winter thought about resisting. But then he knew he wouldn't.

It was quite some time before they were sated.

Winter ordered breakfast to their room. Plenty of strong coffee, fresh orange juice, muesli, toast and fruit. He told Fatima about the grey Lexus and they began planning their visit to Pyramid Investment Partners. Ten minutes later came a knock at the door and at the same time Fatima's mobile rang, this time the honking of a ship's horn.

Winter opened the door and a waiter rolled in the breakfast trolley. Meanwhile Fatima took the call with a 'Hello' and started an animated discussion in Arabic. After the waiter had left with his tip, Fatima said, 'That was Al-Bader's younger brother. He's in Paris. He's not coming today because he's afraid of being arrested in America.'

They had breakfast.

'Pyramid Investment Partners rang him yesterday, advising him not to come. He doesn't want to take any risks until the situation has been defused. His lawyers here in the States are attending to the matter and will probably demand certain guarantees. Although he didn't say anything I got the impression he's pretty furious.'

'So what's going to happen with the letter of intent for the financing?'

'We'll keep going. The younger Al-Bader has authorized Professor Farmer to continue discussions. The professor will meet us.'

'The professor?'

'He's the chief executive here.'

'Did you tell Al-Bader that Pyramid Investment Partners is under surveillance?'

'Yes. And he wasn't in the least surprised.' Sarcastically, she added, 'He thinks it fits the bill. With the help of federal agencies American competitors are putting all possible obstacles in his way. In America the free world only works for white people of the true faith.'

Winter didn't reply. To some extent he could understand the American security authorities. Nobody wanted to see nuclear technology fall into the wrong hands, or extremists directing money into dubious channels with the help of businesspeople.

Irritated by Winter's silence, Fatima flashed her eyes angrily at him.

Fortunately, the ship's horn sounded again. 'Hello? – Nice to hear from you, Professor.' Fatima nodded a few times and repeated his words: 'Okay, Prudential Tower, nine o'clock. I'm very much looking forward to meeting you.' She hung up and said, 'The professor's collecting us in his helicopter.'

Finishing their breakfast, Fatima told Winter about her time as a student in London. They discussed the quality of life in various cities. Winter ordered more coffee and, while Fatima was in the bathroom, listened to his voicemail messages. Tibère had made a few calls and found out something about the detective agency Schmitt, Berger & Partners. It had gone bankrupt twice in the last few years and now consisted of just Schmitt and a part-time secretary.

Fatima came out of the bathroom smartly dressed, with a subtle application of make-up. She closed her laptop and took out the USB stick. She was ready.

They left the hotel via a side exit and Winter hailed a taxi. They drove in silence through the slow-moving morning traffic. After ten minutes they arrived at the Prudential Tower, paid, and took the lift to the twenty-fifth floor.

As they were a little early they had a look at Boston from the viewing deck. Thanks to the overnight rain the air was clear and in the distance they could make out the port and the sea.

At nine o'clock they went to the viewing deck reception. The helicopter with the professor had just landed. An obliging employee showed them through a door and in the corridor beyond a man came towards them. 'What a wonderful day. Please excuse the change of schedule at short notice.'

The professor was wearing a black windcheater, had a deep tan and was one of those people with a permanent smile on their face.

They shook hands in the narrow corridor and exchanged the usual pleasantries. Fatima again introduced Winter as her security adviser. Then they climbed some metal steps, opened another door and hurried, ducking, to the waiting helicopter, its rotors turning. The gusty wind ruffled their clothes and Fatima's hair flew around.

Winter recalled the video images – imprinted indelibly on his mind – of Anne and Al-Bader's transfer at Zürich Airport. The professor opened the rear cockpit door and they climbed in. The pilot ignored them and even before they'd fastened their belts and put on the headphones dangling from the ceiling they were in the air.

The Robinson Raven tilted forwards and accelerated. The street canyons of Boston quickly got smaller. They turned and flew in a north-westerly direction. When the helicopter had reached its air lane the professor's voice came through the headphones. 'Once again, a very warm welcome to you both on behalf of Pyramid Investment Partners. Given the particular circumstances I took it upon myself to shift the location of our meeting.'

'Where are we going?' Fatima asked.

'We'll be there in a quarter of an hour. I'm going to show you one of our investment projects. We're financing the extension of a nuclear power plant.'

During the flight, Farmer pointed out local sights. The settlements vanished. Woods, small lakes and the White Mountains

drifted past. The helicopter descended and the three cooling
towers of a nuclear power station emerged from behind a hill.
A fourth was under construction and surrounded by yellow
cranes and construction machinery. Overhead cables led from
the power station towards the sea.

'This is one of the least seismically active areas in the United
States,' Farmer explained. 'Ideal for nuclear energy production.'

On the access roads the toy cars grew to the size of real
vehicles again as the Robinson Raven landed on a helicopter
pad near the large car park. The professor gallantly offered
Fatima his hand and helped her out. They got into a white
people-carrier waiting there, bearing the logo of an energy
firm. It headed for the steaming cooling towers.

They passed the staff canteen and a visitors' pavilion, with
a large, flashing board illustrating various cycles, and stopped
outside a two-storey administrative building with a flat roof.

Farmer knew his way around. In the glazed reception area
they filled out visitor forms, showed their passports and smiled
into a digital camera. In return they were given a plastic card
to hang around their necks.

Winter watched the security procedures with curiosity.
He knew that every process was only as good as the staff
implementing it. An elderly woman with peroxide-blonde hair
checked their passports. She seemed to know Farmer. Winter
doubted that she'd be able to spot a professionally forged
passport. Every ID could be forged. Passports were stolen.
Embassy personnel lost blank ones.

Farmer said. 'We'll start with a little tour.'

A young guide in a cap appeared and greeted them as if they
were a school outing allowed to visit a nuclear power station as
the climax of a science project week. Winter politely brought
up the rear, listening with one ear only. 'Three-quarters of
energy production in Vermont comes from this plant.' The
guide took them to the visitor pavilion, cheerfully explained

the workings of the power plant, realized that his mini group looked only vaguely interested and so quickly returned to the entrance area.

They came to a security gate. One of the three uniformed guards checked their IDs, then they had to pass through a metal detector and were air-sprayed in an explosives sniffer. Once they'd passed all three tests in silence they were let through a hydraulically controlled sliding door into the next zone. The guide, Farmer, Fatima and Winter were in the inner courtyard.

Winter glanced behind him. The entire plant was protected by a tall, concrete wall. Along its edge ran a thick pipe that jutted out a considerable way from the wall, making it difficult for a climbing intruder to get a grip. The wall had probably been erected by the same firm that put up the one between Israel and Palestine. Unimpeded by the barrier, black crows landed on the flat roof of a warehouse.

They passed a turbine hall, transformers and buzzing, high-tension lines.

The area was dominated by the cooling towers. The enormous cylinders towered almost one hundred metres into the air, overshadowing the plant. In parts the concrete was dirty. Weather debris or algae.

Winter felt small and at the mercy of the plant. Although he knew that the concrete shell could withstand an attack by an aeroplane packed with explosives or a rocket strike, an uneasy feeling came over him, a cold shiver running down his spine. What can happen, will happen, sooner or later. Fukushima was everywhere. His house, too, stood less than twenty kilometres to the east of Mühleberg nuclear power station, one of the oldest in Europe. The westerly wind would quickly blow leaking radioactive material over to him. As a sop to the population within a radius of thirty kilometres, the government had prophylactically handed out iodine tablets. With an effort Winter banished his gloomy thoughts.

They marched through the building with the control rooms, the decarbonisation plant, and from the pump house they peered down at the river, whose water acted as a coolant. No swans. Not even a black one.

The word the guide used most was security. He explained the inherent security, the security principles, the reactor protection system and accident management. Statistical calculations had predicted, apparently, that no major accident was to be expected in the next thousand years. Winter didn't think this was the time for a discussion about risks and probabilities.

After all the fire service was right here.

And Fukushima was a long way away.

Out of sight, out of mind.

But Fatima was impressed and Winter could virtually see a nuclear power station like this, to supply Cairo with energy, taking shape in her mind.

In five or ten years' time the Egyptian president would cut through a red ribbon at the opening ceremony, announcing that power cuts in Cairo were now a thing of the past. The nuclear plant would be a magnificent supplement to the combined cycle power stations. Thanks to this new plant, the Egyptian people and Egyptian industry would in the future enjoy cheaper and more reliable electricity. The president would declare that a new age had dawned for the Egyptian people.

The finance minister would be in attendance too, but he wouldn't say anything, he'd merely be pleased that finally he'd be able to cut the subsidies in the budget to make energy cheaper.

Politicians!

And Fatima would stand proudly beside the energy minister, applauding.

Winter focused back on the present. The embattled guide was seeking to return to the entrance and conclude the tour.

It had served its purpose. Professor Farmer had impressed Fatima. The physical dominance, the complexity of the plant and the electrical tension in the buzzing, high-voltage lines in the air had made an impact. He'd set the scene perfectly for the next stage of negotiations.

They went back through the hydraulic door, the guide gave them a warm goodbye and they entered the administrative building. When Farmer took them into a meeting room with a varnished table, surrounded by black-leather chairs, Fatima took the reins. 'Mr Winter, thanks very much for escorting us. Now if you wouldn't mind we need to speak in private. Why don't you go and have a coffee in the canteen? I'll call you when we're done.' She gave Winter an enchanting smile but then firmly closed the door.

Winter didn't have the opportunity to take a closer look at the fat man in the suit who approached her from the other end of the table. The administrative director of the nuclear power plant? Or an on-site consultant from Pyramid Investment Partners?

Winter walked slowly along the corridor, reading the signs next to the closed office doors. At the end of the corridor he got himself a coffee from the machine and climbed the stairs to the second floor.

An employee coming the other way wasn't fazed by his presence. The moment an administration reached a certain size the individual no longer counted and could move around anonymously, so long as they wore a plastic card around their neck like a dog collar.

On the second floor, Winter slowly went back. At the end of the corridor he came to a sign informing him that this was the office of the power plant's head of security. The door was open and Winter stopped. In the middle of the room stood a metal desk, sitting at it a man in a short-sleeved shirt, who looked up when he realized someone was standing in the doorway.

With a grin, Winter knocked sheepishly at the open door. 'Hello,' he said, 'my name is Winter. Tom Winter. I'm responsible for the security of a Swiss Bank and thanks to Professor Farmer I've just had a tour around your impressive plant.' He pointed to the cooling towers. Compliments had never hurt.

The man behind the metal desk stood up, peered at Winter's visitor's pass, and then waved him in.

The head of security was a small but powerful man. Winter crossed the office and they shook hands. To the right was a wall with document files. The left-hand wall was full of diplomas, certificates, photographs of important people and trophies from shooting competitions. Behind the desk, a glass wall gave a view of the cooling towers. The security chief had the light at his back.

'I'm Jeff. So what brings you from beautiful Switzerland to Vermont?'

'Tom. I'm accompanying a client I advise on security matters.'

'Oh yes, the chief said that the professor would be coming by with guests. Please take a seat.'

The fat man he'd seen in the meeting room must be the head of the plant. Winter sat in the chair by the desk, gave Jeff his business card, and fielded questions about his home country. He'd visited Switzerland on a trip through Europe, Jeff said. The whole of Europe in ten days, probably, Winter thought.

'What's that town called again – the one by the lake that has the magnificent, wooden bridge?'

'Lucerne.'

With a grin the head of security added that he'd loved the Jungfrau mountain most of all. Winter told him that Lucerne and the Jungfrau were excellent choices.

Jeff had time on his hands and, after an animated discussion about how small Switzerland was in comparison to the expanses of America, and Winter throwing out some non-contentious titbits to do with problems in banking contingency planning, designed to win Jeff's confidence, Winter tried to steer the conversation to the subject of the power station's security. He might as well take advantage of being here and learn something.

When Winter probed a little deeper, the head of security said, 'We're a PPP, a Public–Private Partnership. Which means everyone wants to have their say, but nobody's keen on taking responsibility.'

Judging by Jeff's tone, Winter had evidently stirred up a hornet's nest. 'Sounds familiar,' he said encouragingly.

'The whole thing is very tricky politically. The state of Vermont is looking to save money and so it sold the power station to private investors years ago. We were public property. Then, a year ago, Farmer bought into the power station. He's got three clear priorities: profit, profit, profit.' The man laughed scornfully. 'Security shouldn't cost anything. Farmer very neatly outsourced the entire risk to an insurance company, which in turn outsourced it to a reinsurer, which sold it on again, using structured products from banks. Nobody under-stands the real risks.'

Winter gave an understanding look.

Weapons of mass destruction.

'Because of the shareholders' agreement with Farmer and the nuclear energy law, the governing board is a political committee that just nods its head and hasn't got a clue. The Republicans want a slimmed-down state, and to make savings wherever they can. The Democrats and darned eco-terrorists don't want any nuclear power stations at all. And the unions forbid me from running detailed checks on staff here, pleading data protection and privacy rights.' Jeff had talked himself into a rage.

Winter nodded his agreement. 'Which means there's no way of guaranteeing comprehensive security in the long term.'

Then Jeff told a story which made the hair on the back of Winter's neck stand on end.

'A few weeks back we caught a sleeper. In conjunction with the NSA we were testing the beta version of a new face-recognition software on the photos of our employees. And bang!' Jeff fired a shot with his fingers. 'Our candidate was an innocent American citizen with family roots in the Middle East. He studied here at our best universities and has a wonderful family. But he also has a brother who looks like him, who's assumed a new name and is a religious fundamentalist prepared to use violence. Although he's got a beard, the matches on the facial features were clear. And the engineer, who's been working in the highly sensitive zone, kept it quiet of course.'

'Christ. It makes those high walls redundant.'

The black sheep of successor generation immigrants are difficult to identify. Third generation, 3-G terror. The melting pot has its advantages and disadvantages.

'The authorities searched his workplace, house and car. His lawyers gave us hell. They scoffed at the family liability stuff. But luckily they detained him and after three days someone remembered that he also had a hunting cabin. Bang!' With his index finger Jeff fired a shot at his desk lamp. 'They found it all there.'

Recalling Ben's computer programme, Winter said, 'Motive?'

'Unclear. Some massacre in the family during the Iraq–Iran War twenty years ago. Apparently the CIA was operating in the Kurdish area and was a bit too rough when interrogating some members of our engineer's family. Because of oil they're filthy rich and do business throughout the world. Apparently the entire Baktar clan swore revenge. But that's just hearsay, and of course you have heard nothing from me.'

It struck Winter that he knew very little about Al-Bader's background. Discretion also meant asking no questions.

Rummaging around in clients' backgrounds was taboo. Could the bank have been abused and made an accomplice?

His phone rang: Fatima. Flying in five minutes.

Half an hour later Farmer, Winter and Fatima landed on
Nantucket Island. The professor had invited them to lunch
at his second home by the sea. On the flight back Winter had
seen the suburbs of Boston and the characteristic outlines of
Cape Cod.

The helicopter spat them out behind some dunes and took
off again promptly. The landing might not have been entirely
legal, but the authorities probably turned a blind eye. The
professor apologized that they had to go the last three hundred
metres on foot.

A wooden walkway with railings led across the dunes to the
sea. Tall grasses clung to the sand and trembled in the wind.
Wobbly fences sought to keep the drifts of sand in check. Winter
could see sailing boats and motorboats cruising off the coast.

The professor stopped abruptly and pointed at the sand.
'Look, late plover eggs.'

Winter couldn't see anything. It wasn't until he bent down
that he spotted three eggs in the sand. No nest for protection.
In shape, colour and size they were identical to the stones
around them.

'Perfect camouflage, wouldn't you say?' The professor had
admiration in his voice. 'They lie there, before our very eyes
and we can't see them. There's so much we can learn from
nature.'

Winter and Fatima nodded their agreement. Like a sleeper,
Winter thought. Then another thought shot through his head:
for Tiger the eggs would be easy prey.

The Victorian house emerged from behind the dunes. Wooden and freshly painted, it had grey walls, a white door and window frames and a gable roof of black Eternit tiles. A stone chimney rose from the side of the house, puffing out smoke. From a mast a large American flag fluttered proudly.

Between the house and the sea lay a beach of fine sand, shining yellow with the odd brownish tuft of grass. Along the coast stood more houses in the same style. All wooden, in different, subtle shades, and almost all with an American flag. Winter looked back and saw a concrete road that led from a pine forest, accumulated drifts of sand as it crossed the dunes and ended up in a double garage behind the house. Soaking up the fresh sea air, Winter wondered what this property cost.

They went onto a large wooden deck with elaborate garden furniture and light-brown cushions. Three broad steps led down to the sandy beach. The deck didn't have any railings, but was defined by a good dozen dark-brown, rusty, iron stands with half burned torches.

'Please take a seat. What can I offer you to drink?'

Fatima asked for an orange juice, Winter a beer. 'I much prefer to cater for my guests here in my modest second home,' the professor said, 'than in a packed restaurant. For these special occasions I have a chef fly in. Please excuse me for a moment. I'm going to see that we get a bite to eat.'

Fatima and Winter made themselves comfortable in the armchairs.

'Didn't the Clintons sometimes spend their holidays on this island?'

'No idea, I don't read the American gossip mags.'

'Did your conversation with the director and Farmer go alright?'

'I think so. Kaddour – may Allah show him mercy – had prepared the ground well. We signed the letter of intent and now can embark on the next phase. But we're still in the early stages. The planning's going to take time. From the broad brushstrokes to the fine detail. Everyone wants to cover their back. I'm going to send specialists from Orafin, reinforced by staff from the ministry. And the director of the nuclear power plant is keen to sell us his consulting services via a private firm.' Laughing, Fatima made the shape of the director's fat belly with her hands.

For a while they gazed out at the sea in silence. The water and the infinity of the ocean were relaxing.

Winter thought of his terrace at home, the unused loungers and Anne. He felt sad and wondered how the loss of Anne was influencing his relationship with Fatima. The expanse of the sea reminded Winter how insignificant he was. It was comforting somehow.

A young waiter dressed in white wrenched him from his thoughts, served the drinks and set the table for three. After a few minutes Farmer came back. He'd swapped his windcheater for a V-neck jumper and was holding a tomato juice.

'Food's on its way.'

Although they'd spent the morning together this was Winter's first quiet moment with the professor and, after loosening up with some compliments about the beautiful house and its wonderful position, he said, 'Please excuse me for sounding intrusive, but what exactly is Pyramid Investment Partners' speciality?'

Leaning back, the professor began a lecture. 'Mr Winter, it's all quite simple in theory. You must have heard that Harvard University has invested its money very successfully. We're reliant on monies from our benefactors and donors being utilized as effectively and securely as possible, to guarantee the university's survival. We realized early on that it's dangerous to put all your eggs in one basket.'

When two waiters arrived with a cold salmon starter and a bottle of white wine from the neighbouring island, the three of them sat at the large wooden table. After they'd toasted Winter asked, 'But what's that got to do with Pyramid Investment Partners?'

'Years ago Harvard invested in alternative sectors. Property and gold. You know that. But we also invested in platinum, silver, foodstuffs, orange juice,' Farmer said, pointing at Fatima's glass. 'Oil, gas, wood, cattle and much more. The aim is to minimize the correlation between investments and improve the risk profile of the portfolio.'

'Risk profile?' Winter said, thinking of criminal profile.

'Yes, the art is to invest in things that complement each other. Direct investments in oil and transport counter each other. If oil goes up in price, oil rigs yield greater returns, but rising fuel costs mean the transport firms drop in value. The Harvard investment fund has systematized and profession-alized this approach and implemented it consistently. Over the last ten years it's allowed us to beat all key benchmarks.'

The salmon was fresh.

'So what does Pyramid Investment Partners do better than its competitors?'

'We specialize in direct investment in essential infrastructure. And on a global scale. Using our knowledge we build a bridge between investors eager to follow the Harvard approach and locally rooted infrastructure projects, such as the nuclear power plant we visited this morning.'

Fatima knew this already and said, 'Here in the US, Pyramid Investment Partners has opened doors for Orafin that would otherwise remain closed.'

The professor was flattered by the compliment. But he didn't like being interrupted, and so continued, 'The combination of infrastructure, energy and emerging nations is promising for the future. In America and Europe infrastructure needs renewing for billions of dollars. Whether it's boom or bust. The governments are happy to get rid of their concentration risks.

We're always going to need energy. The global population and its prosperity is growing.'

The professor formed an imaginary globe with his hands. 'Just imagine what would happen if the entire world population only used half the energy of your average American. And then the emerging nations! In the future they're going to be growing at five, ten per cent a year too. They need energy for their factories to satisfy the growing domestic demand. Either it's too cold or too hot. It's like the conquest of the Wild West in America – the gold-rush atmosphere. Shortages are inevitable.

*In the crosshairs it was easy to see the professor brandishing his cutlery in the air. The distance was six hundred metres. A slight cross-wind.*

*Through his high-definition binoculars the man focused on Farmer, Fatima and Winter in turn. He was wearing an earpiece and listening in to the conversation. With his upper body, he compensated for the swell that gently rocked his speedboat up and down. Without taking the eyes off his prey he said to his colleague, 'Now it's getting interesting.'*

*'Yes, I'm fed up to the back teeth with this endless waiting. I hope they stop pussyfooting around.'*

The two waiters came out of the house with the main course. Beneath silver cloches they brought three, bright-red, hot lobsters with potatoes. As well as three bowls with tepid water and a pile of clean, cloth napkins. Winter wasn't used to eating fresh seafood so he was pleased to be able to copy Fatima's and Farmer's methods and limit himself to brief questions in the conversation: 'So you help families like the Al-Baders invest their money?'

'Yes, Al-Bader has the money and we have the technical

expertise. They bring the contacts from the East and we bring those from the West. We help each other.' Farmer cracked open the shell of his lobster and said, 'We connect peoples and invest in peace.'

And get rich in the process, Winter thought.

Staring at Winter, Farmer said, 'Did you know that over a century ago, in 1903 to be precise, the first wireless telegram was sent across the Atlantic to Europe from here?' With his lobster shears he pointed towards Cape Cod.

Of course Winter didn't know that, but he didn't think it necessary to answer rhetorical questions.

'We ensure that money flows between continents.'

Winter ran his thumb along the inside of the shell, detaching the meat, and asked casually, 'How much money would I need to have to be able to participate?'

'We only work with a handful of investors. But because it's you – a hundred million and you're in.' The professor smiled and dipped his finger into the bowl of water.

He was gradually getting on Winter's nerves. 'I'll speak to my bank tomorrow.' Maybe this really was a business opportunity for von Tobler. 'But why only a handful?' he asked. 'Surely you could roll out the business model?'

'It's a product of history. Originally Al-Bader asked me whether I might help out with the management of his family's fortune. He'd heard of the Harvard investment method and wanted me to look after the alternative investments in his portfolio.'

Farmer kept playing with the shears and cut an imaginary cake in the air.

'Our analysis showed that the chances of success increase once you reach a critical size. Large projects need large investments. So then Al-Bader persuaded allied families to redistribute part of their fortunes. The clans like a smaller circle. And in terms of the amount of capital available, Pyramid Investment Partners is already number one globally.'

Appearing impressed, Winter squeezed lemon into his bowl, washed his hands and ever-so-innocently tested the water by asking, 'Are the Baktars involved at all?'

Winter gained the impression that Farmer's joviality and aura of self-confidence had vanished for a millisecond. But he swiftly rallied. 'Out of principle we don't speak about our clients. As a Swiss banker I'm sure you can understand that.'

The crustacean shells piled high on the plates and Fatima, who sensed the cooling of the atmosphere and had already made neat work of her lobster, changed the subject: 'As an Egyptian I'd naturally be interested to know why you called the private equity fund Pyramid Investment Partners.'

'Pyramids are wonders of the world, aren't they?' He laughed and was back in his element. 'And the pyramids have survived for millennia. Wars, social unrest, political upheaval couldn't touch them. They are unique.'

A discussion arose between Fatima and Farmer about the different perceptions of brands across the globe. Winter leaned back, unsure whether the professor was a megalomaniac or a brilliant visionary.

Although Farmer appeared to be a very affable man with a permanent laugh, Winter could not shake the hunch that this was a masquerade. The wavelengths didn't match up. Winter mistrusted people who were so convinced of themselves and their ideas that they allowed no room for doubt. Religious zealotry made you blind. In business too. Sooner or later the professor would overlook something and crack his head. Or step on a bomb.

Farmer dried his hands and reached for a toothpick. When the professor picked up the silver toothpick holder, the mini receiver whistled in the ears of the two observers on the motorboat. Then the reception turned clear again.

The professor clicked his tongue and pushed his plate away. 'Mmm, that was delicious. For dessert we have a sorbet. I love simplicity!' At least as far as pudding was concerned Farmer and Winter were in agreement.

Fatima peeped at her elegant gold watch and Farmer reassured her, 'Don't worry. We'll fly back in time. The helicopter's going to pick us up in half an hour.'

'I'm sorry, but I have to catch the evening plane to San Francisco.'

The sorbets and pot of coffee arrived and Farmer told them how the profession of lighthouse keeper almost died out within a few years of the invention of the electric bulb.

Then Farmer had to 'attend to something inside the house'. His guests took the opportunity to enjoy a little walk by the sea. It felt good for Winter to move his legs. Alcohol, food, wind and jetlag had made him sleepy. They were strolling across the sand to the water when Fatima asked him, 'How do you know the Baktar clan?'

'Does that mean they're involved?'

'I asked first.'

'I know. But a question is always an answer.'

She made a dismissive gesture.

Winter laughed. 'I have my sources and they say that the Baktars aren't to be taken lightly when it comes to the Americans.'

Fatima appeared satisfied with the answer and said seriously, 'Yes, Kaddour told me that they're involved with Pyramid Investment Partners too. The Baktars have Egyptian roots and are very wealthy. They have stakes in Egyptian firms, but these days do most of their business from Abu Dhabi.'

'What happened in the Iran–Iraq War?'

'I don't know. But I've heard that several members of the Baktar family who were on the run in the war were tortured by American special forces. Another version of the story says that their minibus was blown up by a US rocket in the desert because the Americans mistook it for a different vehicle. But that's more than twenty years ago now.'

'Sometimes twenty years are not enough for the dust to settle on such dramas.'

Revenge is a strong motive, Winter thought. Is it coincidence that through Pyramid Investment Partners the Baktars are investing in an American nuclear power station and other vital infrastructure and planting a family member in a key position? Was this a case of nepotism and corruption? Or was there more behind it? In the worst-case scenario, the signs pointed towards a terrorist attack by the Baktars. Was he just being paranoid perhaps and seeing a terrorist in every Arab? But no sensible person wanted uranium to fall into the wrong hands. What was the score with the engineer in the Vermont nuclear power plant?

Thoughts were churning in Winter's mind. The facts were sparse. He couldn't seize on one theory, nor exclude another. He didn't even have any clear theories.

'Yes,' he heard Fatima say. 'But many people lost family or friends in the war.' They were standing side by side at the shore, looking out at the boats.

'Fatima, please be careful.'

'Don't worry, Winter. Look, I've no intention of shutting myself away, but I'm not alone, am I?'

'I just don't want anything to happen to you.'

'I know.' She paused. 'Thank you.' Fatima stared at Winter for a moment. He was far away in his thoughts.

For a while the two of them gazed out at the ocean. In the distance Winter saw a motorboat, with two men on board, set off in a westerly direction. The hair on the back of his neck stood up. From this distance he couldn't see that both men were wearing Coast Guard jackets, had put down their binoculars and were in the process of sending the recorded conversation, along with their report to the NSA, via an encrypted frequency.

Shortly afterwards, the Pyramid Investment Partners

helicopter set them down at Logan Airport. Amidst the engine noise Farmer wished them goodbye with a grin and a thumbs up.

In the car from the helicopter to the terminal Winter listened to his voicemail. During the flight von Tobler had left a message, the content and tone of which were unequivocal. The tone was that of 'Colonel' von Tobler issuing an order and brooking no dissent. And the content dashed Winter's hopes of a few days with Fatima in San Francisco. He turned to her. 'The younger Al-Bader rang my boss earlier and said he wants to meet me personally in Geneva. Two days ago if possible. I expect Farmer put him in the picture.'

'Good idea. It'll give you the opportunity to get to know him. All part of client service,' the businesswoman said with a wink.

'Have you already had the pleasure?'

'Yes, for a long time he had a reputation as a playboy and he's quite macho. In his youth he wrote off a few Ferraris. Apart from that he's quite nice. He's responsible for the Al-Baders' hotel business. He got married recently so maybe he's grown up since. He's supposed to be a superb horseman and breeds them too.'

The hotel had brought their luggage and now Fatima and Winter were sitting in a lounge with a wooden floor, drinking tea and waiting. That evening Fatima had an appointment with Orafin's head of Latin America. A Brazilian telephone company was interested in a partnership with Egypt, with the aim of getting a toehold in Africa. And Fatima wanted to meet personally the man who was doing the groundwork for the joint venture.

She was working on her laptop and when she noticed Winter watching her she smiled, threw her hair back and said, 'Shame you can't come to San Francisco. As an advisor on security matters you cut quite a figure.'

Winter didn't really know what to say and so just echoed her words: 'As an advisor on security matters?'

Fatima leaned towards Winter. 'Maybe I'll come and visit you in Switzerland.'

Before Winter could reply her flight was called.

After a very short night a crumpled and weary Winter landed in Zürich. Ben let him through customs unhindered and in the underground car park he found his Audi. He drove home on autopilot, showered, changed and was in Geneva just before noon, on time for lunch with Al-Bader's younger brother.

He parked and was informed at the hotel reception that Mr Al-Bader was not there, but wished to let the esteemed Mr Winter know that he was awaiting the pleasure of his company for lunch in the Château de Plaisance. In the smart envelope was Al-Bader's business card. At the gilded hotel bar, with its Russian waitress, Winter drank a criminally expensive double espresso. Then he patiently fought his way through the traffic and out of the city.

The château was at the foot of the Jura Mountains and turned out to be a stud farm, golf course and Gault Millau restaurant. All very tasteful, and with no lack of staff. Even the car park was in landscaped grounds that would have been the envy of many gardeners.

At various points in the past, buildings had been added to the original farm: a mill, stables and a large manor house. It was only after the two ivy-clad towers were built, however, that the property became a château. In the cobbled inner courtyard Winter saw stable boys grooming horses. Two riders with breeches, tall boots and bandy legs were chatting at the well.

The restaurant was in the manor house. Attached to the wall, beside the restaurant door with its crown glass, were plaques with stars, chef's hats and other distinctions. In the restaurant, Winter encountered a music stand, with a leather-bound menu and a *maître de table* who welcomed him in French.

'Good afternoon,' he said in reply. 'My name is Winter.'

'Ah, Monsieur Winter, you are most welcome. Monsieur Al-Bader is waiting for you in our garden.'

They walked through the baroque gloom of the restaurant and re-emerged into the sunshine on the other side. On the terrace a few tables were set for lunch, at which sat young, rather slim women and older, rather corpulent men. The colourful polo shirts of the golfers, the fleeces of the riders and the light summer suits of the businesspeople on duty pretty much balanced each other out. All of them had a view of an artificial pond, which served both as water hazard for the golf course and a water reservoir for the fire service.

Al-Bader was sitting alone at a table, his legs outstretched and a bottle of mineral water before him. Al-Bader the younger was the spitting image of Al-Bader the elder; they were bewilderingly similar. For a moment Winter thought his acquaintance had risen from the dead. It took him aback, and then he thought of Anne.

The hair and moustache were identically styled. And they must wear the same brand of sunglasses. Maybe the pilot spectacles had been bought on a joint shopping trip. Al-Bader was wearing breeches and a light-green polo shirt. Green, the colour of Islam.

Al-Bader stood up, put his sunglasses on the table and offered Winter his hand with a smile. 'Mr Winter, It's an absolute pleasure to meet you.'

'Mr Al-Bader, the pleasure is all mine and many thanks for the invitation. First of all I'd like to express my deepest sympathy. I'm very sorry for what happened.' They shook with both hands. 'We're doing everything we can to find out what occurred.'

For a moment Al-Bader's eyebrows and the corners of his mouth twitched with grief. 'Many thanks. Yes, it's tragic; I miss my twin brother very much. Allah have mercy on his soul.' Winter nodded and Al-Bader continued, 'We often came here together with our families.' He made an expansive gesture towards the golf course, Geneva and the rest of Switzerland. They sat down.

'I didn't know you were twins.'

'Oh yes. I'm just a few minutes younger.'

'He was a wonderful person indeed. Although I only met your brother a few times I always enjoyed his visits to Switzerland.' Winter looked around and decided on small talk for the time being. 'Magnificent château. I take it you ride too?'

'Yes, we keep a few horses here. This morning I went out on my brother's favourite horse. I'm looking after the entire family now.'

Winter nodded sympathetically and let Al-Bader talk.

'I've written a poem about my brother's death: *A bolt from the blue strikes an olive tree atop a hill, splitting it in two. One half dies, the other survives, continues to bear fruit and in a few years thrives once more.*' He then shook his head as if wanting to erase the memory and changed the subject. 'Let's have something to eat here then play a round of golf together.'

Winter had started playing golf ten years ago. He was a decent-enough golfer with a handicap in the low twenties, but over the last few years had only played a few rounds, restricting himself to the tournaments sponsored by the bank. He nodded. 'Good idea.'

Al-Bader was clearly sporty: riding in the morning, golf in the afternoon. Winter wondered what the sheikh did in the evening? Swimming? Or more intimate pleasures? Mineral water appeared and was poured.

'Many thanks for coming to Geneva. I actually wanted to meet you in Boston.'

'My pleasure. The conversation with Professor Farmer was most insightful.'

'Oh yes, dear old Professor Farmer.'

They were handed a heavy, leather-bound menu. The wine list ran to twenty pages and Winter saw bottles he would have to work an entire week to pay for.

'It can't always be easy in the US if you come from the Middle East.'

'Yes, there are a few misunderstandings. The West still harbours many prejudices. Personally I would avoid the USA for the time being. Better safe than sorry. I simply have no desire to be taken into custody under some pretext or other, just so that I can give away business secrets.' Al-Bader grinned. 'As someone who represents a Swiss bank, I'm sure you can understand that.'

Winter could.

In recent years the American financial authorities had placed bank executives and advisers of rich clients under house arrest, or just taken them into custody, in order to access their data of rich US citizens. Swiss law had long made the distinction between tax avoidance and tax fraud, between gentlemen and criminals. Winter's bank, too, was in the process of disposing of bad debts. The new magic term was 'white money'.

Both men decided against the business lunch, choosing instead the fitness menu. Tomato soup and steak with a bouquet of salad, decorated with a strawberry.

When the waiter had gone Al-Bader said, 'The Americans don't know what they want. They preach the free market, but the moment you try to invest they turn protectionist.'

'First food, then morals.'

As if from nowhere a tomato soup appeared with a dot of cream and a herb garnish. The service was rapid.

'The misunderstandings are fuelled by crypto-fascist conservatives. They already think it's a crime if an Arab invests in a Western firm.'

'Please don't take this the wrong way, but I can understand some of their fear of terrorists.'

'You're confusing your categories. I hate terrorists just as much as the Americans do. Extremism, on the left or the right, is bad for business and it harms society.'

Resolved to be more diplomatic, Winter asked cautiously, 'Aren't the boundaries hazy?'

They unfolded their starched napkins.

'There are grey areas, of course. And those are brutally exploited for political gain.'

'What do you mean?'

'First and foremost, the religious, nationalist conservative forces in America are protecting their business interests. They see to it that the various security services receive selective information. They even claim that we're financing terrorists.'

'Mhm?' Winter's mouth was full.

'All wealthy people give donations. We too give money for good causes. Philanthropy is a social obligation and it gives me and my wife pleasure.'

On his wrist Al-Bader wore a Chopard tourbillon. Winter nodded. 'Yes, many wealthy people do that. At the bank we have a department dedicated to it.' A little self-promotion couldn't do any harm.

'We have built wells in areas of poverty, financed hospitals, founded schools and provided seeds for crops. But if one of ten thousand pupils in the schools we support blows themselves up in Israel, the secret services point their finger and accuse us of training terrorists.'

'The same rules are not always applied.'

'There you go. But actually, it is you I wanted to get to know better.'

The soup finished, they set about their steaks as Al-Bader started questioning Winter, and until pudding arrived he felt as if he were under cross-examination. Al-Bader was well informed about his past, very well informed. He had the knack of being able to ask the most indiscreet questions with the greatest politeness. Perhaps it was his stilted Oxford English. He knew about Winter's visit to Bergen. His uncle had given him the lowdown. He knew about his time in the special unit. Clearly his assistants had dug around in the internet archives.

He wanted to know exactly why Winter had abandoned his career with the police.

Winter explained that he'd had enough of stupid bosses and orders. That was almost the whole truth. Al-Bader swore by loyalty and honour and Winter wondered where the conversation was going.

The restaurant emptied; the businesspeople had to get back to work. Winter's digestion got to work too, and tiredness set in again, crawling up his spine to the back of his head. He ordered a ristretto and was happy to be able to stand up ten minutes later. The *maître d'* intercepted them and obliged Al-Bader in the politest way for a signature.

The nice people at the golf club kitted Winter out, handing him a bag full of clubs. He bought a pair of golf shoes, a leather glove, three balls and a red polo shirt.

The changing rooms were in a modern side annex. Winter studied his appearance in the mirror. His head wound had practically healed and the reddish-blue weal from the garrotte was barely visible. He stuffed the .45 SIG in his golf bag. It would hinder his swing otherwise.

They hung the golf bags on the electric buggy and Al-Bader drove off with a laugh. 'The acceleration over the first few metres is almost as good as a Ferrari.' Holding on tight with both hands, Winter remembered how Fatima had described the sheikh.

Al-Bader didn't think a warm-up necessary, so he drove straight to the first tee. He crossed his hands and pressed his palms outwards, producing an audible click in his fingers. Then he rolled his head and shoulders and was ready to start, though he insisted stubbornly in allowing his guest the honour. After three refusals Winter accepted.

'Best of luck!'

'Thanks. Same to you.'

The first hole was a long par four with plenty of bunkers. Desert. In spite of his jetlag, his digestion and unfamiliar kit, Winter remained relaxed and hit the ball cleanly. His ball landed after one hundred and eighty metres, then rolled off the fairway.

Al-Bader swung and his ball came to rest a few metres away from Winter's.

Trees guarded the green. Both missed it and needed a chip. On the well-tended green they holed out in two putts.

The game was on. Both men wanted to win. Al-Bader might be a good client of the bank, but Winter didn't intend to let him triumph. His competitive nature wouldn't allow that to happen. They concentrated on every single shot. As they teed off on the fourth, a short par three, they were still level. With a grin Al-Bader asked, 'What are we playing for?'

'For fame and honour.' Winter didn't want to get into a game of poker with an oil sheikh.

'Agreed. I like that.'

Winter's ball landed in the greenside bunker. Al-Bader found the green, about eight metres from the hole. When they got back into the electric buggy, Winter asked, 'What gave you the idea of setting up Pyramid Investment Partners?'

'It was simple. For good business you've got to get in early and have professional structures. In the last few years we've been looking intensively at how we can spread our risks globally. We concluded that the best thing would be to do it ourselves, so this fund pretty much suggested itself. Here we are. I think you're in the bunker.

Al-Bader parked behind the green. The bunker was deep and reinforced by a wall. Winter took a practice swing, emptied his head and focused on an imaginary point behind the ball. The ball rose in a cloud of sand and stopped a couple of metres from the pin. Al-Bader missed the hole by five centimetres. Winter managed a single putt. Two pars. They were still level-pegging.

The fifth hole was a par four dogleg. On the way to the tee Al-Bader asked, 'Have the Swiss police actually made any progress in their investigation of the crash?'

'Not that I know of, I'm sorry. I heard that they identified the explosive.'

Al-Bader polished his ball. 'And?'

'Probably from army supplies.'

'Surely you don't think the Swiss army has my brother on its conscience?'

'No, I don't believe that.'

Winter resolved to make enquiries with the police in the coming days. He drove off and his ball flew into the long grass. Al-Bader sensed his chance but he sliced his drive too. Both men fumed in silence. When they finally had a view of the second part of the dogleg fairway they could see four men putting on the green and had to wait. Winter leaned on his iron and asked casually, 'How's the collaboration with the Baktar family?'

Al-Bader took a practice swing and said, 'Good. Why do you ask?'

Winter took a practice swing too. 'I can imagine it's not always easy to agree on the projects you should be putting your money into.'

'Professor Farmer and his people do the sums on the projects. He does all the groundwork and the committee decides.'

'Unanimously?'

'Most of the time.'

'And the Baktars don't have a problem entrusting their money to the Americans?'

'In truth, the Baktars don't think much of the Americans. There's history there. But nor do they want to be on the sidelines if there's money to be made.'

'History?'

'I wasn't there, but in the Gulf War some family members got rough treatment from American special forces. Now, of course, it gives them a certain satisfaction to buy up and control American firms and infrastructure. I can understand that.' Al-Bader laughed thoughtfully. The green was free and the two men tied the hole again.

At the next few tees they had to wait again because of the foursome. They chatted about different tax systems. To their surprise they realized they'd both studied law.

At a frontal water hazard, each of them played a risky shot and each lost a ball. Al-Bader complained about the slow players ahead of them. 'These beginners ought to let us through.'

The ninth hole was a tricky par five, lined on both sides by tall trees. When Winter and Al-Bader reached the corner of the dogleg, the group in front was on the green. Forty metres from the green they had to wait once more.

Al-Bader leaned against the buggy, trying to look as bored as possible. One of the men looked back, waved and gestured to them to play through.

'Finally!' Al-Bader exclaimed.

The men withdrew to their buggy.

Al-Bader hit a good pitch that hit the green, but rolled away from the hole. Winter heard him curse in Arabic. His own ball flew high in the air, landed on the green, rolled on a bit and stopped near the hole.

Al-Bader and Winter drove to the green, parked, nodded at the waiting men and stepped onto the green. Al-Bader headed for the pin, while Winter took out the tiny metal fork to repair the pitchmark.

As he bent down he could see from the corner of his eye that three of the four men had left the buggy and were making for the green. Instead of golf clubs they were carrying pistols. Al-Bader had his back turned to them and was removing the flag from the hole.

Winter repaired his divot.

He had his principles. He never acted without analysis. On this occasion the analysis required no more than a split second. The men were around forty years of age and fit. They moved nimbly and there was determination in their faces. They held their pistols with both hands around stomach height. His own pistol was in his bag in the buggy. The green was surrounded on three sides by trees. Gunshots in the woods wouldn't raise any eyebrows. Stuffed hunting trophies hung on the walls of the gloomy restaurant in Château de Plaisance. Moreover the pistols were equipped with silencers. The men had reached the fringe of the green.

A four-step plan formed in Winter's head. It wasn't perfect, but better than nothing.

Al-Bader had pulled out the flag and was strolling along his putting line, unaware.

The men stood apart. The boundary between the fringe and the green made them stop. Different rules applied on the green.

The men on the flanks momentarily looked at the man in the middle, the leader.

Winter embarked on step one. In a single movement he stood up straight and with a twist of his right wrist threw the sharp metal fork at the left flank. The fork spun around and hit one of the attackers in the face.

Time for step two. 'Al-Bader! Watch out! Take cover!' he called out. Al-Bader turned around and dived straight into the bunker. At the same time three shots were fired. Two bullets flew over Al-Bader, one in the air. Winter's metal divot fork was stuck in the shooter's cheek.

Step three was easy. Before the men could get moving again Winter had ducked, picked up his golf ball and hurled it at full pelt at the right flank.

This man was staring as if mesmerized at the gap where Al-Bader had been. The golf ball hit him in the temple and he screamed in pain.

Step four: Winter overcame his instinct to flee, and narrowed the distance to his opponent. The man in the middle fired a second shot. In the firing line, Winter did a diagonal dive roll and switched the putter from his left to right hand. He was glad the green was so soft and springy.

Now back on his feet, Winter swung his putter at the hand gripping the pistol. Moving faster than in a normal putt, the heavy, metal club head smashed into a few small bones.

There was a crack.

The pistol fell on the green.

'Watch out!' Al-Bader yelled.

At once Winter dropped flat onto his stomach, swapping the putter for the pistol in front of him. The shot from the man with the fork in his cheek hit the central attacker in the heart region. A bullet in the heart was worse than a broken hand.

The man who'd been hit grabbed his chest and slowly tipped backwards. The greenkeeper's not going to like this, Winter thought.

When the man toppled over it gave Winter a sight of the attacker whom he'd struck with the golf ball. He was wearing a red polo shirt and had a flat top.

He stared at Winter, who was waiting patiently on the ground with a finger on the trigger of the pistol. Unable to hold back, the attacker cocked his finger on the trigger of his own gun.

The moment Winter saw this he fired a bullet through the man's eye.

In actual fact Winter had been aiming between the eyes. But he didn't have any time to wonder why he'd missed. Survival, rather than prizes, was his aim.

Winter rolled to the side. The man with the fork in his cheek fired two shots into the green beside Winter. These divots were deadlier than those made by balls.

Taking his time, he aimed carefully, pulled the trigger and shot the man's hand and weapon to pieces. The attacker screamed and doubled up in pain.

Winter stood and looked for the fourth man, who in the meantime had clambered back into the buggy. When Winter turned around towards Al-Bader, he saw the left flank rushing at him with a flick knife. Winter was just able to get out of the way, but the blade gashed his left upper arm.

They fell to the ground.

Winter lost the gun.

The knife came swishing down, but Winter was able to grab the forearm of the attacker who straddled him and stared into his eyes, baring his teeth.

The divot fork was still in his cheek.

With a head butt, Winter rammed the fork deeper and up into the man's eye socket, but the injury didn't seem to stop him.

Using all his bodyweight he pushed the knife against Winter's throat.

Winter braced against the attacker with both hands. Blood ran from the injured hand down the blade and dripped onto him.

Winter's arms were burning.

The tip of the knife blade was scratching Winter's throat.

He heard a dull crack.

His opponent went limp and fell to the side.

As Winter peeled himself away from under the lifeless attacker, he saw Al-Bader twist his old-fashioned putter from the dead man's ear.

Relieved, Winter stood up, took the pistol, wiped it on his polo shirt, which wasn't so fresh any more, and put it back in the hand of the central attacker. An old joke came to mind, even though originally it had been about football: Golf isn't a game of life and death. It's more than that.

Following his example, Al-Bader took a tissue from his trouser pocket, wiped the putter and muttered, 'Not rust-proof.'

The last thing they needed was the police on their backs.

Winter did a quick search of the corpses and took three wallets. They grabbed their putters and ran to the buggy.

Two more lost balls.

'I'll drive,' Al-Bader said.

Winter held on tight again and they raced off in pursuit. The fourth man already had more than a hundred metres head start, but there was less power left in his golf buggy's battery as it had been ferrying four men. And now the escapee was alone. They drove back to the Château de Plaisance.

'Thanks for saving my life!' Al-Bader said.

Without taking his eye off the man in front, Winter said, 'Thank you too.'

'Are you alright?' Al-Bader asked, pointing his chin at Winter's arm.

'Yes, it's just a scratch.'

The flesh wound was bleeding, but it would heal quickly. The adrenaline helped numb the pain. As they crossed a narrow bridge over an artificial water hazard they were jolted around. 'Any idea who they were and what they wanted?' Winter asked.

'No. Not a clue. I've never seen those men before and they didn't introduce themselves. Clearly they didn't want to talk to us.'

Al-Bader stood bent forwards with all his weight on the pedal.

'They weren't friendly at any rate. Contract killers in all likelihood.'

Although the attackers hadn't uttered a word Winter somehow had an inkling that they were ex-soldiers. There was something of the military about their poise and haircuts.

The distance between the two golf buggies hadn't narrowed, and it was pointless to start shooting.

On the long, straight fairway of the thirteenth hole Al-Bader said with a grin, 'You always get to meet such charming people playing golf.'

Winter laughed and admitted to himself that he liked Al-Bader. 'Yes, but I'd imagined holing out on the ninth somewhat differently.'

'I was actually going to wait until we got back to the clubhouse, but given the circumstances it would be better if I asked you now.' Al-Bader was sounding formal. Winter gave him an inquiring look, and Al-Bader said, 'I wanted to get to know you while we were playing golf to find out whether you would work for me. Could you imagine that?'

Winter was taken by surprise. He wasn't used to getting job offers in the middle of a chase.

'Oh. Thank you very much. I feel flattered. I'd like some time to think about it. Perhaps we should discuss it after our round.'

Al-Bader nodded, laughed and adjusted his sunglasses. The

man they were chasing was still a good hundred metres ahead and he turned onto a woodland path that led away from the course. 'This path leads to the car park.' When they got there, they saw the abandoned golf buggy and the taillights of a dark, Range Rover. They leaped out, Winter grabbed his SIG pistol from the golf bag and Al-Bader asked as they were running, 'What do you drive?'

'An Audi.'

'Let's take my car.'

'It *is* a Quattro,' Winter protested.

Without replying, Al-Bader pressed his remote control to click open a silver Porsche 911 turbo. Winter didn't comment.

'Hire car. Belongs to a company at Geneva Airport that specialize in exclusive models,' Al-Bader explained, adding with a grin, 'I always rent with fully comprehensive insurance.'

'Thank God,' Winter said, strapping himself into the red sports seat.

Al-Bader sprayed gravel everywhere.

The Range Rover hared down the narrow drive of Château de Plaisance, which was lined by a low, stone wall and originally built for horse-drawn carriages. The heavy four-by-four swerved perilously on the uneven cobbles. In the curves, the car's wheels skidded through the mud at the roadside. The pursuers in the Porsche saw the red tail lights flash between the trees.

Al-Bader drove with the nonchalance of a playboy unconcerned about scratches, let alone insurance.

Winter was pleased his seat had side supports. The Porsche lay close to the ground and the way he was being thrown around meant it would only be a matter of time before they caught up with the Range Rover. When the four-by-four reached the main road, they turned right and zoomed through a little village with stone houses.

On the village square, stood the off-road patrol vehicle of the local policeman.

A few villagers were chatting outside the grocer's.

Three women with shopping bags staggered to the side.

They exited the village at the same high speed.

A team of elderly mountain-bikers were so terrified they ended up in the roadside ditch.

Then they were on the pass that zigzagged up the mountain, alternating between long straights and tight hairpin bends. The centrifugal force on the tight bends thrust Winter to the side, while the subsequent acceleration pushed him back into his seat.

The Range Rover overtook without any regard for the traffic heading back down into the valley. A few drivers managed to avoid a head-on collision only by veering onto the mountain pasture, where grazing cows galloped to safety.

Al-Bader was forced to throttle his speed, change down gear and swerve around a Citroën Picasso that stood across the road. Very Picassan parking.

'He's trying to make it to France,' Winter said.

'They'll stop him at the border.'

'I doubt it's manned.'

Al-Bader accelerated again and overtook a horse transporter. He hooted and flashed his headlights to warn an old camper van chugging in the opposite direction.

Not used to mountains, the overweight Dutchman was sweating from every pore. He slammed on the brakes and drove into the mountain. The heavy rear of his camper van skidded sideways across the road and blocked them.

The Arabic curses came impressively thick and fast. It took the Dutchman almost a minute to collect himself and find the right gear. Only then could the Porsche wriggle around the back of the camper van.

When they had an unimpeded view of the road again, the Range Rover was nowhere to be seen. They shot past a dozen cars in the traffic, took two more hairpin bends, drove alongside a horse pasture and then headed into a sparse fir wood that covered the mountain ridge.

'What now?' Al-Bader asked.

Winter tried to put himself in the mind of the Range Rover driver. What was he thinking? What was his goal? He would try to get himself to safety, probably in France. The attack had gone pear-shaped. The aggressors had been careless, surprised by the counter-attack and hadn't banked on such a rapid escape.

'Slow down!'

'What? We've got to catch up with the bastard.'

'He's in a Range Rover, we're in a Porsche. What would you do to shake off a Porsche?'

'Go cross country,' it dawned on Al-Bader. 'Shit!'

He reduced his speed a little and the two men kept their eyes peeled for signs of the Range Rover. The forest was thin, interspersed with huge moss-covered boulders and low under-growth. Every few hundred metres a muddy track led off from the road. These were used by foresters to tow away felled trees. The tracks were not meant for sports cars and had deep ruts. With every rainfall the tyres of heavy tractors had dug in deeper and deeper. No fresh tracks were visible.

The forest opened out completely. They were nearing the highest point of the pass, marked by a low farmhouse, in front of which a pop-up restaurant had set some tables and umbrellas.

The Porsche stopped with a screech. Leaning out of the window, Winter smiled and asked, 'Have you seen a Range Rover?'

The cheerful group that was sharing some bottles of white wine conferred and several hikers pointed to the ridge to the west.

Winter thanked them and said to Al-Bader, 'He turned off on that track.'

The Porsche's bonnet juddered as they left the main road for the path along the ridge. Fresh tyre marks were visible in the mud.

The sports car skidded. Stones scratched the undercarriage. Winter's head hit the low roof of the car. Maybe the Audi would have been a better choice, after all, he thought.

They re-entered the forest, almost knocking over two young, unsuspecting hikers who had to yank their dog back by its collar. The young man stuck his middle finger up at the Porsche as it raced past.

The track rose fairly steeply and Al-Bader had to cut his speed even more as he wound his way through the trees.

Luckily the forest opened out again.

They arrived at a gently sloping meadow. Down to the left a few horses were grazing and beyond these stretched the mountain chains of the French Jura. To the right was a wind fence. Like in Nantucket.

And further ahead, about half a kilometre away, they spotted the Range Rover. It was heading at normal speed down the slope, perpendicular to the ridge.

'There!' Winter pointed ahead. 'He thinks he lost us.'

Al-Bader put his foot down, left the track and smashed through a loose, wooden fence. The Porsche lost its right-wing mirror and the wooden slats flew everywhere. They were skidding diagonally down the pasture.

The gap was closing.

Further down, the horses started moving. They accompanied the unfamiliar vehicle at a gentle gallop, more curious than scared. Winter had always wondered why horses, who could jump fences with ease, allowed themselves to be penned in.

In the rear-view mirror Winter saw some of the herd dash through the hole in the fence. There would be a furious horse breeder today, as well as a livid greenkeeper. Venturing a sideways glance, Al-Bader said approvingly, 'What magnificent creatures!'

'Watch out! Ditch!'

Al-Bader wrenched the steering wheel to one side and they just missed a water ditch.

The sports car leaped back onto the sloping track.

Now only thirty metres ahead, the Range Rover accelerated again.

Al-Bader put his foot down.

Winter released the safety catch.

The track was tarred again. Advantage Porsche. Leaning

out of the window, Winter balanced his body with his legs and shoulders and fired two shots at the rear tyres of the Range Rover.

The second bullet shredded the right-hand tyre.

The heavy Range Rover skidded, but regained control.

They were back in the forest and speeding towards a hairpin bend, branching off from which was another mud track. As the off-roader swerved, Winter thought it would overturn. But the vehicle merely mowed down a post that held in place a pile of logs.

The logs rolled towards the Porsche.

Al-Bader cursed loudly in Arabic.

The poles clattered past, under and over the Porsche. Unperturbed about losing any further parts Al-Bader careered the sports car further up the slope.

From experience, Winter knew that these forestry tracks generally got narrower, turning into footpaths that could only be navigated by off-road vehicles or not at all. In winter the loggers would let the felled trunks, cleaned of their side branches, glide down the snowy path on a winch.

Al-Bader was more optimistic: 'We've got him.'

The track scratched the Porsche's undercarriage.

Despite its burst tyre, the Range Rover continued to head up the slope at full pelt. Black smoke billowed from the exhaust. The track climbed three hundred metres in a straight line. At the end of the forest, the track made a sharp turn to the left and became an impassable path that wound its way between the last few trees and the steep limestone face. Millions of years ago this had been part of a sea. These days, school groups came here looking for fossilized animals. Winter sensed the forest was thinning out. 'Slow!' he urged.

The driver of the Range Rover saw the danger a fraction of a second too late. He yanked the steering wheel, but his tyres no longer had any grip and he went shooting over the abyss at eighty kilometres per hour. The first thing he saw was the white light of the summer evening sky.

The car seemed to hang in the air for a long while, like the coyote in the Road Runner cartoons.

Slowly the Range Rover started to spin around its own axis. The driver saw the panorama of Lake Geneva, then the forest one hundred metres below. He was screaming. Then came the crash. When Winter and Al-Bader got out the man's cry, mingled with the bang, was still echoing off the cliff face.

The two men stood on the edge of the chasm.

'Shame about the Range Rover,' Al-Bader said.

'Yes. It lost its grip despite the four-wheel drive.'

At that moment the wreck exploded.

Exhausted, they sat on a park bench at the viewing point. Looking at his golf shoes, Winter said, 'What did they want? The four men were after you. At least you were the one they shot at first.'

'I really don't know. I admit that not everyone is fond of me back home. But those attackers didn't look like religious funda-mentalists.' He stroked his clean-shaven chin with his palm.

'No, I got the impression that they were soldiers. Mercenaries perhaps.'

Remembering the three wallets, Winter took them out and emptied their contents onto the bench. Three driving licenses, well done, but probably forgeries with blurry photographs and nondescript names. No personal photos. Change and banknotes: euros, Swiss francs and US dollars – about a few hundred francs worth overall. The card from a Geneva hotel. In one wallet they also found a return ticket for the railway up to the *Jungfraujoch* – 'Top of Europe'. The man had obviously been doing a bit of sightseeing.

Hearing a vehicle stop, they turned around and saw three officers get out of an off-road police car. Once Winter's arm had received medical attention, he and Al-Bader spent the

evening, and half the night, explaining to the various authorities what had happened.

The need for explanations increased with the discovery of
the corpses on the golf course. Coordinating the two cantonal
police forces involved took time, and things slowed down even
more when the federal police stepped in.

It was agreed that the Geneva police would head the
investigation. The three bodies on the golf course in Geneva
outweighed the driver who had plummeted to his death in the
canton of Vaud. Vaud and the federal police each nominated
one liaison officer. At three o'clock in the morning, the officer
in charge escorted Winter out of the interrogation room. Both
men were overtired and only still able to function because of
large amounts of coffee.

'Monsieur Winter, thank you for your cooperation. A
puzzling affair. Please remain at our disposal.'

They shook hands and Winter asked, 'Have you any idea yet
who the four men were?'

'We've identified the three at the golf course. Two Americans
and one Italian. The Americans were in the military for a long
time. Amongst other things they were involved in dubious
operations in Honduras and the first Gulf War. Then they
became freelance security consultants. Colleagues of yours, so
to speak.' The tired, but friendly wink in the eye of the stout
police officer told Winter that this wasn't a serious comment.
His suspicion that the attackers had a military background had
been proved right. 'What about the Italian?'

'A Tyrolean. An arms fanatic and militant Nazi, with a string
of previous convictions. Last year he beat up foreigners in
Berlin.'

'Were the IDs forged?'

'Yes and no. The documents themselves were genuine. Just
the names weren't right. Either they had blank ones or they
were helped by an accomplice working for the authorities.'

'And the fourth man?'

'We haven't identified him yet. His body is pretty charred, but there's no record of his fingerprints.'

'Shame. Would you call me if there are any developments?'

'I will.'

Al-Bader appeared from the neighbouring room, accompanied by another officer. He said goodbye, clearly not resentful and seemingly in a good mood. It was fate, a game. And he was happy to be alive. Al-Bader appeared fairly relaxed about the attack.

He clapped Winter on the shoulder. 'Well, Winter, that's that over with. Fancy a drink?'

Winter nodded and looked the policeman in the eye again. 'One final question. Have you managed to work out where the men came from?'

'The trail of the Italian is cold, but in the hotel rooms we found plane tickets. They flew into Zürich yesterday evening, no...' the officer paused, checking the time, 'two evenings ago, under their real names, from Boston.'

Before Winter opened the door to the bank's headquarters, he closed his eyes for a moment. The night had been short, very short. His blood was throbbing from the stab wound in his arm. The degree of residual alcohol in him was high.

Al-Bader and he had taken a taxi from the police station to Geneva. Much to the annoyance of the rental company, the Porsche had remained in the custody of the police.

The hotel bar was already closed, but Al-Bader called room service, ordered a bottle of whisky to be brought to his suite and insisted that Winter join him in a toast to their adventure.

He'd told Winter that he received regular threats from religious fundamentalists and now increasingly from Western fascists. Although the two groups loathed each other they both feared that their homelands would be sold out.

After the second, exceptionally large, whisky Al-Bader said that the most difficult thing was to find out which competitor was behind the threats. After the third, he poured out his heart and Winter had to promise the drunk sheikh that he would consider his offer very seriously. Fear and alcohol.

Shortly after four o'clock Winter had made himself comfortable on the sofa and slept for three hours. When he left the suite, Al-Bader was snoring away in his huge bed. Winter took a taxi to Château de Plaisance and then drove his Audi straight to the meeting that the bank had convened at short notice. Yesterday evening Känzig had summoned him to Bern in less than flattering tones. Maybe he should give Al-Bader's offer serious consideration. The pay would definitely be better.

Winter took a deep breath. Fresh morning air. The massive door opened with the assistance of an electric motor and Winter climbed the steps to reception. He smiled at the two women behind the flowers, and with his security card opened the side door that led to the back offices. In Bern, the conference rooms were named after famous men, rather than mountains. No women. Winter was ten minutes late when he entered the Einstein room.

In the centre of the room stood an elegant table with six chairs. Schütz, Känzig and Baumgartner on one side, Hodel and Helfer on the other.

With a nod to his colleagues, Winter sat in the remaining free chair.

Without interrupting his rant, Känzig turned and fired a broadside at Winter: 'Ah, our esteemed head of security is back. While our clients are being bumped off, you're gallivanting on holiday. Not acceptable. From now on I expect you to be a more visible presence to reassure our clients that they and their money are safe with us in Switzerland.'

Winter smiled, waited for Känzig to pause in his lecture for breath and said, 'Al-Bader's younger twin brother is fine. I had a long chat with him this morning and he's most satisfied with our work. Yesterday I saved his life. In my job that's all part of client service.'

Känzig was speechless, but smart enough to keep quiet.

'Explain the corpses on the golf course,' Helfer said. 'A prying crime journalist from Geneva wants to know what you were doing there.'

'Playing a round of golf with a client,' Winter said. 'To my knowledge we don't comment on individual client relations. Check the bulletin of the Geneva police.' Winter gave a broad outline of the previous day's events, finishing with the words, 'Most likely a radical nationalist faction from America.'

His colleagues nodded.

'And they have some connection or other with our bank,'
Winter added.

Now he had the undivided attention of everyone, even
Känzig.

'It's just conjecture, but I'm starting to ask myself where the
attackers got certain confidential information from.'

'But I can't say that to the media,' Helfer said. He tailed off
towards the end of his sentence, as if muttering to himself.
Everybody knew he wasn't exactly brimming with intelligence.

Hodel fixed Winter with crystal-clear eyes. 'My God, Winter.
If that's the case then trust in our bank will be irreversibly
eroded. What proof have you got to back up your suspicions?'

'It's a gut feeling.'

'Be more precise!'

'How could the attackers have known that Muhammed
Al-Bader was going to get into a helicopter laid on by us? Only
a select group of people were privy to this information. How
come the attempt to kill his brother took place exactly when I
went to meet him on von Tobler's orders? It's not easy to get
up close to the Al-Bader brothers. They're always on the move,
and they rarely appear in public. These attacks were not just
coincidental.'

'Are you saying we've got a mole in the bank?'

'Yes,' Winter said tersely.

Silence around the table.

The room became smaller, the walls crowding inwards
menacingly, threatening to squash them. The men stared at
the table top, documents were rearranged. Nobody dared look
anyone else in the eye. After a minute that seemed like an
eternity, Hodel said, 'Let's assume Winter's right. What does
that mean for our bank?'

'Negative headlines, loss of reputation,' Helfer blurted out.

'And?' Hodel looked at Schütz, who said, 'Security-conscious
clients, especially those from India, China and the Arabian

Peninsula, would withdraw their money. For them Switzerland
is a safe haven. We'd get into a downward spiral. Our business
is based on trust, trust is based on human behaviour and once
negative rumours start circulating it's very difficult to counter
these.'

Baumgartner cleared his throat.

Hodel looked at him.

The liaison man stroked his slicked-back hair and said in
his deep voice, 'If you'd allow me, I'd like to mention another
factor that mustn't be ignored at the moment. You won't be
surprised to hear that I don't always regard our cooperation as
frictionless. In the current circumstances those voices at head
office demanding a total integration of the bank will be getting
louder. We might go so far as to abandon the name, completely
merge the back offices and only retain the very best people.'

Winter had heard a few times about the aspirations of the
much bigger financial group. Those in favour of total integration
argued that it would cut costs. Opponents believed that the
bosom of the parent company would squash the small bank.
Over the past few years von Tobler had always managed to scotch
these attempts. He emphasized the bank's close relationship with
its clients, its intimate atmosphere and illustrious name.

Winter recalled the last lunch he'd had – over a month ago
in Zürich – with Hugentobler, the financial group's head of
security.

The head office was working with McKinsey consultants
to put together a cost-cutting programme. You didn't have
to be a fortune teller to predict that the external firm would
recommend centralizing and standardizing everything. Perhaps
the bank would be allowed to keep the name as a consolation
prize. All the same, Winter was taken aback by the liaison
man's threats. The shark had smelled blood.

'Gentlemen, gentlemen,' he heard Hodel say. 'Let's not
throw the baby out with the bathwater.'

Undeterred, Baumgartner continued with extreme politeness, 'Well, perhaps the simplest thing would be to sweep the entire matter under the carpet, and then quickly forget about it. An internal mole. Pffh.'

He shook his head in contempt. 'We must learn to trust each other. It's our job to motivate and inspire our employees, not suspect them.'

Baumgartner smiled at Winter.

Winter, the whistle-blower.

Känzig nodded and was about to speak again.

Hodel, the former general staff officer, was quicker. He didn't want to be having this discussion and said tersely, 'Actions?'

Helfer took the floor. 'I'll get on the phone and ask my journalist contacts what they know. That'll allow me to get a sense of the extent to which the scant facts are now common knowledge. I can also set out our version of events.' Maybe the man isn't as stupid as I imagined, Winter thought.

Aligning his document folder to the edge of the table, Schütz said, 'I think we ought to go on as normal. If a client asks, we say we're horrified at the thought we could be involved in any way and we reject any connection. We have to focus on our annual conference at the end of the week. May I remind you that we have invited lots of top-notch clients. Perhaps,' he continued, looking at Hodel, 'it would be a good idea if Herr von Tobler went out of his way to make plenty of time for them.'

'No worries,' Hodel replied. 'Herr von Tobler will spend most of his time promoting our three new private equity funds to the guests.'

Winter's ears pricked up. 'What does that mean exactly?'

'The deliberations are still at an early stage,' Hodel said, 'but we're looking to increase direct investment. We plan to create three global vehicles: one for raw materials, one for infrastructure and one for property. Opportunities for buyers are good at the moment.'

'In Boston I met Professor Farmer from Pyramid Investment Partners. He assists Al-Bader and other Arab families with their investments in the United States.'

'Yes, he and others are stiff competition for our investment management team,' Schütz said. 'They promise far greater returns. Albeit without any evidence. They don't have any history. But they're making life pretty tough for us.'

'To stop the money drain, we have decided,' Hodel said, meaning himself and von Tobler, 'that we can do the same. Fees for special services are better than for off-the-peg products.'

Hodel turned to Winter. 'What additional security measures would you consider implementing?' An order formulated as a question.

'This conference was organized long ago, but I'm going to double-check and reinforce personal security.'

The discussion continued for a while longer. Helfer was desperate to know what the language arrangements were. Winter zoned out and tried to put his thoughts in some sort of order. He too found it hard to believe that an employee of the bank could have collaborated with extremists. Winter was responsible for checking security. But no system was perfect. Maybe someone had recently got a new girlfriend? Maybe someone was in debt and all of a sudden open to bribery? Maybe someone had employed a consultant, or temporary employee, and skipped the security check?

Or maybe someone was just really pissed off? The working environment wasn't bad and the bank paid its staff a decent salary. Ever since an employee of a Zürich bank had run amok a few years back and shot several colleagues dead, they'd been making an effort. Theoretically at least. Although they'd promoted Känzig.

Now on his feet, Känzig was trying to summarize the discussion on a whiteboard.

Baumgartner received an urgent call and excused himself.

Winter wondered whether he'd faked the call so he could leave the room. After all, almost anything was possible with today's smartphones. Then a shiver ran down his spine. He'd completely forgotten to check who had rung Anne in the final hours before her death.

A few minutes later Hodel closed the meeting. 'I don't believe I need to remind you that everything we've said in this room is absolutely confidential.'

When Schütz opened the door, Winter grabbed him by the arm and nodded in the other direction. 'Can I ask you something?'

Schütz nodded. They went into Winter's office. He opened the window that gave onto the rear courtyard. As ever it smelled of pizza. Making himself comfortable on the leather sofa, Schütz put his folder on the floor and said, 'Nasty business, isn't it?'

'Schütz, in Boston and Geneva there was talk of the Baktar family. What do you know about them?'

'Oh, the Baktars,' Schütz said with a knowing smile. 'They're a very specific case. Dallas in Arabic. To my knowledge there was quite a lot of squabbling between the young heirs. Part of the family has rediscovered Allah and the *Qu'ran*; the other part couldn't give a shit about that stuff and is enjoying the jet-set life. We administer a small portion of the latter's fortune via our Geneva branch. Their petty cash for Europe.'

'Ever met any of them personally?'

'No.'

'Any rumours?'

'Our Geneva colleagues weren't unhappy to pass on the mandate.' After a dramatic pause, Schütz continued, 'Apparently the odd rumour was floating around that the Baktars divert money into channels we ought to have nothing to do with.'

'What does that mean?'

'Financing of terrorists and arms. The usual, I assume.' Schütz pulled a face. Although he found it distasteful, he operated according to the principle of 'What I don't know can't hurt me'. Also known as 'discretion'.

'Could you ask Geneva what the current state of play is? I don't want us to get a nasty surprise. Especially not after the attack yesterday. The authorities and journalists will undertake their own research.'

'Will do.' He slapped his thigh, checked the time and said, 'But I have to go now. I've got a client coming in two minutes.'

'Thanks.'

'My pleasure. And take care of yourself.' Schütz pointed to the scar on his neck and must have noticed that Winter was moving his injured arm more gingerly than usual. Touched, Winter gave him a coy smile and muttered, 'Occupational hazard.'

After Schütz had left, Winter set about checking the phone numbers.

According to Dirk's list, Anne took a brief call from the bank at 16:55 on July 24.

Winter accessed the list of the bank's telephone extensions in the computer system. The number belonged to a telephone in room 107: first floor, room seven. Winter knew it, an unflashy conference room for internal meetings. It was right beside Anne's office, a few metres from where he was now.

Did someone from the bank go looking for Anne, find she wasn't there and then call her from that conference room? Why hadn't the bank employee used their mobile? Practically every member of staff had a mobile, on which they were required to be contactable at all times.

Sometimes that room was used for temporary project work by external consultants or interns, but he couldn't remember if it was currently in use. He stood up and went over to room 107. The door was closed. He knocked and entered without waiting for an answer.

The room was furnished with the bank's standard furniture and looked tidy, unused. The wastepaper basket was empty,

the small, plastic tray full of office stationery and the obligatory flip chart blank. Winter opened the sliding door of the
sideboard: empty.

Then he turned the key of the cupboard and opened the
metal doors. Inside were a dozen empty files as well as two
boxes for printer paper, stuffed full of old documents. Winter
pulled out a few pieces of paper: documents relating to the
'Futura' IT project. As far as Winter knew, very highly paid
consultants from a specialist firm were developing IT archi-
tecture recommendations for the outdated trading platform
for Dirk.

As Winter was stuffing the papers back in, one of the sides
of the box broke and its contents came spilling out.

'Shit.'

Winter crouched and gathered up the bits of paper.
Notes, calculations, internet analyses, minutes of project and
sub-project management meetings. All of a sudden he stopped
what he was doing. An extraordinary sub-project management
meeting had been held here in room 107 on the Friday
afternoon of July 24.

According to the minutes, three consultants had been here
from two till half past four to discuss options for raising the
transmission capacity of the dedicated lines between branches.
Did the consultants leave the building immediately after the
meeting or did they stay in the room afterwards?

Winter kept the minutes, pushed the cardboard box into
a corner of the cupboard, returned to his office and called
the consultancy firm. He obtained the mobile number of the
sub-project leader and managed to get hold of him. In the
background Winter could hear the noise of a rail journey.

Having introduced himself, Winter asked, 'You were working
at our offices on July the twenty-fourth, in project room 107.
Did you leave straight after the meeting?'

'No.'

'Can you remember what time you left the bank?'

'Just before five o'clock. We took the train. Why? Is there something wrong with the bill?' Hourly billing by consultants was a sore topic. The more hours calculated, the more revenue. When calculating their hours, consultants usually only erred in one direction: upwards. Not wanting to enter one of these discussions, Winter said, 'No. Did you use the conference room landline?'

'No. I always use my mobile.' The consultant's tone was a mixture of irritation and curiosity.

'We're just in the process of trying to clear up an internal transaction that doesn't have anything to do with you or your firm.'

The train went through a tunnel and the connection hissed. This gave Winter a few seconds to think. When the reception improved again, he continued, 'After you finished the meeting and packed up, did you notice anything? Bump into anyone?'

'Wait a sec.' Winter heard the man stand up and walk through the train. 'Now you ask me, I *do* remember something. We'd put our laptops away and were about to go when a man came in without knocking. I expect he thought the room was empty.'

'Could you describe him?'

The IT consultant leaned against the wall in a quiet corner of the train and described the man. Winter thanked him and hung up. The description matched.

Schmitt, Berger & Partners detective agency was in an industrial area of Zürich. Winter had a job interview with Schmitt at half past one. Or, more accurately, an informal meeting so they could get to know each other.

A call from a phone box, and a casual mention that he was a police officer in search of a new challenge, had sufficed. The managing partner was curious and agreed to a meeting in spite of his packed schedule.

Having located the old factory building that housed the offices of Schmitt, Berger & Partners, Winter drove around it twice. The Audi crossed railway tracks and passed building sites, warehouses and temporary car parks. The factory was in of one of the key zones of Zürich's urban redevelopment.

The area behind the station was in the process of reinventing itself. Some of the old buildings dating back to the beginnings of the industrial era had already been converted into expensive lofts. Others had been occupied by short-lived clubs, restaurants and alternative shops. All on the hunt for inexpensive rents somewhere central.

Besides a few bleak warehouses only a local brewery seemed to be still fulfilling its original function.

Winter parked beside a wine shop which had placed a few barrels outside for decoration and was advertising organic wines. Construction vehicles started clanking away; it was one o'clock. The noise signalled to everybody within a radius of five hundred metres that the lunch break was over.

He let a tram rattle past, crossed the street and entered the factory complex. In the huge former assembly hall with its jagged roof, filthy roof-lights and steel supporting columns, a few cheap dividing walls had been erected.

A sign at the entrance listed about forty shops, companies and restaurants. As he was not in a hurry, Winter took a stroll through the hustle and bustle inside. In the middle of the factory hall, some restaurants were grouped around an artificial courtyard.

Dozens of decorative olive trees stood outside a florist's. Other shops were striving to create a Mediterranean atmosphere too. A travel agent had laid out a beach with real sand and sun loungers, and another vintner's specialized in Tuscan wines and antipasti.

The Schmitt, Berger & Partners offices were in the quieter area to the rear of the hall, in a side passage between the toilets and an architect's office for wooden buildings. A discreet sign announced that Schmitt, Berger & Partners offered consulting services in personal protection and security matters. Drawn blinds on three of the windows blocked Winter's view of the office interior. Through the fourth, he caught a glimpse of an empty reception area with yet another olive tree, a computer and a modernist painting.

Winter did a tour of the factory floor, made a few purchases and then approached Schmitt, Berger & Partners again. But before the meeting, he went into the toilets. He locked himself in the farthest cubicle, put down the lid and prepared for his visit. Three minutes later he exited the cubicle, closed the wooden door and stuck a note on it saying, 'Broken!! Out of order!!' That would keep people out.

Winter washed his hands and glimpsed in the mirror. The small moustache as well as the chewing gum in his cheeks disguised his appearance. To change a few details was often enough. Satisfied, he left and entered the Schmitt, Berger & Partners offices. The olive tree had been joined by a brunette, typing away. She paused, looked up and said, 'Hello. Who should I say is here?'

'Summer. I have a meeting with Herr Schmidt.'

With a smile she picked up the phone and announced that Herr Summer had arrived. Summer was the perfect alias, nondescript but more believable than Müller or Meier. Herr Summer smiled back.

'Just a moment, please. Herr Schmitt is on his way.' She indicated a designer chair beside the olive tree, but Herr Summer preferred to stand.

Soon afterwards a door opened and a man in his early fifties invited Winter to come in. He was tall, suntanned and had short, grey hair. He wore jeans with a large belt buckle, and a white shirt with an embroidered monogram and rolled-up sleeves. The man's handshake was firm and his teeth polished.

'Good afternoon, Herr Summer.'

'Good afternoon, Herr Schmitt. Thanks for agreeing to meet me at such short notice. I have a business meeting at the airport this afternoon and on the way here I thought there's no point in having good ideas if you don't follow them through. Your firm has an excellent reputation in our circles, which is why I rang out of the blue.'

In Schmitt's office were two further olive trees. The large desk was dominated by three screens, arranged as in a flight cockpit. Noticing Winter's interest, Schmitt explained, 'Today it's impossible to underestimate the importance of IT in our business. Schmitt, Berger & Partners specializes in professional security consulting, especially in the digital world.'

Winter gave a theatrical sigh and said, 'What happened to the good old private detective? When I was still on the beat we would spend days observing a suspect.'

'Well, that's progress for you. But please, take a seat.' Herr Summer sat in one of the two steel chairs in front of the cockpit.

'Can I offer you a coffee?'

'Espresso, please.' Winter hoped that Schmitt would leave the office, but he ordered the coffees by phone. Two minutes and three exchanges of small talk later, the assistant came in with a tray carrying two espresso cups in a minimalist design, and put these beside the screens.

As Winter bent forwards to pick up his cup he got a glimpse of the three screens. Two of them were divided into quarters, displaying stills from security cameras, while various windows were open on the third screen. Schmitt stirred his sugar and said, 'So you could envisage leaving the police force and working in the private security industry?'

Winter leaned back in the steel chair, placing his left hand on the armrest and the right in his jacket. 'Yes, I know a few colleagues who've made the move already. After the third beer, however, they admit that it's difficult to get jobs working alone. I prefer working as part of a network, where a variety of specialists complement each other. Personal protection, digital security etc.'

As he was gabbling away and gesticulating with his left hand, his right found the new mobile in his pocket and the correct button to send the two emails he'd written earlier.

One to the anonymous Herr Müller, the client of the private eye in Winter's slurry pit.

And the other to Harald Schneider, the freelance journalist and client of the helicopter company that specialized in infrared photos.

'... over the past fifteen years with the police, I've had the opportunity to work in a wide variety of departments. Drugs, child abuse, murder, abduction. Everything you could imagine.' Schmitt was now leaning back too, his eyelids slightly drooping. His digestion was probably drawing the blood from his brain.

After Winter's emails had been sent it took twelve seconds for them to be picked up by the nearest radio mast, encrypted and hurtled through half of Switzerland via two servers of the telecom provider before finally being forwarded to the recipient via the Hotmail server.

A soft 'Ping! Ping!' announced the arrival of two new emails on Schmitt's computer.

'... I can also definitely see myself working in personal protection. I'm fit and a second-degree black belt in karate...' Winter heard himself say. Schmitt's eyelids lifted slightly and he peered at the new emails. Winter carried on regardless, registering with satisfaction the dilation in Schmitt's pupils.

Winter paused, bent forwards and picked up the espresso cup by its minimalist handle. Unfortunately it slipped from his hand and clattered back down on the saucer. Out of the corner of his eye he glimpsed sender, subject and the first two lines of his emails on the screen.

A double hit.

'I'm really sorry,' Winter said with an embarrassed smile and pointing at the cup. He was playing for time, preventing Schmitt from dealing with the two emails immediately. A glance at his watch told him that he'd left the toilets nine minutes ago. Not long now. 'How does the Schmitt, Berger & Partners network function?'

Schmitt was torn between the computer screen with those emails and his guest. He finished his espresso and opened his mouth to embark on an explanation when the belated August 1st firework went off in the toilets.

The candle had burned down as planned and the wick reached the fuse of the bangers that Winter had bought on sale at half price after August 1. When Winter was a child they used to call them 'ladies' farts'.

The farts made a hell of a racket.

Schmitt stared in bewilderment at the wall that separated his office from the noise.

There were wisps of smoke too.

This was phase two of Winter's plan. As the smoke rose in the cramped cubicle, it reached the fire detector and triggered the alarm. The terrified people in the toilets scarpered. Nobody switched off the alarm. The sprinkler system was programmed so that that twelve nozzles in the vicinity of fire would automatically be activated once the alarm went off. Winter knew how the system worked; the bank was fitted with one too.

It started raining.

On the computers.

'Shit!' Schmitt cursed.

'Quick! Have you got anything to cover them? A plastic tablecloth or something?' Winter suggested.

Schmitt got up and dashed out of his office.

This was the moment Winter had been waiting for. He snatched Schmitt's mobile from the desk. With a paper clip he removed the SIM card and replaced it with another he had bought from an electronics shop stuffed with goods of dubious origin. Winter wiped off his fingerprints, replaced the mobile, and hurried into the dry lobby.

The racket from the toilets had stopped, but the water was still drizzling unchecked onto the computers. Schmitt came back with plastic tablecloths from the nearest restaurant, his assistant in tow. Ignoring Winter, they started covering the computers and the desk.

Winter left.

The job interview was over.

He made his way swiftly through the crowd of onlookers. Fire officers came running to the scene. When he left the factory hall he ripped off the moustache and spat out the chewing gum. Once at his car he took off his wet coat and threw it onto the back seat.

Safely in the dry of his car, Winter inserted Schmitt's SIM card into his own phone and copied the contact data. He put his SIM back in again and tucked Schmitt's into his wallet.

Schmitt's mobile was wet and it would take some time before he discovered that the SIM had been switched. Winter scrolled through all the new contacts, hoping to come across names and numbers he recognized.

Nothing.

The phone rang. Fatima. Winter pressed the green button straightaway. 'Hello, Fatima!'

'Hello, Winter. How are you?'

'Fine, thanks. Yesterday I played a round of golf with Al-Bader's brother' – it seemed longer than twenty-four hours ago – 'and just now I got caught in a downpour.'

'But you're back in the dry now?'

'Yes. It's a long story and I'll tell you about it some other time. Where are you? How are you? Everything okay?' he asked, concerned.

'I'm fine, thanks. I'm at the airport in San Francisco and wanted to know if you'd mind me coming to see you?'

Taken by surprise, Winter didn't respond. He had mixed feelings. He was pleased that Fatima had called, but unsure where it was all heading. In truth a large part of him had assumed that after Boston he'd never see her again. Any hint of a relationship felt like a complication he didn't need so soon after Anne's death.

And the day after tomorrow he had to go to the bank's annual three-day conference in Interlaken.

Still, Fatima would love Interlaken, nestled between Lakes Thun and Brienz in the heart of the Bernese Oberland. They could go to the mountains together, he supposed, as friends. Before Winter had fully thought through the implications he heard himself say, 'Fatima, when are you landing?'

'I could be in Zürich at ten thirty.'

'I can pick you up.'

'Thanks, Tom,' Fatima said. She didn't seem to want the conversation to end. 'The Brazilian business is on course. But

I'm not making progress with Farmer. Smith's people are putting pressure on Pyramid Investment Partners. They're threatening them with the tax authorities, who apparently have the right to examine every single transaction on the basis of the slightest suspicion.'

Winter was unfamiliar with the jungle of American regulation. 'And?'

'Farmer has entrenched himself with his lawyers. The problem is that the NSA has raised the national terror threat from Yellow to Orange. Elements of martial law come into force and it means that the NSA gets more power.'

'Orange is the second highest level?'

'Yes, the probability that America will suffer a terrorist attack in the next seven days is now judged to be higher than fifty per cent.'

For a moment neither of them said anything, reluctant to discuss it further over the phone. Winter thought of Anne and wondered whether the helicopter crash could be classified as a 'terrorist attack'.

Eventually Winter ended the conversation abruptly. 'I'll see you at the airport.'

Winter left Zürich and once he'd swung onto the A1 motorway he put on 'Sarah McLachlan Live in Concert'. The music helped him think.

Tomorrow he'd drive back in the other direction and pick up Fatima. What would happen then? he wondered.

There was little traffic on the roads. Many people were still on holiday. Winter gave free rein to his thoughts and replayed in his head the events of the last few days. He fell from the bridge again and fought for his life on the golf course. The image of Angela, who had placed one hand on Anne's coffin, popped up.

The anticipation of seeing Fatima mingled with his grief over Anne. Winter recalled the happy photo in Anne's office with the three As in the pizzeria: Anne, Andrea and Angela. Three sisters, similar and yet different, but it seemed as if they'd all been close. Like the Al-Bader twins.

Winter imagined the three women chatting away to each other for hours on end. In the garden at Fraubrunnen, or on the phone. He knew virtually nothing about them.

Angela was studying in the US.

And Andrea?

Maybe Anne had told Andrea something about her secret admirer.

Had Anne been responsive to him? The melancholy gave way to a bitter taste in his mouth. Was it possible that Anne hadn't been completely honest? Had there been someone else?

The simplest thing would be to ask Andrea.

He called directory enquiries.

Andrea lived in Kölliken, which was pretty much halfway between Zürich and Bern. Winter didn't believe in telepathy. It must be coincidence that he'd thought about Andrea now. A smile darted across Winter's face. Five minutes later he indicated and left the motorway.

The confusion of his emotions dissipated.

He focused on the next step.

Anne's sister lived with her family in the middle of the village in a large renovated farmhouse that now consisted of several apartments.

Winter parked and got out.

An elderly couple doing some gardening. A dog. Then he saw Andrea, who was attaching a hose to a garden sprinkler.

Andrea's apartment was in the former barn. It had a large, modern glass front that connected the garden and kitchen-diner.

Andrea looked up and gazed at Winter with an expression of curiosity and interest, and as though he seemed somehow familiar. He closed the car door, smiled and walked across the lawn to her.

'Good evening. I'm sorry to bother you. My name's Tom Winter.' He smiled again. 'Anne's colleague.' They'd shaken hands at the funeral, but she'd had tears in her eyes at the time and he had been wearing a formal suit. From her eyes he could see that she recognized him.

She nodded, wiped her hands on her jeans and came up to him. 'Hello.'

They shook hands.

'I'm really sorry,' he said softly.

Andrea shook her head and pointed at the sprinkler. 'For some reason the hose doesn't fit properly.'

'Let me take a look.'

As the two of them crouched, Winter eyed Andrea. She

looked uncomplicated. Jeans, sleeveless T-shirt and loose ponytail. Her bare feet had unpainted toenails peeping out of her hiking sandals.

Winter recalled Anne telling him that Andrea worked in a home for troubled children, which was integrated in a farm with lots of animals. Or was it disabled children? In any case he could well imagine Andrea shepherding snotty adolescents, or caring for the disabled. Winter twisted the connection between the hose and sprinkler.

It clicked and Andrea said, 'Wow! How did you do that?'

Winter shrugged and they stood up. Andrea went over to the house, said, 'Watch out!' and turned the water on.

When they were on the paved terrace between the lawn and the kitchen, Andrea asked, 'Something to drink? I've got iced, peppermint tea.'

'Sounds good. Very good, in fact. Yes please.'

She pointed to an ancient wooden bench by the wall, went inside and Winter sat. Two minutes later he had in his hand a big glass of peppermint tea, ice cubes and a slice of lemon. It tasted wonderful.

'Thanks. The ideal drink for a summer's day. Tastes great.'

'Thank you.'

'Homemade?'

'Secret recipe.' A fleeting smile flew across Andrea's face, but vanished quickly. She sat at the other end of the wooden bench, leaning against the tall armrest, into which countless initials and hearts had been carved over the decades.

For a while they watched the sprinkler and the curved lines of the water. The drops of water formed rhythmic waves that fell on top of each other, glittering colourfully in the sun. Winter took another sip.

'I don't like ambushing you like this. But I was on the motorway from Zürich to Bern and I thought I'd drop in. A telepathic brainwave, so to speak.'

'It's fine. I wondered when someone from the police or bank might pay a visit.'

'Has no one come to see you yet?'

'No.' Monosyllabic.

'I'm sorry.' Winter didn't know who he was apologising for. He felt a responsibility not only for the bank, but because of his past in the police too. A little, at least.

'Have they found anything out yet?'

He'd have loved to tell Andrea everything he knew. But he didn't want to arouse any false hopes and so said, 'I'm sure the authorities are doing all they can to get to the bottom of the crash. But a thorough analysis takes time. The bank is only involved on the fringe. We're waiting too.' Eager to regain the initiative, Winter added, 'I didn't just come here as her boss; I also really liked Anne.'

'I know. Anne liked you too.'

Winter felt a warm feeling spreading inside him and for a moment he thought he was going to have to hold back tears. He looked away and squinted at the rainbow-coloured fountains of water. He wondered what Andrea knew, but didn't dare ask her directly. Maybe he'd find the courage to do so later.

Then Andrea started talking about her sister. She aimed her words more at the rainbow than Winter. She spoke of how much she missed Anne. They'd always called each other on Wednesday evenings and at the weekend.

Andrea said that both she and Anne had shared a passion for sport and nature. Sometimes they'd go riding together on a neighbouring farmer's horses. Now, Andrea didn't feel like riding any more, but she was missing the horses. Her husband worked for an insurance company and was not particularly sporty.

She smiled, almost apologetically, and Winter just nodded. He knew that once people had started talking it was better to let them tell their story rather than interrupt with words or questions.

Anne had often sat on this wooden bench, she continued. She'd also accompanied her to the home a few times. Anne had said that the people she'd encountered with the police were surely easier to deal with than the disabled children. Andrea hadn't agreed. She could never work for the police. Too dangerous.

It wasn't fair that Anne should have been the victim. Anne had left the police to study law, and then work in her supposedly safer job for the bank.

Andrea found it hard to use the past tense when talking about her sister.

In her memories Anne was still alive; in her soul that was true.

The neighbour's dog came slowly trotting past. In dog years he must be as least as old as the pensioners who lived next door, and his eyes with their droopy bags looked at Winter trustingly. Could dogs cry? The black-and-white Bernese mountain dog had arthritis and his movements were stiff. He doubled back and pushed awkwardly between Andrea and Winter, wanting to be stroked.

Andrea bent forwards and fondled him below the muzzle with both hands.

'I can't be sure,' Winter said, 'but I always got the impression that Anne liked working for the bank.'

This was actually a question to Andrea, but Winter had wrapped it up in a statement. He hoped to get her flow going again.

Andrea let go of the dog, who turned to Winter for more petting. He laid his head on Winter's knee, which clearly didn't smell of cat. Or perhaps the dog was too old to pick up any traces of Tiger's scent. Or he didn't care. At any rate Winter dutifully ruffled the dog's well-groomed fur. His behaviour mirrored that of Andrea.

After a sip of peppermint she said, 'Yes, she did like working for the bank, especially meeting new clients. She told me that

in spite of their money they were often astonishingly nice.'
Andrea broke off abruptly and Winter sensed there was more
she wanted to say.

'What did she think of me?' he asked, in the meantime.

'Anne always said you were a good boss. She learned a lot
from you.' Smiling, she continued, 'In spring she said it was a
shame that she'd had to meet you as her boss rather than in a
different capacity.'

Winter waited. When no more was forthcoming he said,
'At the bank, relationships between employees are very much
frowned upon. We can't forbid them – nor do we want to – but
they raise eyebrows. Especially in my role as head of security
I've done all I can to ensure that they're regarded as undesirable.'

'I understand. And I think Anne appreciated this too. She
always wanted to do the right thing.'

'Sometimes it doesn't work.'

'I know.'

They fell silent again. The dog lay now on the warm paving
slabs, folded his aching legs under his body and yawned. In
the animal's wide-open mouth Winter could see yellow, worn
teeth. Then he felt Andrea's hand on his right forearm.

'I think you would have made a good couple.'

'It wasn't to be.'

'I'm really sorry, Tom,' she sympathized.

'Thank you.' Sometimes the world was a cruel place.

Andrea nodded, and she looked a little uncomfortable.

'Seeing as Anne's no longer here, you ought to know that
she had another admirer,' she said then.

Winter tensed inside and Andrea retracted her hand.

'We discussed a few times in the last few weeks whether
she ought to tell you or not. We weren't sure how you would
react. When we went on our final ride, along the stream to
*Oberentfelden* and back through the woods, we almost had an
argument.

'I don't understand.'

'Although I only knew you from what Anne had said, I thought that you definitely wouldn't have a problem with it. She thought a lot of you and I thought you'd understand. Anne didn't want to talk to you about it. Or felt she couldn't. At least not while everything was still up in the air. It was too private. She didn't want to put a strain on your relationship before she knew how far it might go.'

'When was this exactly?'

'I don't know. Hold on, yes I do. On July the twenty-second. I was working in the morning and we celebrated Ralph's fifteenth birthday at the home. He's in a wheelchair and I held the cake for him so he could blow out the candles. Yes, it was the twenty-second.' Shaking her head pensively, she wrapped her arms around her body. 'It seems like an age ago. Anne told me that you'd invited her to dinner. You're renovating your house, aren't you?'

'Yes, but I haven't got as far as you,' Winter said, nodding at the farmhouse. His terrace wasn't even finished. But at the moment that was irrelevant and he asked, 'What did Anne say? Was there anything else?'

This second sentence, in particular the 'else', had slipped out unwittingly. He'd been struggling with the unwritten, internal rules of the bank. She had been his colleague, and that's why he'd been restrained. Too hesitant, maybe. And so it was no surprise that there'd been another relationship. Anne was an attractive woman. The love letter alone spoke volumes.

Andrea shook her head, smiling. 'No, it wasn't what you think. It was not reciprocated. You were the only one.'

Winter looked at Andrea in relief. Until she said, 'But that old fart von Tobler, he was after Anne.'

'J' as in Josef von Tobler.

'Shit!'

The dog lifted its head in shock.

Winter was out running.

On the motorway home he'd got annoyed by drivers who stuck to the speed limit. Now he was annoyed by von Tobler. But deep down he knew that he was annoyed at himself. Why hadn't he been more open towards Anne with his feelings? Why had he listened to his sense of duty rather than his heart? Why hadn't he been more honest with her?

He hoped that running would allow him to let off steam.

As ever the river flowed peacefully and unperturbed. A never-ending cycle. He'd worked up to a fast rhythm, breathing quickly through his mouth to fill his lungs, and feeling the tension in his thighs.

The angling rays of the evening sun cast long shadows through the sparse wood. The pattern of these shadows flitting past Winter gave him the illusion that he was running even faster. The blue of the river, the cool temperature and the endorphins calmed him down.

Winter started to relax.

Now he knew that Josef von Tobler had been after Anne, it was obvious.

He'd just been blind.

His insight had failed him. You didn't have to know von Tobler particularly well to realize that even at his age he was still chasing after women. He probably hunted them like trophies. And he probably had some sort of arrangement to this effect with his third wife, the blonde Swede.

And a marriage contract.

In any event, now Winter understood von Tobler's touching eulogy. Maybe the bank's CEO had loved Anne in his own sort of way. Anne was almost the same age as von Tobler's daughter, Miriam. Perhaps it was a kind of paternal affection, although the passionate love-letter, whose handwriting had looked familiar to Winter told a very different story.

The letter was excellent insurance.

He would guard it in a safe place.

How had Anne reacted to von Tobler's advances? Had she unambiguously turned him down, or had she kept her distance diplomatically? Both a blunt rejection and a vague maybe would have fuelled von Tobler's hunting instinct.

As an employee Anne had been in a difficult situation. Although there'd been two levels in the hierarchy between her and von Tobler – Winter and Känzig – life would have been tricky for her if she'd got on the wrong side of the CEO.

Von Tobler was used to getting whatever he wanted. More than once, Winter had seen the old man give disagreeable employees a public roasting, or furiously badmouth other people. He was generally a very jovial fellow, but there was another side to him. He had high blood pressure and a quick temper.

Had von Tobler lost his temper because Anne had rejected him? Winter couldn't imagine that. But nor could he imagine the CEO seriously wishing to have a relationship with Anne. For him women were mere distraction, or decoration. Money, the bank and business always had priority.

Should he confront von Tobler? No. Not yet. Winter wasn't sure what the point of such a discussion would be. He had a good relationship with the boss. And although Anne was dead it would be weird for him to discuss her with von Tobler. He decided to postpone the matter.

Winter came to the covered wooden bridge and crossed

the Aare to begin his way back. He dropped his speed slightly, began to breathe more deeply and settled into a rhythm of four steps per breath. The soft woodland path ran ever so gently downwards and the water was now flowing in Winter's direction. The sky was still light and cloudless.

He decided that Anne should occupy a place of honour in his memory.

For half an hour he stopped thinking, applied himself exclusively to his running and made his way back along the river.

When he came level with home it was time for the final spurt. A dusty, narrow path zigzagged up to his house, climbing one hundred metres along the way. Winter used this last stretch to get his pulse properly racing again.

After an hour of running, his thighs were burning.

But the end was in sight.

Winter focused on the steep path, overgrown with roots. No tripping. Panting and sweating he made his way up and didn't see Meister until he'd arrived at the top.

'Hello, Winter. Fit as ever.'

Meister regarded sport as murder.

This is all I need, Winter thought.

Between breaths he managed gasp a 'Good evening'. Supporting his back with his hands he greedily took in the evening air.

'I live nearby, and when I saw you were back I thought a little visit wouldn't hurt.'

The 'nearby' was meaningless and Winter didn't believe him one bit. Meister didn't do coincidences. He was wearing the same summer shoes with tiny holes and the same shirt from a supermarket multipack.

'I'll change my number tomorrow,' Winter panted.

Meister just smiled.

Winter began stretching his right leg. He put his heel on a tree stump and bent forwards over his knee.

'You've been pretty busy over the last few days, Winter. You could have told me about your afternoon of golf with Al-Bader in Geneva.'

'I never got round to it. But it seems as if communication between the various authorities has been working flawlessly, even across the language barrier of the rösti border.'

'Winter, we have a problem.'

Switching legs, Winter bent over his left knee and slowly stretched his warm muscles. 'Just one?'

'Listen, I'm being serious. I've spent the whole day smoothing the information flow and then I went with the director to see the minister. He's going to inform the Federal Council tomorrow.' His minister was ultimately responsible for Switzerland's internal security. Meister had Winter's attention. Getting an early night is out of the question now, Winter thought. He stood back up and extended his left arm.

'I'm all ears.'

'With the Americans' help we've identified the fourth man from Geneva. He was one of the leaders of a political splinter group from the Midwest: True and Armed Americans, TAA. They see themselves as following in the tradition of the crusaders. The 'T' is written like a cross. They represent a mixture of nationalist, ultra-religious and arch-conservative thinking. You know the sort of stuff: 'America for the Americans', 'Weapons for the free' and 'Abortion is murder'. It's a registered party, it's legal, but insignificant. It evolved after 9/11 from dissatisfied Republicans, unemployed racists, bankrupt farmers and disappointed soldiers. In their frustration the True and Armed Americans hate blacks, Jews, Asians and Arabs, in short everyone who isn't like them. Our colleagues have had them under observation for some time and suspect that members of the party have carried out attacks on moderate politicians, and high-level government officials. Their preferred methods are threats, slander and letter bombs.

Max would slot in perfectly, Winter thought.

Meister let his words sink in. 'The TAA has many members who fought in Afghanistan and the second Gulf War. It's also integrated with European nationalists.'

'The Tyrolean,' Winter said.

Nodding, the spy continued, 'The NSA informers believe that the True and Armed Americans modified their strategy about a year ago. This information was classified as reliable by the experts. Their principle is: an eye for an eye, a tooth for a tooth, for which you can find justification in the world's most read book. In practical terms, it means that because the evil Arabs killed Americans, we're going to kill Arabs. But as they can't kill them all at once, they're focusing on a few high-profile individuals. Al-Bader wanted to invest in the US. As far as the TAA is concerned, that represents a selling-out of their homeland and must be prevented at all costs.'

Winter just nodded. He'd used almost exactly these same words that morning. Stretching his right arm instinctively, he encouraged Meister to go on.

'Put yourself in the minds of these madmen and tell me how you would select your victims.'

'Enlighten me.'

'They're revolutionaries taking on the establishment.'

'Aren't we all?'

'What holds the world together at its core?'

'Now you're getting philosophical.'

'Money.'

Although Winter didn't agree with this answer, he was starting to understand where Meister was coming from. He froze.

'Do you have any concrete proof that our bank is in particular danger?'

'No, but the Americans believe that attacks are planned against the global financial system too. As Swiss banks administer a substantial share of global wealth, they are of course particularly vulnerable. A whole string of TAA members have gone off the radar. Some have been sighted in Europe. This afternoon I spoke to the president of the banking union and asked him to instruct his members to be especially vigilant.'

'And you think that Al-Bader was a victim of this True American sect?'

'Yes.'

'Why?'

'He's buying up America. As a prime mover he was – and his brother is – in serious danger. Apparently there's a list of names. I haven't seen it, but everyone who's anyone in business is on there. And it doesn't matter how much they've given away in donations or what good deeds they've done.'

'But how did the rednecks get at Strittmatter's helicopter?'

'That's what I was going to ask you.'

'I've no idea.' This wasn't altogether true, but Winter was sure that Meister knew more than he was giving away.

'The Federal Aviation Safety Investigation Board and the laboratory in Spiez have released the first draft of their report. It's provisional and highly confidential.'

'Don't keep me on tenterhooks. I'm starting to get chilly here.' They took the path back to Winter's house.

'The laboratory in Spiez came to the conclusion that the helicopter was brought down by an incendiary device. It was supposed to look like engine damage. The chemists in Spiez reckon that in all likelihood between one and two litres of accelerant were sprayed throughout the cockpit and ignited in an instant. Al-Bader and Anne caught fire immediately; their clothes are burned almost to a cinder.'

This explained Anne's final words. Horrific.

'Strittmatter was further away from the source of the fire. It took longer with him.'

'But how did they do it?'

'Do you drink whisky?'

'Do I need to get drunk for this?'

'Maybe. You've seen the airport's security video.' This was a statement rather than a question. Winter nodded. He didn't want to get Ben into trouble.

'The eggheads at the laboratory didn't find any shards of glass or a bottle.' Winter remembered the cylindrical carton under Anne's left arm. 'According to the report the accelerant was in a plastic rather than glass bottle. Remains of the molten plastic were found, containing bubbles with trapped accelerant.'

'You think Anne took the bomb aboard?' Winter choked out this awful suspicion.

'Yes.'

Winter was speechless.

'The detonator reacted to air pressure and exploded as soon as the helicopter had reached a certain height. Bang.' Meister irreverently puffed up his cheeks and with his hands made a childish gesture to signify an explosion. 'Al-Bader arrived in his private jet. Strittmatter with his helicopter. Both of them flew.'

Had Anne really brought the deadly bomb on board?

'Where did your colleague get the welcome gift for Al-Bader?'

'The chocolates are standard for these clients. Al-Bader loved them. I brought him boxes like that myself a few times. Every branch gets a monthly delivery. One of the assistants is responsible for them.' He'd question the assistants at the first opportunity.

'Would anybody have had the chance to tamper with the box?'

'They're not stored in the safe.' Lots of people had access. They were usually kept in the cool basement, alongside the wine. When Meister didn't reply, Winter knew what he was waiting for.

'I can't explain the bottle in the gift box. Muslims don't drink alcohol.'

'And all Christians are monogamous.'

'The Al-Bader brothers might enjoy the odd glass in private,' Winter conceded; he recalled Al-Bader's suite and how they'd toasted their adventure in the early hours. 'The bank does all it can to avoid embarrassing situations.' Meister nodded sympathetically.

'The first time I saw the carton was on the security video and I've no idea where Anne got it from. Perhaps Al-Bader ordered the bottle as a present for a business partner or to toast a deal with them? We often end up being gophers. It's all part of the service.'

Winter noticed that he was desperately looking for excuses to exonerate Anne.

'Have you already analysed the other airport videos?'

Winter was ready to clutch at any straw.

'No, but the Zürich police have detailed two men to work with airport security. They're studying all the videos from the period in question. It's going to take a while yet.'

Meister and Winter were on the unfinished terrace. The folded loungers were leaning against the wall. The spade stood on its own in the earth. Granite slabs scattered around. The sun had set.

Winter's sweat had dried. His T-shirt was stiff.

He shook his head and went up the wooden steps. Meister followed. They walked along the creaking balcony and Winter opened the door.

'Watch out!' he said, pointing to the low, seventeenth-century doorframe – from an era when people were shorter, and died at forty.

Meister stayed in the middle of the sitting room while Winter put on a jumper. Then he went to the fridge, poured himself some orange juice, diluted it with half water and drank thirstily.

'Cosy place you've got here,' Meister said.

'Want some?' Winter lifted his glass.

Meister shook his head and returned to his car. A very ordinary white Opel with a 'Baby on Board' sticker. Halfway there he turned around. 'Winter, find the mole in the bank, would you? Time is running out.'

Winter nodded in the twilight.

Winter drank some more diluted orange juice, took a shower, tidied up a bit and then decided to view the DVD from Zürich Airport again. When he'd watched the recording with Ben and then again on his own, he hadn't really paid attention to the carton.

Prior to the sheikh's visit, Winter and Anne had discussed looking after Al-Bader and what his penchants were. She'd also asked him whether their guest drank alcohol. Winter had said that Al-Bader might drink a glass or two at business meals.

He'd assumed that Anne had taken it upon herself to supplement the usual welcome box of chocolates with a bottle.

He'd assumed that she'd bought the whisky at the duty-free shop at Zürich Airport.

Never assume, ass-u-me! Christ.

He fast forwarded until Anne appeared in the picture, then focused on the two presents. She arrived in the customs car. Winter first spotted the box of chocolates just before she got out. She'd put the bulky box on top of the dashboard so she could get out unencumbered.

The Lindt & Sprüngli chocolates were wrapped in gift paper, decorated with a large bow, in the bank's livery colours. The proximity to the bomb explained the residues on the bow, which the explosives detector at airport had picked up.

Then he saw the carton on her lap.

Anne got out. She held the carton in her left hand and clamped the box of chocolates under her arm. Intuitively, she made sure she kept the bottle vertical. She'd felt the shifting of weight of the liquid inside.

The cylindrical carton wasn't gift-wrapped. At the top was a plastic lid and there was writing on the side.

Winter paused the DVD, copied the freeze-frame image into his photo processing software, and used this to enlarge the part of the picture until the label on the carton filled the entire screen. Single Malt, Laphroaig, ten years old, bottled in 2004, forty-three per cent alcohol. It all looked genuine.

Meister was right.

Winter grimaced.

In his mouth Laphroaig tasted liked the dentist's. This single malt was more medicine than pleasure.

A pharmaceutical.

Maybe even flammable.

Winter preferred Talisker.

He stood up, fetched a heavy glass, took a couple of ice cubes from the freezer and the bottle of Talisker: twelve years old, double matured. He poured himself a generous measure, swirled the drug around the glass and dreamily admired the golden-brown colour. Where had Anne got that carton from? Did Al-Bader call her to order the bottle? For himself or the Egyptians?

He fished out the list with Anne's telephone calls. Al-Bader's number didn't appear on it. Maybe one of his assistants had called. No, there weren't any numbers with similar prefixes either. It was possible that Al-Bader had called from a withheld number.

Anonymized and digitalized.

Maybe his brother knew something.

He called the younger Al-Bader from his mobile. It took an age for the signal to come through, but then it rang. 'Hello, Winter. Have you decided to accept my offer?'

Winter had almost forgotten Al-Bader's offer.

In the background he could hear the hubbub of voices and the clinking of glasses. The younger Al-Bader appeared to be in a good mood, so Winter decided on a witty response.

'The bank is asking for a transfer fee that not even you'd be able to rustle up.'

'Try me.'

'Are you travelling?'

'Yes, I'm in St Petersburg. At the reception of an oil magnate. But good entertainment.' Peroxide blonde, Winter thought.

'I've got a question about your twin brother.'

'Fire away.' All of a sudden Al-Bader sounded serious.

'Did he have a favourite brand of whisky?'

'No. If he had to order whisky, it was always Glenfiddich. I think it was the only one he knew. But why?'

'It's likely that the helicopter was blown up by an incendiary device disguised as a whisky bottle.'

'By Allah, the Almighty!' Winter could hear the party guests chatting in the background. Then Al-Bader stammered, 'Who, who?'

'I don't know. Not yet. It was a Trojan Horse.' Winter didn't want to enter into a discussion over the phone. 'So your brother didn't have a particular fondness for whisky, then?'

'No, he was more serious than me. At business meals he would have the occasional glass out of politeness to his hosts. But he never ordered whisky himself.'

'Not even Laphroaig?'

'No, certainly not. He couldn't stand dentists!'

'Thank you.'

'By the way, when are we going to play the remaining nine holes?' Al-Bader was the playboy again.

'Tomorrow afternoon?'

'I'm with Putin. But I'll give you a call.' And he was gone. Winter wasn't sure if the Putin comment was true or whether Al-Bader was just pulling his leg. But now it was clear that

Al-Bader hadn't ordered the whisky for himself. As a gift for his
Egyptian partners? Unlikely.

He stared at the screen. The black, plastic lid was stuck down
with tape in the colours of the whisky and bearing its logo.
In its original packaging. There was no reason for Anne to be
suspicious of the carton. The whisky wasn't anything particularly special; you could buy it in any decent shop.

He couldn't make out any barcode or price tag. The carton
couldn't be traced.

Winter restarted the film, keeping his eyes on the bottle
until Anne entered the helicopter. Al-Bader let Anne go first.
Through the windows Winter could see that she'd put the
carton on the seat protecting it from tipping over with the box
of chocolates.

The helicopter took off.

There was only one possible conclusion: someone Anne
trusted had given her the whisky bomb as a present for
Al-Bader.

Winter wandered out onto the creaky wooden balcony,
emptied his glass pensively, took a deep breath and stared
motionless into the darkness for a few minutes.

He went into the bedroom and put fresh linen on his double
bed. It was a distraction. He laid out a set of towels, checked
the drawer of his bedside table for condoms, and placed a
bottle of mineral water and a bowl of apples from the neighbour's garden beside the bed.

With the palm of his hand he wiped dust from his antique
chest of drawers. An heirloom. There'd been an old chest
of drawers in his room in Cairo, too. Taking a step back he
surveyed the room. It wasn't the Ritz but, as Meister had said,
it was 'cosy'.

As he looked around Winter couldn't quite decide if he was
looking forward or not to seeing Fatima. It would be clearer
tomorrow, he guessed.

Back in his kitchen-diner he caught sight of the mobile phone, which reminded him of Schmitt's contacts from the detective agency. He intended to study them this evening. Winter made some coffee, went through his post and watched CNN. A car bomb outside a government building, blurred pictures from a civil war, a flood in Asia with people on corrugated iron roofs, a group photo from another EU summit, the stock market data and the weather. Then an advertisement for an airline. He switched off and poured coffee into his favourite cup.

Work was pending.

He took his mobile phone containing Schmitt's data.

He had about three hundred new contacts.

Winter connected his phone to the computer and tried to transfer the numbers to an Excel file.

The computer crashed and Winter had to go through the entire process again. Finally, he had a clear table in front of him. Around two thirds of the numbers had surnames and names attached, including Schmitt's family members with pet names. The remaining third of the numbers just had initials.

Most numbers had a Greater Zürich prefix, which was to be expected. Schmitt, Berger & Partners operated mostly this region.

An initial survey of the names and numbers before him didn't ring any bells in his memory.

He compared them with the bank's telephone directory. It was a random attempt. Was there really an accomplice at the bank? And would this person be so inept as to call from a landline inside the bank? His eyes were burning, but he couldn't find any matches. Schmitt hadn't saved any of the bank's numbers in his contacts.

After the third cup of coffee, Winter looked at the list of Anne's telephone calls. Maybe the client had rung Anne from Schmitt's phone. He compared all the numbers Anne had been called from with Schmitt's contacts. No match. Once more, nothing.

Winter went systematically through all the numbers without complete names, one by one. Using the electronic telephone book on the internet he tried to get a name for them. But many of the mobile numbers weren't listed. This search too failed to produce anything noteworthy. No familiar name.

After the fourth cup of coffee he gave up.

He was frustrated.

He knew it was going to be hard work. But he hated it when hard work didn't produce results. Maybe he'd call the anonymous numbers over the next few days on a pretext and try to find out more names. If nothing significant came up he could always give the list to Ben and ask him to compare the numbers with his database.

He stretched and wandered back out into the fresh air on the balcony. He felt as if he'd reached a dead end. The stars were twinkling, almost as clearly as when he'd been at the pyramids. He thought of Fatima, as Tiger weaved around his legs. He picked up his cat and gave him a stroke. Tiger began to purr. The telephone rang and Tiger leaped off into the night. Winter went back inside, wondering who might be calling him at this hour.

Al-Bader's name was on the display.

'Hello. Party over already?'

'Winter, I've got to tell you something.' Al-Bader was slurring his words; he was clearly drunk. In the background it was quiet, but Al-Bader's voice echoed.

'Where are you?'

'In the hotel. I wanted to call you before I kick the bucket too. I'm not feeling well.' A pause. Footsteps. Then Winter heard Al-Bader throwing up. He was in the bathroom. The mobile phone clattered onto the floor and transmitted more

waves of vomiting from St Petersburg to Bern. A tap was
running. Throaty noises. A flush. Then Al-Bader's voice again.

'Winter, are you still there?'

'Yes, are you okay?'

'I'm sorry. Yes, no. Yes, I'm alright. That bloody vodka.
Sorry. But I was going to ask you whether you want to work for
me now or not? You still haven't given me an answer. Are you
planning on killing me, too?'

Ignoring the question, Winter said, 'Listen. You'd best go to
sleep now. Shut the door and lie down.'

'I can't sleep!'

'Is someone with you?'

'No, I'm all alone.' Self-pity. 'The tart has buggered off.'
Loneliness, giving way to fear. 'They're going to kill me. I'm
scared!' Crying, Al-Bader was on an emotional rollercoaster.
Perhaps he'd had more than just alcohol.

'Take some deep breaths and sit down.'

Winter could hear Al-Bader plonking himself down.

'Now drink some water.'

Winter could hear Al-Bader unscrew the lid from a bottle
and drink. Water? Or more booze?

'Winter, my brother is dead and back at home everyone's
after me. I don't know what to do. Could you start tomorrow
on whatever terms you want? Please.'

Instead of responding to the renewed offer, Winter asked,
'Who exactly is after you?'

'I don't know. Everybody!'

Winter's thoughts were interrupted by another plaintive
statement. 'The Baktars killed my brother. They were at
loggerheads, and he absolutely had to come out on top. I told
him to leave it. But I couldn't protect him. I always thought that
if something happened to us, it would be me that got it, not
him. He was the head of the family. I was just the little brother,
even though I'm only a few minutes younger. He was careful,

whereas I would bash my head riding when we were children. And now he had to provoke the tigers.'

Winter tried to make some sense out of this. 'Tigers?'

'The Baktars. They've got cousins who take the *Qu'ran* literally. They call themselves the Holy Tigers of Islam. They'd rather fight than do business.' Al-Bader snorted contemptuously.

'But why your brother?'

'He was the head of the family. Pyramid Investment Partners was his idea. He persuaded the others to join in. And now I've got to do it.' Winter heard Al-Bader sigh and fall backwards, presumably onto the bed.

'You can rely on Farmer, surely,' comforted Winter.

'He's not on top of things.'

'I got the impression that the professor knows his stuff...'

'That's what my brother always used to say too. But I've found papers. My brother wanted an independent auditor to check the investments.'

Winter listened more closely. 'Why?'

'The NSA says we're financing terrorists. That's nonsense, but it's why I can't travel to the States at the moment. I wanted to drive IndyCar races. I can't do that either now.' Al-Bader was feeling sorry for himself.

'Did the auditor find anything?'

'No, no. My brother was going to start using him from the next board meeting.'

'Were your investments really legitimate?'

'Of course!' Al-Bader cursed in Arabic, and Winter was glad not to have a simultaneous translation.

'I'm sorry. It was just a question and clearly your brother had his own suspicions. Are you saying that the Baktars channelled money into suspect sources?'

Al-Bader hiccupped.

'You said that some members of the Baktar clan were unhappy about investing in Western infrastructure,' Winter pressed on. 'Maybe they told themselves they'd make the best of it and use these channels for their own purposes. If you can't defeat the enemy, you might as well embrace him. Old Chinese proverb.'

After a lengthy pause Al-Bader said thoughtfully, 'Yes, that's a possibility.'

'Just so I understand this correctly, Pyramid Investment Partners is a collection pot, isn't it? At one end acquaintances of your brother paid into the fund, so that at the other end investments could be made in infrastructure projects. It means the risk is spread. What I don't quite understand is how Pyramid Investment Partners is run. Am I right in thinking that each partner is responsible for a few projects? Was your brother – and now you – responsible for the Cairo nuclear power station?'

'Yes, the projects are divided up. Each partner has the lead in a few projects.'

'Which are the Al-Bader projects?'

'The nuclear power plant in Cairo. We have connections with Orafin. The wind farm in the hills above San Francisco. My brother didn't think we could rely on oil in the long term. And a few others, but I can't remember now.'

'And which projects are being run by the Baktars?'

'The Baktars are chiefly interested in IT stuff. The fibre-optic networks in Dubai and Philadelphia. Or Dallas. Some dump in the States. And something in Europe too.'

'And how does Pyramid Investment Partners ensure that a project is profitable?'

'We have people for that.'

'But you don't relinquish control altogether?'

'No. Pyramid Investment Partners always has seats on the non-executive board.'

'And it has access to all the information?'

'Yes, as a director I can see everything at any time. If I wish,' Al-Bader proclaimed with proud conviction.

Winter found it hard to imagine Al-Bader the younger grappling with the finer details of company management. He seemed to work according to the helicopter principle. Fly in quickly, make a lot of noise, stir up dust and then fly away again. But what did Winter really know of how Al-Bader ran his investments?

'That means you'll have access to the nuclear power plant in Cairo.'

'Of course.'

'Have you got a list of the investors and directors of Pyramid Investment Partners?'

'It's probably back home with my brother's papers.'

'Could you send it to me?'

'Only if you work for me.'

'I have to give three months' notice. The list would be a great help in finding out who was responsible for your brother's death.'

'Why?'

'Motive.'

'We're related to the Baktars. There's no way they would have killed Muhammed.'

'Are you sure?'

'Yes, absolutely.' What had happened to the Holy Tigers? Was Al-Bader still drunk, or was he sobering up?

'Send me the list all the same.'

There was no reply.

Winter doubted that Al-Bader would send the list. Once he'd slept off his drunkenness he'd feel so ashamed that he would want to put a lid on this particular conversation. He heard a click as Al-Bader terminated the call.

It was another short night and Winter slept deeply; this time his dreams left him in peace. He woke up refreshed and was already dressed and on his way to the neighbouring farm before his alarm went off. The farmer, busy with the milking machine in the cowshed, just nodded when Winter wished him a good morning. He found the farmer's wife in the vegetable garden where she was cutting the last stalks of rhubarb.

'Good morning, Frau Mettler.'

'Good morning, Herr Winter.' She slowly stood back up.

'Is that for compote, jam or cake?' Winter asked, pointing at the rhubarb stalks.

The maternal Frau Mettler gave Winter the occasional jar of jam from her mouseproof store cupboard. A large, warm-hearted woman, she was usually in a good mood and wore her long, greying hair in a bun. Beneath her shabby, work apron, she was wearing a floral, summer dress with short sleeves. Winter sensed that she liked him, even though he worked in the city and – worse – for a bank.

'These are only good for compote. You're up and out early this morning.'

'Yes, I've got to go to Zürich. I'm picking up a girlfriend from the airport.' Winter bit his tongue. His choice of words would be grist to the Mettlers' rumour mill.

'Oh, anything serious?' she said, beaming at him hopefully.

'No, no. We know each other through work.'

'Oh, what a shame.'

'She's going to be staying with me for a few days.'

'I see.'

'And so, I thought it would be nice if I could brighten up my sitting room with a few flowers. As a sort of welcome.'

'I understand.' She gave Winter a knowing smile.

'I thought—'

'Just tell me when your friend's arriving and I'll sort it out.' Frau Mettler interrupted him, good naturedly.

On his way out Winter waved to the farmer, who ignored him.

Fifteen minutes later he was on the motorway heading for Zürich. In the cocoon of his car and part of a convoy of vehicles on its way from Bern to Zürich, Winter had time to think.

Had Pyramid Investment Partners been involved in a bribery scandal? Why had Al-Bader looked for an independent auditor? Had there been a clash of cultures? Or was it simply greed?

Winter sighed.

When Winter entered the underground car park in Zürich it was just after eight o'clock. He used his black security card and the lift took him up to the fourth floor of the bank. He wanted to talk to Frau Obrist, the head of administration responsible for client gifts.

The woman at reception was just rearranging the flowers on the counter. In their short life the orchids had probably undergone a long journey: grown in a greenhouse in Israel, flown to the flower market in Amsterdam, and then driven by lorry along the motorway here to Zürich to delight clients for a handful of days. Globalization.

'Good morning, Frau Fischer. What beautiful orchids!'

'Good morning, Herr Winter. You're right there. They really brighten up the room. What can I do for you today? Coffee?'

'Later perhaps. Is Frau Obrist here?'

'She's in her office.'

He said thank you, and walked around the discreetly lit, oval screen to Frau Obrist's realm. She was dressed, as ever, in an austere suit, and her very short, blonde hair sticking out in all directions would have suited a footballer. She was sorting through her post and turned around when Winter approached. 'Hello, Winter. Haven't seen you in a while.'

'Morning. I've been away quite a bit.'

'Because of the helicopter crash?'

'Yes, it's more complicated than I thought.'

'I know, come in.'

Winter shook her hand and sat at the round table.

'Coffee?' she said, raising her eyebrows and nodding towards the reception.

'No, thanks.'

'Too much caffeine isn't good for you anyway.' Frau Obrist was well known for rigorously trying to avoid all the world's toxins. She was a vegan and cycled to work.

Winter winked at her. 'I just wanted to ask how it works with client gifts here in Zürich.'

'Well, you can read about that in the process description.'

The two of them grinned because they were well aware of the discrepancies in the bank between theory and practice.

'It would be easiest if I showed you.'

They took the lift to the third basement level. On the way Frau Obrist explained, 'The client account managers, or more accurately their assistants, help themselves, but they have to specify what they've taken. This allows us to order replacements in time.'

The lift door opened and they entered a cool, concrete cellar with ventilation and water pipes on the ceiling. Winter knew that the heating system and a water tank were housed at the end of the corridor. Frau Obrist opened the unlocked door to the store and switched on the light. The neon strip flickered a few times then lit up the room.

On the left-hand side stood a wooden wine rack that reached to the ceiling, in front of which stood a few unopened crates. Someone had tried to create a bit of order with little signs. A few particularly valuable bottles were in individual wooden crates with sliding lids.

No cylindrical cartons.

No whisky.

On the other side was shelving, with boxes containing printer cartridges, paper, envelopes and promotional material.

In one corner stood head-height aluminium banner stands, which the bank used to advertise their presence on official occasions.

Beside these was a pile of about a dozen boxes of gift-wrapped chocolates. On top of this very neat tower sat a box of decorative bows.

A charred decorative bow sat on Winter's desk at home.

Winter took out a bow, turned it around and stared at the self-adhesive label on the underside.

Remove the plastic film, stick on the bow and the gift is ready.

Frau Obrist stood by the door, watching Winter. After a while she said, 'If someone takes something from the store they mark it here and sign.'

She took a slim, ring binder from the shelves beside the door and handed it to him. It contained various lists: 'A4 paper, 500 sheets', 'HP printer cartridges', 'Wine: Burgundy'– with dates, quantities and names. Winter perused the list headed '1kg chocolates (inc. bow, separate)'. Anne's entry from July 24 was the third last.

As he continued leafing through the folder, Winter asked, 'Do we have whisky here too?'

'No, only wine.' She looked around. 'But the Etter plum schnapps from the jubilee must be here somewhere.'

'No, I'm looking for a Laphroaig.'

'A Laff...what?'

'A Laphroaig. It's a single malt.'

'Can't help you there.'

'Don't worry about it. Did you see Anne on July the twenty-fourth, the day of the crash?' Winter lifted up the folder with the lists.

'Yes, she popped in briefly.'

'About what time?'

'We'd already closed up and the weekend was upon us. I'd say a little after seven that evening. But she was in a hurry. She said she had to meet a sheikh at the airport.' Frau Obrist ran a hand through her hair. 'I can remember asking her, if he was a fairy-tale prince? Anne laughed, as only Anne could. But Anne said she was already taken.' Pensively, she added, 'Those were the last words we said to each other.'

She looked at Winter. 'Do you know the unlucky man? She didn't want to tell me who it was. All she said was, "It's still very new".'

His eyes fixed on the ring binder, Winter closed it, rapped it with his knuckles and said, 'I think I do.'

Frau Obrist looked at him. 'She was such a warm person. Why is it always the good ones?'

'Yes, it's fate, I suppose.' He thought of Allah. Suddenly he felt a chill in the cool cellar and turned around. 'I'm going to make copies of these lists.'

They turned off the lights and went back up to the fourth floor. In the lift Winter stared at the security-card reader.

All employees could go to the third basement level. But very few were allowed access to the vaults on the fourth basement level.

'When Anne was here, was she carrying a cyclindrical carton?'

'In all honesty I can't really remember. She just poked her head around the door. Didn't she write anything in the file?'

'Just a box of chocolates.'

Winter photocopied the lists in the folder. He put the piece of paper with Anne's entry on the top of the pile that was still warm.

Then he drank a coffee in Frau Obrist's office. She had a herbal tea and gave Winter the lowdown on the latest rumours.

The hottest topic was the complete takeover of the bank by the financial group, especially concerning which of the branches might be merged or axed. A few account managers hadn't reached their targets, the inflow of new monies was below expectations and as far as many people were concerned it looked to be now no longer a case of whether, but when and how. Frau Obrist was horrified at the idea of these prospective changes.

Winter tried to reassure her. 'I'm convinced that von Tobler will fight tooth and nail against integration.'

'Integration?' Frau Obrist snorted. 'It's a hostile takeover! Von Tobler's going to retire soon and Känzig has already changed sides. He keeps scurrying back to Mama.' She made a scornful gesture in the general direction of the financial group.

'Känzig is a politician who doesn't want to spoil his relationship with any party. That's networking.' Winter smiled to himself at his diplomatic language.

'You're getting old, Winter. Once upon a time you would have called that arse-licking.'

He laughed and said, 'Thanks for the drugs; I've got to get to the airport.'

Winter arrived half an hour early. He went to the confectioner's and bought two hundred grams of handmade, champagne truffles. Virtually the same price as gold. But in Boston Fatima had wolfed these down in no time.

He sat in a quiet corner and made a few telephone calls. Assumptions were gradually turning into facts. Every human being inhabits space and time. Victims and perpetrators always left traces. Every criminal made mistakes.

Winter took the lists from the folder, looked through them again, turned the pages over and jotted down a timeline of Anne's final hours. The exact times had branded themselves on his long-term memory:

16:00: visit to parents in Fraubrunnen.
16:55: call from room 107 of HQ in Bern (Dirk's list).
Anne's mum: 'just before five o'clock'. 'Anne back to work'. Why?
17:02: call from withheld number (see Dirk's list). Who?
17:20: approx. arrival in Mini at underground car park in Bern. About 40 mins. Where? HQ? What? Whisky? Find out!
18:00 (latest): Anne gets train or drives (which?) to Zürich.
19:00: arrives in Zürich. Main station? Where? Verify? How?
19:15: Obrist: 'after seven o'clock' Anne gets chocolates in Zürich.
Train from main station to airport – ten mins every five? Or taxi? Traffic?
19:47: Strittmatter lands at airport.
20:14: Gulfstream lands.
20:19: meet & greet Al-Bader. Ask customs official!
20:41: last call from Anne!

Still so many question marks. Winter rolled his head and relaxed his shoulders.

The arrivals board showed that flight LX9 from Chicago had landed. Fatima was here.

Fatima had been travelling for twenty hours. She'd flown yesterday from San Francisco to Chicago, and two hours later from Chicago to Europe through the night. The border official in his glass box checked her entry papers and said in a friendly tone, 'Welcome to Switzerland!'

Winter stood behind the barrier amongst relatives, tour guides and drivers with signs. Through the large pane of glass he spotted Fatima in the throng of passengers. Feeling tense, he followed her slim silhouette, long hair and open, white collar through the hall with the luggage carousels. Fatima just had her small, wheelie suitcase and laptop bag. She vanished, only to reappear a few moments later as the automatic sliding door opened. Fatima stopped and Winter could see the eyes of the waiting men drawn towards her.

Then she saw him and gave a shy smile of greeting.

'Hello, Winter!'

He gave a restrained wave back.

This time they hugged. Not intimately, but more formally, as you might greet a friend's wife in Europe, or as two businessmen embrace in Egypt. Winter went for three kisses and caught a strand of hair in his face.

He smelled the perfume. Cinnamon.

'Finally!'

Unsure what that meant, Winter replied, 'I hope you had a good journey'

She shook her hair from her face. 'I hate aeroplanes.'

From close up Winter noticed the rings around Fatima's

chestnut-brown eyes, which even her carefully applied make-up couldn't hide completely. She still looked ravishing and far too good for him. They walked side by side through the arrivals hall, Fatima insisting that she could manage her luggage herself.

On the escalator Winter heard an anonymous voice over the public address system: 'Herr Winter, please report to the airport information desk immediately.' And after a short pause: 'Herr Winter, please come to the information desk on the first floor.'

What did that mean?

They went to find out. 'Good morning, I'm Herr Winter. You've been looking for me?'

'Oh yes, good morning, Herr Winter. Herr Halter would like to speak to you. He just rang and asked if you'd wait for a moment. He's on his way.'

'Thanks.' Turning to Fatima, Winter said, 'Ben Halter's responsible for security here at the airport.'

'Did you tell him we were coming?' Fatima asked, taking a small bottle of mineral water from her laptop bag.

'No, but he has his methods.' Winter leaned back against the information desk and felt the chocolates in his jacket pocket.

'Here, Fatima – I nearly forgot. Something sweet for you.'

'How lovely! Thank you very much.'

Fatima opened the box and took out a truffle. As she was about to put it in her mouth it occurred to her that she was being impolite. 'Would you like one?'

Winter laughed but shook his head.

She placed it on her tongue.

The arriving and departing passengers hurried past, baggage trolleys squeaked and the PA voice blared out above their heads. They waited in the crowds for Ben, and Fatima talked about San Francisco and the seals by the pier and the bendy road where Steve McQueen had made a film.

Then Ben appeared, looking as if his huge body were dividing the waves in the sea of passengers. 'Hello, Winter.'

A shake of the hands, a slap on the back. 'Please excuse me,' Ben said, out of breath, 'The director and I were in a meeting with opponents of the airport who are particularly sensitive to noise. When I saw you were here I wasn't able to leave immediately.'

'Ben, this is Fatima. We met in Egypt.'

Ben held out his hand. 'Good to meet you.'

'Delighted,' she replied.

Winter looked at Ben. 'What I'd like to know is how you knew I was at the airport?'

'Digital facial recognition,' Ben said, and Winter nodded, having guessed this to be case.

'Next time I'll remember to wear a hat or have a beard.'

'Theoretically it wouldn't make any difference because the software analyses the features of your skull. And it gave me the opportunity to say hello.'

Winter elbowed Ben in the ribs. 'You old charmer.'

Ben looked at Fatima. 'I'd very much like to include you in our database too, if you would so allow.

Fatima gave him a professional smile, and Ben took this for acquiescence. He photographed her on his mobile. Then he said, 'If you wouldn't mind I'd like to talk business with Winter for a moment.'

Winter said, 'Fatima was there when Kaddour was blown up. Tell all.'

'Okay. We analysed the video recordings of the relevant time period again using the facial recognition software and with the help of the cantonal police. They kindly seconded a few officers to us.'

'And?'

'Anne got off the S16 from Zürich at nineteen fifty-eight.

Mentally Winter added a further entry to his timeline. Anne had taken the train.

'She was carrying the carton with the incendiary device and

the box of chocolates. As far as we know she didn't go into any shop. She can be seen on two further recordings as she heads straight for the private check-in.'

'Thanks. Could I have a quick word with Heinz? He may have noticed something.' To Fatima, Winter said, 'Heinz is the customs official who drove Anne to the helicopter.'

Through a side door they left the hustle and bustle of the arrivals hall and found Heinz behind the scenes in a windowless green room enjoying an early lunch of a sandwich. On one side of the room a head-height one-way mirror was set in the wall, allowing the customs officials to observe passengers. Heinz was sitting at a table with a colleague, watching the people walk past.

Winter recognized him straightaway, and after Ben had made the introductions he said, 'Thanks for giving me a moment of your time. A colleague of mine was in the helicopter that crashed. Anne Arnold. You accompanied her on the twenty-fourth of July to the helicopter landing area, didn't you?'

'Yes, but as I already told the police I didn't notice anything out of the ordinary. It all seemed routine. The helicopter pilot made the usual announcement of the transfer from the Gulfstream to the Bell helicopter on the apron and asked us to pick up a guest from the private flight check-in.'

'Do you know when the call came in?'

Winter knew to ask simple questions first, so that the person feels comfortable and the conversation gets going.

'Yes, the helicopter landed a couple of minutes ahead of schedule at nineteen twenty-two. The VIP Helicopter Transportation Corporation is a regular client.'

'Then you went to pick up the passenger?'

'Yes, I went to the check-in at eight o'clock as arranged. She had just arrived. I like it when people are punctual.'

'How did she seem?'

'Slightly out of breath. I assumed she was late and had run through the airport.'

'She wasn't running on any of the videos,' Ben said, 'but two minutes from the station to check-in is pretty athletic.'

Winter nodded and asked, 'What did she have on her?'

'The police were interested in that too. A large, gift box and a bottle of whisky.'

'A bottle of whisky?'

'Yes, a Laphroaig.'

'Are you sure?'

'You bet. I've confiscated enough of them and I don't mind the odd dram myself either. As we were driving out to the apron I asked her if she was a whisky fan.'

'What did she say?'

'That she preferred chocolate.'

'Did anything strike you about her? Was she nervous?'

'No, well, maybe a little. Tense. She was like a sprinter before a race. You know, when they're hopping up and down behind the starting blocks.'

'Yes, I understand what you're saying. Do you do athletics yourself?'

Heinz gave an embarrassed laugh. 'No, I've been a member of the gun club since my youth. Some people say it isn't a proper sport.'

'Nonsense. Anne was a good shot too.' Winter paused to give Heinz the chance to think about his meeting with Anne again. As a customs official, he had a professionally honed skill for observation, but on the other hand he saw thousands of people every day. When Heinz shook his head apologetically, Winter asked, 'Do you have any inkling where the gifts came from?'

'The box was in the same colours as the bank's logo,' Heinz remembered

Winter nodded. 'And the whisky?'

'It wasn't packed. That's why I noticed the brand.'

'The bottle wasn't packed?'

'No, I mean yes. The bottle was in one of those round cartons. But the carton wasn't wrapped in gift paper.'

'And Anne didn't say anything about it?'

Heinz stared into a corner of the room.

'When I asked the lady whether she was a whisky fan and she said she preferred chocolates, I also said that I'd happily have it. She just laughed and said, "Man gifts". I dropped the subject because we'd arrived at the apron and I didn't want her to think I was after some sort of tip.' Heinz looked at Ben in embarrassment, but Ben was busy watching passengers through the one-way mirror.

' "A man's present",' Winter echoed.

'Exactly. I didn't think any more of it. I'd be more likely to give a woman chocolates than whisky too.'

'Depends on the woman,' Ben grunted at the mirror.

Winter glanced at Fatima, who couldn't follow the conversation in German and was nibbling chocolates.

'She didn't say anything else?'

'Just the usual: good evening, thank you and so on.'

'What about Al-Bader's security check, how was that?'

'Routine. His papers were in order.'

'Anything else?'

'I know you shouldn't speak ill of the dead, but I always get the feeling with these rich foreigners that they behave as if we weren't there. This guy was polite, however, and didn't make any trouble. But there are very different types. I could tell you...'

Then Ben turned around, and Heinz left his sentence hanging in mid-air.

'Many thanks. You've been very helpful.' Winter shook Heinz's hand. 'You've got a terrific eye for detail. If anything else occurs to you, even something tiny, I'd be very grateful if you would let either me or Ben know.' Heinz gave a satisfied smile. Compliments were a rarity in his profession. They said goodbye.

Ben escorted Fatima and Winter out.

In the corridor, Winter asked, 'Ben, have you ever heard of the TAA?'

'Do you mean those nice rednecks, the True and Armed Americans?'

'Precisely.'

'Of course. Those lunatics are rising unstoppably through the rankings of the most dangerous groups out there. It's just a question of time before they catch up with Al-Qaeda. A few years ago the TAA mostly consisted of trigger-happy village idiots who occasionally blew each other up. Now the TAA is far better organized. Under Bush they became acceptable amongst some high-ranking military figures and national–conservative intellectuals. And now they're refining their skills with survival training in the desert.'

'Shit.'

'Exactly. The American security authorities have given me a few nice pictures for my album, amongst which are some TAA members. Their clean-shaven heads are simple to identify.' Ben grinned, then turned serious. 'Why do you ask?'

'Our friend Meister thinks they're behind the incendiary bomb.'

'Christ. One thing for certain is that these sect members know how to blow something up.'

The drive to Bern was fairly silent. Although they'd only met recently, the two of them felt as if they'd known each other for ages. There was no need to make polite conversation. Fatima chose the same music that Winter had last played.

On the motorway she leaned back, adjusted her hair with a circular movement of her arm, and closed her eyes. Winter pondered space and time. In the silence they felt a connection. Then Winter switched off the music. Fatima stirred, sat up and looked around.

He ventured a sideways glance.

She blinked, rolled her neck and combed her shining hair with her fingers.

'I propose we make a brief stop in the city centre for something to eat.'

'Sounds good. I'm starving.' She smiled.

'Afterwards I've got to check something in headquarters. I'm sorry but I can't take whole days off at the moment. I'm just an employee.' Fatima looked sceptically at Winter and saw him grinning. 'And tomorrow sees the start of the bank's annual conference. In Interlaken. I'm going to have to show my face. As a client of ours you're invited, of course.'

'Thank you. I will place my destiny in your hands with confidence.'

That's what Anne had done, too, Winter thought. He looked over at Fatima to see whether she was being serious.

She added, 'So long as I'm in Switzerland. I'd love to go to the mountains. Up to the snow or, even better, a glacier. I've never been on one before.'

'Well, I could offer you a rather nice glacier in the Bernese Oberland.'

'Isn't it cold there? I've only got summer dresses with me.'

'No worries,' Winter said. 'In summer and with this fine weather we'll manage. I can lend you a jumper if needs be.'

They left the motorway, wound their way around the one-way system and parked the car in the underground garage. When they emerged from the concrete they were in Bern old town.

The historic, sandstone houses were bordered on three sides by the River Aare. Winter loved his home town because it was a manageable size and relaxed. Sometimes, on the way to the office, he'd take a detour and wander through the cobbled streets and arcades, or through the fruit, vegetable and flower market.

Today they sat on the casino terrace, with its overhanging plane trees. Fatima's eyes grazed on the lush green of the trees. 'Beautifully cool.'

'It's bearable in the shade,' Winter said.

They laughed, ordered two light lunches and began planning the coming days.

'Can I visit the vault?'

Winter shook his head and said seriously, 'For security reasons I'm afraid that's not permitted. But of course we'd be happy to open a deposit box for you.'

'Can I choose my neighbours down there?'

Winter was perplexed. 'Why?'

'I don't want my valuables lying next to a dictator's stolen gold. I'm very fussy about those sorts of things.'

Fortunately, just then the waiter came with the bill, allowing Winter to evade the question.

'Come, I'll show you the town.'

They strolled to the huge square in front of the federal

parliament. Children skipped around, screaming in delight, running through the water features and trying to avoid the fountains that sprayed vertically into the air.

'Underneath here are the Swiss gold reserves,' said Winter. 'Look, that's the national bank. Can you see the house number?'

'The national bank is Number 1?' Fatima said in surprise. 'Not the parliament?'

'That shows you the priorities in Switzerland.'

'And in a democracy, too.'

'Money rules the world. Even in the Middle Ages we had the best mercenaries.'

A female minister crossed the square.

Winter nodded towards the woman. 'Here comes our justice minister.'

Now Fatima was sure Winter was pulling her leg. 'I don't believe you.'

'Our ministers even take the tram sometimes. In Switzerland, executive power is shared between a number of people.'

They walked across the flower market. He showed Fatima the *Käfigturm* with its mediaeval prison cells and large clock. Then they arrived at the bank. They arranged to meet again at six o'clock. Winter felt bad about letting Fatima explore the city on her own. He felt less bad when she told him with a grin what a shame it was that he couldn't accompany her to all the clothes shops.

Watching Fatima vanish into the crowd, Winter studied the people walking behind her, but then decided against feeding his paranoia.

He climbed the stairs to his office, trying not to think about Fatima. An unfinished puzzle was awaiting him.

In his office, Winter listened to his phone messages as he started up his computer. A woman from Communications, whom he'd never heard of, wanted him to call back immediately to discuss the security measures in the contingency plans of the annual conference. Dirk was asking where he was and whether he'd like to come for lunch. Winter parked both messages and focused on the case at hand.

The first piece of the puzzle was the list of numbers from Schmitt's mobile. Late afternoon was a good time to call the unidentified, anonymous numbers. Winter opened Skype on his computer, put on headphones and microphone, and dialled the first number.

'Yes?' a voice asked.

Winter assumed an affable tone. 'Good afternoon, my name is Schneebeli. I've got some good news for you: you've won a great prize! Congratulations!'

'I'm sorry?'

'A few weeks ago you let us ask you some questions about your consumer habits. Today we picked a winner from all those who were kind enough to take part in our survey. The draw took place in the presence of a lawyer.'

'I didn't take part in any survey, and I don't want to buy anything either.' It was a man's voice, guttural and already annoyed.

A picture formed in Winter's head of an unshaven alcoholic. He carried on regardless, 'I'm not selling you anything, and I'm really sorry to disturb you, but it's my job to notify and congratulate the winners, and send them their iPad minis.'

'iPad?'

'Yes, you've won one of the ten iPads in our draw.'

It took a little persuasion but eventually the man gave his address, Winter asked which finish he would prefer – white, black, or metallic – congratulated him again and said goodbye. Not bad for starters. He drank a mouthful of water then made his way through the list.

About every third call ended in a conversation, where the person on the line gave him their name and address. The prospect of a small gift worked. Bribery.

Another third of the numbers went to answerphone or
voicemail. He didn't leave messages, but noted down any
names that were mentioned.

The final third brought Winter in contact with people who
were decidedly curt. An elderly lady with a snooty manner
fired obscene but imaginative insults at him. One man said
Winter could shove his 'iPad' up his arse.

After an hour he gave up, pleased that he didn't have to
earn a living in telesales. His ears were hot and his friendly
streak was all used up. None of the names got him any
further. He'd call the rest of the list of anonymous numbers
later.

Winter stood up, stretched and went on the hunt for another
piece of the puzzle. Every child knows that the quickest way
to complete a jigsaw is to start by finding the corners and then
the edge pieces. His puzzle was more complicated, without
edges and without a picture for reference. But time and space
couldn't be ignored.

Winter fetched a coffee.

Many people complained that everything and everybody
was under surveillance these days: video cameras on every
corner, dozens of access codes, passwords and IP numbers.
As far as Winter was concerned, these made the bank more
secure. Security was the prerequisite for trust. And trust was
the bank's capital.

Winter logged on to the bank's access system that covered
the doors with electronic locks. Employees could only open
these with their security cards. All data was automatically saved.
Precisely one minute after midnight the system generated a
new folder for each card reader.

Scrolling to July 24, Winter opened the folder for the card
readers of the Zürich lifts. The lift too could only be operated
by the personalized security cards. Staff with a parking space
could go down to the second basement level. A select group

of employees with security level 3 were permitted to enter the fourth basement level with the deposit boxes and the vault. But almost all staff could access the third basement level with the heating, the archive and the stationery store.

The lift folder had nine subfolders. One for each floor. Winter opened the one for the third basement level. A list of personnel numbers and exact travel times filled the screen. A cemetery of numbers.

In the HR's SAP module, Winter hunted fruitlessly for the names to match the numbers. After five, gruelling minutes he rang the HR department and got them to guide him over the phone to the employee roll. Winter thanked them, hung up and printed out the list. When Winter took the paper from the printer he was once again amazed at how many people were on the payroll.

Anne had not yet been deleted from the system.

At 19:19 she'd taken the lift down to the third basement level and gone up again two minutes later. Anne had been quick in fetching the box of chocolates noted in the file. Another piece of the puzzle.

Winter clicked further through the folders. Anne had opened the entrance to the Zürich branch at 19:10. This suggested she'd come by rail, as the trains from Bern always arrived on the hour in Zürich, and the bank was walkable from the station in ten minutes.

Eleven minutes after entering, Anne had left the bank again. The times confirmed what Frau Obrist had said. Winter wondered whether Anne had meant him when she'd talked about the fairy-tale prince.

Anne's movements in time and space were growing ever clearer. Winter scribbled on a pad. First a bottle of whisky, then a Who? and a Where? Two questions remained to be answered. Who had given Anne the bomb disguised as Laphroaig? And where had the handover taken place? As he pondered these questions he shaded in the whisky bottle and went over the words 'who' and 'where' several times.

Then he checked his watch. The last thing he wanted was to keep Fatima waiting. At that moment his mobile rang. He must be telepathic after all. 'Hello, Fatima.'

'Found anything?'

'Perhaps.' A pause. 'Where are you?'

'In a changing cubicle. I just wanted to let you know I'm running a little late. A few Egyptian minutes.'

'No problem. Found anything nice?'

'Oh yes, you've got wonderful shops here.'

Winter didn't have a clue about clothes shops.

'But I've got to change a few things. See you later.'

He had time for his puzzle. Full of curiosity, Winter clicked through the folders for the card readers at headquarters in Bern.

Between five and six on the evening of July 24, Anne hadn't left any electronic traces there. Where had she got her whisky bomb from?

Back with the folders for the Zürich branch, he started analysing the movements of other employees with the help of the personnel roll. Quarter of an hour later he muttered, 'Interesting.' Egyptian minutes had their advantages.

*Max wasn't late. About one hundred miles to the south of where Winter was sitting, he was driving a fully laden, four-by-four Land Rover. He'd bought the car six hundred kilometres to the west for cash. To make enough room for his cargo he'd flipped down the back seats.*

*The axles groaned under the load covered by a military tarpaulin. The Land Rover slowly climbed the single-track road that snaked through the mountain forest. Max consulted the 1:25,000 map on the passenger seat, then his mobile phone. The red dot wasn't moving and there were four more hairpin bends to the meeting point.*

Fatima was only half an hour late, 'Five Egyptian minutes,' as she emphasized. When Winter put Fatima's shopping bags into his boot, he spied a box with heavy-duty mountain boots, and at the top a dozen chemical heat pads. A padded, winter coat bulged out of another bag. Bright green like a fluorescent marker.

He smiled. 'Are you heading to the North Pole?'

'No, but glaciers are made of ice, and ice is cold, right?'

'Don't worry. It's summer.'

They left town via a rat run, and it wasn't long before Winter took the scenic route. The sun was shining, and a quarter of an hour later they arrived at Winter's little house.

'Here we are.'

Fatima smiled and looked around. Green. It smelled of grass and cows. Winter fetched the bags from the boot and opened the door. Weighed down with the shopping they entered the low-ceilinged room. Fatima's gaze fell on the huge bunch of flowers. 'How beautiful!'

Winter silently thanked Frau Mettler.

He carried Fatima's bags into the bedroom to find a puddle of water on the floor, which had spilled from a vase. Frau Mettler's second bunch of flowers lay beside it; Tiger was stretched out innocently across the bed. Winter shooed the cat out of the room with a sharp word.

Fatima was standing in the doorway. 'Winter, cats are sacred in Egypt. Watch out you don't incur the wrath of the gods.'

Tiger rubbed up against Fatima's legs.

'May I introduce you both? Fatima, from the land of the pharaohs and the sphinx. Tiger, king of the local jungle.'

Fatima tickled Tiger's neck. 'You're a spoiled boy, aren't you?'

Winter pointedly ignored them both.

As well as courgettes Frau Mettler had also put some fresh tomatoes and a head of lettuce in the fridge, and Winter started preparing some food.

Fatima was impressed by Winter's kitchen skills and seemed happy to be cooked for. They ate with relish, spoke about Swiss barbecue culture, the melting ice of the glaciers and Egyptian farmers struggling against the encroachment of the desert.

Fatima stroked her hair behind her ears, put the last mouthful of courgettes in her mouth, and asked, 'What proportion of energy production in Switzerland comes from water – white gold?'

'I reckon we get about half our energy from hydroelectric plants. We have lots of reservoirs. These are our natural batteries.'

'Very practical.'

'Yes, so long as the dam walls hold.'

'Our white gold is the water of the Aswan Dam. Unfortunately, it's not enough.'

Both of them realized that they'd gone in a huge arc back to the Cairo power station. Winter got up and for pudding conjured up some frozen blackberries from his own garden. He served them, warmed in a bain-marie, with vanilla ice cream.

They watched the sun set and the blue sky slowly turn dark. Instead of pyramids, Winter had the crown of the Alps. Above it, threatening towers of dark storm clouds had formed over the course of the evening. As they each drank an espresso, the first flashes of lightning hit the water of the nearby River Aare, accompanied almost instantaneously by terrifying thunder. In the darkness, large drops of rain started to pelt down, but by the time the lightning came Winter and Fatima were too preoccupied to notice.

Early the following morning Winter disinfected his stab wound, laid some fresh gauze on it and re-bandaged his arm. It was another sunny day. Tiger had made himself scarce. His bowl was empty. Winter had given him a particularly generous portion the night before. Not that tomcats can be bribed.

His mobile phone didn't show any urgent messages. The financial group's head of security wanted to meet him at the annual conference. The communications department had sent him the conference programme.

Winter screwed up his eyes and tried in vain to decipher this on the small screen. There wasn't a peep to be heard out of Fatima, and Winter crept silently to his car to get some fresh croissants.

Outside the bakery he bumped into the postman who handed him his post and the newspapers. A hedge fund of a large Swiss bank was being shut down by the authorities because of dramatic losses in its share price. The investors had lost ninety-five per cent. The fund's speciality was leveraged investments in mining shares. Winter thought of Farmer and the different colours of gold: black, white, yellow.

Back home he threw the papers on the sofa, puffed up the squashed cushions and put some coffee on.

Fatima appeared, gave Winter a dozy wave, and vanished into the bathroom without a word.

In the various newspapers, Winter read different versions of the hedge-fund collapse. Thanks to big leverage the managers had rapidly made huge profits, but when the tide turned they slipped even more quickly into a downwards spiral. Growth couldn't go on forever. Winter didn't have any sympathy. He drank coffee, pressed fresh orange juice and filled Tiger's bowl.

Three-quarters of an hour later Fatima was ready for an expedition to the North Pole. For the three-day conference, Winter placed a dark suit in a protective cover on the back seat, and put his wheelie suitcase into the Audi's boot. For today's excursion, a small rucksack with a few supplies and a spare jumper would suffice.

Now the red dot on Max's mobile started to move southwards.

Winter left the Susten mountain pass and parked beside the base station of the cable car. They bought two tickets and entered the small red cabin, which held a maximum of eight people. Fatima and Winter were the only passengers. Mountain climbers and pensioners went up earlier, family outings were rare during the week.

On the outer wall of the cabin were two bulky luggage crates in which the inspector stacked supplies for the mountain huts.

At half past ten, the small gondola left the base station, wobbled a little and then quickly soared skywards. Winter sensed Fatima tensing up. She was used to flat country, but now bravely held on tight to the poles at the side and tried to look relaxed. Fatima wanted to see a glacier, and that meant going up. As if she could read his thoughts, she asked, 'Where is the glacier?'

'Higher up and further into the mountains. After the cable car we'll have to walk another couple of hours.'

Winter knew the valley and the surrounding mountains from an exercise his special unit had carried out. The scenario was that his team had to free hostages who'd been abducted by a doomsday sect and held captive in a remote Alpine hut. They could only approach it unnoticed at night. During the endless wait his deputy had got badly sunburned.

Beyond the large windows of the cabin, the houses, cars and people shrank. Below them, the lush-green meadows turned into barren pastures. The beech forest became a fir forest.

Winter and Fatima kept yawning to combat the changing pressure in their ears.

Ten minutes and an ascent of three hundred and fifty metres later, they got out of the former works cable car. A cool wind blew through the top station. Once outside they took the fresh air deep into their lungs and marched off.

A dusty path led across an alp with cows and cowpats, both fresh and dried. The well-nourished cattle ignored the tourists, chewing away serenely. They were far plumper than the scraggy cattle on the fields along the Nile.

They crossed a mountain stream via a wobbly wooden bridge. The cows were replaced by more scrawny-looking sheep, each of them with a small bell around their neck; the tinkling delighted Fatima. Then the path became steeper and stonier, the vegetation sparser and hardier. Gentians were in flower.

After a scree slope they discovered to their left a small reservoir. Above the drinking-water reservoir, the glacial stream had dug deep into the bare rock.

Winter felt the sweat running down his back. His shirt stuck to his back beneath the rucksack.

Fatima, who didn't seem to be sweating, followed him step for step. She was fit and had good balance. To start with, Winter stopped at the particularly steep and narrow parts to offer her a helping hand. But after she'd declined a few times he left it. She climbed the tricky bits flexibly too.

The last section to the Windegg hut zigzagged steeply up the mountain. Around midday they reached the lee of the hut. They ate the rolls they'd brought with them, drank tea and looked down into the valley. Far below they could see the Audi in the car park, beside it a green off-road vehicle.

The hut warden came out of his shelter, looked delighted to have company and forced them to taste his spicy alp cheese, which he'd stored for three years up here in a stone hollow. He served them finely-shaved cheese, gherkins he'd preserved himself and two fresh tomatoes on a wooden board. Fatima asked the cheesemaker, 'Is it far to the glacier?'

'Just around the corner,' he replied in English, with a thick Oberland accent.

'Over one hundred and fifty years ago the British discovered the Bernese Oberland as a tourist destination,' Winter explained.

'You get the best view from the suspension bridge.'

'The suspension bridge?'

'Yes,' the hut warden said, 'in the past the Trift Glacier used to extend far into the valley and was easy to cross. Then a large part of it melted away. Global warming. The meltwater lake is getting bigger and bigger. Thanks to the bridge we don't have to make a big detour to get to the hut.'

'Is there another hut higher up?'

'Yes, it's a good two and a half thousand metres above sea level.'

The hut warden nodded. For dessert, there were dried apricots and hot coffee with a shot of strong, homemade plum schnapps.

They thanked him, paid, set off and ten minutes later caught sight of the Trift Glacier glittering in the sun.

The icy mass lapped in massive steps down a col. Lengthways, cracks furrowed the ice, which was covered in scree. In the valley basin, the tongue of the glacier ran into a milky meltwater lake, in which small icebergs drifted. The lake was blocked at the entrance to the valley by a natural dam. On the shadowy northern slope of the basin, individual slabs of snow remained from last winter.

Fatima and Winter stopped to allow the inhospitable but fascinating scenery wash over them. They stood there in silence until Fatima said, 'This is my first glacier.'

'And?'

'It's massive.' After a while, she added, 'I feel really small.'

'I find it calming.'

'Yes, somehow the valley gives off a sense of serenity.'

'I can understand that. But don't delude yourself. The glacier with its cracks is dangerous, the water in the lake is ice cold and the weather up here can turn very quickly.'

Fatima took photos with her mobile. The little bars that showed phone reception had vanished. They were in a dead spot. A helicopter with a low-hanging net flew high above them. Supplies for the hut or building materials to improve a path.

They kept walking and reached the bridge at the end of a ridge. To Fatima's surprise the bridge was endlessly long. A fragile nothing hovering above the abyss. The suspension bridge was almost two hundred metres long and hung one hundred metres above ground.

'Shit!'

Fatima was familiar with wobbly suspension bridges, but only from developing countries. Luckily this one looked new. She bent forward cautiously. Far below, the glacial stream frothed over the natural dam and disappeared into a gully.

She paused and filled her lungs with air. This would be worse than the trip in the swaying cable car. Her head said: whatever happens the bridge will hold, the Swiss are reliable. Her heart said: never! A queasiness spread throughout her stomach. Her innate reflexes were automatically resisting the chasm.

Fatima glanced at Winter, who looked totally relaxed. In the faint hope of being able to avoid crossing the bridge, Fatima said in a deliberately firm voice, 'It looks pretty rickety.'

'Don't be scared. Many hikers have crossed this bridge.' Winter smiled impassively.

'I don't have a head for heights.'

'Me neither. The best thing is simply not to think about it. The bridge is as wide as a pavement and you'd never think about not walking on one of those.'

That was easier said than done for the suspension bridge seemed to lead into nothingness.

Four, thick, steel cables had been stretched over the valley, two at foot height and two at chest height. The two lower cables were connected by cross braces, upon which lay three parallel boards, running lengthways, each about a foot wide. Through the gaps between the boards you could see right down into the valley. Finer cables had been woven between the cables on either side to make a broad-meshed balustrade.

The bridge swung slightly in the fresh breeze. Fatima banished the thought of a gale which might toss the bridge from side to side. 'It's only in storms that you have to be careful,' Winter explained. If the bridge is wet it acts like a lightning conductor, so in an electrical storm you could end up toast. But today the weather's fine.'

He grinned.

Fatima gave a tormented smile.

Winter pointed at the glacier, then down into the depths of the valley. 'Far more dangerous would be if part of the glacier broke off, as that would create a tidal wave and the dam wouldn't be able to hold the water.'

Fatima wasn't interested in hearing such thoughts. Ignoring Winter's words, she braced herself mentally for her passage across the abyss. Two hundred metres would take no more than a few minutes. She decided to walk swiftly, hold onto the side cables and only look straight ahead at where she was heading. Focused, but careful. Absolutely no tripping. There were large holes between the cables on the sides. Fatima was certain that she could fall through one of those.

'Come on. We'll be at the glacier in an hour. Would you like me to go first?'

Fatima nodded and Winter began marching across the bridge without the slightest hesitation. As she stepped onto it, Fatima noticed that the suspension bridge wasn't flat. It went down at first and rose again after the mid-point.

Winter had demonstratively put his arms out like a 'T' and

cast her an encouraging glance over his shoulder. Her palms glided along the rough, cold cables. This calmed her. She circumspectly shuffled one foot in front of the other, ensuring that she distributed her bodyweight between two boards at any one time. Better safe than sorry.

When, after twenty or so paces, the bridge hadn't collapsed, Fatima felt emboldened. The suspension bridge bounced gently. The tension of the cable. The horizontal oscillations were so slow that neither Fatima nor Winter really felt them. Adrenalin shot through her body as she started to enjoy this mini adventure. The view was breathtaking.

Against her good intentions she even ventured a glance down into the valley. But when she saw the eddies of the glacial stream far below, her stomach convulsed again and she fixed her gaze squarely on Winter's rucksack five paces ahead of her. To compensate for the up and down movement she had adjusted her rhythm to Winter's and was now walking in step with him. The sky was blue, the air fresh. It was glorious.

In the middle of the suspension bridge they stopped and marvelled together at the blaze of colour. From this vantage point the milky green of the glacial lake was even more intense. They stood beside each other quietly. The bridge swung. Far above, a bird of prey was circling, keeping an eye out for groundhogs. A buzzard, a kite or even an eagle. Freedom.

All of a sudden their peace was disturbed. On the other side, a group of mountain climbers stepped onto the bridge.

It started to sway.

They had to cross each other.

Fatima and Winter shifted carefully to one side, holding on tight to the steel cables with both hands. The bridge tipped sideways slightly. Inadvertently they looked down into the depths.

The mountain climbers, all men around forty with checked shirts, heavy-duty shoes, ice picks and ropes over their shoulders, marched past. The last in the group raised his cap by way of a greeting.

Now Fatima was keen to get off the bridge and feel the glacier beneath her feet. She pushed her way past Winter. The bridge led gently upwards. In her knees she could feel the vibrations of the mountain climbers.

Winter paused for a moment. It was about another hour to the glacier. Maybe they could walk a short distance on the glacier ice. In summer the crevices weren't covered in snow and so clearly visible. The local tourist board may have marked out a safe section for visitors. Winter followed Fatima.

The rocky outcrop on the other side was still about thirty metres away when a wooden board split right in front of him. The adjacent boards were ripped from their brackets, opening up a gaping hole. One of the stray splinters bored into his forearm.

Someone had shot at them. Up here they were exposed, without protection.

Human targets.

When she heard the wood crack, Fatima turned around and stared at the hole between her and Winter. Her eyes were wide with horror.

Pointing to the end of the suspension bridge, with his bleeding right arm and outstretched finger, he cried, 'Run!'

Fatima saw the blood and seemed frozen, unable to move.

A second shot destroyed more boards between Fatima and Winter.

Panicked, Fatima ran towards land.

Winter felt surrounded by a peaceful bubble. Calmly, he analysed the situation. The shooter was below them. He hadn't heard a report. The shots had been fired with a rifle from a long distance. A hunting rifle with a telescopic sight. They didn't start hunting chamois until autumn.

A shot from that distance and this angle was tricky. So far the marksman had only hit the wooden boards. Was he a poor shot or just a sadist?

Winter turned around and hurried back to the middle of the bridge.

He was doing the unexpected.

And luring the gunman away from Fatima.

But two more bullets, fired in rapid succession, tore up the boards in front of him. A long hole appeared. Winter stopped abruptly, shielded his eyes with his arms and collected another splinter.

The ground beneath his feet was rapidly shrinking.

He saw the broken boards falling slowly into the bottomless depths.

One question had been answered, at least. The gunman was an excellent shot, and this meant he was a sadist who liked to let his victims suffer. This was the better of his poor options, as it might possibly give Winter time to come up with a plan.

Movement.

Although moving targets are more difficult to hit than static ones, most creatures usually froze. Like the deer in the headlights of an oncoming car. Winter spun around in a flash and leaped back blindly.

It wasn't a moment too soon, for the next shot destroyed the last three boards beneath his feet. The bullet whistled past him. A splinter sunk into the rucksack. He grabbed the right-hand cable with both hands and landed with his feet on the lower cable.

He looked over at Fatima. She was ten metres from the safety of the rocks. The two cables sprung violently up and down and he tried to stabilize his position above the abyss.

Fatima was still five metres from safety when the ground was shot away from beneath her. She plunged through the hole.

It seemed to Winter as if she were sinking in slow motion, as through a trapdoor in the theatre. Or beneath the gallows.

'No!'

Her shrill, desperate scream was a mixture between 'Stop!', 'No!', 'Help!' and 'Allah!' in Arabic.

The protracted echo of her shriek reverberated from the valley basin.

And again.

Then there was silence, and for a second the world stood still.

When Winter opened his eyes he saw that one of the thin cross braces had somehow caught Fatima beneath her arms. Her chest, stomach and legs were hanging beneath the bridge.

Her shoulders and head were where the wooden boards had been just seconds ago. A yawning chasm.

'Hold on tight! I'm coming!'

'I'm slipping.'

With his feet, he pushed himself along the cable towards Fatima. Step by step. The thin cross brace creaked in the side brackets.

'Almost there.'

He'd turned his back on the marksman and was expecting another bullet any second. Reaching a few metres of undamaged bridge, he rushed towards Fatima.

Had the gunman emptied his magazine? Was he reloading? Might the rifle be jammed? He hadn't been able to spot the shooter from this distance. He might even be five hundred metres away. But Winter had no time to contemplate this.

Once again he put his feet next to each other on the lower cable and carefully groped his way towards Fatima.

He heard a whimper. 'Winter?'

He edged his way forward.

Fatima stared at him with opaque eyes. 'I'll get you out of there,' he tried to reassure her.

To keep a firm footing, he dug his heels into the cable and gripped more tightly on the upper cable with his left hand. Then he let go with his right and bent his knees. Grabbing Fatima's left forearm, he slowly pulled her up. The stab wound from the golf course hurt like hell and the scar split open again under the tension. The blood mingled with that from his new splinter wounds.

'Fatima, help me. Put your foot up.'

Fatima's stomach was now level with the lower cable and she tried to get a footing on it. But she couldn't.

Her wrist was slipping through Winter's bloodied grasp as the thick, steel cable scoured his other hand. Time was running out.

Winter gritted his teeth.

He gave it his all.

He swung Fatima upwards, but her feet missed the lower cable again and she fell back down. The cross brace snapped from its bracket. Fatima stifled a scream.

She was hanging from Winter's arm, dangling over the void.

Winter's shoulders were wrenched apart. His fingers dug into Fatima's forearm, but his grip on the cable became weaker. Winter's knuckles were white and blood flowed between the fingers.

He took a deep breath. The jolt of her slip had set the bridge swinging more violently, and Winter used one of the upwards movements to pull up Fatima with the last reserve of his energy.

She thrashed about with her free arm and managed to grab the upper cable on the other side. That was good. Now she could put a foot on the lower cable.

'Excellent. Now stand up and hold on tight with both hands.'

Fatima got up very cautiously. The cables swung and vibrated, but she was able to pull herself up and get her other foot onto the cable. She stood in a strangely contorted pose, gazing into the valley far below. She seized up and one foot slid outwards, but she caught herself in time and regained her footing.

'Stay totally calm,' Winter said. 'We're almost in safety. I'm going to let go of your arm now.' The two of them were standing upright and he added, 'Watch, Fatima. The best thing is to push your feet along the cable like this.'

At that moment, something tugged at his rucksack, the aluminium flask pinged and he felt a blow in his back. A bullet had entered the rucksack and penetrated the thermos.

The blow reeled Winter around.

He lost his footing. The bridge lurched perilously to the side. He swung outwards. This time there was no bungee rope.

'Aargh!' he cried.

'Winter!'

Fatima wanted to hold out a hand, but had to get a grip on herself. The cables were seesawing wildly. A bullet shot through her hair, but she didn't notice it. The movement was making life difficult for the marksman. As the bullets flew the targets were yo-yoing.

'Quick!' Winter cried.

Fatima pushed herself in rapid strides towards the outcrop, reached the last intact metre of bridge and ran. Behind her the boards shattered. The gunman had followed her with his rifle, but he'd been too late. She dived to safety, landing on her stomach, and immediately turned around to Winter.

He was still suspended a few metres from the rock face, manoeuvring himself along the cable with his hands using the oscillations of the bridge. A bullet shredded Winter's trouser leg on his inner thigh. He felt the puff of air and was relieved that the bullet had missed his most sensitive part.

Then he too reached the concrete anchoring of the bridge, pulled himself up, reached shelter behind the rocks and crawled over to Fatima. His forearms left a trace of blood on the bare rock.

Drained, Fatima closed her eyes. 'What was that?'

He pulled splinters from his arm. 'Someone's hunting us.' He placed his uninjured arm around Fatima's shoulder.

'Why?'

'I don't know.'

'Did you see the gunman?'

'No. Thankfully he was far away. Somewhere below us. There's a direct path to the bridge that doesn't make a detour to the hut. I expect the shooter went that way. But with no bridge he can't follow us.' Winter crawled to the edge and peered down into the valley. Unable to spot anybody, he pulled himself back. He was dripping blood.

'You're bleeding. Let me see.'

Winter slipped off the rucksack and removed his shirt. Feeling his arm he said, 'It's not so bad, just a few scratches.

The muscles are unharmed.' He clenched his fist several times. His fingers were in perfect working order.

Fatima cleaned his arm as best she could with a tissue. Winter tore the sleeves of his shirt into strips and together they bandaged the flesh wounds.

Then he pulled the rucksack over and first removed the large splinter. He took out the thermos flask, which bore a bullet hole. The tea had leaked out. The flask and the liquid had checked the bullet.

Winter shook the thermos. The bullet rattled around and rolled out. 'A .308 calibre. These bullets are used for hunting and sniper rifles. You can easily buy them here. All you have to do is show your ID and wave a bit of money in the air.'

Winter let the events play out again in his head. First the boards in front of him, then the ones behind. A shot for the boards below him and then the hole beneath Fatima. Then a pause for reloading.

A hunting rifle, maybe a Remington. A weapon like that wouldn't stick out around here. The US Marine Corps used a similar model. With the police Winter had tested custom models with which he'd been able to hit a coin from eight hundred metres in good conditions.

'What are we going to do now?' Fatima asked, holding her mobile phone. No reception.

'We'll just stroll across the glacier,' Winter said dryly.

'See the glacier and die,' Fatima retorted. The steel cables hung serenely over the chasm, swinging back and forth. A solitary wooden board dangled from it.

'Come on, then.' They got to their feet and climbed up to the glacier. They washed and refreshed themselves at a small mountain stream. Winter still had two apples and a bar of chocolate.

As they walked, they wondered who might be behind this. The most obvious theory was that someone wanted revenge for the events on the golf course. These TAA madmen were bound by the Old Testament. An eye for an eye.

How had the marksman found them? Were they followed? Winter hadn't noticed anything on the way here. But he hadn't been looking in his rear-view mirror the whole time. Or had someone located them via their mobiles? That was routine for Meister. But there wasn't any reception up here. The helicopter earlier on had just flown past, transporting something. Winter had another suspicion, but he couldn't confirm it until they were back down in the valley.

They reached the glacier. After the suspension bridge Fatima wasn't particularly impressed any more. They crossed the ice on a marked path. Hours later and with weary knees they got back into the cable car that took them down to the valley. They didn't meet a single person the entire way.

Winter asked the young cable-car employee whether he'd seen a hunter. He said he hadn't but he'd only replaced his colleague at three o'clock. He told them where the employee lived who'd been on the morning shift. Winter and Fatima found him just around the corner from the base station, in the garden of an ancient farmhouse made crooked by wind and snow. Winter stopped beside the fence. 'Hello, do you mind if I ask you something?' The man with the pitchfork looked up and just nodded. He wasn't the talkative type.

'This morning we took the gondola up the mountain.'

'Yes, I know,' he said, wiping sweat from his brow.

'Just after one o'clock someone mistook us for a chamois. So I'd like to know: did you see a hunter?'

'The hunting season doesn't begin till September.'

'This hunter was ahead of the times.'

Unflustered, the mountain farmer rested his chin on the pitchfork and had a long think. It was hard work. 'One man went up about an hour after you.'

'Did he say anything?'

The farmer shook his head.

'But he wasn't a hunter?'

'No.'

'So he didn't have a rifle on him?'

The farmer had another long think. Winter waited in silence until the other man felt uncomfortable. After a minute that seemed endless, the farmer said, 'He was a sort of punk.'

This astonished Winter. 'A punk?'

'Yes, you know, dressed all in black. And as pale as an albino calf. Too many computer games, I'd wager. And too little hard graft.' He disdainfully dug the pitchfork into the ground and skewered a potato.

'Hair colour? Height?'

'Are you a policeman?'

'Not any more.'

'He had short, blond hair and was fairly tall. I only saw him briefly at the ticket desk.'

'Did he speak Swiss German?'

'Yes, but he wasn't from around here.'

'Rucksack?'

'No. Wait. Yes, now that I come to think of it, he did.'

'What does that mean?'

'I think he was carrying a paraglider. In a rucksack.' You could easily hide a rifle in that.

'Notice anything else?'

A long pause. He scratched his back. 'His shoes. He was wearing army boots. The ones that only officers used to be allowed to wear.'

'You mean lace-up combat boots?'

'Yes, that's right. I suppose that's all part of a punk's get-up.'

They thanked him and walked to the Audi.

Fatima, who hadn't understood much, said, 'A punk?'

'Punk is dead. That must have been Max. Same shoes, same hair.'

The green off-road vehicle was no longer there.

Winter bent down and examined the Audi. He didn't find a bomb, but on the inside of the right rear hubcap he discovered an inconspicuous-looking transmitter, attached with a strong magnet. It was the sort you could buy in any electronics shop and favoured especially by detectives who specialized in divorce cases, but also used for tagging lynxes and bears.

'This explains how Max found us.' He left the transmitter in place and looked around. The valley was quiet.

The fake eyelashes of the smart women at the reception of the Grand Palace in Interlaken didn't flicker when a sweaty Winter checked in with his bandaged arm. These women had seen all manner of things in their time. It was part of the five-star hotel's successful business model that their employees kept a tight veil of secrecy over the whims and eccentricities of their clientele.

The bank valued this too and had commandeered half the hotel for three days. Winter had invited Fatima along as the new CEO of Orafin. Both were on the printed guest list.

The Grand Palace was an old, nineteenth-century hotel that could boast monarchs, actors and presidents amongst its guests. In that order. The place had been extended and renovated countless times, the most recent overhaul being the restoration of the ballroom. Rich Russians and Indians, especially, loved hiring the hall, done out in pastel colours, for their parties.

The security guard beside the lift made a decent impression from a distance. It was Anne who'd organized the security firm that would keep onlookers at a distance. The detailed contract was in Winter's suitcase. He'd do an inspection of the hotel with the local person responsible.

One of the receptionists asked if Winter had any particular requests. He selected two neighbouring rooms with parquet flooring on the fourth floor and ordered two litres of mineral water, two slices of cake as well as tea and coffee to be brought to his room. And a first aid box. Winter thanked the woman and took the documents and plastic cards she handed him.

He looked around.

Fatima had disappeared.

But he could see Schütz, deep in conversation with an Asian client.

The bank enticed clients to their annual conference with an exclusive programme. The men loved racing across the mountain pass in Jaguar sports cars under the instruction of an aging rally driver. The women usually preferred the guided excursions to see the nearby mountain flora, and of course the spa with its beauty treatments. This evening there was a genuine Swiss cheese fondue on the *Jungfraujoch* to mark the opening of the conference.

Schütz gave a nonchalant wave.

Grinning, Winter waved back with his uninjured arm and saw Fatima on the phone in an armchair.

Looking at Winter's arm the receptionist recommended the hotel doctor in the spa area just around the corner.

When Winter just shook his head, all she could do was wish him a 'wonderful stay'. The well-meaning woman had acquired her affected way of speaking during role-play sessions. In many languages.

Fatima, who'd finished her call, got up and was heading towards Winter. He admired her elegant movements but she looked straight past him.

Behind him he heard von Tobler's resonant baritone.

'Winter! What the devil have you been up to?'

Von Tobler clapped Winter on the shoulder and he flinched involuntarily. The boss was wearing a bespoke, black suit and a starched, white shirt with a billowing silk tie fastened by a gold pin. On his lapel was a Rotary Club, wheel badge. As he shook Winter's hands his golden cufflinks with the bank's logo gleamed. Von Tobler was making his presence felt in the hotel lobby, personally greeting as many of the arriving guests as possible. When his gaze alighted on Fatima, Winter said, 'Herr von Tobler, may I introduce Frau Hakim from Orafin?'

Before Winter could finish talking, von Tobler had switched on his male charm. 'Ah, what a pleasure to meet you finally. It's a special honour for me to welcome such a distinguished personality to our humble event. You are even more charming in the flesh.'

Fatima swept the hair from her face and gave von Tobler a professional smile.

'The pleasure is all mine.'

'Did you have a pleasant trip?'

'Yes, thank you. Herr Winter has been looking after me.'

'Allow me once again to congratulate you on your success. I'm sure that you are a shining example to Egyptian women – and the entire business world.' With both paws, von Tobler now clasped Fatima's slim hands. He moved a few centimetres closer to her than what would be deemed a polite distance.

'Many thanks, Dr von Tobler. Mr Kaddour was an excellent mentor.'

'Enough. Enough of business. How do you like our little country?'

'It's wonderful.' Freeing her hands with an expansive gesture in the direction of the Alps, Fatima took a step away to recover some distance. 'I was deeply impressed by the Trift Glacier.'

As he spotted another client, von Tobler took Fatima's hand again, bowed slightly and said in an unmistakeably lascivious manner, 'I'm looking forward to seeing you later.'

In the mirrored lift, Fatima touched Winter's arm. 'I don't think I'll come this evening. It's been a white-knuckle day.'

'I'm sorry about the attack. I didn't see it coming.'

'The gunman or von Tobler?'

Winter laughed. 'Both. But I meant the sniper.'

'Fate. Allah willed it to be so.'

Winter admired Fatima's pragmatic fatalism and wished he could pack away his past so easily. His father had told him from an early age that you create your own success and you also have to take responsibility for your mistakes. Memories he'd prefer to keep hidden surfaced, and then he noticed Fatima looking at him thoughtfully in one of the mirrors.

The lift went 'Ping'.

When they stepped out onto the soft red carpet in the corridor Winter looked at his watch. 'I've got a meeting in an hour. With the financial group's head of security. If it comes to a takeover, he'll be my line manager.'

'Those are just rumours, aren't they?'

'Where there's smoke, there's fire. I hope von Tobler will shed some light on it in his speech this evening. The rumour mill's going crazy.'

'He seemed very confident just now.'

Winter maintained a diplomatic silence. They walked down the long corridor, round a cleaning trolley, turned two corners, went down the two steps between the old building and the extension and came to their rooms.

Winter handed Fatima her card.

'Here.'

'Thanks.'

They opened their heavy, bedroom doors and met inside between the connecting doors. Five minutes later the tea, coffee, cake and first-aid kit arrived. The waiter came from Morocco and spoke French. Winter gave him a handsome tip.

Winter took a shower and tried to keep the burning soap away from his injured arm. Beneath the warm stream of water he was overcome by tiredness. He turned the temperature control to ice cold. His heart leaped and his pulse throbbed. Icy water. Glacial lake. He was awake again. Who wanted him dead? Stretching out his arms, Winter supported himself against the wall and let the cold shower patter on his back. This evening he would demand answers.

He turned off the water and put on the hotel dressing gown, but it was too small. He took it off again, wrapped a towel around his waist and drank a cup of coffee.

Fatima came through the connecting door. 'Shall I patch you up again?'

Nodding gratefully, Winter sat in an armchair and raised his arm. Fatima opened the box with the red cross and attended to Winter's flesh wound. She was a pitiless nurse. Winter could not help flinching when she applied disinfectant. Ten minutes later he looked as if he were advertising plasters.

The movement and strength of his arm were not impaired but the flesh wounds were sensitive to touch. This opened up a whole array of new possibilities to avoid falling asleep later on during the speeches in the muted lighting. He'd just have to press on his forearm and the pain would keep him wide awake.

He got dressed. Dark suit, white shirt and understated tie. The uniform went with the evening.

He took a small plastic bag from his wheelie case and attached the holster with his semiautomatic .45 SIG to his belt behind his back. The spare magazine in his left trouser pocket, the flick knife in his right. This time he also tied the holster with his .22 Mosquito to his right lower leg. Not carrying the Mosquito during his round of golf with Al-Bader had almost spelled disaster.

Today they had tried to kill him and Fatima.

Better safe than sorry.

In the early days Winter had hated carrying weapons, but over time he'd learned to live with them. And after having fired thousands of rounds he was now a good shot. Shooting was a technique that was as much part of his job as conversational skills or shadowing people. The SIG had twice saved his life.

Winter took out the .22 and checked it. The .45 was all in order too. The SIG pistols produced by the Schweizer Industrie Gesellschaft were reliable, precise and indestructible. The beavertail grip lay reassuringly in his hand. He hoped he wouldn't need to use it.

Winter closed the door and headed to the reception. He

was on time to the minute: 19:45. The financial group's head of security, looking bored in one of the chunky, leather chairs, put down his *Financial Times* and stood up. They shook hands.

Live and let live. Hugentobler was fourteen years older and at least thirty kilos heavier than Winter. The financial group's security chief was waiting for retirement. He was notorious for his long coordination meetings and he chaired a variety of committees. Winter liked him all the same, particularly his wily eyes and sharp tongue. It was traditional to invite him to these events.

Winter had booked two seats in the 19:50 helicopter shuttle.

'How are you?'

'Seeing you in one piece makes me glad.'

'How was Florida?' Hugentobler regularly played golf in the States.

'Hot, but good. Alligators with no inhibitions about biting. That's what you call real water hazards.' He grinned and bared his teeth.

They left the lobby via a side exit and hurried to the hotel's helipad, which was hidden behind tall, fir trees. While they waited briefly Winter filled Hugentobler in about his investigation so far. Before the helicopter had arrived Hugentobler was in the picture.

Beside them, one of the hotel's hospitality staff was struggling by turns with her skirt and hair, all the while talking with a broad smile and animated hands to two Japanese clients, who were having great fun and had already drunk a glass or two.

The helicopter landed, the pilot gave the thumbs-up sign and the hospitality woman pushed the Japanese men in. Winter and his colleague followed and belted up too. The helicopter took off again straight away. They flew across the dark Lake Brienz, turned and crossed a high-voltage power line. Then up to the Jungfrau. The two Japanese men chatted excitedly.

Then they took out small, ultra-modern video cameras and filmed in awe.

Winter looked absentmindedly out of the window. The low sun bathed the mountain tops in orange light. In his childhood there'd been an ice lolly called the Rocket, which was the same orange colour as the mountains. Winter's mouth started watering.

It grew dark. The light disappeared behind a grey dam wall and Winter was overcome by an oppressive feeling. The helicopter rose slowly and almost vertically up the concrete wall. The pilot had taken the scenic route, wanting to impress his passengers – not only with mountains but with one of the tallest dam walls in the world too.

Down in the valley the turbines rotated, producing electricity from the dammed water. The demand for energy had led to this monumental construction. Tons of concrete and reinforcing steel had been transported up the mountain and assembled there.

It was regarded as an architectural masterpiece, despite the submerged village behind the wall. And in local pubs, rumours still went around that foreign construction workers who'd suffered fatal accidents were concreted into the dam.

After almost three hundred vertical metres the spook was over and the passengers started breathing easily again. The helicopter reached the top of the curved dam and roared across the full reservoir that wound several kilometres through the mountains. Further on, the sun was only just still slanting through the mountaintops.

The helicopter spat out its passengers in the snow on the Jungfraujoch, almost 3,500 metres above sea level. Beneath them, the Great Aletsch Glacier stretched out majestically. Another hospitality woman was waiting to greet the guests. She showed them the way and the helicopter went to pick up its next load. The Japanese were filming again. Winter and Hugentobler trudged through the wet snow to the rocks, where once pioneers had drilled the mountain station of the cog railway. Winter took his mobile from his chest pocket and saw that Ben had tried to call.

'Go ahead,' he said. 'I'll be there in a minute.' He gazed down at the Aletsch Glacier with its moraines and waited for Ben to pick up.

'One of our TAA friends came strolling through my airport today.'

'What do you mean?'

'The facial recognition software was checking our rogues' gallery. At midday we had a TAA match. I thought it might interest you.'

'Absolutely.' All of a sudden the glacier was far away. 'What does your picture look like and what's written beneath it?'

'Military. Leather jacket, combat trousers and short hair. He was in Afghanistan. Logistic corps. Dishonourable discharge because of embezzlement. Sentenced a number of times for drunk driving, affray and illegal possession of weapons. The NSA thinks he belongs to the military core of the TAA and carries out the dirty work.'

'Where was he coming from?'

'From Dallas to Zürich, via London. Hand luggage only.'

'Did you see him personally?'

'No, only the photo. It's not great quality but I'd spot a thug at low resolution. Do you want me to email it to you?'

'Yes. This afternoon Fatima and I were shot at by a sniper.'

'Where?'

'The Trift Glacier. He almost got us.'

'What time?'

'Around one.'

'That couldn't work time-wise. Are you alright?'

'Just a few scratches. How good is this facial recognition software?'

'Good, but not perfect.'

'Do you have any idea what he's after? What's rustling on the electronic grapevine?'

'In all honesty I've no idea. The Americans say that many of the TAA brothers have vanished into thin air. On holiday, hunting, in the desert or gone underground. Somehow it's all gone very quiet.'

There was a pause in the conversation. The email arrived, the telephone beeped and Winter opened the fuzzy snapshot of the TAA thug.

'Nice.'

Prejudices confirmed. The sun had set. Winter thanked Ben and hung up. Preoccupied, he cast a final glance at the glacier.

Winter walked down a bleak tunnel and came to a lift that took him to the party. As he entered the restaurant he paused for a moment. The guests were tightly packed. At a bar, champagne and white wine glasses were being filled and then eagerly accepted by men in dark suits and women in glittering robes.

In one corner a quartet consisting of accordions, clarinet and double bass was playing traditional folk music. The occasional whooping was drowned out by the chatter of the party guests and the clinking of glasses. It sounded as if everyone were trying to toast everyone else.

The waitresses wore traditional Swiss dress even though most of them came from Austria or even further to the east. The important thing was that they were buxom blondes. Around two-thirds of the guests were clients with their spouses or partners. The rest were managers at the bank.

The two Japanese men from earlier were gesticulating with an account manager from Geneva.

In this throng Winter felt lonely. He missed Anne. Or was it Fatima he missed? Putting on his party face, he threw himself into the fray. He hated parties. But the annual conference was a good opportunity to chat to colleagues who Winter normally never met.

He circulated for a few minutes, shaking some hands. This weekend was also about being seen, something von Tobler was a master at. You got the impression that he was everywhere at the same time.

Soon after Winter had finished his round a cowbell rang.

The music and guests went quiet.

Von Tobler gave a witty welcome speech and announced that dinner would now be served. Everyone streamed into the room, with its tables covered in red-and-white checked cloths, steaming pots of cheese fondue placed on each.

'Stir! Stir! Stir!' someone ordered.

Laughter rang out and the mob fell on the molten cheese with cubes of white bread speared onto their forks.

Winter sat with a Russian couple from St Petersburg near the exit. The Russian had grafted away as a plumber under the 'bloody communists' and now owned his own company that specialized in pipes. As he explained, in St Petersburg there were many piping systems for all manner of things.

The Russian was having a wonderful time apparently. He particularly liked the fact that the cheese soaked up the alcohol.

He also loved the rule whereby anyone who lost their chunk of bread had to buy the next round. It was something he wanted to introduce in Russia. Maybe fondue could be exported on a large scale, too? After the cheese they tried to distil the difference between kirsch and vodka.

For that there had to be experiments – a whole string of experiments.

About ten o'clock, Winter found himself again out in the fresh air on the viewing terrace. The cheese lay like a lump in his stomach and the alcohol had affected him slightly.

The two Japanese at the other end of the terrace appeared to be in a worse way.

Winter breathed in deeply. The sky was clear, the stars glittering and it was peaceful here outside. The mountains all around were merely a jagged pattern.

He heard footsteps behind him and he turned around slowly.

The silhouette of a small, slightly stooped man was moving across the terrace. He was smoking a cigar, its end glowing. He went in an arc and came over to Winter, who leaned back against the railings and said, 'Good evening, Herr Marti.'

'Hello, Winter.' Marti puffed with relish on his Cohiba. The bank's chief economist was a sprightly old man, way beyond pension age, who'd long given up his directorship, but still turned up to his office every day. His network of connections was second to none. Winter thought of Yoda from *Star Wars*.

'Lovely evening, isn't it?' the old man said.

A touch of irony.

The two of them looked down at the mighty glacier.

'Most interesting. A Russian plumber drank me under the table. He earns a fortune renovating pipes.'

'Then he must understand something about the circulation of money.'

'He understood how to adapt after 1989 at any rate.'

With a wistful smile Yoda said, 'The helmsman navigates his ship through the rocks with the help of the rocks.' After a pause, he added, grinning, 'Homer's words, not mine.'

'*Our* helmsman was in top form again tonight,' Winter said, pointing at the brightly lit restaurant.

'Yes, he's in his element. The man's a natural talent when it comes to selling something. Himself and the bank.' Marti seemed to have no inhibitions when it came to talking about von Tobler. 'He's always been ahead of his time. Did you know that he flew to Dallas straight after he graduated and devised options trading for oil?'

'No. I just knew about his time on Wall Street.'

'May it rest in peace.' Marti blew a cloud of smoke skywards. 'It's like your Russian plumber. Money flows through the pipes of capitalism. Money instead of shit. And sometimes the pipes are simply blocked.'

'We live in a crazy time.'

Marti shook the ash from his cigar. 'Ashes to ashes.' Then he said, seriously, 'What really worries me is the shifting of capital into undemocratic hands. Over the last few years the Americans have run up alarming debts. Too many expensive wars. The Europeans have far too high levels of debt as well. And they're still arguing. Only the rest of the world has earned money. Money is power. And I don't trust governments that aren't democratically elected.' After a pause, he added, 'It's an age thing.'

'But they're undeniably successful.'

Marti pointed his cigar at the restaurant with its guests from every corner of the globe. 'Don't get me wrong, Winter. I was and I still am in favour of the free market. Whether it's the cattle or stock market. But not at any price. Because the market consists of greedy people there will always be egotistical, monopolistic, protectionist and nationalist excesses.'

Yoda took another puff of his cigar. 'It's the nature of the beast. We're all mercenaries.'

The smoke came back out of his lungs and curled up into the night. The master gazed up at the stars. 'The question is how much society is prepared to tolerate.' Turning to Winter, Marti looked him straight in the eye. 'Winter, if we don't watch out the extremists will win and things will get out of hand. Chaos. The radicals, whether they're fascists, communists or religious fundamentalists, are the modern rocks of today's helmsman.'

Like the TAA and the Holy Tigers of Islam? Winter thought.

'You don't believe me? Didn't it hurt you too when Lufthansa bought our oh-so-proud Swissair for a song?'

'The main thing is she's still flying.' But Winter had to admit that at the time he'd felt some patriotic pangs too.

'For several years now,' Marti continued, the cigar pointing at Winter, '*our* Toblerone has belonged to the Americans. Sheiks are buying up large chunks of UBS. I could give you examples from every country. I'm not deluding myself about this. It's globalization. The question is: where are the boundaries? Or even: is there a boundary at all?'

'As far as I'm concerned the key thing is that it works,' Winter said.

'That's easier said than done. In California, the private electricity supply of thousands of households failed. Like in developing countries! Entire bridges collapsed. Catastrophic.' Marty shook his white hair. 'Infrastructure is either a monopoly or an oligopoly. The prices are distorted. Top management is filled with figureheads. They say market, but they mean power. The actual helmsmen stay in the background. But I want to know who makes the decisions about the basics of my day-to-day life. That is the foundation of power.' Marti gave a slight shrug. '*Veni, vidi, vici*. Money came, saw and bought.'

He took a final, glowing puff.

Then tossed the cigar over the mountainside.

It sizzled out in the snow.

Winter thought about what Marti had said. Anne, Al-Bader, Strittmatter and Kaddour. What was the bunch of TAA thugs doing in Switzerland?

Winter needed to empty his bladder. To keep up with the Russian while they were trying the kirsch he'd drunk plenty of water. And after the cold this was now demanding to be let out. He was standing alone and in mid-flow at the urinal when all of a sudden the music got louder and von Tobler reeled in, his tie loosened.

Although the lavatory had a dozen urinals, the CEO positioned himself next to Winter. Their shoulders touched. In spite of the urine Winter could smell the booze on von Tobler's breath. The CEO was drunk.

Winter glanced at his boss, who didn't notice him. Instead, von Tobler stared glassy-eyed at the fly painted onto the urinal, which he tried to hit with his jet. Winter did up his trousers, turned around and washed his hands, keeping an eye in the mirror on von Tobler behind him. Winter was drying his hands on paper towels when the bank's CEO finished his business and acknowledged him at last.

'Ah, Winter. The world is just too small for the both of us.'

Winter said nothing. He wondered if von Tobler's comment was an allusion to Anne, or whether the man was just drunk. Both, probably. Winter pulled another paper towel from the dispenser.

Von Tobler came up to him and said, 'Where's your Egyptian friend?'

Winter smelled the combination of alcohol and cold cheese. Although he'd drunk too much himself, he knew that the anger rising inside him was pointless. Talking is silver, silence is golden. He scrunched up the paper towel and threw it scornfully into the white basket. Clearly von Tobler hadn't been expecting an answer. He staggered over to a basin menacingly and washed his hands very thoroughly. Was he trying to wash away his guilt?

Jerking back up straight, von Tobler made a brisk lurch for the paper-towel dispenser. Halfway there he slipped in a puddle of water and fell down hard on his back. His head hit the linoleum floor with a dull thud. Absolutely plastered.

Winter helped von Tobler back to his feet. The CEO muttered something to himself. Perhaps his fall and the knock on his head had ousted his drunkenness.

He didn't curse, just felt his head out of curiosity. He looked down, examined the damage to his bespoke suit and said in a normal voice, 'Thanks.'

'Are you alright?' Winter was still holding onto the elbow of the bank's founder.

Von Tobler nodded. 'Have you got a five-franc piece?'

Winter took the coin from his wallet and gave it to von Tobler. He pressed it against his bump with an impish grin. He fingered the bump and put the coin in his trouser pocket. 'Come with me, Winter, I've got something to show you.'

Winter was speechless. But as his silence had proved successful over the last few minutes he opted to maintain this tactic.

Von Tobler went ahead, up some stairs and along a corridor with lights set into the floor. Passing through two double doors they entered the labyrinth of the caves, a tourist attraction hewn from the eternal ice of the glacier. Ceilings, walls and floors – everything was made of ice. The floor was slippery, but fortunately there was a handrail.

They shuffled their way along the ice tunnel. It shone blueish in the light from the lamps. The last time Winter had been here was as a teenager on a school trip, slithering through the maze of corridors. Fatima would have liked this too. You got a view of the glacier from the inside.

Where was his boss going? They were alone, sliding quietly down the ghostly tunnel. Apart from von Tobler's panting it was utterly silent. The ice cut them off completely from the outside world. No more folk music. Small clouds of condensation formed in front of their mouths. They passed a niche with an igloo and an Eskimo family carved from ice with an ice seal. The figures glistened like glass.

Winter was shivering in his suit. The warming effect of the alcohol was wearing off.

Then a niche with three eagles. For the Americans. Specific figures were probably cut from the ice for each target group. Two polar bears standing on their hind legs silently offered a photo opportunity.

Von Tobler slid around another corner, stopped abruptly and said, 'There!'

Winter followed his outstretched arm and trembling index finger. They were in the ice chapel. Von Tobler was pointing at the ice altar.

'There! Mari and I got married at this altar.'

In front of the altar stood massive ice benches with insulated cushions for the guests. In a niche hung a wooden box for donations. The altar was decorated with enormous ice roses. Behind, stood two earnest-looking angels with huge candles. The angels' breasts were especially smooth and shiny from having been touched.

Winter nodded while his mind was firing on all cylinders. What on earth was von Tobler doing here? The best thing was to let him do the talking. 'It must have been very romantic.'

The old man was still staring straight at the altar, his face in a grimace. 'Winter, I don't want to lose Mari.' His jaw was quivering, either out of fear or cold.

'I'm sure that will never happen,' Winter tried to sound reassuring.

Von Tobler moved away from Winter, held onto the altar and kneeled carefully before it. He put his hands together and began praying fervently, but silently. He leaned his head against the icy altar. Between his knees and the ice, a thin layer of meltwater formed. The suit was ruined anyway.

Winter stood where he was for quite a while, then moved behind the altar with his arms crossed. Now he knew what von Tobler wanted: atonement.

Von Tobler looked up pleadingly. 'You helped me out with my daughter back then. And now you've got to help me again.'

Winter nodded and opened out his arms. 'Tell me about Anne.'

The boss looked relieved rather than surprised. 'The moment you introduced Anne to me I couldn't get her out of my head, no matter how hard I tried. A man in my position can't afford to have rumours floating around. But I wanted to see Anne again. I agonized over it for ages. I thought the big difference in age would solve the problem by itself.

'But?'

'I asked Anne, Frau Arnold, out to lunch. I said that it was part of the bank's programme for advancing female staff.'

Von Tobler had now reached the point of no return. Winter was standing between the two ice angels, listening to his torrent. 'She was reticent to begin with. She wasn't quite sure. Then she warmed up and we had a great time. I asked her to call me Josef.'

A pause.

'I'd hoped I could forget Anne, but the opposite was true. She settled in up here,' von Tobler knocked his forehead against the altar several times and then said, 'A few days later I called her to ask whether she'd accompany me as bodyguard to the Bregenz Festival. She declined. And I didn't want to go to Bregenz with you.' Von Tobler looked at Winter and laughed awkwardly. 'But I did invite her to dinner. What an idiot!' Angrily he knocked his head against the altar again.

'What happened then?'

'Nothing. We just talked. But over pudding she told me she'd prefer it if I didn't invite her out again. Anne had realized that the programme for the advancement of female staff was just an excuse, and that in truth I was attracted to her. I became furious at the rejection. I was drunk. We left and things calmed down for a few weeks. She kept out of my way. Then she seduced me again.'

'I don't think she did seduce you.' Winter struggled to keep any tone of menace from his words..

Von Tobler looked up in astonishment. 'Yes she did. At the beginning of July. She sent me a birthday card.'

Winter remembered. Every member of staff knew von Tobler's birthday. It was part of the bank's patriarchal tradition to send the boss a birthday card. Winter had written one too. Anne had asked him for advice about hers, and he'd suggested she send von Tobler a simple card, wishing him the best of health and success.'

'She wrote me a really lovely card. I thought she'd changed her mind. I thought she'd forgiven me.'

Winter walked around the altar and helped von Tobler stand. They sat in the front row on the green, insulated mats. Now von Tobler was nothing more than a cold, old man in a dirty suit.

'You wouldn't guess what I did next, the old fool that I am.'

'You wrote a love letter?'

'You know?' Von Tobler sniffled and wiped his eyes.

'I read it. It was very beautiful.' That was true. Winter had admired the old-fashioned, but gallant style. He wished he'd had the courage to confess his love to Anne in such words.

'Really?'

'Yes.'

Atonement.

Von Tobler took out a handkerchief with his embroidered

initials and wiped his brow. With a shallow smile and calm voice, he said, 'She didn't respond. I expect she didn't know what to say. I couldn't bear it any longer so I called her.'

'On the afternoon of the crash.'

'Yes. First I wanted to tell her in person. I went to her office, but she wasn't there and it was locked. I called her from the conference room next-door and we arranged to meet.'

Winter nodded. The call at 16:55. The IT consultant had given a pretty accurate description.

'She wanted our relationship to be clarified immediately. We met in a café. She was agitated and threatened to resign.'

Winter couldn't help smiling. Anne could be terribly frank if necessary. Obviously she'd decided on that fateful July day to spell things out clearly to von Tobler. In the underground car park she'd read the love letter once more, put it under the sun visor and forgotten her pistol beneath the seat.

'I just wanted us to talk it through. But Anne simply got up, said, "Enough is enough" and left. Those were her last words. That evening you rang to tell me about the crash.'

Von Tobler put his head in his hands and, judging by the sounds he was making, had started sobbing. 'If only I'd stopped her.'

'There was nothing you could have done. It was fate.'

After a while, von Tobler sat up straight again and composed himself.

'I think we ought to go back now,' Winter said.

They stood up. Their limbs were stiff from the cold and fatigue.

'Please keep it to yourself.' From von Tobler's tone, this wasn't a plea, question or an order, but just a plaintive statement. Von Tobler knew that he could trust Winter.

'Only if you give me my coin back.'

Von Tobler picked it out with clammy fingers. 'Here. Money rules the world.' And after a long pause: 'Thanks.'

They went back.

Past the cold eagles, polar bears and Eskimos.

When the sliding doors came into view, Winter asked, 'When did you actually see Muhammed Al-Bader for the last time?'

'I wondered when you'd ask me that question,' Von Tobler said, pausing for a moment on the slippery ice. Turning to Winter, he continued, 'I met the head of the Al-Bader family on July the twentieth, in Oslo, to persuade him to invest in our new private equity fund. I flew there especially.'

'And? Was it a success?'

'I think so. Switzerland as a neutral, secure and stable country was a winning argument. He promised to give the offer serious consideration.'

'Did Al-Bader want to withdraw the money from the States and transfer it to us?'

'I've no idea. Why?'

'Supposedly, Al-Bader was no longer satisfied with Pyramid Investment Partners.'

'You mean with that Farmer chap?' He snorted. 'His pyramids are just a trick to lure the sheikhs. All smoke and mirrors.'

'Do you know Farmer?'

'No, but my old friends in America don't think much of him. He's a wolf in sheep's clothing. Al-Bader wasn't sure either. At any rate he asked me about Farmer in Oslo.'

They went through the first of the sliding doors. A dimpled, rubber mat. Now they had a proper grip. Von Tobler paused again. 'We have to fight for every client, you know. If the Al-Bader family stays with us and invests more, I might not have to sell my share of the bank to those amateurs in Zürich. They're putting me under terrible pressure at the moment.' Von Tobler fixed Winter with his familiar look. 'Winter, I'm counting on you.'

Von Tobler stepped through the second sliding door. 'Right, now I'm going to get changed.' One of his principles was *Gouverner, c'est prévoir*. Leadership is the art of anticipating. The old fox had brought a spare suit with him.

But he hadn't seen the murders coming.

Or had he?

At midnight the party was over. Winter sat in the last carriage of the train that was running specially for the party and pretended to sleep. The side of his head leaned against the cool, fogged-up window.

The cogs, and his brain, juddered.

Was von Tobler's confession in the ice cave genuine, or had the old man just put on a big show? Was he trying to set him on the wrong track?

His thoughts drifted to Anne. Unlike von Tobler, he hadn't had the courage to admit his feelings to her.

And now it was too late.

With a rude jerk the train stopped in the dark night.

In the deserted hotel corridor Winter carefully opened the door to his room. His senses were keen. All was quiet. One of the lamps beside the double bed was on. In the muted light he could see the connecting door to Fatima's room, almost closed. It was after one o'clock. Was he expecting anything else?

He stood for a while by the connecting door and listened, but couldn't hear anything.

Winter removed his tie, took a bottle of mineral water and sat on the bed.

On the pillow he saw a piece of paper, folded once. 'Dear Tom, thanks for showing me the glacier today and saving my life.' A smile spread across his face. 'I had a cosy evening in the spa and now I'm so relaxed that I have to go to sleep! Hope your party was fun. Goodnight. Fatima.'

Winter felt kind of happy. The little note meant a lot to him. Was their friendship going to blossom into a relationship? But how could a relationship work with the jobs they had, and at that distance? Maybe he ought to accept Al-Bader's offer after all.

Anne.

Had von Tobler really been in love with her? Was the letter with those timeless phrases meant seriously? Or had von Tobler, the gifted actor and salesman, just feigned it all? Feelings couldn't be measured. Winter closed his eyes. His brain sat inside his head like a heavy, black lump.

He got up, switched off the light and went out onto the balcony with his water. His mind free of thoughts, he stared into the night. He'd become dead tired during the journey back from the party. But the mixture of unanswered questions and unprocessed alcohol kept him awake.

His eyes accustomed themselves to the darkness. The contours of a pointed, garden pavilion and the fir trees in the hotel park stood out. The rustling of the trees mingled with the gurgling of the nearby River Aare that fell over a low weir beyond the park.

He sat on a wrought-iron bench and reflected. The cool silence and security of the darkness freed up his thoughts. Unbound, they flew right through time and space. In his mind Winter made connections that he hadn't been able to see during the turmoil of the day.

His walk with Fatima, which had begun so peacefully, the wooden boards falling into the depths, the glacier and the dark dam wall. The powerful financial group and the little bank. Would he soon be getting a new boss? Poking into the cheese fondue, the system of pipes, full of shit, beneath St Petersburg. Marti's Cohiba glowing like a lit fuse in the snow. The altar with the two archangels. Von Tobler kneeling before it in the eternal ice.

Winter gave a start and woke up.

He'd nodded off.

A sound had awoken him.

Had someone opened the bedroom door?

Winter didn't stir. He didn't want to give his position away. His first thought was: flee! His second, informed by experience, was: stay cool! What time was it? How long had he slept? It was still the middle of the night. Had the intruder come back to finish off the job from the suspension bridge?

Winter had surprise on his side.

And this time he was armed. Fortunately, he hadn't taken off his weapons. The .45 was in its holster by his side, the .22 strapped to his right leg. The glass water bottle would also serve him well in close combat. Winter turned his head very slowly and strained to hear what sounds were coming from the dark room.

Through the gently wafting curtains he saw the hazy shadows of a tall figure. Winter sought the angle that gave him the best view.

In the dark, your periphery vision was better.

Different receptors.

The uninvited guest stood motionless in the middle of the room. In the night people looked taller and more menacing. Time passed. Now Winter was certain that the intruder was looking at his bed and had his back to him. He was wearing a black hoodie. Winter couldn't make out the hands.

Slowly lowering his right arm Winter inched his hand towards the butt of his pistol. The figure turned around and took two quick paces towards the balcony.

'Winter?'

Winter pulled his hand back and sat up. 'Fatima?' His pulse was racing with relief. 'Is that you?'

She stood in the doorway and poked her head through the curtains, which played with the untied hair that Winter had mistaken for a hoodie. Fatima's gaze fell on the weapon in the holster, then roamed across the dishevelled Winter, the park and up into the sky. She took a deep breath and stepped barefoot out onto the balcony. The concrete floor was cold.

Fatima picked up the bottle and took a swig of mineral water. 'How was the party?'

Winter was not in the mood to give a detailed account of the evening. He was annoyed that Fatima had woken and startled him. Somehow he felt as if she'd interrupted his thoughts, just before they'd reached their conclusion. He rubbed his eyes, took the bottle from Fatima and also had a gulp of water.

'Interesting. Von Tobler was pretty drunk. How well do you know Farmer, actually?'

'Not that well. We always spoke directly with Al-Bader. Why?'

'Von Tobler called him a wolf in sheep's clothing.'

'Von Tobler and Professor Farmer are rivals.'

'Yes, I know, but still.'

'The professor wants to invest his money in our nuclear power station.'

'It's not his money.'

'Yes, it is. Some of it is his money. He's put his own capital into Pyramid Investment Partners.'

'How much?'

'I don't know, but he kept emphasising it in Boston.' Fatima mimicked the professor's voice: '"The investors' money and my own assets are working hand in hand, ensuring that we've all got the same interests".'

Smart questions are the sniffer dogs of intelligence gathering.

'And where does Farmer's money come from?'

Fatima didn't know, but she promised to enquire when on her next trip to the States.

This gave Winter an idea. He plucked a business card from his wallet and took out his mobile.

'What time is it in the States?'

'East or west?'

'East?'

Taking hold of Winter's left wrist, Fatima looked at his watch. 'Take away five hours... that makes it five past nine. Who are you going to call?'

'Smith. Or whatever he's called. He said I could reach him twenty-four seven.' Winter dialled. It took a while before a woman's voice answered.

'How may I help you?' Winter could hear the sound of typing on a computer keyboard.

'I'd like to ask Mr Smith a few questions. My name is Tom Winter.'

'One moment, please.' Winter was put on hold. After a minute the woman's voice returned. 'What is it you would like to talk to Mr Smith about?' Clearly Winter wasn't listed in the computer system.

'I met him a few days ago in Boston. I'm responsible for security at a private Swiss bank.'

Winter heard a few clicks, followed by Smith's East Coast English across the Atlantic. 'Good evening, Mr Winter. How are you?'

'Good evening, Mr Smith. Sorry to disturb you,'

'No problem. Is it an urgent matter to make you call me at this hour?' Smith had traced Winter's call back to Switzerland.

'Perhaps. This afternoon I was shot at by a sniper. I wanted to ask you something about the relationship...'

'Mr Winter,' Smith interrupted, 'I'd best call you back. Are you near a landline?' The NSA man didn't trust the satellite transmission through the air. Winter went inside, gave Smith the name of the hotel, and then sat on the bed and waited.

Fatima sat beside him.

Shortly afterwards the hotel phone rang.

'Thank you for your patience,' Smith said. 'What was it you wanted to know?'

'I know that your people are monitoring the activities of Professor Farmer's Pyramid Investment Partners. A few hours ago I found out that members of True and Armed Americans entered Switzerland via Zürich. Is there any connection?'

Winter could hear Smith thinking.

'Good question, but I'm afraid I can't answer it.'

'Can't or won't?'

'Both.'

'Then tell me what you can.'

'I'm responsible for the Middle East. As I told you in Boston, we're fighting the terrorists there who use religion to justify their actions. We're trying to nip it in the bud. And so of course we're also keeping a close eye on the money that finances this terrorism. You can be sure that in the course of these investigations Professor Farmer's company has appeared on the radar too. As far as we can make out, it hasn't been involved in any illegal activity.' A pause.

'But?'

'Let me pose a question of my own. You had lunch with Professor Farmer in his lovely, weekend house.' In spite of the helicopter, Farmer evidently hadn't managed to shake off Smith's people. This was the first time Winter had detected a sarcastic tone to Smith's voice. Was Smith, a public employee, envious of Farmer's wealth? 'What impression did you get of him?'

'A good one. Professional businessman with an interest in nature. He was cultured, funny, he loves his puddings. Where are you going with this?'

'There are hints that in his youth he sympathized with right-wing nationalist extremists. But there's never been anything on file. Just chatter, rumours, old stories. And now he runs a company specialising in investments that bring people together. I'd put a question mark there.'

'A Damascene conversion?'

'In our business I'd call it an anomaly.'

They promised to stay in contact and hung up.

Von Tobler had called Farmer a wolf in sheep's clothing. Farmer's comment in the dunes of Nantucket about the plover eggs suddenly took on a new meaning. More to himself than to Fatima, Winter murmured, 'The solution is right before our eyes and we can't see it. The camouflage is perfect.'

Winter's mobile phone rang. He opened his eyes. The vibrating had taken the mobile to the edge of the bedside table and Winter grabbed it just before it toppled off. An unknown number with the prefix 971. Winter pressed the green button. 'Hello?'

'Winter?' Al-Bader's voice.

'Yes, it's me. How are you?'

Beside him, Fatima turned around. Winter got out of bed and went over to the other room.

'Fine. I'm at home. All peaceful here.'

Al-Bader the younger wasn't drunk this time. The vodka from St Petersburg had evaporated. He sounded relaxed. No background noises. Winter pictured Al-Bader nestled in oriental cushions, talking on the very latest model of mobile phone, in a large desert tent with handwoven carpets.

Winter sat down naked on a chair, screwed up his eyes to drive away his sleepiness and heard himself say, 'Are you in the desert?' Privately he cursed his curiosity having got the better of him.

Al-Bader didn't resent Winter for having asked it, but remarked on the two different parts of his country: 'Yes, out here in the desert I get an understanding of my roots. Much better than in our offices in Riyadh.' He paused before adding, 'Winter, you really must come and visit me some time. I'd love to show you my horses and falcons. And we can finish our round of golf.'

No more word about the job offer, but an invitation nonetheless. Also no apology for calling so early in the morning. Saudi Arabia was three or four hours ahead of Switzerland. But

Al-Bader looked to be one of those people who expected his staff to be on call twenty-four hours a day.

'Thanks. I'd love to. How can I help you?'

'I just spoke to Sheikh Baktar, and I recalled our last conversation.'

'Yes?'

'You wanted Pyramid Investment Partners' project list, didn't you? I found it. Where shall I send it?'

'Oh, thanks very much.' Winter was surprised.

'We share the same goal.'

'Have you heard anything from the other investors?'

'I had a long talk with Sheikh Baktar and he told me that he met my brother shortly before the crash. Muhammed tried to persuade Baktar to vote on the board in favour of the special audit.'

'Special audit?'

Winter was wide awake.

'Yes, clearly my brother suspected Farmer of having siphoned off money for himself. Only minor sums, a few million dollars.' Everything's relative, Winter thought. Al Bader continued, 'He probably smelled a rat and wanted to get the other directors to agree to a special audit. Muhammed had lost confidence in Farmer and was considering getting rid of him as the administrator of the funds.

That was a motive. But was it enough to kill someone?

'Did you talk to Farmer, too?'

'Yes, we spoke on the phone. He advised me again not to come to the States. Farmer said there's still too high a risk that the American authorities would arrest me on a legal technicality. Now I'm no longer sure if that's just his way of keeping me at arm's length.'

'What does he say about the criticism?'

'I haven't talked to him about that yet. First I want to see the documents my brother left behind and get a better understanding of the whole thing.'

'When's the next board meeting?'

'I can call one any time. The next ordinary meeting is already scheduled for...' Winter heard the rustling of papers, 'September the fifteenth. In Riyadh, probably. I'll be formally voted in as president.' Al-Bader gave a short, scornful laugh. 'This time Farmer's coming to me.'

'How well do you know Farmer?'

Al-Bader thought for a moment, then said, 'Not well. Muhammed was the one who did business with him. I only met him once, around six months ago at the George V in Paris. My brother introduced him as the man who'd open doors for us in America. We shook hands and exchanged a few words. That was all.'

'Do you know why your brother put his trust in Professor Farmer?'

'To my knowledge, Farmer has an outstanding reputation as a fund manager. My brother spent quite a while trying to find someone with the right connections.'

'Did your brother find Farmer, or was it the other way around?'

Al-Bader pondered this question then said, 'I don't know.'

'But your brother convinced the other families to invest their money in Pyramid Investment Partners?'

'Yes, he called the Baktars, and other families, and sold the opportunity to them. Why do you ask?'

'I've heard rumours that Professor Farmer used to sympathize with extreme right-wing nationalists. They're not exactly known for their love of people outside America.'

Another pause while Al-Bader digested this information.

'Are you saying that Farmer's a fascist, who only set up Pyramid Investment Partners to get at our money?'

'I'm not saying anything. But maybe Farmer hasn't made *himself* rich, but *has* siphoned off money for extreme right-wing causes. These extremists need money too. They used to rob banks; maybe Farmer founded one for the same purpose.'

'And I was thinking it was for rotten tax dodges or to get himself rich.' A pause. 'Where did you get this from?'

Farmer, the wolf in sheep's clothing, has been ripping off Arab sheikhs, Winter thought. 'The NSA,' he said.

'Is their information trustworthy?'

'Up to a point, but everyone always has their own agenda.'

'I'm going to follow up these rumours right away. If they're correct we need to act immediately.'

Winter was sure that this 'we' didn't mean him and he wondered who Al-Bader was thinking of. 'Call me if you find out anything.'

'I will, Winter. By the way, have you given the other matter any thought?'

The job offer. 'Yes,' Winter said. 'I've decided where it would be best for you to send the Pyramid Investment Partners project list. I'd be grateful if you could email it to me.' He heard Al-Bader's throaty laugh.

'Winter, Winter. I'm coming to understand why my brother valued your bank so highly.'

'Always at your service! I hope we can continue to be there for many more generations of the Al-Bader family.'

'Enough advertising. You're starting to sound like that von Tobler.'

Winter gave Al-Bader his email address. They said goodbye. It felt as if his relationship with Al-Bader was gradually evolving into a friendship. Maybe he really would visit him in his desert tent.

All of a sudden Winter felt he was being watched.

Fatima had propped herself up on her elbows and was looking over at him.

Impassively she asked, 'What did he want?'

'He wants to arrange a special audit so that Pyramid Investment Partners' transactions can be checked by independent experts. Muhammed suspected Farmer of siphoning off money.'

'That's definitely a motive. Damn! I hope it's not going to delay our Cairo project.'

The email from Al-Bader pinged through. Winter opened the attachment. Four badly-scanned pages. Fatima slipped out of bed and sat beside him. On the little screen they studied Pyramid Investment Partners' portfolio. There were handwritten remarks in an illegible scribble, a few items were underlined and certain investments had been marked with a highlighter.

'Can you decipher this scrawl?'

Fatima bent lower and shook her head. 'No, not a chance. They look like abbreviations.'

Winter enlarged the list and began studying the investments, by scrolling up and down. There were three sections.

The first section was entitled 'Financial holdings: listed companies'. It listed shareholdings in companies such as the German EON or the American Verizon. Amongst the thirty or so firms Winter spotted, two were from Switzerland: a telecoms company and an energy provider. After each holding was listed the value in US dollars and the percentage of the company owned. The shares were in the thousandths. A number of asterisks referred to footnotes in small type that were impossible to make out on the grainy scan.

The second section contained roughly fifty direct investments in businesses Winter had never heard of, many of them with made-up names that sounded like they were related to new technologies, environmental protection and the internet. These firms weren't traded on the stock market but in private hands. In this section the share of the business owned by Pyramid Investment Partners was substantially higher, ranging between seventeen and one hundred per cent.

Winter found three Swiss firms. Pyramid Investment Partners owned one hundred per cent of TheNewEnergy AG and had large shares in two other Swiss companies: Secer AG and TraPoCom GmbH.

Investments in the tens of millions, which was rather small fry given the entire picture. Winter didn't have a clue what these businesses did. Overall Pyramid Investment Partners had made direct investments across the whole world, although the focus was clearly on America, followed by Europe. What had Al-Bader said about Farmer? 'The man who'd open the doors for us in America.'

'There!' Fatima exclaimed.

She pointed at Orafin in the third section of projects. Two to three hundred million. But no percentage share. Negotiations hadn't yet been concluded. In the 'in charge' column stood Muhammed Al-Bader's name. He was responsible for this project.

Someone had marked this project with a hand-drawn arrow. Sheikh Baktar was in charge of the fibre-optic projects in Dubai and Philadelphia.

'Interesting,' Fatima said.

'Yes, something von Tobler could only dream of.'

Farmer and his people had been busy over the past few years. In terms of value the shareholdings and direct investments were evenly matched. All in all, the portfolio included investments in the tens of billions. With the professor's help the families around Muhammed Al-Bader and Sheikh Baktar had accumulated a vast fortune inside the pyramids. In the funerary chamber.

Going back to sleep was out of the question now. Peering out of the window, Winter saw the first modest rays of the sun. It was going to be a lovely day. Good for flying. The most successful account managers and a few clients were going tandem paragliding with experienced pilots. Winter knew a few account managers whose nerves would have kept them awake most of the night.

The man with the green Land Rover had got up even earlier.

Winter braced himself for a long day. A schedule of duties. Känzig had called a coordination meeting for seven o'clock. Winter ordered breakfast in the room: tea for Fatima and a pot of coffee for himself. When he came out of the shower, Winter saw that Fatima had made herself comfortable with breakfast in bed. He sat beside her with his tray.

'I haven't even asked you. Did you sleep well?'

She spread butter onto a roll and said, 'Yes, the hike, the fresh air and the massage in the spa while you were out last night did me the world of good.'

Winter took his first sip of coffee for the day, ate a croissant with jam and said, grinning, 'There's a visit to an old military bunker on the programme for this morning. Would you like to go?'

'Why should I be interested in military bunkers?'

'It's living history. Before the Second World War mountains were hollowed out completely. If Hitler had invaded with his tank divisions, the army would have withdrawn to the bunkers and defended Switzerland against the superior force of steel.'

Holding his croissant jokingly to his chest he lowered his voice,
'Till the last drop of blood.'

'What about the women and children?'

'No idea. It never got that far. The Nazis got enough without
taking possession of Switzerland.'

'But what am I going to do in a bunker?'

'Many of the tunnels in the mountain have been sold by the
military over the last few years. Today we're going to visit a
firm who've bought one of these bunkers and maintain servers
in them. Tradition meets cutting-edge technology. Dirk, our
head of IT has organized the visit. We secure our data there.'

'What else is on offer?'

'Well, if you joined the ladies' programme you could go on a
hike with a suntanned mountain guide and admire rare plants.'

'I'd rather stick with you and the bunker.'


Fortified, Winter entered the small conference room in the
hotel basement at 06:59. Känzig and Helfer were standing in
one corner, talking in hushed tones. Baumgartner, the liaison
man for the financial group, was sitting red-eyed at the table
with a pile of printed out emails in front of him.

'Morning.'

His colleagues muttered a greeting and nodded to Winter.
Hodel shook his hand.

'Fighting fit? The Russians are hard to drink under the table,
aren't they?' His laughter lines doubled in number. Hodel
had seen him drinking with the plumber from St Petersburg
yesterday evening.

Winter quoted a phrase from the bank's mission statement:
'Every client receives a personal service tailored to their
individual needs.'

Hodel merely raised his eyebrows.

Känzig clapped his hands. 'Morning, everyone. Right, the
quicker we start, the quicker we'll be finished.'

They sat down.

'Schütz just called me. He can't come. But he said that he's done a poll of colleagues and established that our clients are no longer mentioning the minor incident.'

So the helicopter crash caused by an incendiary device that had claimed the lives of Anne, Al-Bader and Strittmatter had shrunk to a minor incident and soon would be forgotten altogether.

The table was round and covered with several layers of white linen tablecloths, some of which reached the floor and hid wobbly legs.

Fortunately, someone had brought coffee.

The liaison man poured it.

Inside this windowless room the men felt cramped. They couldn't stretch out in their habitual manner and mark their territory on the table with notepads, folders and devices. Baumgartner had lined up two mobile phones and a tablet in front of him. Känzig delineated the left-hand boundary of his personal space with a heavy bunch of keys, the right-hand one with his mobile.

Hodel and Winter were the only ones without any items on the table, while Känzig rested his elbows on it and was holding a smart, fountain pen horizontally between the fingertips of both hands. He looked around the table and jutted out his chin. 'Update?'

Helfer said, 'The crash isn't a media story any more. Over the last few days the incident hasn't been mentioned in the print media or online. The shooting in Geneva,' he continued, frowning at Winter, 'is only a story in Western Switzerland, although the name of our bank isn't mentioned. We've been able to steer the issue towards the question of how much money the public purse should spend on security for rich tourists in Geneva.'

He gave a narcissistic smile, ran a hand through his pomaded hair and sneered, 'Thanks to the excellent relations we have with the Geneva authorities, our colleague Herr Winter was referred to as a personal bodyguard.' The pretty boy was good at presenting ideas that he hadn't thought up himself. 'That sort of security is quite normal in those circles, so no connection has been made to us, at least not yet.'

'Excellent.' Känzig turned to Winter. 'And I'd be grateful if you'd let us know if you intend take this further. Personal bodyguard.' Känzig laughed. 'That would be a career move.'

'I'll bear it in mind,' Winter said. 'Al-Bader would definitely be a good boss.'

Hodel mediated. 'Now, gentlemen.' He only had to raise his hands briefly and the squabbling ceased.

Helfer wasn't done, however; he was bursting to continue with his commentary. Winter eyed the group of tired men. Five minutes and a whole lot of hot air later: '... overall,' finished Helfer, 'I get the impression that our communications strategy based on containment has worked well from the outset and we have the situation under control. People are quick to forget.'

'Winter?'

Winter didn't have the slightest intention of telling these men about yesterday's attack, nor was he going to articulate his thoughts about the events of the last couple of weeks. His warnings of a connection between the murders and the bank had fallen on deaf ears and Känzig's strategy was clear. He wanted to sweep the incident under the carpet as quickly as possible and get back to normal. Winter restricted himself to a brief summary of the facts, which would be in the police report anyway.

Turning to the liaison man, Känzig asked, 'Any observations from the financial group's point of view?'

'No.' Baumgartner looked ghastly. His voice was hoarse, his face as white as a sheet. He'd probably drunk too much yesterday and now was feeling the effects. Served the son of a bitch right.

'Thank you, gentlemen. On the basis of what you've said and if nobody objects…' – a quick glance at Hodel, who didn't stir – '… I conclude that we can put this sad incident aside and turn to address more important matters.'

Känzig looked at his watch. 'Thirteen minutes. Not bad. Must be the early start. Hope you all have a lovely day.' He flipped shut his folder and stood up.

Staying seated, Winter poured himself another coffee and watched Känzig point at the liaison man and ask whether he could spare another five minutes. Helfer was the first to leave. He was responsible overall for the annual conference and in no danger of being bored today. Känzig placed a hand on the liaison man's shoulder and guided him to the door.

Winter was about to put the pot down when he noticed that Hodel was still in his seat too. With his chiselled, inert features he reminded Winter of the Sphinx. He lifted the pot again. 'More coffee?'

'Love some.' Winter poured him a cup.

'Do you think the bank is out of this mess?'

'Maybe.'

'No mole? No accomplice under our roof?'

'I don't think so. I expect Al-Bader must have unintentionally shared his travel plans with the murderer or murderers.'

'Now you're making me curious.'

Winter told Hodel about the rumours concerning Professor Farmer's past.

'Yes, Josef once mentioned something along those lines.'

Winter voiced his suspicion that the professor was using the opaque private equity vehicle of Pyramid Investment Partners to pilfer money from the enemy's pockets. 'Muhammed Al-Bader got wise to Farmer's tricks and arranged a special audit. To preserve the cash cow, Farmer saw no other option than to get his chairman out of the way.'

'But who put the bomb in Anne's hands?' After decades as

a lawyer, Hodel was committed to logic and he couldn't bear any loose ends.

'Farmer and Al-Bader were in regular contact. Al-Bader was in charge of the project in Cairo. So it's safe to assume that Farmer knew about the meeting between his chairman and Orafin. Farmer must have sent Anne the bomb by courier. Or had an accomplice send it. Simple, but effective.'

'But how could Farmer or his accomplice know that the bomb had to go to her?'

'That I don't know for sure. But I can speculate. Al-Bader knew that Anne was going to escort him. As always I emailed him the logistical details of the transfer and locality. It's conceivable that Farmer saw this email. Al-Bader may have even forwarded the message to Farmer to let him know how the project was progressing. Maybe Al-Bader forwarded it unwittingly as part of a long, email thread. Maybe Farmer had someone close to Al-Bader. After all, they do business together.'

'Do you have any evidence to prove this? A digital footprint or paper trail? A witness?'

Winter shook his head. Hodel drank his coffee pensively, holding the saucer directly below the cup to prevent any stray drops from falling onto his conservatively cut suit. 'We live in a crazy world,' he said with a gentle shake of his head. 'But given what's happened, do you think that we're going to be able to keep the Al-Bader family as clients?'

'I think so. Al-Bader's brother is getting to the bottom of things in America with a special audit. The pendulum is swinging back in our favour.'

'Good. Stay on it. We can't afford to lose any more money. The financial group is just waiting for a sign of weakness to take us to task again.'

'Is it that bad?'

'Yes.' He carefully placed the cup and saucer back down on

the table and got up. No more discussion. Were the negotiations already at a critical stage?

Winter returned to his room. Fatima had gone. The meeting had been shorter than expected and now he had a little free time. The bus to the bunker with the server farm wasn't leaving till nine o'clock.

He lay on the bed, stretched, crossed his arms behind his head and relaxed. At this very moment there was nothing to do. Tiredness was creeping up again. Maybe Känzig was right. The best thing would be to file the case away and focus again on day-to-day operations. Al-Bader was warned and had his bodyguards. Sooner or later the Swiss police and American authorities would do their work.

Anne.

Her murderer had probably been a professional and Winter was under no illusions about the evidence. And who was Max? A friend of the dead men from the golf course? Was he after revenge? An eye for an eye, a tooth for a tooth. How was he going to rid himself of these ghosts? Winter had no desire to be continually looking over his shoulder.

After all that coffee he now felt restless. He leaped up, prowled around the room, put on his two holsters again and checked his weapons. What else had to be done? He still hadn't identified who had hired the detective agency. A few more calls couldn't hurt. He dug out the list with Schmitt's telephone numbers, connected his laptop to the hotel's network, started Skype and called the next anonymous number on his list.

As the computer dialled Winter got his story straight. At this time of day, inventing competitions with iPad prizes wasn't the best way to engage someone in conversation. Should he pretend to have rung the wrong number?

The first person answered with their name. Winter couldn't believe his ears. After a brief pause he heard a 'Hello?' in his headphones. Winter held his breath. The caller asked, 'Hello? Who is that?'

Then the line went dead.

Winter recognized the voice.

And the name that went with it.

The coach, packed with a mix of guests and managers, left the hotel a few minutes late. Dirk sat in the front row, playing tour guide. He'd forgotten to specify a dress code. Some had opted for suits, others sporty jackets and another lot jeans.

The passengers beside Fatima and Winter were discussing the great evening they'd had high up the mountain and speculating about their visit to the military bunker.

The coach left Interlaken and turned off the main road a short while afterwards. It swayed as it wound its way along a stony, dried-out stream bed, the water dammed far back in the valley. After a tank trap, whose concrete prongs looked like a stone Toblerone, the road narrowed even further. The driver had to work hard to navigate the tight bends.

Some of the guests fell silent when they realized how close the coach was driving to the edge. Others, following the fondue and breakfast buffet, were struggling with the contrary movements in their stomachs and kept quiet too. On its pneumatic suspension the heavy coach slowly lurched this way and that, up and down.

Fir branches grazed the windows. Dirk explained to the two Japanese men in the second row that everything was fine. The bunker, he said, was sited to defend the entrance to the valley, which was why it had been built at the narrowest point.

They turned off and parked on a shadowy patch of gravel. The doors hissed open. The passengers streamed out of the coach in relief and stood beside a wet rock face with a rusty iron door. Decades ago the loose rocks had been secured with sprayed concrete. The cliff, overgrown with lichen and small shrubs, towered upwards. Everything was dripping.

Winter and Fatima stood at the edge of the crowd, examining the guests and the rock face. The entrance to the bunker looked decayed, frail and unused. The shabby appearance is good camouflage, Winter thought.

A helicopter flew low over the trees; they could hear the rotary blades come to a halt after the landing in a nearby clearing. The visitors were shivering. Some were on their phones, others chatting. The desolate bunker had steered the men's conversation to war stories. Many of the managers were officers in the Swiss militia army.

Around thirty metres above him, Winter could make out two recesses reinforced with sandy concrete for artillery guns protecting the entrance to the valley during the Second World War and the Cold War.

Winter saw von Tobler, Hodel and four Arabs coming through the forest. The four Arabs had rolled up their white robes to protect them from the forest floor, which was marshy in places. The expressions on their faces suggested that they hadn't particularly enjoyed themselves so far this morning. They were used to different routines. But the motto of the annual conference was: 'Unforgettable days in the Bernese Oberland'.

For today's outfit, von Tobler had gone for English gentleman out grouse shooting. He strode towards them.

Winter took out his phone, activated the 'number withheld' option and dialled a number with his thumb. The small screen showed that the call was going through. Ten metres to the side of him, somebody put their hand in their pocket and pulled out a vibrating mobile. Winter hung up.

The entrance to the bunker creaked open and the crowd of guests turned their heads.

A man of around forty, in a swanky pinstripe suit and

gleaming shoes, had stepped out of the bunker. He shook hands with Dirk, who requested the group's attention to introduce the man as Herr Torhorst, managing director of Europe's largest server farm for the secure preservation of bank data.

Torhorst greeted his highly esteemed guests with a deep voice that echoed off the cliff behind him and said smarmily, 'Please enter the realm of secure data preservation.'

The crowd thronged through the rusty entrance, behind which an astonishingly roomy cavern opened up. It was sparsely lit with lamps behind grills.

It was dripping.

Winter saw three corridors.

'Ladies and gentlemen, it is my great pleasure to be able to welcome you to our sacred halls.' In priest-like fashion Torhorst raised his hands to the cavern's vaulted ceiling. 'All of us value discretion and security. With the help of the Swiss mountains our firm offers you both of these. In this bunker your data is more secure than in Scrooge McDuck's Money Bin.'

Muted laughter.

The managing director gave them an overview of the firm and how volumes of data were rapidly growing. Mega. Giga. Tera. He motioned to his guests to enter one of the tunnels carved straight from the rugged rock. The temperature rose, the dripping stopped and after five minutes they reached another cavern with a cloakroom.

Two armed men in combat boots were guarding a bolted steel door. Video cameras hung from the ceiling.

Torhorst stopped and said, 'For understandable reasons we set great store by security. So we will have to pass a number of security doors. If I may ask you to come this way?'

Two unarmed pensioners manned the cloakroom. They gave each guest a grey cloth bag with a number. The mood soured slightly. 'Worse than the airport,' someone grumbled. Politely, but firmly the elderly cloakroom attendants asked them to hand in all electronic and metal items, cameras and mobiles. The filled bags were exchanged for a plastic numbered token and hung on a rack behind the counter. Then the visitors had to pass through the latest thing in metal detectors.

The guards opened the fireproof steel door and stepped aside. Behind it ran a sterile, harshly lit corridor. The contrast was baffling. The mood and sense of expectation rose. 'Almost like in hospital,' Winter said to Fatima.

'The idea that there are millions of tons of rock above my head makes me feel queasy.'

After fifty metres they came to a multifunctional space that served as canteen, staff room and classroom. Simple wooden tables and benches, a whiteboard, a coffee machine and a vending machine with chocolate bars and fizzy drinks. Two employees in white overalls fled from the invasion of visitors. On the tables were baskets with fresh croissants and the two pensioners from the cloakroom started handing round cups of coffee.

'This is the communal area,' the managing director said. 'Our maintenance and security staff work around the clock for you. We have a kitchen and bedrooms. No luxuries, but more comfortable than in the army.' More restrained laughter. Torhorst always had the right words at his lips. 'We're a welcome employer in the valley.'

'Are there still cannons here?' an American asked.

'Most of the heavy artillery was scrapped but we have the two largest in our mini museum.'

A question-and-answer discussion ensued about the change from military bunker to data centre. 'The world has changed,' the managing director said, 'but the threats are still there. In the past we were afraid of the Russians.' The Russian plumber made a voluble protest, and the managing director corrected himself: 'Excuse me. In the past we were afraid of the communists. Today people are afraid of losing their data. And I'm not talking about a few digital holiday snaps, but data absolutely vital for business. In our knowledge-based society, data is the capital of many firms.'

Torhorst was in full flow. 'Seventy-two per cent of all Swiss bank transactions and over forty per cent of European bank transactions are stored here in absolute security. And although this bunker once belonged to the Swiss army, the tax authorities have no access here. That's why we've got the spring-guns.' Now he had the bankers and their clients in his pocket. Looking at the visitors with a winning smile that had probably been practised in the mirror, he said, 'And we still have spare capacity.'

Then came more advertising. 'We are totally self-sufficient.' The managing director pointed at a poster showing a cross section of the bunker. 'We have our own supply of drinking water, emergency power generators, a pressurized system to prevent gases from entering, sensor and filters against nuclear, biological and chemical attacks, air purification and screening from electromagnetic waves. All these things mean we're secure against earthquakes, terrorists and atomic bombs. We're equipped to deal with the absolute worst-case scenario and can keep functioning for months without contact with the outside world.'

Winter wondered who would still be worried about data in the case of a nuclear war.

Schütz raised his hand. 'And what do you do to combat hackers?'

'Aha, that's a very good question. The data only comes to us encrypted. And we use the very newest security methods. Each client has their own server here to which they have exclusive access. As a banker you could liken it to a safety deposit box. Depending on the volume of data you need to store, you can hire a small or large data deposit box. We give you a totally unique keycode that runs to more than a thousand characters, which allows access to nobody but you. It's our job to maintain your deposit box, that's to say your server.'

The visitors were divided up into four groups and taken by staff in white overalls through the bunker's tunnels. The employee leading Winter's group was called Martin and was responsible for marketing.

The deeper they went into the mountain the more impressed the visitors became. Generators, thick, cable harnesses, flat screens, closed steel doors.

After several more security doors, which their guides could open only with retina and hand scanners, they were allowed a brief glance at the actual data storage centre, through a thick pane of glass. This was less spectacular, consisting of racks with servers and cables. No entry. 'Sterile,' Martin said apologetically.

Soon afterwards they all met up again in the canteen.

A snack with speciality cheeses, cured meats and the obligatory white wine was waiting for them. Torholst gave a short speech and recommended that by way of a contrast they take the detour to the small military museum, where the old life of the bunker had been reconstructed and where you could admire the two remaining cannons.

Dirk sat beside Winter, who said, 'Good idea, this tour, Dirk. Really interesting. The security measures are impressive. It's an excellent calling card for the bank.'

Dirk poured Winter and himself a glass of white wine.

'Thanks.' They toasted and Winter said, 'I envy that guy who had the business idea. Right on trend.'

'I don't know. He's suffered too. We first assessed him as a provider eight years ago. At the time,' Dirk said, pointing with a little roll of *Tête de Moine* at Torhorst, doing the rounds, 'he was on the verge of bankruptcy. He started during the dot-com boom, and when the bubble burst he only survived because Secer came up with an injection of fresh capital.'

'Secer?' That couldn't be a coincidence.

'Yes, they're a leading provider of security technology in IT. Their HQ is in Zug. Have you never heard of them?'

'Yes, I have.' This morning.

'Secer kept Torhorst going in return for shares.'

'What about us?'

'We – and the financial group too, by the way – only got involved later when the long-term viability of the company was secured. We're already completely integrated here.' Dirk laughed. Winter took a piece of Emmenthal from the mixed platter and put it thoughtfully in his mouth. Behind Dirk, Winter saw Torhorst and Baumgartner enter a neighbouring conference room. 'And are you absolutely sure that nothing can happen to our data here in the mountain?'

'One hundred per cent.'

'You fantasist. There's always a residual risk.'

'Agreed. Let's call it ninety-nine point nine per cent.'

Dirk and Winter clinked glasses again. 'Cheers!' The noise level rose and as the wine flowed, the quality of jokes deteriorated.

After a while the retinue made its way back through the corridors and the security gates, where they reclaimed their valuables. Winter discreetly put his guns away. One of the pensioners turned out to be a veteran; he took the visitors along another corridor to the bunker museum.

Fatima was talking to a Chinese businesswoman. Winter had no desire to see dusty wax soldiers and yellowed photographs of stony faces. It was dripping from the ceiling again and he allowed himself to fall to the back of the group.

They turned into a narrower tunnel, and went through a number of heavy, concrete doors with ankle-high thresholds. Five minutes earlier they'd still been in the air-conditioned light and dry server factory. Now they were climbing up poorly lit, slippery steps inside a narrow tunnel.

The group passed an embrasure. Through its narrow slit you would have a view of the valley, but this one was overgrown with foliage. All that remained of the cannon here was a completely rusted turntable, set in concrete. The veteran explained how they'd organized the supply of munitions. It was crucial that each cannon had enough, but not too much, to avoid the risk of explosion following a direct hit. This is why each battle station had a small, separate entrepôt. A few visitors quickly stuck their heads into the musty, adjoining room before moving on to the next battle station.

Winter stood beside the rusty door and said to the man in the smart suit next to him, 'The procedures in the bunker are interesting, aren't they? Shall we have a closer look at the munitions room?'

The man gave Winter a bored look and said, 'Why would I want to do that?' Winter smiled back.

They were alone.

Winter effortlessly grabbed the man's neck, clamped his other hand over the mouth and shoved him into the small room, slamming the door shut with his foot. Without freeing the man's mouth, he rapidly turned him around. The man's head cracked against the rock face. With his right hand, Winter seized the collar and jammed his voice box with his forearm. The fingers on his other hand dug through the man's cheek in to his jaw. Taken completely by surprise, the man had offered no resistance.

Winter listened.

The footsteps were getting further away and growing quieter.

A dirty, caged bulb dimly lit the decayed munitions store. In the wet, hung the pungent smell of munitions sulphur, urine, putrefaction and mould. The visitors' footsteps faded away and it fell silent. The ideal interrogation room, Winter thought. When he took his hand away from the man's mouth, Känzig started protesting immediately. 'Winter! What the hell has got into you? Have you gone mad?'

Winter increased the pressure on Känzig's throat and said, 'I'm the one asking the questions here.'

'Let me go at once!' Winter just shook his head and his boss gasped wretchedly, 'You're hurting me.'

'If you tell the truth nothing will happen to you.'

'Are you threatening me?'

'That comes later.'

'You're fired, with immediate effect,' Känzig hissed, spitting with anger.

Winter ignored the slobber on his superior's chin. With his forearm he slowly rolled Känzig's throat up the wall until he was standing on tiptoe. The smart suit was chafing against the rough rock. 'Very good, so now I'll ask you the first question in a private capacity. Why did you murder Anne, Al-Bader and Strittmatter?'

'How did you get that nonsense into your head? I won't stand for such an outrageous accusation!'

'Why not?'

'I... I didn't do anything.'

'Then you won't mind answering a few questions.'

'You're a lunatic. You must have lost your mind. I'm going to sue you.'

'Lunatics aren't responsible for their actions.' The lanky Känzig was intelligent enough not to resist with force. He knew that in a one-on-one fight with Winter he would come off worse. After the initial shock, therefore, Känzig resorted to making a deal. A deal is always give and take. But for that to work he needed to know what Winter was after.

'Just tell me what you want!'

'I want you to answer a few of my questions,' Winter said patiently.

'I'll try, but first you have to tell me why you're being so violent. This morning we were chatting like civilized individuals.'

Winter said nothing.

Känzig looked down at himself. 'My suit is all filthy now.'

Vain old bastard, Winter thought, pressing Känzig more firmly against the rock face. 'Now, listen carefully. I'll ask my first question again. Why did you blow up the helicopter?'

Winter loosened his grip slightly. Gasping for air, Känzig coughed, 'I didn't blow up the helicopter.'

'So who did?'

'I told you. I don't know.'

Maybe Känzig was telling the truth; maybe he was lying. With his left hand, Winter took out his phone and tapped in the number he'd found on Schmitt's SIM card at the detective agency. Another mobile phone vibrated. Känzig didn't move. His arms were hanging down, his palms pressed against the cold rock. Winter put away his phone and fished out Känzig's from his jacket pocket.

'What are you doing now? Are you going to steal my phone as well?'

It was a cheap model. Probably prepaid. Winter declined his own call. Then, from the short contacts list, he selected a

Zürich number and pressed the green button. Together they listened to the celestial sound of the ringing tone. Just for once Känzig was silent.

After a few seconds they heard, 'Schmitt here from Schmitt, Berger & Partners detective agency. Good morning, how can I help you today?' Winter wasn't in the mood for a chat so cut the connection.

'That is the second question,' Winter said, raising his eyebrows.

Känzig's gaze darted upwards and to the left, past Winter. He was about to concoct a lie. Shaking his head, he stuttered, 'That's a pr...pr...private matter. My wife, you know. I suspect her of cheating with another man and so I thought...' A bad liar *and* a bad actor. Winter put Känzig's phone in his pocket. He needed a free hand.

The earlobe isn't a vital part of the body, but it's extremely sensitive. It has a plentiful supply of blood and consists mainly of tissue, skin and cartilage, between which thick nerve pathways run. With thumb and forefinger Winter folded Känzig's earlobe and twisted it one hundred and eighty degrees. The cartilage transferred the pressure to the nerves and these shot a clear signal into the pain centre. Känzig held back a scream, then gasped for air.

'Wrong answer. Second attempt.' He stared at Känzig without letting go of the earlobe. When no answer was forthcoming, Winter twisted the folded lobe a little further. Now Känzig was breathing heavily. Winter noticed the sweat on his brow.

Then Känzig stammered, 'I just wanted to be sure.'

'And?'

'The crash affected all of us badly. I just wanted to do all I could to...'

'Bullshit!' Winter twisted the lobe even further. 'Shall I rip your ear off altogether?' he said, taking a deep breath.

'Stop, stop! I just wanted to know what you were up to. As the man in charge I like to be in the picture. I wanted to be sure that you really were doing the right things. I'm sorry. I ought to have told you. Can you let me go now – please?' Känzig was begging.

'No.'

Winter was calmly thinking of the next question when Känzig asked, 'How did you find out the thing with my phone. That's my private number. What made you start meddling in my affairs?'

Winter wouldn't dream of answering that question. Känzig was tougher than expected. The sly bastard. The anger Winter had suppressed till now bubbled up. His eyes narrowed slightly. He knew this was no clinical action from the handbook. He was in danger of losing his professional distance. Too many emotions. It was personal. Focus. In theory it was all very simple.

Anne was dead.

And Känzig had to talk.

Winter had experience of psychological warfare. He nodded, let go of the earlobe, collar and neck, and smoothed Känzig's lapel. 'Okay.' As expected, Känzig tried to exploit his new freedom immediately and push past Winter. The latter had been expecting this and kneed Känzig in the balls. Fuelling false hopes was a cornerstone of psychological warfare. Another was the deliberate combination with physical force.

Känzig groaned and slowly started collapsing down the wall. His suit was now totally ruined. Winter wanted eye contact. Grabbing Känzig's hair, he pulled him back up.

'A simple extra question. Who is Max?'

Känzig's glazed eyes told Winter that his resistance was burning out. With deep breaths, Känzig just shook his head. Again Winter asked, this time with gentle encouragement, 'Max?' No answer. Winter shook the hair a little. 'Max? You know, like Mad Max.'

'I don't know a Max,' Känzig wheezed. 'Really I don't.'

For the first time Winter believed Känzig.

Max was good, too good for Schmitt, Berger & Partners.
Max was in a different class from the snooper, Romero, whose
romantic excursion to Lake Geneva had come to an abrupt end.
The ass-licker might be capable of discreet commissions over
the phone to a detective agency in Zürich, Winter thought, but
he couldn't imagine him hiring Max.

Winter let go of Känzig's hair and stroked his cheek. Känzig
had learned not to move.

'Third question. Where were you on July the twenty-fourth?'

'On July the twenty-fourth?' Känzig was trying to play for
time.

'Don't play the fool with me.'

'Was that the day of the helicopter crash?' Winter raised his
hand slightly.

'Okay, okay. On July the twenty-fourth I had a lunch in
Zürich, a business lunch in the *Baur au Lac*.'

'And in the afternoon?'

'I don't know.'

Winter gave a slight shake of the head.

'Oh yes, now I remember. I was with Hediger and in the
evening we were entertaining at home.' Hediger was high
up in the financial group, three or four rungs higher than
Hugentobler, the head of security.

'And in between?'

'I was on my way back. Yes, that's right, there was a traffic
jam at Egerkingen. I had to hurry because I'd promised my
wife to help with the preparations. But where is all this going?'

'Did you stop off at the Zürich branch?'

'I don't think so.'

Winter slapped Känzig's cheek with his palm and hit the
other one with the back of his hand. After all, didn't it say in the
Bible to turn the other cheek? Känzig's head flew one way, then
the other, his eyes like saucers. Winter was gradually losing
patience. 'Wrong answer. Have a think.'

'Yes, I totally forgot. I popped by quickly. I had to fetch a few documents.'

'... and deposit a bottle of Laphroaig.'

Känzig's eyes fluttered for a millisecond. Winter had him.

'You can't prove that.'

'You were in the lift. The data from your security card proves it. You entered the building on Bahnhofstrasse at 17:27 and took the lift straight to the third basement level. You put the Laphroaig beside the other client gifts in the store. Just before that you called Anne and told her to pick up the whisky in Zürich and give it to Al-Bader.'

Känzig shook his head in disbelief. He looked crestfallen. He couldn't understand how he'd been found out.

Winter gave Känzig a piercing glare. 'Why?'

'It wasn't me.' Resignation took hold.

Very softly, Winter said, 'The fingerprints on the carton prove it.' That was a bluff. The carton had been totally destroyed in the explosion. Burned to cinders and scattered as ashes in the Höllentobel. But it worked.

'Yes. Yes, I gave Anne the whisky.'

'Why, Känzig? Tell me why you did it.'

Winter let go of his hair. Känzing was still shaking his head mechanically. Winter stepped back and leaned against the wall opposite. The two men looked at each other in the gloom. 'Why?'

Känzing collapsed, and crouched on the floor. Seconds passed, then he said, 'I was just the messenger.' Then he made a half-hearted, semi-circular gesture with his hand. 'But the murderer is still out there.'

Now it was Winter's turn to be surprised. 'What do you mean?' He knew that an initial confession opens a small window of time in which the person confessing feels they can explain their perspective. It was like opening the vent on a steam boiler. Winter had heated the boiler, and now Känzig wanted to let off the pressure that had been accumulating for days. Winter was the confessor, saying nothing, just nodding occasionally.

'I'm no murderer. I was just the messenger. I didn't know it was a bomb. I thought it was a present. Honestly. If I'd known I would have gone straight to the police. Or to you.' Känzig looked at Winter and gave him a tentative smile. 'I'm sorry. I ought to have come to you much earlier. The whole thing got out of hand.'

'That happens.'

'After the crash I wanted to get my own idea of what had happened. Von Tobler was applying the pressure. So I commissioned Schmitt to do some research. Discreetly. Better safe than sorry. The first thing he did was to send a helicopter. I already felt uneasy then.'

'You'd worked with Schmitt before?'

'Yes, once or twice. He helped out with a divorce case for a college friend of mine in Zürich.' Känzig gave a brief laugh. 'To begin with I thought it was a pilot error or bad weather, but that same night von Tobler was breathing down my neck. When you said the following day that Al-Bader and Anne had been murdered, and that the police were unofficially confirming that the helicopter had probably crashed as the result of a deliberate explosion, I got scared.'

He was still moving his head slightly from side to side, as if trying to shake off the story. If it shouldn't have happened, it couldn't have. 'I didn't want to get dragged in. My wife would never have forgiven me. And our marriage isn't the best. You know, Winter, I'm being devoured by work.'

Winter remained impassive.

When Känzig didn't get any acknowledgement, he continued, 'But none of that is of any interest to you. Anyway, I told myself it's better to be safe than sorry and extended Schmitt's assignment. I got him to keep an eye on you.'

'And hack into my computer?'

'That was Schmitt's idea. He told me about the new possibilities. It's quite easy these days to monitor emails. I let myself be persuaded.'

Winter didn't challenge the excuses, but thought, Känzig is never to blame. Instead he asked, 'What did you tell him?'

'Something about an internal audit and money laundering.' Slowly, but surely Känzig seemed to be regaining his composure. The emotional leaps were subsiding. Horror, shock, fear and relief were levelling out.

Winter decided not to listen to his drivel any longer and instead asked the key question. 'Who gave you the whisky bottle?'

A disdainful snort from Känzig.

'Well, that's a strange story.'

The fool just can't get to the point, Winter thought. But he allowed him to speak.

'As I said, I was at lunch with Hediger. First lunch, then a meeting. That's simplifying it. We talked about the merger. You know, Winter, Hediger is a key figure and we discussed how we might achieve a smooth integration. Here too, the devil is in the detail.'

Winter could scarcely believe how brazenly Känzig was spouting all this. But it made complete sense. Känzig was preparing himself for the rumoured takeover and had crawled up Hediger's arse. Känzig was doing all he could to climb the career ladder. Winter wondered if von Tobler knew of this.

'After lunch,' Känzig continued, 'we drove to Hediger's office and examined the scenarios further. At four o'clock he had an appointment and I left. In the corridor I ran into Baumgartner.'

'And?'

'He gave me the bottle.'

'Baumgartner?' Winter let the name hang in the room. He hadn't thought of him for a second.

'Winter. You know him. He's here. In the bunker. He works for the financial group's chairman's office and has access to their CEO. How could I refuse?' Baumgartner had always been present when Winter reported back to his colleagues. And this morning he'd spoken to Känzig after the meeting. Winter recalled how his superior had waved Baumgartner over.

'You got the bottle from Baumgartner?' Winter still couldn't believe it.

'Yes. He bumped into me in the corridor as if by chance.'

'He knew that you were meeting Hediger.'

Känzig nodded. 'He must have had access to his diary. Of course I didn't think anything of it at the time. His office is on the same floor. "I'm glad I met you", he said. "You wouldn't mind doing me a little favour, would you?".' Känzig imitated Baumgartner's voice and it occurred to Winter that the liaison man had virtually said nothing the whole time.

'We went into his office where there were several cartons with bottles. All identical. I assumed the chairman handed them out on a daily basis. Baumgartner put a carton in my hand and said, "For Al-Bader from the boss. For the summit meeting this evening in the mountains. The CEO thinks that a little gift is called for. I mean, we want to keep out best clients sweet, don't we?".. I couldn't turn him down.' Känzig slumped.

'Are you telling me that the bomb came right from the top?'

'I don't know. The big boss wasn't anywhere to be seen.'

Baumgartner had orchestrated things skilfully. The first line of defence was to disguise it as an accident. After the crash there weren't any direct witnesses; they were all dead. The second line of defence was the clearly clueless messenger, Känzig. A Trojan Horse. The ass-licker had faithfully taken the bomb to the store in Bahnhofstrasse. The third line of defence was the knowledge that Känzig would do all he could to keep the matter under wraps. As a careerist, Känzig was a good choice of agent. And if necessary Baumgartner would be able to claim in court that Känzig's story was an unbelievable pack of lies. Nobody could prove anything; it would be one man's word against another's. The evidence linked Känzig to the explosive carton. If the case ever came to court.

'So you put the bottle in our gift store on Bahnhofstrasse and called Anne?'

'Yes. To begin with I thought about handing it over personally, but unfortunately we had this dinner party. I'd promised my wife to be back home punctually. I couldn't get hold of you. So I called Anne.' The 17:02 call from a withheld number.

'She was in Bern and I was in Zürich. My first suggestion was that we meet at a motorway service station somewhere along the way. But she wanted to take the train because of the traffic around Zürich. So she said I should leave the CEO's present in our gift store. She had to pop into the branch anyway to pick up the chocolates, so she could grab the whisky too. That suited me fine. I didn't have to wait at some service station on the motorway and I'd be at home on time. I didn't suspect a thing. I'm so sorry. I liked Anne.'

Anne had unwittingly organized her own death. Efficiently

as ever. Fate was unfair. Fate was cruel. 'I was terrified you'd find me out,' Känzig said with an awkward grin. 'Justifiably so.'

'What about Max?'

'I've no idea who you mean. Who is he? What's he got to do with all this?'

'He threatened me and yesterday tried to shoot me.'

'Good God. I always sensed that Baumgartner wasn't alone. This morning I confronted him, threatening to go to the police if he didn't hand himself in. He just laughed, said he didn't have a clue what I was talking about and recommended I spent some time recuperating in a sanatorium with mountain air.'

'What's he actually doing here at the annual conference?'

'Standing in for the CEO, as always.'

'Come on. Let's bring this story to a close.'

Winter moved away from the wall and helped Känzig up, who dusted down his ruined suit. They left the munitions room and walked through the bright rays of sun that shone through the embrasure, dividing the bunker into two. In the tunnel beyond it was dark again. On the way back they could hear nothing but their own footsteps resonating in the silence.

After a few minutes they came to the steel door and stepped outside. Screwing up their eyes in the midday sun they looked around. The coach was parked to the side in the shade of the fir trees. The driver was nowhere to be seen. They were alone.

Winter looked at his watch. 'We'll wait here. They'll be back soon. Leave me to sort it out.'

'Why do you think Baumgartner did it?' Känzig asked.

'I don't know.' Before Winter could speculate any further his phone rang. On the small screen he saw three missed calls and one coming through now. He moved away from Känzig and took the call. 'Winter.'

'Hello Winter, it's Smith here. I've been trying to get hold of you for an hour. I hope I haven't woken you after last night.'

'Good morning. I was inside a mountain.' He calculated the time difference. On the east coast of America it was six o'clock. And Smith had already been up for a while. What did the NSA man want from him at this hour? It must be important. Känzig walked across the clearing and sat on a tree stump at the edge.

'Everything alright with you?' Smith asked.

'Yes. Magnificent sunshine and I'm making progress. Why do you ask? Should I be worried?'

'I think so. The Securities and Exchange Commission has detected something that will interest you. As you know, after 9/11 the SEC introduced a notification system for unusual share and options transactions. Since then we've improved it after every financial crisis. It prevents certain types of speculation and stops terrorists from getting rich after an attack.'

'I know the early warning system. Which thresholds were crossed?' If, for example, the volume of shares or options being traded exceeded certain limits, a computer-operated alert was triggered.

'Pyramid Investment Partners has massively sold short a variety of large banks but especially the financial group behind your bank. It's betting with options on a sinking share price.' For the financial group, whose shares were listed on the Zürich, Frankfurt, London and New York markets, there were more than two hundred different call and put options.

'Are you sure?'

'Yes, so far as I can see,' Smith said, rustling some papers, 'over the last two weeks Pyramid Investment Partners has itself and via a number of shell companies bought massive options from issuers on all the important stock markets. They're trying to spread out the purchases and so keep below the radar. But the total sum of purchases got the alarm bells ringing.'

'Average expiry?'

'All short. Most only run till the end of the month, and none of the options is valid for longer than three months.'

'Strike price?'

'Most deep out of the money. The average strike price is way below the current share price. And many with big leverage. All in all, the transactions add up to more than one hundred million.' If the share price fell substantially then Farmer would earn a fortune. With such sums you could pay for murder out of petty cash.

'Farmer knows something we don't,' Winter said.

'Yes. The notification only came through an hour ago. I've been on the phone ever since, trying to find out what's going on.'

'Is the TAA behind it?'

'I don't know.'

'Is that your official opinion?'

'Yes.'

'And what's your personal opinion?'

'It's not relevant, but the answer is "Yes". In the past, right-wing extremists used to rob banks; these days they speculate and manipulate stock market prices. It's more profitable.'

Winter's synapses were red hot.

First the True and Armed Americans fraudulently got hold of their enemies' money, from Al-Bader and other rich Arabs. And now Farmer was trying to multiply this cache. Al-Bader had seen through the professor and demanded the special audit. Farmer had had to get him out of the way to win time.

But for what?

'Winter? Are you still there?'

'Yes. For that sort of money, you'd normally have to rob several banks.'

'You're telling me. And up till now everything's been legal.'

'I know.'

'Winter, for Pyramid Investment Partners to be successful the share price of the financial group has to fall dramatically. How can Farmer exert that sort of pressure on the share price? He has to manipulate it somehow.'

The rusty door of the bunker creaked. Dirk came out, followed by a beaming von Tobler and his guests. They were blinded by the sun, but convinced that their data were secure with Secer AG, deep in the mountain, protected by old artillery cannons.

Winter stared at them.

'Smith! I know what Farmer's planning! He's bought shares in Secer. This firm stores data for various banks, including ours and the financial group's. Imagine what would happen if we lost the data. It would be a catastrophe. The share price would hit the floor.'

'Are you sure?'

'Yes. Just this morning I got the list of Pyramid Investment Partners' investments. They're big shareholders in Secer AG. Farmer isn't digging a tunnel into the vault; he's simply bought access with his oil money.'

'Sophisticated.'

'Right now I'm standing outside the bunker that contains Secer AG's server farm. Investment in vital infrastructure. Do you remember? I was always thinking of something on the lines of 9/11 or the oil rig. But Farmer's planning an attack from the inside that would also have devastating consequences. And it would be so easy for him to do, because as a major share-holder he has access.'

As he spoke Winter felt annoyed at himself for not having listened attentively during the tour. Dirk had told him that only very few people got to see the inside of the server farm. The head of IT was proud that he'd managed to organize this special visit.

'What are you doing there?'

'We're visiting the bunker as part of our annual conference.'

'Isn't that a good opportunity to smuggle something into the sensitive area?' Smith asked from the other side of the Atlantic.

It was a question that the security planner of the annual conference had no answer to.

More satisfied bankers and clients came pouring out of the bunker. They were physically safe at least. Or were they?

In the stream of people Winter spotted Fatima's black hair. She was looking out for him. He waved and she began heading towards him.

Where was Baumgartner?

'Maybe Farmer has bought access to other data storage centres. If several of these places were to break down, the stock markets would collapse. The security measures in the data centres need to be checked immediately. The biggest danger is from moles right at the top of the hierarchy. Warn the other banks.'

'Okay. I'll see to that and I'll get the cyber boys out of bed too.'

'When does the New York stock market open?'

A pause. Smith looked at his watch. 'In three hours and seventeen minutes.'

Winter swallowed, and then he hung up.

Fatima was standing beside Winter. 'Hello. Where did you get to? The bunker museum was really interesting. I didn't know that Switzerland was encircled by the Nazis in the Second World War.' Fatima noticed the deep furrows between Winter's eyes. 'Everything okay?'

He put his mobile away, shook his head and looked her in the eye. 'Now I know who gave Anne the bomb.'

Fatima's eyes grew wider. 'Who?'

'Later. The murderer is here. Somewhere in the crowd.' Fatima slapped a hand over her mouth and closed her eyes. 'And he's planning an attack on the server farm. Wait here!' When she opened her eyes again Winter was making his way through the visitors, who were chatting as they waited to go back to the hotel and enjoying the sunshine after the stale bunker air.

Grabbing Dirk, Winter said, 'I need to talk to you now. Now!'

The head of IT excused himself apologetically from a client and was hurried to the edge of the crowd by Winter.

'Hey, Winter, what's going on?' Dirk protested. Then, seeing from Winter's face that this was no time for any backchat, he shut up.

'Dirk. Two questions. Where's Baumgartner?'

'Baumgartner?'

'You know, the oily one in the suit – the liaison man for the chairman's office. He was here. I saw him.'

'Oh, him.' Dirk made a dismissive gesture.

'Do you have any idea where he might be?'

'No, but I could call him.'

'That's not necessary. Give me the number.' Dirk accessed the contact details on his phone and Winter copied the number in his.

'Second question to Dirk the IT expert. What would be the easiest way to bring Secer AG to its knees?'

'Are you going mad?'

'No. It's very likely that an attack is imminent. As an insider how would you incapacitate the servers?'

'It's not possible. Everything is backed-up twice, three times.'

'Come on, Dirk. The Titanic sank, didn't it?'

'You can't just pull a plug.'

'Dirk. Use your imagination.'

Dirk rubbed his nose and closed his eyes. 'It's all backed up several times. The data are constantly mirrored and saved. This compensates for a possible server failure. All systems are duplicated. Even with today's processing power you couldn't crack the access codes in a million years. The entire complex is secured with armed guards. Nobody can enter with a weapon. You've seen that yourself. If the alarm goes off the security doors shut automatically and seal the whole thing off.'

Dirk energetically waved his hands either side of his head. His eyes still closed, he continued, 'The automatic system can only be overridden by two senior managers. The two-man rule works there too. Biometric data for your iris and palm. The entire complex can function with emergency generators, has its own water supply and filters the air. The excess pressure system protects against poisonous gases. The bunker is nuclear bombproof. With the best will in the world I can't see any holes.'

'Use your imagination, Dirk!' Winter insisted.

Dirk opened his eyes and shook his head.

'They've continually been improving the security system over the past ten years and closed every hole. You can't mess that up in a minute.' Looking around, Dirk pointed up at the cliff. 'You'd have to take the whole mountain away. But the bunker was cut out of granite. An earthquake would have to have its epicentre right here,' he said, pointing at the ground and ruffling his hair.

Winter gestured to hurry Dirk along.

'A hurricane,' Dirk joked. 'Or how about an ice age. We could just freeze the entire thing.' Winter still didn't completely believe Dirk.

'Bad joke.'

Joining them, Fatima said, 'What's up?'

Winter put her in the picture. 'Dirk says that only an earthquake with its epicentre directly under the bunker could paralyse the servers. But you can't order a natural catastrophe like that.'

'Natural catastrophe? In Egypt we have sandstorms...'

'A hurricane. I told you,' Dirk interjected.

'... and floods,' Fatima continued. 'Everything is dried out. As the rain falls it floods, taking everything with it. All of a sudden a wadi becomes a torrential river.' She looked up the valley. 'But what would happen if the dam broke and the reservoir inundated the valley here?'

Dirk shook his head. 'Impossible. They've thought of that too. First, no dam like that has ever broken and second, the ventilation dampers would close automatically.'

Winter dismissed the idea of a flood and said, 'We're not getting anywhere here. Our best bet is to ask the CEO.' He nodded to the bunker. 'He'll know how you could disrupt the plant.'

Dirk and Fatima exchanged glances and nodded. Both of them knew that once Winter had set his mind on something he was hard to deter.

They made their way through the throng to the bunker entrance, prised open the rusty door and hurried along the tunnel inside the mountain. The damp floor was slippery, and in their haste they kept sliding. They reached the visitors' lounge again, where one of the guards was getting himself a coffee. Winter explained who they were and asked if they could see Herr Torhorst.

'I'm sorry, but Herr Torhorst can't see you at the moment.' The guard looked nervous; his finger anxiously kept stroking the safety catch of his machine gun.

'Then take us to the head of security,' Winter insisted.

'He can't see you either.'

'Why not?'

'That's confidential information.' The finger twitched again.

'Do you know where he is?'

'That's confidential information,' the guard repeated.

'You don't know where your boss is, do you?'

'I'm sorry, but I'm going to have to ask you to go back to the entrance and submit your request another time.'

The guard was playing strictly by the rules.

Winter looked at his watch. Three more hours till the New York Stock exchange opened. He went up to the guard, looked him in the eye and asked with a friendly smile, 'Your weapon, please.'

Winter's request took the guard completely by surprise.

He stared blankly at Winter until he realized that the short machine gun had been yanked from his hands. Winter engaged the safety catch and put a reassuring hand on the guard's shoulder. 'Keep calm. You're not going to come to any harm. We suspect that an attack has been planned on the servers. So I'll ask again. Where's your CEO?'

For a moment the guard stared at his empty hands before dropping them and unintentionally brushing the holster with his pistol. Winter shook his head and could see the guard processing the risk analysis. After a few seconds the man dipped his head in resignation and crossed his arms.

Winter sighed and the guard said, 'The boss and the head of technology have disappeared. I couldn't find them just now.'

'Take us to your boss's office.'

They left the visitors' lounge and hurried along a corridor with several doors. The guard unlocked a door to a small, functional office. 'He's here, normally.' They looked around. Empty.

The guard opened a second door on the other side of the corridor. 'That's the head of technology's office. He's our head of security too and he's not there either. Strange.'

'Maybe they're in the server rooms?'

'No, nobody's in the sterile areas at the moment. The technicians are in the staff room. Lunchbreak.' They returned to the visitors' lounge. Winter, Fatima, Dirk and the guard stood helplessly beside the coffee machines. The last time Winter had seen Baumgartner and Torhorst was by the door to the adjoining conference room. He tried the latch. Locked.

'Open it!' he ordered the guard, who grabbed his bunch of keys again and unlocked the door. Winter entered the conference room, furnished sparingly with a round table, six chairs, a white board and a cupboard. Glancing incidentally in the wastepaper basket he saw a cup half filled with brown liquid. Winter opened the cupboard.

'Christ!'

Torhorst was lying on the floor of the cupboard.

Crooked.

His throat and carotid artery had been slit, his white shirt full of blood. Another suit ruined.

Where the eyes should have been were two dark, gaping holes. Someone had gouged out the eyeballs.

Winter instinctively took a step backwards.

Fatima, Dirk and the guard took sharp intakes of breath.

'Call the police and sound the alarm!'

The guard started running.

A siren went off.

Winter crouched and examined Torhorst's dead body again. On the metal floor of the cupboard was a pool of blood that had started to congeal. The CEO of Secer AG had been killed about an hour ago. And his right hand had been chopped off.

The hacker had obtained the biometric access data to Secer AG.

All hell was let loose inside the bunker. Service technicians in white overalls and guards scurried into the visitors' lounge. Some thought this was a drill, others were scared. Those who'd been on night shift had been torn from their sleep and were rubbing their eyes in bewilderment. They were in frantic discussion and crowding around the conference room with Torhorst's body.

A lean, grey-haired man took control and attempted to bring some order to the chaos. By the tone of his voice he must have been a sergeant. He ordered the guards to search every room, hand around gas masks and prepare the generators.

I've got to find Baumgartner, immediately! Winter thought.

Handing Dirk the machine gun, he abandoned him and Fatima and ran to the offices, passing more technicians on the way. He shook locked door handles. The first thing he needed was a telephone. The fourth door was unlocked.

A telephone stood on the desk, beside it rock samples. Maps hung on the walls. In one corner was a tripod with a half-covered surveying instrument. A geologist's office. He sat and picked up the receiver. No dialling tone. He pressed zero. Still no dialling tone. Double zero. Wrong. Winter growled then, right under his nose, noticed a list of telephone numbers on the wall. You had to press * for a line. He called Meister's number.

It took an age for his call to be answered. 'Hello?'

'This is Winter. Meister?'

'Yes. May I ask where you're calling from?' The Secer AG telephone number from the former military bunker had clearly made Meister and his surveillance computers uneasy. 'From the Secer bunker. Someone here has slit the Secer CEO's throat.'

'Most disagreeable,' Meister said impassively.

Ignoring the understatement, Winter said, 'You have to pinpoint a telephone number for me right away.'

'I'd need a court order for that.' Meister was not the person who made the law but who implemented it in practice.

Winter knew that Meister knew that he knew.

'Don't give me that, Meister. We don't have time. The man that number belongs to gave Anne the bomb and killed the CEO here.'

'Interesting,' Meister said dryly. 'Which number?'

Winter gave him Baumgartner's mobile number and a summary of Smith's call. The Americans had probably warned him too. One hand washes the other.

Meister played it cool. 'But this only works if the mobile telephone in question is switched on and it accepts a call. You need a four-second connection to make a triangulation. Otherwise you cannot identify a location.'

'Four seconds. Understood. As soon as I'm out of the bunker I'll call from a number Baumgartner won't decline. Give me ten minutes.'

'Alright.'

'As soon as you've got him, call me back on my mobile.'

'Good luck, Winter!' Meister hung up.

For a second Winter wondered whether the cynical Meister had meant that seriously. Tearing a map of the Bernese Oberland from the wall, he left the geologist's office and in the corridor bumped into a corpulent man in overalls. His glasses were fogged up, his face red and he panted in horror, 'He's dead.'

Stepping back Winter saw that the man had a wet floor cloth in his left hand, while the right was full of blood. Both were dripping onto the lino.

'Calm down. Who's dead?'

'Meierhans.' The man in overalls helplessly raised his blood-smeared hand.

'Who?'

'Meierhans.'

'Who is Meierhans?'

'My boss.'

'What does he do?'

'He works with the computers.' The head of technology. 'When the alarm went off I was just putting away the cleaning trolley.' As proof he held up his arm with the wet cloth. Tears were streaming down his round cheeks. His chest was heaving up and down briskly. Winter put his arm around the cleaner's neck in comfort.

'Keep nice and calm.' A gentle squeeze of the shoulder. 'Where is Herr Meierhans?'

'In the cleaning room.'

'Would you take me there please?'

The shocked man in white overalls nodded, turned around, walked mechanically down the corridor, turned left, then right. He stopped beside a trolley laden with detergents and a bulky, blue tub full of dirty water and a mop. The man pointed to a door that was standing ajar.

He screwed up his eyes. 'There.'

Winter carefully opened the door.

A narrow storeroom with stuffed racks. Bright, neon light. Traces of blood on the floor. The cleaner had stepped in the pool of blood that was spreading from the far corner.

Wedged between the last rack, which had been shifted slightly, and the wall stood a man whose white overalls were slashed with red. His head was tilted back onto the rack on a jumbo pack of loo roll, his throat was slit and the blood had run out. In the gape of the man's bloodied neck Winter could make out the round outlines of the severed carotid artery and windpipe. Baumgartner had attacked Meierhans with a very sharp knife, a cut-throat razor or more likely a scalpel.

His eyes and right hand were missing.

The two-man rule.

Winter turned around, raced down the corridor past the cleaner to the control room, which he remembered from the tour. The door was half open.

The gaunt sergeant was standing behind a technician who was hacking around on a keyboard. The six flat screens of the control console were working. Still. Winter couldn't help thinking of the control room of an underground rail network. But instead of symbols for tracks and trains, here you saw cables with data flows. Putting a hand on his holster the sergeant said sharply, 'Who are you? What do you want?'

'Winter.' He showed the man his ID. 'We were just here on a visit.' He pointed to the consoles. 'Has anything been manipulated?'

The sergeant stared at Winter and the ID, then said 'Yes.' He pointed to two glass plates set in the middle of the console.

Bloody handprints.

A frayed optic nerve on the iris scanner.

'What has been manipulated?'

The sergeant gave Winter back his ID. 'We don't know yet. The sterile areas have not been entered. All systems are functioning. The emergency generators are ready. Data cannot be deleted without the client's agreement and their code. For the moment it looks as if we're secure.'

'No. Look here!' The technician frantically pointed at a screen full of codes. 'They've uploaded a virus.' He ran his finger along the lines of code. 'The moment a client logs in the worm changes the time protocols.' His finger left a sweaty mark on the screen. 'Which always gives our timestamps priority. Shit!'

'What does that mean?'

'Nothing for the moment. But the next time a client logs in, their data will be automatically prioritized here in the bunker. The balancing safeguard has been overridden.'

'What happens if the data is lost here?'

'Then we lose all the data. Everywhere.'

'I don't understand. Isn't the data secured in the other locations too?'

'Yes. But those data will be automatically deleted. It's like the hard disk on your PC being overwritten by completely blank documents.'

The sergeant cursed. 'Do something!'

At that moment a warning lamp flashed.

The technician rolled over to an adjacent screen.

'The air-conditioning! It's also interfered with the programme for controlling the air-conditioning.' He typed hectically and brought up a diagram of the ventilation system. The bars in the chart were all in the green, none of the values too high or low. The technician breathed a sigh of relief and leaned back. 'All seems to be okay. It just opened the ventilation valves. The air supply is working perfectly. The oxygen level is right. We're breathing fresh, unfiltered mountain air. So long as we don't have a cow crapping into the ventilation pipes we'll be fine.'

'What would that do?'

'No idea.'

'Close the ventilation valves again and restore the programme's default settings,' the sergeant barked.

'I can't. It can only be authorized by...' The technician's eyes glided over to the blood-smeared glass surfaces. The three men exchanged glances and then looked around. Prudently Baumgartner hadn't left the hacked-off hands and gouged-out eyes lying around.

The sergeant growled in annoyance and asked, 'Are they going to gas us?' The technician looked more closely at the code. 'We do have the gas masks,' he said to his own relief.

'Explosive gas, perhaps. The servers wouldn't survive a fire or explosion in here,' the sergeant ruminated.

Another diagram appeared on the screen. 'The fire suppression system is functioning at any rate.'

'All the same we're going to evacuate. Quick march!'

They hurried back to the visitors' lounge where the staff had assembled. About thirty men were standing around, putting on gas masks. They were talking to each other in muffled voices. An eerie atmosphere. The heads covered in grey-green rubber and with glass eyes turned to the newcomers. 'Listen up, everyone,' the sergeant bellowed and began his assessment of the situation.

As he made his way over to Dirk and Fatima, someone handed Winter a gas mask. Dirk lifted his rubber nose and asked, his face already dripping with sweat, 'What the hell is going on here?'

'I'll tell you later. We've got to get out as soon as we can. Let's go.'

Fatima, Dirk and Winter slipped out of the room, passed the unguarded security door and hurried along the by now familiar tunnel into the fresh air.

The sun was high in the sky.

Without a tour guide Dirk, the bankers and their guests had become restless, and half of them had already taken their seats on the coach. Von Tobler was standing in the middle of the forecourt, trying his best to entertain his guests. When he saw Dirk he waved him over impatiently.

Winter called out, 'Dirk, get these people away from here!'

He took out Känzig's mobile as well as his own and called Baumgartner. Hopefully Meister was ready. It rang four times. The ringing tone cut out. No connection. Was Baumgartner still inside the mountain?

'Shit!'

Winter looked around, then at his watch. Still a good two and a half hours before the stock markets of the Western world were all open. Where could Baumgartner be? What was he planning? Explosive gas?

Känzig's phone rang. Winter stared at the screen. Baumgartner's number. Clearing his throat, Winter pressed the button with the little green phone icon. Disguising his voice, making it extra deep and putting on a Bernese Oberland accent, he said, 'Hello, who is that?'

'Did you just call me?' No name, but Baumgartner's voice for sure.

'It's Bettschen here. Good afternoon. I found a mobile phone here on a bench. I rang the first number on it and wanted to know if you could help me...'

'Sorry.' Click.

More than four seconds. That should be enough for Meister to pinpoint the location. Winter closed his eyes and ran through the conversation again in his head. Background noises? None. Had Baumgartner recognized his voice? It had been a pretty good attempt to imitate the dialect, and he hadn't detected any indication that Baumgartner had recognized him. But Baumgartner was ice cold. His own mobile rang. Meister.

'Winter?'

'Did you get him?'

'Yes.' Meister relayed the coordinates.

'Wait a sec.' Clamping the phone between his ear and shoulder, Winter kneeled down and spread out the geologist's map on the gravel. He ran his finger along and down the latitude and longitude lines. 'He's right on the dam.'

Winter looked up the narrow valley. What had Fatima said?

In his head, he pictured a dry riverbed in the desert, and a torrent suddenly roaring through it. The dam wasn't far away and behind it lay huge volumes of water.

There was a terrible predictability to this horrifying thought. Winter felt sick.

'What's he doing up there?' Meister asked from what sounded like far away.

'Baumgartner's going to blow up the dam. If I can't stop him the valley's soon going to be overrun by a tsunami.'

A 'shit' escaped from Meister's mouth. 'I'll organize the evacuation.'

'Hugentobler is somewhere here. He's the financial group's head of security.'

'I know him. But why is Baumgartner doing this?'

'He's opened Secer's ventilation valves and overridden the controls. The bunker housing the servers will be flooded and all the data destroyed. We have two and a half hours. Then the American stock market opens and by then he wants the market ready to plunge into freefall.'

'A catastrophe.' Meister said, with rapid understanding.

Winter looked around. The forecourt was emptying. Von Tobler shook hands, clearly intent on keeping up the façade that everything was as it should be. He was excellent at that sort of thing. Dirk was standing beside the coach, which would be setting off shortly, to judge by the driver letting the engine warm up. Hugentobler was nowhere to be seen.

Fatima was beside him. 'Come on!' Winter said, grabbing her hand.

They ran through the forest to the clearing where von Tobler's helicopter was waiting. The sliding doors of the bright-red Alouette III were open. On the back benches sat two Arabs in conversation. The pilot was reading the *Blick*. Winter yanked open the cockpit door.

He had Fatima speak to them in Arabic before they made any signs of moving; Winter had factored in that her language skills might come in useful.

'I'm the bank's head of security,' Winter said meanwhile to the pilot. 'We have an emergency. You have to fly us up to the dam immediately.'

The pilot lowered his tabloid, looked at Winter calmly and asked, 'What's wrong?'

He was around forty years of age, with weather-beaten skin and a peaceful demeanour. Although greying at the temples, his Lech Wałęsa moustache was still black. He didn't look as if he would be easily fazed. The man probably flew rescue operations for injured mountain climbers.

Whipping out his ID, Winter said in a low voice, 'Two men
have been killed in the bunker. We've just located the murderer
up by the reservoir. He's going to blow up the dam. You need
to fly us up there immediately.'

The pilot put on his helmet, switched a few levers and the
rotors began turning. He radioed the control tower. 'Panther 2
here. Housi, there's an emergency. I'm flying quickly up to the
dam. Out.'

The rotors reached takeoff speed. Fatima and Winter climbed
in and the helicopter rose into the sky. The Arabs' no-longer-
quite-so-white robes wafted in the clearing.

Winter checked the .45 SIG, the .22 Mosquito down by his
right calf and the flick knife in his right trouser pocket.

He turned to Fatima. Their faces were only a hand-width
apart. 'Listen to me. You were right earlier. Baumgartner is
trying to flood Secer. He's overridden the air-conditioning and
opened the ventilation channels so the water can get in. Now
he's up by the dam. I don't know how he plans to do it, but if
it ruptures it will look like an accident.'

'By Allah the almighty!'

'And this morning Känzig admitted that he gave Anne the
bomb. He got it from Baumgartner.'

'Who is this Baumgartner?'

'He works for the chairman of the financial group. He told
Känzig that the whisky was a present from the chairman.'

'So what now?'

'I'm going to stop him.'

'How?'

'Somehow.' He could see the fear in Fatima's eyes. 'I'll
improvise. We haven't got a second to lose.' Still almost two
and a half hours.

'Be careful!' Fatima said, stroking Winter's knee. It was the
first time they'd touched like this other than when they were
alone.

Just above the treetops, the helicopter hurtled up the valley, angled forwards. Side valleys and a few farms flashed past. They gained altitude and headed straight for the dam.

Winter peered through the windscreen and stared at the slightly curved concrete wall. It rapidly grew bigger.

He scanned the huge edifice for explosives, but all he could see was a maintenance platform, similar to the lifts used by window-cleaners on skyscrapers. In some places water dripped down. Water and microorganisms were eating into the concrete and would finally defeat it in a few million years. Man was far more effective. He could blow up the dam in just a few minutes.

How high would the wall of water rushing down the valley be? One hundred metres? Two hundred? It would hit the bunker at full force and flood the ventilation pipes. Mudslides would come crashing down, tearing apart the data cables. Buildings and homes in the valley below would be annihilated. Many lives would be lost.

The pilot turned around halfway. 'Where would you like to be put down?' They flew along the crest of the dam. Not a soul was to be seen.

'Down there. While you hover,' Winter replied, pointing to a small car park at the edge of the dam.

'Roger.' The flight had only taken a couple of minutes and the landing was pure routine.

'Thanks.'

'My pleasure.'

'And then take the lady straight back,' Winter said.

'Where should I send the taxi bill?' the pilot asked. Even – especially so – in a crisis, money could not be forgotten.

'To the bank.' It wouldn't break the budget for the annual conference. Assuming the bank was still solvent, that is.

The pilot slowed down for landing, curved round to the left and slowly approached the car park. Winter pushed open the side door and prepared to jump out. On the other side of the helicopter someone got out of a green Land Rover.

When the pilot saw that the man in black was holding a pistol and aiming at his head he immediately jerked the helicopter around.

The bullet entered via a small window on the underside of the helicopter and exited the cockpit through one of the curved ceiling windows. Apart from the additional ventilation holes there was no damage.

Surprised by the sudden lurching of the helicopter Winter slipped and skidded out. His fingers tried to dig into the lightly ribbed rubber mat on the floor of the helicopter. Without success.

Wanting to help, Fatima bent over. But the safety belt held her back. She was jammed.

Slipping further, Winter made a desperate grab for the sliding door, but only grasped at air and fell completely from the twisting helicopter, which was once more above the chasm of the valley. Before Winter's eyes, a three-hundred-metre deep, dark-green hole opened up.

Fatima's cry of horror was drowned out by the noise.

'What the hell was that?' the pilot asked.

'Winter fell out of the helicopter!' Fatima screamed.

'What?'

'Winter is gone!'

'Where is…?'

With one hand Winter was gripping onto the runner. He was dangling in mid-air. With his other he tried to reach the metal bar, but the helicopter was racing upwards in a wide arc. Gravity and acceleration were working against each other.

Swinging back and forth, he used the momentum to grab the bar with his free hand. The sharp blades cut into his hands, but he felt marginally safer. The gaping, green hole was gone.

They were flying above the water. With a pull-up he heaved himself up and to the side, and hooked his leg over the runner.

The pilot stabilized the helicopter out of firing range. Then he noticed Winter's leg through the floor panel. 'He's hanging onto the runner.'

'What?'

'He's still there.' The pilot pointed down.

Fatima bent carefully through the open door and could see only Winter's hands, one foot and his fruitless attempts to clamber onto the runner. Her hair was blowing all over the place and blocking her view.

'Land! Fly to the other side of the dam.'

'I can't.'

Fatima turned her head. On the other side the dam abutted the rock face. No space anywhere. Far too steep for a helicopter.

'Can you land directly on the dam?'

'Too dangerous.'

'Why?'

'Because of the cables and the wind.'

'Try. Please. There's no time to lose.'

'Okay, I'll see if I can do it.' Slowly, and with finesse, the pilot manoeuvred the helicopter back to the dam wall. Right above the edge, a strong downwind was blowing. Fatima bent over again.

Winter had disappeared.

The water slapped above Winter. He didn't feel the cold in the initial moments. It was only when the water soaked through his clothes that it felt as if a vast fist of ice threatened to crush his chest.

Winter surfaced, took a deep breath and drew the mountain air into his lungs. He blinked the water from his eyes. The helicopter circled high above his head and disappeared behind the dam wall. He swam to a rusty ladder, climbed out and scrambled over to the deserted dam.

Winter discarded his sopping jacket.

Freedom of movement.

Shivering, he shook the water from his face and hair. He sucked his lips into the warmth of his mouth and clenched his fists several times to warm his fingers.

On the other side of the dam he cast a vertiginous glance down into the depths, instinctively holding his breath and steadying his foothold. Two small puddles formed at his feet.

The wall fell vertically downwards and curved slightly inwards. A concave shape against the reservoir was better able to withstand the water pressure. In the shadows far below he could make out the stony, dried-out bed of the stream and the white dots of grazing sheep.

Who had fired the shot?

Pulling the .45 from his holster, Winter checked the slide and began to jog across the dam. The movement got his blood circulating and warmed him up. The helicopter was far below in the valley. He could make out the rocky outcrop on top of the Secer bunker. To his right, the water was like glass and reflected the midday sun. The waves caused by his jump had subsided.

In the middle of the dam, Winter came to the frame for the maintenance lift. The lift ropes were vibrating. He stopped and carefully looked down over the edge. Way below he could see two members of the service crew in orange helmets. The lift was moving slowly upwards.

With no time to wait, Winter ran to the car park. If someone started shooting he could leap into the water at any moment. As he neared the end of the dam he slowed down and bent behind a low wall for cover.

Some steps led down a few metres to the empty car park. The Land Rover was a good fifty metres away. A flat, aluminium boat with a small outboard motor lay half in the water, covered with a blue tarpaulin. It was probably used to fish driftwood from the water.

His shooting hand out in front, Winter climbed over the wall, giving him a view of the blind spots behind it. Nobody. He hurried down the steps.

From there to the Land Rover was pure, open terrain with no cover.

Glancing back, he saw that a massive steel door gave access to the dam's innards.

Vehicle or dam? Prioritise.

First the Land Rover, then the vaults of the dam. Maybe there'd be clues to Baumgartner inside the all-road vehicle. With both hands clasping the SIG and pointing it at the filthy Land Rover, Winter approached the car from the rear. A quick glance beneath the vehicle revealed that nobody was hiding behind it.

But wasn't someone sitting there in the passenger seat? The windows were dirty, and the headrests obscured his view. Was someone perhaps calmly waiting there, his finger on the trigger, until Winter came close enough for a clear shot? The car park offered no protection. It was utterly silent, not a breeze stirring.

Winter changed his angle of approach, which gave him two advantages. First, his opponent would be forced to move. Second, it would make the shooting angle more difficult, as the rear roof brace now offered a little protection.

Twenty metres.

Suddenly Winter sped up. He did two side steps. Saw the figure sitting in the passenger seat. Tugging open the driver's door, Winter ducked to offer less of a target, and aimed his gun inside the car.

Baumgartner. Although he was in white Secer overalls, he was unmistakable. Only the little hole in the side of his head was new.

Winter put his pistol away. Adrenalin and blood coursed through his veins. He walked around the car and opened the passenger door. No pulse. But still warm. Baumgartner's eyes were staring into space, in search of his soul.

Winter unzipped the overalls, beneath which the liaison man was still wearing his pinstripe suit. In the left breast pocket he found an extremely sharp, ceramic knife, which a metal detector wouldn't pick up. If challenged, he could say it was a letter opener. No blood – wiped clean.

In the right breast pocket a slim, leather wallet with banknotes and business cards. In his trouser pockets just the usual odds and ends: change, chewing gum, bunch of keys and a car key. Evidently Baumgartner drove a BMW.

Used to drive.

There was no key in the ignition. An accomplice had probably been waiting for Baumgartner with the Land Rover at the bunker. Max? And once the banker had fulfilled his purpose he'd become redundant. Max, or whoever the killer was, obviously didn't want any living witnesses. Perhaps Winter's call from Känzig's telephone had sealed Baumgartner's fate. At any rate, his mobile was missing.

Winter looked around. Baumgartner's death saved the state a huge amount of money. Everything had its pros and cons.

He searched the car. In the glove compartment, only vehicle documents and a road map of Switzerland. Winter closed the door, went back around the car and opened the tailgate. Nothing in the boot but a scrunched-up military tarpaulin, beneath it brown drag marks from a heavy load. Splinters from boards or wooden crates?

Suddenly he could hear voices from the dam.

Laughter.

First Winter saw a pair of orange helmets, then beneath these the two maintenance crew in their blue windcheaters. Around their waists they wore thick, leather belts with all manner of tools, and around their shoulders safety ropes with metal hooks. The men were chatting as they came down the steps.

Winter closed the tailgate and hurried over to the men with a wave of his hand.

'Hey! Wait!'

The men fell silent and stopped at the bottom of the steps. The elder one put his toolbox on the side wall. They eyed the soaked Winter with suspicion. 'What are you doing here? Did you fall into the water? Can we help you?'

'Don't worry. I'm fine. But you do have to help me. A madman is about to blow up the dam.'

The two men exchanged puzzled glances. Winter couldn't blame them for assuming that *he* was the madman. Wet, alone in the mountains, armed with a pistol and spouting crazy ideas. But in the head technician's expression Winter could detect a touch of concern and uncertainty too. They'd just been hanging from a three-hundred-metre high wall and were professionally trained to deal with risk.

'What makes you think that?'

'It's a long story. We have to search the dam straight away.'

'There's nobody apart from us.' The head maintenance man cast a glance at the steel door, firmly locked. 'Why should anyone think of blowing up the dam?'

'They're trying to flood the old military bunker down there,' Winter said pointing into the valley. 'And destroy the servers inside. If we let that happen the people living in the valley will die. It could be about to blow.'

The head technician screwed up his eyes, scratched his head thoughtfully and ran his finger along his upper lip. He was clearly giving the matter some thought. He looked at his colleague. Second opinion. The younger man shook his head almost imperceptibly. He wasn't convinced either.

'Sound the alarm at once! Evacuate the valley!'

The man shook his head. 'Look, anyone could come up here and say that. I think you're in shock. Where did you fall into the water?'

Winter took a step towards the elder man and grabbed his arm. 'Come with me!'

'Hey! What are you playing at?' Angrily, he shook himself free.

Winter was insistent. 'Come with me. There's something I want to show you.' Baumgartner's corpse inside the car would get these lame assholes going. He pointed to the green Land Rover. 'There's a dead man in there.'

'Wait here!' the head maintenance man said to the younger man who looked relieved not to be going with them.

'Are you sure about the dead body?' the elder man asked Winter, as he followed him to the car park.

Winter opened the passenger door and pointed at Baumgartner. Bending over, the technician saw the exit wound and froze. 'Shit!' he said.

'They're serious about this. Will you help me now?'

'Who is that? Did you kill him?'

'No, I found him like that, but he was going to blow up the dam. He was a banker who backed the wrong horse.'

'We need help,' the technician stammered, clearly very suspicious.

'Yes, and we need to search the dam at once.'

Keeping a watchful eye on Winter, the service technician fiddled with his belt and took out a radio. 'Hello? Hello? It's me. We've got a problem up here. Can you hear me?' The radio crackled. Static. The head technician looked at Winter and shook his head. Then his gaze wandered down, alighting on Winter's pistol. 'Who shot him?' he asked again.

'Not me. If I was going to cause you trouble, I'd have done it by now.'

The man took a few steps back to get better reception. He clamped the radio to his ear, bent his head towards the dam and pressed the transmit button again. 'Hello? Hello? Can you hear me?'

'Yes, what is it?' the radio hissed.

'Boss, we've got a problem. There's someone here saying the dam is about to be blown up. He found a dead body in the vehicle. What should I do?'

'Kill him.'

'Now!' the voice crackled from the radio. The maintenance technician put the radio back on his belt, placed the rope carefully on the ground and unzipped his blue windcheater.

Winter hadn't heard the order. He was bent over Baumgartner again, examining the compartments in the central console. Just bits and pieces.

He flipped down the sun visor. Maybe the murderer had left something here. In the visor mirror he saw the maintenance man approaching with a pistol.

The fake technician was about ten paces away. From that distance anybody could hit. But he came closer. Winter had his back turned to the man and was restricted by the confines of the car. The .45 SIG was clearly visible in its holster.

Not good.

But he had surprise on his side. Good. This advantage, however, would go up in smoke if the attacker cold-bloodedly shot him in the back.

He flipped the visor back up.

Suddenly Winter felt a fool.

It was all so obvious really.

The orange helmets and blue coats were all brand new, with no company logo – neither of the energy company nor a maintenance company. Also, there were no other vehicles in the car park apart from the Land Rover. It was unlikely that the maintenance men had walked here with all their equipment. Why hadn't his instinct warned him? The cold water must have had affected his mind too.

Winter crawled further into the car. Baumgartner's white overalls rustled. Inside the car it smelled of artificial air freshener and something sour. Baumgartner himself was still fresh.

Tiger, his cat, could detect the slightest changes in air pressure with his whiskers. Winter only had his neck hairs, but they too stood on end when the man with the pistol came closer.

Four more paces, three.

Was the man going for a shot at point-blank range, or would he be happy with two or three paralysing shots into the spine?

Winter hated unnecessary risks.

Which is why he fired his Mosquito beneath his left armpit. Winter ducked onto Baumgartner's lap and turned around. He saw the right shoulder of the man being kicked back by the bullet from the Mosquito.

The blue windcheater puffed up, the barrel of the gun that had been aimed at Winter was thrown skywards and the man's eyes were wide in horror. A second shot wasn't necessary.

In general Winter wasn't particularly keen on firing the first shot. Shoot first and ask questions later was rarely a successful tactic. But the exception proves the rule. Winter climbed out of the car, his Mosquito pointing all the while at the service technician. 'Don't move.'

The man's mouth opened. Perhaps he was going to scream. Or curse. Or call for help. His lips closed again. He stared at Winter in disbelief.

The door to the dam slammed shut.

The second maintenance man was gone.

Winter kept the Mosquito aimed at just above the man's nose. He felt significantly more comfortable in this changed situation. Having his own finger on the trigger was reassuring.

'Drop the gun.'

No movement.

The Heckler and Koch P10 was hanging from the half-raised arm. Barrel pointing down. A German police pistol. Winter studied the man's face. Had he shot Baumgartner? The first shock had dissipated at any rate. A bullet through the shoulder wasn't the end of the world. Was he annoyed that he hadn't dispatched Winter with a shot from a distance? Behind the man's glassy eyes, a complex calculation was being made.

'Now!' Winter said incisively.

The man's features suggested someone who was used to obeying orders. The Mosquito came to within a few centimetres of his face, making him go cross-eyed and feel discomfort in his brain. The gun clattered to the ground and Winter kicked it away with his foot.

'Hands behind your back!' With his left hand Winter pulled the injured man's jacket down halfway. The man let out a cry of pain, and his upper arms were now impeded in their movement.

'Kneel!' The man obeyed immediately. Keeping an eye on him, Winter picked up the rope.

He tied a noose, placed it around his prisoner's neck, pulled the man's head back by his short hair and forced him into a police armlock. Then he tied together the hands and forearms. With the rest of the rope, he quickly bound the man's feet. The technician groaned, offering only minimal resistance. 'Right,' Winter said, admiring his handiwork. If the man stretched his arms or legs the noose around his neck would tighten. A bent salami, ready for drying.

He searched his prisoner, pocketing the flick knife and putting the pistol in his belt. Winter placed a hand on the man's shoulder and asked, 'Where is the explosive device?'

He shook his head. Winter pressed his thumb into the wound; the technician gritted his teeth in pain and grimaced.

'How many of you are there?'

'More than you think.'

Winter knew that time was against him. And he knew that the sausage in front of him knew that too.

His watch said 13:17. In two hours and thirteen minutes, the New York stock market would open. He had to prevent the dam from being blown up at all costs.

Taking the radio, he hurried to the dam, then slowed when he was a few paces from the steel door to the catacombs.

At least two other men were involved in this: the younger technician and the man on the radio.

Maybe more. Expect the unexpected, Winter reminded himself. Were they waiting behind the door?

Reinforcements. He squeezed his mobile out of his damp jeans. The screen was flashing crazily. The electronics had been defeated by the water in the reservoir. Känzig's mobile wasn't working either. Great. So much for modern technology.

It was good that SIG pistols were waterproof.

Winter took a deep breath.

When he put his hand on the round door knob, the metal felt cold and sent a shiver down his spine. Winter raised the .45, took another deep breath and tried the door. Locked.

The radio on his belt hissed. 'Hello? Jochen? Where the hell are you?'

Winter recognized the voice. Max, his friend from the bridge with the bungee jump. Max, who'd been hunting him yesterday. He had two options, the first being to ignore Max altogether. This would make him suspicious and send someone to check the situation.

Or he could give Max a fright. Winter pressed the transmit button. 'Hello Max.'

Static hissing. Poor reception. Apart from the echoing of footsteps Winter couldn't hear any background noises. Max was somewhere in the concrete bowels of the dam.

'Winter. What a pleasant surprise. How's Jochen?' Max

asked soberly – there had been a pause but Winter could detect no nervousness in his tone.

'Ready for consignment.'

'I was going to send that amateur back. He was pretty useless.'

'Wasn't he? How are you, anyway?'

'Can't complain. My holiday is just around the corner.'

'Dreams are but shadows. *I* am just around the corner.'

'Well, well, a funny guy.'

The reception kept getting weaker; Max was moving further away from Winter. With every step Max was putting more concrete between them. Had he already set the explosives? Was he already escaping? Winter gained the impression that Max was slightly out of breath. From running, from carrying the explosives?

'So where are you going? Beach or mountains?'

Max gave a guttural laugh. 'You know what, my dear Winter? I'm more of a beach type. Put your feet up, a cool drink and a few girls.'

'But it's so beautiful here in the mountains!'

'We all need to get away once in a while.'

'If you're lucky they'll let you stay here and you'll end up in prison, rather than in the electric chair in the States.'

For the first time Max sounded slightly irritated. 'Shame we can't have a longer chat, but I'm afraid I don't have the time to give you a walloping today.' Was Max leaving already? 'My holiday begins in precisely...' Max said, consulting his watch, '... seventeen minutes.' Winter had hoped to have at least two hours before something drastic happened to the dam, but now such luxury seemed to be vanishing into the thin, mountain air.

There was no nearby beach with cool drinks and girls. How was Max going to abscond? Winter paused and heard him add, 'And your holiday in the eternal hunting grounds will begin too. Enjoy rotting in hell!'

The radio went silent.

The bomb had been set.

Winter sprinted back across the dam. With each step Max had been moving further away, assuming he was going to leave the wall from the other side. Winter would prepare a nice reception for him.

The crown of the dam was almost five hundred metres long and there was no help anywhere near. A cloud floated in front of the sun. The blue water turned dark grey. The strip of concrete seemed endless. Winter's lungs were burning and his thighs hardening. He approached the service lift.

This consisted of an open, metal cage with a large hanger and fat, rubber reels. It was let down by a winch on steel ropes.

Winter peered down. Far below him he could see a bulky, grey mass. There could only be one explanation: the two fake technicians had used the lift to mine the dam wall from the outside.

Should he go down? The buttons that operated the lift were in a massive, weatherproof box that couldn't be forced open without tools. The key for the console was missing. Of course. Winter slapped it in anger. Time was running out.

But Max was inside the dam.

That meant there must be explosives inside as well. And a way out, as Winter didn't think Max was planning on sacrificing his own life by staying inside the dam.

Winter kept running. Max had to be his priority. During the long sprint he focused on the end of the dam, which bordered a steep granite rock face. Around twenty metres before this was a small, cube-shaped, concrete structure containing the access steps to the inside.

Winter slowed, then stopped. The door was on the leeside, the other side from Winter. There was no cover on the dam and Winter didn't want to fall naively into a trap.

Where were Max and the younger technician? Did Max have more accomplices? He tried to get a view of the blind spot behind the stairs.

Beyond, at the end of the dam, a narrow path led into the mountains. The first section of path had been blasted into the rock face and in places made safe with ropes. At the steepest part, the path even led through a small tunnel. Had something just moved in that black hole? Winter aimed his gun at the shadowy aperture of the tunnel.

At that moment, from the corner of his eye, Winter glimpsed a blue windcheater appear from behind the cube of concrete and aim a pistol at him. Fortunately he was ready to shoot too. Swinging his .45 to the left, he fired a shot.

A scream. A hit. Windcheater and pistol disappeared behind the steps.

Winter had no cover between himself and the steps, and he didn't want to push his luck any further. He only had a tiny window of opportunity. The shooter hadn't expected to take a bullet. Winter sprinted to the concrete structure. Pressing his back against the wall, he glanced around the corner to the footpath.

There! A man, all in black, was exiting the small tunnel and hurrying up the mountain. Max was carrying a heavy, almost rectangular rucksack. He had a several hundred metres head start and had left behind at least one accomplice to stop Winter.

Max was out of reach. For the moment.

One thing at a time, Winter thought. The next opponent was waiting on the other side of the structure. Winter didn't know how many men he was dealing with. He felt the coarse and cold concrete against the back of his head. He listened carefully.

Wind.

Alpine choughs.

Silence in the mountains.

But time was running. Against him.

In his trouser pocket Winter found the tied-up technician's flick knife. He weighed it in his hand, flicked out the blade, then tossed the knife in a wide arc over the concrete structure. The knife spun several times, almost came to a stop at the highest point, then made its way downwards, blade first. When it disappeared from Winter's view he moved away from the wall and slinked around the cube of concrete.

The metal blade clanked on the ground.

Distracted, the shot man turned his head.

Winter came around and aimed the SIG at the technician's torso. Right at the heart. 'Drop your gun!'

He hadn't seen this left-hander before. The man's shooting arm started moving upwards. Winter couldn't be sure if this was deliberate or just a reflex, but he had no time to weigh up the risks and certainly no time for diplomacy.

Without any further ado he shot the man in the hand. The pistol fell to the ground. Another Heckler. Maybe the guns had been bought in a multipack.

Where was the third maintenance man?

Winter chucked the Heckler into the reservoir and motioned with his SIG for the man to move from the door to the edge of the dam. He took off the technician's belt and tied him provisionally to the balustrade.

Suddenly, the door creaked.

In a flash, Winter was back, flying the last metre through the air and ramming his shoulder against the door.

The third maintenance man was wedged between the steel door and the frame. Winter grabbed his outstretched forearm and prised the pistol from the hand of the surprised attacker with a sharp twist away from the body. This gun flew into the water too, increasing the reservoir's lead content.

The young technician from earlier made an attempt to fight back, but Winter elbowed him with full force in the side of the head, his knees buckled and he fell unconscious.

During this struggle the second man had freed himself from his belt and was running away. Despite the grazing wound to his shoulder and the hole in his hand, he refused to accept that it was over for him.

Aiming carefully, Winter shot him in the thigh. The man staggered a few more paces forwards, fell and stayed put. Winter shook his head. Learning difficulties.

He tied up the unconscious man and gave him a fleeting search. He didn't have a mobile that Winter could have used to expedite the assistance he'd requested.

Max was gone.

Doubting that the chopper pilot and Fatima would be able to muster an official back-up in time, it looked as if he would have to defuse the explosives himself. Winter prayed his explosives know-how hadn't gone rusty.

A black crack opened up behind the door. Winter held the pistol in front of him at the ready. He opened the door fully. A surprisingly broad staircase led down. Stark light. No saving energy here.

Winter raced down thirty or so steps and arrived in a five-by-five metre concrete catacomb. Concrete and nothing but concrete. A few ducts on the ceiling. It was cool and musty like a wine cellar. He stopped for a moment and listened inside the dam. It was silent. Eerily silent.

He could hear nothing but the blood rushing in his ears.

There were two narrow, vaulted tunnels. Winter took the one that led to the centre of the dam. His shadow followed him, then a moment later leaped ahead. Another catacomb. Tunnel, catacomb, tunnel. A small catacomb every thirty metres. In the fourth or fifth vault Winter came across a narrow, spiral staircase that seemed to lead downwards *ad infinitum*. Beside it lay an orange helmet and some abandoned empty wooden crates. They'd obviously been too unwieldy for the narrow metal stairs.

Winter put the pistol back in its holster, placed both hands on the banister and ran, slid, stumbled down as fast as he could, taking three or four steps at a time. He'd watched sailors use this technique. His palms burned. It wasn't half as easy as the sailors made it look.

About forty metres down he reached another chamber with two horizontal tunnels leading off from it. The curvature of the dam made it impossible for Winter to see more than fifty metres in either direction.

Down here it was warmer and stickier than in the upper tunnels. Winter stayed on the spiral staircase. The bomb device on the outer wall had been attached about two hundred metres below the crown. The explosives on the inside were probably at the same depth.

With increasing confidence Winter slithered ever faster down the spiral stairs. He stopped at the fourth tunnel.

Not a sound.

But no explosives to be seen either. Winter dashed into the adjoining catacomb. Nothing. He hastened back and glanced into the catacomb on the other side. At least the attackers couldn't hide the explosives in these bleak caves. Turning back again, Winter descended another forty metres down the staircase.

He smelled the bomb before he saw it. The sour tang he'd detected in the Land Rover was worked into the explosives by the manufacturer for safety reasons. When he entered the catacomb a few steps later, it was impossible to miss the device. Dozens of blocks of white C-4 plastic explosive were stuck to the wall with thick industrial tape. Each block was about forty centimetres long, five-wide and eight-deep. Winter gave the device a careful examination.

A capsule containing the initiating explosive was stuck into each block. Stiff, black-and-white copper wires connected the detonators. The wires came from a roll that lay half finished in a corner. The C-4 explosive and the wires spun a deadly spider's web inside the catacomb.

The central detonator hung in the middle of the web: a small metal box. On three sides it had copper clips, into which the wires from the individual blocks had been stuck. On the front of the box was a number keypad and a small screen like pocket calculators have.

Red digits: *00:11:03, 00:11:02, 00:11:01, 00:11:00, 00:10:59, 00:10:58.*

Winter wiped the sweat from his brow.

Defusing bombs was definitely not his favourite pastime.

Plastic explosive was robust.

You could shoot at it and nothing would happen. The blocks would only explode if the much more unstable, initiating explosive were detonated by a gentle, electrical shock. The problem he faced was the central timer – he had no idea about its mechanism or programming.

No risk, no fun.

With his index finger Winter pressed the * button.

The little black box was beeping. *00:10:52, 00:10:51, 00:10:50.* Jesus Christ! Winter tried the # key. The box was welded shut and couldn't be opened without the right tools.

Should he just rip out the wires? During explosives training, the instructors had always impressed on him that with many modern detonators the explosion was triggered early if there was electrical feedback.

There must be a way of overriding the central detonator with the right combination of buttons.

Winter pressed the # key several times.

Beep, beep, beep. Nothing.

Where were the instructions?

Winter wiped the sweat from his face.

His only hope was trial and error.

He pressed the * and # keys together.

Beep. The two zeros denoting the hours started flashing. Winter pressed two then three for twenty-three hours, then pressed the * and # keys again. Now the minutes were flashing. Five, nine, * and #.

Winter breathed a sigh of relief.

It wouldn't go off for another twenty-three hours and fifty-nine minutes. Long enough for the experts to defuse it. Part of the disaster had been postponed. But that was the easy bit. The more difficult part was waiting on the outside wall. He had just ten minutes and no idea how to operate the lift and get to the other bomb.

Running up the spiral staircase took longer. Winter struggled, taking more steps at a time. He had to force himself to ration his energy. The bomb was about two hundred metres down the dam. Each step was twenty centimetres. Five steps were a metre. A thousand steps. Too many to count.

He wouldn't be going jogging after work today.

Winter was breathing heavily.

He was short of oxygen.

A stabbing in the lungs.

Cramp in the ankles. Winter felt giddy from spiralling up the staircase. It was the same feeling he'd had as a child when his father had held him by the hand and ankle, and he'd flown through the air with centrifugal force like a plane. Back then his only fear had been that he might bang his head against the plum tree. At that moment he stumbled and cracked his right kneecap against the edge of a metal step.

A few minutes later, he finally reached the exit.

Bright light.

Winter paused, panting heavily. The unconscious man he'd tied up didn't appear to have moved, and the technician with the learning difficulties was leaning against the railings like a boxer after a knockout. As Winter sped past him he curled up into a defensive position.

The service lift was the only access to the second bomb. He had no idea how to get it working. He had to improvise.

From the valley he could hear the drone of a helicopter. At last. The helicopter zoomed over the dam wall. It was the same bright-red Alouette III that had flown him and Fatima here half an hour ago.

The helicopter turned and hovered over the reservoir.

Beside the pilot's moustache, Winter recognized the financial group's head of security. Winter waved, happy that he'd updated Hugentobler on the investigation yesterday evening. Fatima and two men were sitting on the passenger bench. The pilot was reticent about approaching the car park again, but Winter waved to signal that it was safe now and he should land there.

He set off at a pace. When he reached the car park, the doors were opening and the passengers getting out. Winter checked his watch. Less than five minutes. No time for detailed explanations.

The helicopter noise grew deeper and duller. The rotors slowed. Hugentobler was the first out. Grabbing him by the shoulder, Winter shouted in his ear, 'In four minutes a massive load of C-4 will go off.'

'Where?'

'Down there,' Winter replied, pointing at the dam. 'I've managed to reprogram the other load inside the dam. It's in the fifth underground level. In the middle. You've got to fly in the explosives experts from Spiez immediately.'

'Right. What about you? Are you okay?'

'I'm fine. But time's running out.'

'What's the situation?'

'Baumgartner dead. Four others, one on the run, three incapacitated. One's there,' Winter said, pointing to Salami by the Land Rover. 'The other two are injured and lying at the other end of the dam. Get them out of here. But not till we've defused the bomb!'

The two other men, wearing grey-orange fleece jackets with the logo of the operating company, joined Hugentobler and Winter, who shook two coarse, powerful hands and asked, 'Do you have a key for the service lift?'

'No. Not here. Why?'

Winter ignored the question.

'Where's the spare key?'

'In the maintenance room.' The man's chin pointed to the dam wall. Winter did some calculations. The service lift only moved at a snail's pace.

One of the men in fleeces tried to open the steel door to the dam. Without success. The fake technician had bolted it from the inside or just left the key in the lock. They didn't have time to break open the massive door.

Improvise.

Winter looked around.

Situation analysis.

The mission was clear. Defuse the bomb in four minutes. Little time. Speed of the essence.

How?

Fatima stood beside Winter, looking anxiously at him. He smiled at her, but in his mind saw Anne, who gave him an idea.

'Winter!' Fatima cried when he ran from her.

He half turned around and gave her the thumbs-up. Fatima wouldn't forget her minibreak in Switzerland quickly.

Anne's laughter flashed in his head. Winter felt anger and upset brewing inside him. Focus. He yanked open the door of the cockpit. The pilot with the Lech Wałęsa moustache grinned at him, baring his yellow teeth. 'How was your swim?'

'Refreshing.'

The pilot put out his hand. 'Hari.'

'Winter.'

Fixing the pilot's eyes, Winter couldn't detect any nervousness. Just professional curiosity, a touch of mischief at the corners and the concentration of a man who can't afford to make a single mistake. Ever. Over a beer this evening he'd light a long, thin cheroot, twiddle his sweeping moustache and serenely tell his colleagues another hair-raising story. Winter could be sure that their collaboration would work. He was in reliable hands.

'Do you fly mountain rescue missions?'

'Yes, of course.'

'Do you have the right equipment on you?'

'Always. Who do you want to rescue?'

'The dam wall.'

'The dam wall?'

'In the centre, about a third of the way up, a bomb has been fixed to the wall. It's going to explode in less than four minutes. Where's the gear?'

Lech Wałęsa pointed his thumb at the passenger area. 'In the box beneath the benches.'

'Let's go!'

Winter slammed shut the front cockpit door. The rotors started to accelerate again. He hauled himself into the passenger area and closed the sliding door. One bath a day was enough. He put his helmet on and positioned the microphone. The helicopter took off and the pilot said, 'Hello, Winter. Can you hear me?'

'Yes, loud and clear. Give me instructions.'

'Open the bench.'

Inside, Winter found a climbing harness with loops and several carabiner hooks. As they flew across the reservoir he put on the harness and pulled the loops tight. 'Where's the rope?'

'The winch is between the benches. The red carabiner to the red ring, and the blue one to the blue ring,' the pilot instructed.

By now they were facing the wall and the pilot said, 'I see the target area on the wall. It's quite far down. It's going to be tight. We've got two hundred metres of rope at most.'

'Should be enough,' Winter said optimistically. If not, he thought, at least we'll have a box seat for the explosion. He hooked up the red and blue carabiners and checked they would hold.

'Open the hatch,' the pilot said. In the middle, between the two parallel benches, Winter unbolted a security mechanism. Now he was able to push part of the floor to one side. A rectangular hatch about eighty centimetres by one and a half metres opened.

The wind blew in.

When Winter opened his eyes again he could see the sheep grazing far, far below. They had no idea of the danger they were in.

'Are you ready?'

'One sec.' Winter sat at the edge of the hatch, opposite the winch. Both his legs were hanging out of the helicopter. The wind was ruffling his damp trouser legs. They would dry very quickly.

The pilot maintained a hover. 'When you're hanging on the rope I won't be able to see you. I'm reliant on your instructions. And make sure that you don't swing too hard. No jerky movements. Good luck!'

Winter swallowed and supported himself with both arms either side of the hatch, like a gymnast on the horizontal bars. 'I'm going to let you down now,' he heard the pilot say. The winch jolted into life, and the red, synthetic rope began to unwind quickly. Winter let go of the helicopter and clung onto the rope with the harness. When his head was level with the floor he saw the ribbed, plastic mat and the metal bench legs.

The wind blasted into his face. Instinctively he looked up to check that the rope was holding, but all he saw were the bright-red metal plates of the underside of the helicopter and the braced chassis.

With both hands on the rope Winter slowly started spinning. The valley with its green fir forest, the dried-out stream bed, further down the Secer bunker and Lake Brienz in the distance. Alpine meadows on the mountain slopes with thinned, low woodland, then the dam wall again. Behind it the reservoir. Winter tried in vain to stop the spinning, with a gentle counter-movement of his torso. After the second full turn he heard Hari's voice in his helmet.

'Everything okay, Winter? How's the view?'

'Not bad.' Winter let his gaze roam the panorama. In the sky with its grey clouds he could see a single paraglider circling. The puffed up glider didn't sport the usual bright rainbow colours, but was a military green. The pilot was just a tiny black figure.

Max!

That was all he needed.

The bulky rucksack had been a paraglider. The rat could land anywhere on a meadow far below, jump into a waiting get-away car and drive away as cool as a cucumber.

By now, Winter was a hundred metres below the helicopter, gently swinging back and forth. One thing at a time. The bomb was still below him.

'Can't this thing go any faster? We don't have much time.'

'The winch is at maximum speed. We're almost there. I'm approaching the edge of the dam wall.'

Hari let the hovering helicopter lose height. As Winter passed the crown of the dam, the water vanished behind the concrete wall. He was now about thirty meters from the wall. It was shady and cool. All of a sudden the winch juddered; the two hundred metres of rope were fully extended.

'That's the end of the rope,' he heard Hari say.

'I'm thirty metres from the wall and fifty metres above the explosives,' Winter explained.

'Your wish is my command.'

The distance to the concrete shrunk to twenty, then ten metres. Now Winter could clearly see the black seams of the concrete formwork. He kept calm to reduce the spinning and swinging to a minimum. He looked straight up the wall. The helicopter was partly obscured by the edge of the wall and the red rope swung slowly back and forth. The C-4 explosive device was still about thirty metres from his feet.

'I'm still thirty metres above it.'

'It's getting tight.'

Hari meant the metres, but Winter looked at his watch. One more minute, assuming that the devices had been set to explode simultaneously. 'Yes.' The rope swung away from the dam wall.

'Wrong way. Closer to the wall!'

'Apologies. The wind is pretty unpredictable up here above the edge.' And the helicopter was a plaything for these downwinds. Winter was getting inexorably closer to the concrete wall. He tried to absorb the impact with his feet and forearms. Then he knocked against the wall, his helmet clanking against the concrete.

'What's going on?' Hari said.

'I'm at the wall. Three metres to the left, away from the car park, and five metres lower.'

'Impossible.'

'There's no such thing as impossible.'

'I'm almost touching the railings.'

'I need another metre to the right and two down.'

The rope now pulled him against the concrete and he had to brace against it with hands and feet. The service lift might have rubber rollers, he didn't. Above Winter's head the synthetic rope fluttered and nervously slapped against the dam wall. Hopefully it wouldn't wear through and break.

Now Winter could almost touch the outer ring of the C-4 plastic explosives with the tips of his toes. The central detonator was the same model as before. The black box hung on a climbing hook that was sticking from a neatly drilled hole. Grey, industrial tape criss-crossed the whitish blocks of explosive, holding it fast to the wall.

His feet were at the level of the central detonator. If he stretched in the harness and bent forwards his hands could reach the outer explosives but not the detonator in the middle.

'Hari! Just another half metre lower!'

The rope tore Winter away from the wall.

The helicopter jerked Winter upwards. The harness cut into his thigh and trussed his chest. At the end of the rope he flew back into the valley. The unexpected movement sent him into a spin, which he couldn't control. He swung from the end of the long, now wild pendulum, helplessly rotating back and forth. Thrashing about with his arms and legs in the air proved useless. Winter's pulse was at the upper limit of the optimal zone.

The mountains circled around him. He was in the middle of a carousel that had sprung its axis and was now turning too quickly.

He held on tight to the rope with both hands.

'Hari! What are you doing?'

'The rope almost snagged on the service lift. It could have brought the chopper down. I had to get away immediately.'

'The next attempt has to work. Quick!'

Hari flew straight back to his old position; with a slight lag the rope also swung back, slowly at first, then faster. Winter careered towards the concrete wall, lifting his legs at the last moment to avoid getting entangled in the explosives. He smacked hard into the wall.

His palms and right cheek scraped against the rough surface. His hands left bloody streaks and prints on the concrete. Finger painting.

'Slightly lower! One metre!'

Hari set the helicopter with the front end of both runners gently onto the service lift. He couldn't go any lower. The rope was vibrating. Winter felt a jerk. The rope was still too short.

'I'm touching the service lift. I can't go any further.'

'I need another half a metre.'

Winter pulled himself and stretched in the harness.

He looked at the red numbers on the central detonator relentlessly decreasing. Four zeros already. Less than a minute.

His arms were too short.

In the changing downwinds, Hari kept the helicopter as steady as possible over the edge of the dam. The small waves on the water showed him when the wind changed direction. With the cyclic he adjusted the helicopter's direction to the millimetre. He tried to lower the tail with the rope slightly, to give Winter the extra length he needed.

From a distance Fatima, Hugentobler and the two men from the operating company watched the helicopter perch on the railings, its rear section hanging over the abyss.

Fatima forced herself not to put her hands over her eyes. She felt she owed Winter that.

Everyone held their breath. But then the runners started skidding on the edge of the service lift and Hari had to manoeuvre the helicopter back to the horizontal.

The rope bobbed up and down.

Winter got closer to the central detonator.

But not close enough.

And there was no time left.

The plastic explosives were stuck in a circle.

Like a tornado.

When the charge exploded he would be in the eye of the storm. A quick death. What would happen to the helicopter? Would the rope break? Would the violence of the explosion make Hari lose control of the helicopter?

For a moment time stood still.

Then it clicked. Winter was trapped in the harness that was fastened to the rings of the rope by the carabiner hooks. The red hook was at belly button height, the blue one up by his chest, an arrangement that was keeping Winter upright. He pulled himself up slightly and unhooked the blue carabiner.

The laws of physics immediately spun Winter around the red carabiner at his navel. Upside down, he was now secured to the rope by a single hook. The unfastened blue carabiner smacked against his chin. Coins fell out of his pocket, clinking against the stone wall as they fell. Winter felt for the rope with his feet and stabilized himself.

'Hari, don't move! I'm at the detonator.'

The keypad was now level with his chest.

*00:00:34, 00:00:33, 00:00:32.*

Blood rushed to his head.

As the rope seesawed he compensated for the movements with his arms. Carefully he stretched his hands out to the black box. With blood-smeared fingers he watchfully cupped the detonator.

Then, using both thumbs, he simultaneously pressed the * and # keys.

Nothing happened.

Winter's heart missed a beat. Not the ideal time for cardiac arrest. At least with this pilot he was in good hands. The helicopter must have a defibrillator too.

*00:15, 00:14, 00:13.*

Had he slipped? Had his fingers trembled? Did this detonator have a different mechanism?

He pressed both buttons again, this time with greater determination. Together.

*00:12.* Beep.

The digits for hours started to flash and Winter reprogrammed the detonator. He breathed a sigh of relief. Close, but better than *00:07.* The explosives experts would have twenty-four hours to defuse the device properly, via the service lift.

'Bingo! Hari, you can go up now.'

'Congratulations! Very good. Hold on tight.'

The helicopter rose backwards. Hari flew over the valley in an elegant arc and Winter swung gently by the mountainside. The winch started to reel him back in. Tensing his stomach muscles, he pulled himself up the rope with his arms, fastened the blue carabiner again and gave the thumbs up with an outstretched arm to the onlookers in the car park. Fatima waved back.

'How about a little Alpine flight?' Hari joked.

'Maybe later. It's not over yet,' Winter told Hari. Where was Max? Winter's eyes scanned the valley. The rapidly moving clouds cast dappled shade onto the Alpine meadows.

There!

'Can you see the green paraglider over there on the right-hand side of the valley. At about three o'clock.'

Confirmation came after a few seconds. 'Yes, I see it. Military. What about it?'

'That's the fourth terrorist. Stop the winch. We're going to get him.'

'I'm not so sure. It would be better to call the police and they can catch him when he lands.'

'He'll be long gone by then. We'll be quicker in the chopper.'

'Alright. We'll have a go. But I'm going to call the police anyway.'

Hari stopped the winch and turned into the valley. The rope tensed. Winter was now hanging about fifty metres below the helicopter. He heard Hari radio the police and explain the situation.

When he'd seen the camouflage paraglider for the first time it was circling peacefully. Max wanted to watch the performance he'd staged himself from the air. But now that the programme had changed, the paraglider was speeding away into the valley in a faint wavy line.

The helicopter followed the paraglider from above, like a

bird of prey. The gap quickly shrank. They flew above the rocky narrow section. Winter saw the forest, the bright stream bed and the little road leading to the bunker. On the gravelled forecourt stood cars with flashing blue lights. A few heads looked up momentarily.

The valley opened again and Winter could see Lake Brienz glittering far in the distance. Behind the bunker lay a huge, gently sloping cone, the result of a powerful landslide. A recent storm had scarified the dense fir forest. Beyond the forest, stretched a plain with lush meadows, scattered farmhouses, a railway line and a busy road. It was the ideal place for Max to land and make his escape.

He was still about three hundred metres ahead of the chopper and one hundred metres below. Despite the camouflage the paraglider was easy to spot. Maybe it was from military supplies. It wasn't just the chemical traces in the explosives from Strittmatter's helicopter that suggested an army connection.

Winter could clearly make out Max's blond hair and the pale face which had impressed itself indelibly on his mind a moment prior to the bungee jump. The fugitive didn't seem to have noticed the helicopter above him. The noise of the wind must be drowning out that of the rotors, Winter supposed. He was gliding a hundred metres above the treetops. For the time being.

'Lower,' Winter instructed. 'Before he lands. We'll get him above the forest.'

Although the two men had only been collaborating for a few minutes, they worked together seamlessly. Winter directed and Hari immediately translated the instructions with supreme accuracy.

Max looked around, and Winter thought he sensed a moment of panic. Then the paraglider contracted for an instant, before turning left abruptly. He was trying to sidestep them. At once Winter and Hari corrected their course.

Soon Winter was almost able to touch the wing of the

paraglider and he heard it flapping. He caught the occasional glimpse of Max between his feet and through the puffed-up wing. As Max tried to evade them he had to watch out that he didn't lose height too quickly above the trees. Leaning forward in the harness, Winter tried to grab the wing.

'Drop five metres, and two metres to four o'clock.'

Hari reacted so quickly that Winter virtually fell onto the nylon wing.

It collapsed.

It felt silky, smelled synthetic and blocked his view.

Max yelled.

Then the material was torn from Winter's fingers and puffed up again below him. Winter's landing on top of the wing had crumpled it, nothing more.

Max plummeted, but was able to regain control of the paraglider just above the treetops.

'Up twenty metres,' Winter commanded.

But Max was hovering to his right at the same level. He was holding a pistol, its barrel pointing straight at him.

Winter heard two shots in rapid succession. The bullets missed. Even for Max, hitting a moving target in flight was tricky. But if he wanted a shoot-out in the air, he was most welcome. The advantage lay with Winter; he had a helicopter reliably piloted by Hari. Max just had the wind.

He reached for the SIG on his hip. Felt for it. The holster was empty.

Max bared his teeth and laughed.

The gun had fallen out when Winter had defused the explosives.

A bullet whistled past his head.

Unwilling to take any risks, Winter shouted, 'Up! Fifty metres. Quick!' Max disappeared beneath his paraglider.

'What's going on down there?' Hari asked. 'The distance to the trees is not strictly regulation.'

'Don't worry,' Winter reassured him. 'We're going to make a second attempt. Twenty metres to ten o'clock, thirty metres down.' Winter was pursuing the paraglider in Max's blind spot. 'Excellent. Now, ten metres to eleven o'clock and, when I say, drop five.'

Once again Winter's feet were getting close to the wing from above. 'Now!'

This time, Winter was better prepared, having scanned the wing for a handle or a loop. As he dropped he grabbed a green, nylon cord and immediately clipped this to one of the free carabiner hooks on the support rope. Max was on the lead.

The forest came rushing towards them.

Winter was enveloped by the wing. 'Up! Now!'

He was yanked upwards again, the material of the paraglider was stretched vertically, and he saw Max aiming at him. For a split second the two men stared at one another. Then the terrorist was hit by the full force of the jolt upwards and the shot missed to the side.

Max dropped his gun, and Winter understood from his defeated expression that he didn't have another weapon.

'Hari? We've got him.'

'Great. What now?'

The patrol cars on the forecourt of the old bunker were nearest. Their best bet would be to drop Max off there. He checked that the cord of the paraglider was still hanging securely in the carabiner. Like a fisherman he pulled in more of the wing's cords and clipped them in. Max was safely trussed in his harness, dangling ten metres below him. They'd done it!

'Winter? You still there? Where are we going to deliver him?'

'Did you see the police cars by the old bunker?'

'Yes. Good idea. We'll be there in a minute.'

'No need to land. We'll just drop him off.' Winter had no desire for interrogations and paperwork. He could do all that later. 'Then back to the dam.'

'Roger.' The helicopter turned, once more the rope above Winter tensed at an angle and they flew back at a leisurely speed, about twenty metres above the fir forest. Winter heard Hari notify the police and announce their arrival.

Winter looked around. The dam wall stood unscathed at the far end of the valley. The grey clouds had cleared away behind the crest of the mountains and the sky was impeccably blue. It was going to be a lovely afternoon.

He took a deep breath and closed his eyes. It was all over. How he would have loved to take a secluded walk now with Anne, down one of these peaceful side valleys. That had been his plan. Their plan. On that ill-fated Friday. Anne had accepted the invitation for their second date at his house and hadn't objected when he'd courageously added, 'And on Saturday we can go walking in the mountains.' Anne had just given him an impish look, smiled with her eyes, and said, 'We'll have to get up early.'

Now, for the first time in a fortnight, Winter felt free, relieved and unburdened. The hunt was over. For him at any rate. Baumgartner was dead, Max was on a leash and Farmer... it was just a matter of time.

He glanced down. Max had gone.

'Hari, wait! The guy's gone!'

'What do you mean, gone?'

'I don't know. He's disappeared.' The cords were hanging loose from the carabiner, flapping in the wind. The paraglider harness had vanished too. Max knew he was facing a long prison sentence, perhaps even the electric chair in America. 'He cut himself free.' Max had gambled on the chances of the fir trees breaking his fall.

'Lunatic,' Hari said. Winter nodded, even though the pilot couldn't see him.

'Fly slowly back the way we came.'

The helicopter turned around and Hari cancelled the announcement of his arrival.

Winter gathered up the remains of the flapping paraglider and started scanning the forest beneath him. The firs were growing densely and it was almost impossible to see the floor of this unmanaged forest. The impenetrable undergrowth offered ideal hiding places.

They flew along a storm glade. Juvenile firs were already sprouting between the broken trees, only some of which had been cleared to stumps. The eternal cycle of nature. Surely Max wouldn't be so stupid as to cross the clearing. Screwing up his eyes, Winter scoured the edge of the forest. He tried to get into Max's mindset. The forest extended for about three kilometres to the meadows. Despite the rough terrain a good runner could do it in fifteen minutes. Somewhere down there Max had parked his getaway car.

Then he saw him. At the edge of the glade.

'Down there, Hari. Ten o'clock. Two hundred metres.'

The paraglider puffed up again, obscuring Winter's sight. He shoved the huge, nylon jellyfish to one side. The terrorist had cut the lines as they were flying up the valley above the dense forest. Aiming for the fir trees to break his fall, he'd jumped.

Now Max was lying face-down on the trunk of a fir tree split by a storm. Impaled. The helicopter hovered in the air. Winter could see sharp splinters sticking out of Max's black back. Straight through the lungs.

'Good God,' Hari whispered. 'May the Lord be with him.'

'Not so sure about that,' Winter said. 'He's going straight to hell. Shame we won't be able to grill him ourselves any more.'

Max's head turned. The pale face was ashen. His eyes stared blankly at Winter hovering above him. Max contorted his face into a grin and tried to say something. Blood ran from the corners of his mouth. Winter stared impassively at Max until the life faded from his eyes. One of his arms fell to the side and his body collapsed further onto the stake.

'Winter. He just moved. He's still alive.'

'Not any more,' Winter said, with a hint of disappointment in his voice. Max had died far too quickly for his liking.

'Take us back to the mountains.'

The helicopter turned and they flew back up the valley.

# LATER

That afternoon a large contingent of police cars, fire engines and ambulances flooded into the usually peaceful valley. Baumgartner was placed in a body bag. A group of paramedics and foresters dealt with Max. Hugentobler had gathered up the three fake maintenance men and handed them over to the police.

Explosives experts flew in and defused the devices for good, with the help of experts from the operating company. Sniffer dogs searched the dam wall for hours, but didn't find any more explosives. They were rewarded with their dog treats all the same.

In Boston, Farmer was arrested by Smith and his people as he left his Boston brown stone. He protested against the misunderstanding and the handcuffs, but didn't resist when the plain-clothes officers put him in the car. Two hours later he was walking free again, thanks to his lawyer, a written promise not to leave Boston and a bail of ten million dollars.

Neither the stock markets nor the bank's clients noticed a thing. The latter enjoyed a sumptuous party that afternoon, on a renovated steamer with huge paddle wheels. Von Tobler gave one of his splendid speeches, into which he weaved his brand new investment vehicle, enabling the super-rich to invest directly in global infrastructure projects. After all, von Tobler joked, this venerable steamer, over a century old, still yielded a substantial return. Immune to economic crises and wars. The rich guests from across the world laughed discreetly and applauded.

Winter had driven home in the afternoon and laid the granite slabs. The terrace was finished just before sunset. The sky was already changing colour when he set out the two loungers.

Seven weeks later, on a sunny, September day, Al-Bader and Winter played their second round of golf at Château de Plaisance. This time they reached the eighteenth hole without any notable incidents. Apart from Winter's ball finding water on the fourteenth hole.

Al-Bader won by three strokes.

The old beeches and oaks along the fairways were still in their summer attire. By contrast, the interspersed birches with their white trunks already sported yellow leaves. An Indian summer on Lake Geneva. Since their round in August, which had been rudely interrupted, the temperatures had fallen. Both men wore light jumpers and were now sitting in the half-empty restaurant.

The well-earned beer came accompanied by towering club sandwiches. They hadn't talked much during the round, focusing instead on the little white ball. As they toasted, Al-Bader said, with exaggerated formality, 'Winter, I'd like to take this opportunity to thank you most kindly on behalf of the Al-Bader family. We are pleased that the murder of my elder brother has been solved. Allah be merciful on his soul. Without you, it would have taken far longer and indeed may never have been cleared up at all.'

After the first sip – the one that always tasted the best – Winter replied with overplayed modesty, 'My pleasure. It's my job and all part of the bank's service.'

Wiping the foam from his lips, Al-Bader grinned. 'You know what I mean. It's just a shame you declined my offer,'

'I'm sorry.'

He'd politely, but firmly turned down Al-Bader's generous offer of employment. He wanted to finish renovating his farmhouse and finally furnish his own home.

Winter changed the subject. 'How is the moving of the pyramids from America to Switzerland going? Are you content?'

'Yes, very. Yesterday we formally completed the transactions. Von Tobler is a genius.'

Before Al-Bader's first Pyramid Investment Partners board meeting, von Tobler had made use of the trials and tribulations concerning Farmer to make Al-Bader a detailed offer for administering the investment projects. The CEO had conjured up his own team which was also managing the recently-established investment vehicle. Once again, von Tobler had struck gold with his unerring instinct.

At the board meeting in Riyadh, von Tobler had convinced the other representatives of the rich Arab families that their money would be best looked after by his discreet, totally neutral and traditionally solid Swiss bank. For a modest fee the bank assumed the onerous administration of the investments as well as the back-office work.

At a stroke the volume of the new investment vehicle had increased tenfold.

And von Tobler's success had given him some time and breathing space. In the financial group there was no longer talk of more integration. According to a well-informed source, the chairman of the group had personally engaged Baumgartner on his staff. Even Baumgartner had his advantages. At any rate, rumours of a takeover petered out.

'I'm pleased to hear that, of course,' Winter said.

'Please tell Dr von Tobler that I'd be delighted to welcome him on my stud some time soon. We share a passion for breeding beautiful horses.'

Al-Bader attacked his sandwich.

Winter just nodded. Von Tobler was now his immediate boss. Känzig had left the bank with immediate effect for personal reasons and was looking for new challenges. He had disappeared. But Dirk had told Winter that he'd heard from someone that Känzig had gone to a heath resort in Nice to decompress after the recent stresses and strains. Many years ago it would have been called an 'asylum'. But the main thing was that they were rid of that particular nuisance.

Winding a strip of wild, smoked salmon on his fork, Winter said, 'Yes, a year or two ago von Tobler bought himself a rambling estate in Essex from bankruptcy assets. For his retirement, or more accurately his unretirement.' He left these words hanging thoughtfully in mid-air, then asked, 'What was the reaction of the other families?'

'The Baktars and the other families were furious when the report from the special audit was produced, and Farmer was arrested and released a second time.'

Al-Bader had fired the professor with immediate effect. But he couldn't completely prevent the losses on the options. The special audit ordered by his twin, the one that had cost him his life, had been confirmed by the preliminary investigation of the district attorney. The State of Massachusetts was preparing a case against Farmer for misappropriation. Al-Bader took another sip of beer and gobbled up the rest of his club sandwich. 'We've been asking around. The only documented connections to right-wing extremists date back twenty years. It will be difficult to prove incitement to murder in court.'

'It was malicious intent. With your money and via Secer AG he bought access to our bank. In the past they dug tunnels, now they steal money electronically.'

'Yes. Farmer was planning to rob his friends. He wanted power. And he was greedy. With the Secer project he saw the opportunity to make a few billion. That buys you a lot of power. And all he needed to realize his plans was to call on his old brothers in arms.'

The two men leaned back. Farmer was hard to grasp.

'What do you think? Will the evidence be adequate to convict Farmer?' Winter asked.

As far as he knew, which was based on a lengthy midnight telephone call with Smith and a walk with Meister, all that could be proved was that Farmer and Baumgartner knew each other. They'd met a few years ago when Pyramid Investment Partners sold a share of Secer AG to the financial group.

And Baumgartner knew Max. The two of them, both fatherless, had grown up on the same working-class estate. Back then the two schoolmates were a good foil for each other. The powerful Max protected Baumgartner the weakling, who in return helped him out in school. When they were teenagers, this odd couple discovered a passion for weapons and explosives. Together they tortured small animals and terrorized the children of immigrants.

Max had left school early and, after spending some time in prison for affray, enlisted as a mercenary in Africa. There were several records of him on file as right-wing and, according to unconfirmed reports, he'd taken part in various civil war atrocities in Africa. Max had hired the fake service-technicians from an extreme right-wing splinter group in Langenthal.

Baumgartner had scraped through his business studies degree and had got the job at the financial group thanks to his connections in a duelling association at university. His criminal record was clean.

Whenever Max spent time in Switzerland he stayed in the loft apartment of Baumgartner, who was single. They'd been big-game hunting several times, and in May had spent a week together in Nantucket.

Although Farmer didn't deny their meeting, he claimed that Baumgartner had brought Max along to ask Pyramid Investment Partners about the financing of a solar project in Africa. Farmer continued to play the generous benefactor. As both Max and Baumgartner were dead and buried, they couldn't tell their stories any more.

Smith didn't believe Farmer's account and assumed that the

trio had spent the weekend in Nantucket planning the attack, Farmer taking the lead.

Smith had also arrested and interrogated the TAA thug that Ben had photographed at the airport when they re-entered the United States. But this man kept quiet and eventually had had to be released. Smith suspected that he'd been sent by Farmer to clear up. He was due to meet Max and Baumgartner and eliminate both of them once the work had been done.

According to Smith, Farmer had a whole host of influential friends in the States for whom he'd made lots of money. All in all, Smith was sceptical that the evidence would be sufficient for a trial, let alone a conviction.

Rocking his head from side to side, Al-Bader pushed away his empty plate and said, 'I don't know if he will stand trial for murder. In Western democracies the wheels of the law turn very slowly. But it doesn't bother me any more.'

'Why not? He killed your brother and Anne!'

Very early that morning Winter had visited Anne's grave, bringing her flowers from his wild garden. He still found it hard to think of her and mention her name.

Al-Bader must have read his thoughts, for he said, 'I miss my brother, too. But it was Allah's will. We will meet again in Paradise. And as I can see, you're not up to date with the latest news.'

Winter frowned in surprise.

Holding up his palm, Al-Bader stood and said, 'I'll be right back.'

Winter blinked into the autumn sun. Had something eluded him? Farmer's career was over. Smith would take care of the prosecution personally. For Winter the matter was over. The uniformed waiter arrived, cleared away the plates and Winter accepted the dessert menu.

Al-Bader returned. A confident smile on his lips and a well-read newspaper on his hand.

'Here you go. I read this today at breakfast.'

Al-Bader offered Winter a folded copy of the *New York Times*.

Winter raised his eyebrows and swapped the menu for the paper.

With his manicured finger, the sheikh tapped silently on a small article in the right-hand column: 'Brutal attack on well-known money manager!'

While Al-Bader gave serious attention to the sinfully expensive puddings, Winter read a short report about an anonymous money manager who had been attacked and mugged after leaving a restaurant in Boston old town. Normally this sort of incident would have barely made the miscellaneous stories of a local paper. But the victim in this case was a prominent private equity manager who was also under suspicion of having misappropriated funds from his investors, totalling hundreds of millions of dollars. The law enforcement officers, who'd arrived within three minutes, discovered that both of the money manager's hands had been chopped off. An intensive search for the missing hands in the area surrounding the crime scene was unsuccessful. The man had lost a large quantity of blood and was in shock. He was taken to intensive care in a private clinic, where the senior doctor described his overall condition as stable. Given the nature of the crime, the authorities were not ruling out the possibility that fanatical Muslims could be responsible.

'You think that's Farmer?' Winter asked.

'I'm certain.' He grinned and looked past Winter for a moment.

Winter wondered how far their friendship went. What did Al-Bader really know? Was he behind the attack on Farmer? 'A Muslim who has taken the *Qisas* principle of Sharia Law seriously?' he said.

'Or a Christian who's taken the Old Testament literally? An eye for an eye, a tooth for a tooth.'

Turning to the approaching waiter, Al-Bader took off his sunglasses, tapped them on the menu and asked in French, 'Would you kindly bring me an orange and rosemary *croquant* with...' – he consulted the card – '... poached pear and *Araguani* chocolate duo?'

'With pleasure, sir.' The waiter nodded obediently.

Winter put the paper aside and ordered a *Coupe Danmark*.

Al-Bader pushed his sunglasses back on his head. His brother had worn the same make. The young waiter with the white apron disappeared and Winter asked, 'Are you still on course in Cairo?'

'Ask me again in a few years. It's going to take time. As an investor you need staying power and a little...' – he rubbed his thumb and index finger together – '... *baksheesh*.' Then Al-Bader wanted to know what Winter thought about investing in a further development of Shanghai port.

When the artistically arranged desserts sailed in a few minutes later, Al-Bader licked his lips and asked mischievously, 'And how is Fatima?'

Winter paused, and then said, 'I daresay she would feel safer if they apprehended the men behind the attack at the pyramids.' Nobody had been able to prove a connection between Farmer and the explosion that killed Kaddour.

Two weeks ago, Winter and Fatima had spent a week together in London. Fatima had taken Winter to her favourite restaurant. But on the Sunday afternoon somehow they'd started talking at cross purposes and from there it was only a matter of time before Fatima insisted on catching an earlier flight back to Cairo.

Since then Winter had heard nothing from the very busy diplomat's daughter at the head of Orafin.

But during their walk along the rose beds in Regent's Park she'd told him the Al-Bader family was now the third-biggest shareholder in the newly established project development company, behind the Egyptian state and Orafin.

Now Winter threw the ball back at Al-Bader. 'Didn't you see her at the board meeting of the Cairo nuclear power station?'

'No, I sent a good-looking cousin,' Al-Bader said with a grin, and ordered a *Piedmontese Nebbiolo* grappa to digest his meal. When the waiter returned with the slim bottle, Al-Bader took it from his hand. 'We'll have the whole bottle.'

Winter took out his vibrating mobile. Von Tobler. He ignored the call and put the phone back in his pocket.

Having filled the two little glasses to the rim, Al-Bader toasted Winter. 'To us!'

'To the future!'

They downed their glasses and shivered with the cold. The alcohol burned their throats. The autumn evening had turned cool and soon the first snow would be falling.

'Got any plans yet?' the sheikh asked.

'No, but another winter is on its way.'

# ACKNOWLEDGEMENTS

Despite it being only my name on the cover, many people worked on *Damnation*. In 2008 I wrote the first seventy pages and gave them to my partner (and toughest critic), who silently read them. Today I can still remember the moment when she told me that it reads like a 'real' book. After that, I hunkered down, finished the manuscript and sent it out. The reaction from the publishers was underwhelming to say the least. I reworked the manuscript and gave it to a dozen test readers, who improved it again with their honest feedback.

I also found myself an agent, Katharina Altas, who convinced the German publisher Emons to transform my manuscript into a proper book. I owe a lot to Hejo and Ulrike Emons, Christel Steinmetz, my editor Irène Kost, who whipped both story and hero into shape, and Dominic Hettgen, who told everybody to read my thriller.

Since I've long been reading a lot of crime fiction in English, I started to think about an English edition. The experience, patience and wisdom of Tanja Howarth, my new London-based agent, soon led to Oneworld, where I immediately felt very welcome and I'm particularly grateful to company owners Juliet Mabey and Novin Doostdar. My thanks go to Eva Stensrud and her colleagues from Pro Helvetia for generously supporting the translation and to Jamie Bulloch for so admirably translating my complicated sentences into an elegant read.

I'm greatly indebted to Jenny Parrott, from Oneworld's imprint Point Blank, as it was she who acquired and edited

*Damnation*. Many thanks to Kate Beal, Alyson Coombes, Paul Nash, Margot Weale, James Jones, Hayley Warnham, Caitriona Row and Thanhmai Bui-Van, and my copy-editor Emily Thomas. In my eyes, they and all the others working in the background lifted *Damnation* to another level and proved what good teamwork can achieve.

I also highly appreciate all the book aficionados working in libraries and book shops, running specialized blogs or writing in the media. It's always fun to answer your tricky questions or to do readings. And last but certainly not least, a million thanks to all my readers. For me as an author you are the most important. Thank you!

This book wouldn't be in your hands if my Queen of Hearts, Elizabeth Steele, had frowned sceptically ten years ago discouraging me to continue. Since then, she helped me in more ways than you can imagine. I love you lots!

Peter Beck
www.peter-beck.net/english

# Oneworld, Many Voices

### Bringing you exceptional writing
### from around the world

---

*The Unit* by Ninni Holmqvist (Swedish)
Translated by Marlaine Delargy

---

*Twice Born* by Margaret Mazzantini (Italian)
Translated by Ann Gagliardi

---

*Things We Left Unsaid* by Zoya Pirzad (Persian)
Translated by Franklin Lewis

---

*The Space Between Us* by Zoya Pirzad (Persian)
Translated by Amy Motlagh

---

*The Hen Who Dreamed She Could Fly* by Sun-mi Hwang
(Korean) Translated by Chi-Young Kim

---

*The Hilltop* by Assaf Gavron (Hebrew)
Translated by Steven Cohen

---

*Morning Sea* by Margaret Mazzantini (Italian)
Translated by Ann Gagliardi

---

*A Perfect Crime* by A Yi (Chinese)
Translated by Anna Holmwood

---

*The Meursault Investigation* by Kamel Daoud (French)
Translated by John Cullen

---

*Minus Me* by Ingelin Røssland (YA) (Norwegian)
Translated by Deborah Dawkin

---

*Laurus* by Eugene Vodolazkin (Russian)
Translated by Lisa C. Hayden

---

*Masha Regina* by Vadim Levental (Russian)
Translated by Lisa C. Hayden

---

*French Concession* by Xiao Bai (Chinese)
Translated by Chenxin Jiang

*The Sky Over Lima* by Juan Gómez Bárcena (Spanish)
Translated by Andrea Rosenberg

*A Very Special Year* by Thomas Montasser (German)
Translated by Jamie Bulloch

*Umami* by Laia Jufresa (Spanish)
Translated by Sophie Hughes

*The Hermit* by Thomas Rydahl (Danish)
Translated by K.E. Semmel

*The Peculiar Life of a Lonely Postman* by Denis Thériault
(French) Translated by Liedewy Hawke

*Three Envelopes* by Nir Hezroni (Hebrew)
Translated by Steven Cohen

*Fever Dream* by Samanta Schweblin (Spanish)
Translated by Megan McDowell

*The Postman's Fiancée* by Denis Thériault (French)
Translated by John Cullen

*The Invisible Life of Euridice Gusmao* by Martha Batalha
(Brazilian Portuguese) Translated by Eric M. B. Becker

*The Temptation to Be Happy* by Lorenzo Marone
(Italian) Translated by Shaun Whiteside

*Sweet Bean Paste* by Durian Sukegawa (Japanese)
Translated by Alison Watts

*They Know Not What They Do* by Jussi Valtonen (Finnish)
Translated by Kristian London

*The Tiger and the Acrobat* by Susanna Tamaro (Italian)
Translated by Nicoleugenia Prezzavento and Vicki Satlow

*The Woman at 1,000 Degrees* by Hallgrímur Helgason
(Icelandic) Translated by Brian FitzGibbon

*Frankenstein in Baghdad* by Ahmed Saadawi (Arabic)
Translated by Jonathan Wright

*Back Up* by Paul Colize (French)
Translated by Louise Rogers Lalaurie

*Damnation* by Peter Beck (German)
Translated by Jamie Bulloch

*Oneiron* by Laura Lindstedt (Finnish)
Translated by Owen Witesman

*The Boy Who Belonged to the Sea* by Denis Thériault
(French) Translated by Liedewy Hawke

*The Baghdad Clock* by Shahad Al Rawi (Arabic)
Translated by Luke Leafgren

*The Aviator* by Eugene Vodolazkin (Russian)
Translated by Lisa C. Hayden

*Lala* by Jacek Dehnel (Polish)
Translated by Antonia Lloyd-Jones